# A Fondant FAREWELL

## ENCHANTMENTS & ENDINGS

BEWITCHED BY CHOCOLATE
MYSTERIES

BOOK NINE

# H.Y. HANNA

# CONTENTS

# PART ONE

# CHAPTER ONE

Caitlyn Le Fey had often heard the famous movie quote about life being like a box of chocolates—"you never know what you're gonna get"—and in the months since she'd come to England searching for answers about her real family, she'd often felt like she was living that well-known saying. *Literally*, in her case, since her search had led her to an *actual* chocolate shop filled with many boxes of chocolates! And it had been no ordinary chocolate shop either: situated in Tillyhenge, a village deep in the Cotswolds countryside, *Bewitched by Chocolate* had a notorious reputation as being owned by a local witch. It was assiduously avoided by the locals, who whispered that the chocolates there were so delicious, they just *had* to be enchanted...

*Well, they're partly right*, thought Caitlyn as she gazed out the window of the taxi. She'd quickly discovered that the mysterious chocolate shop was owned by a cranky old woman named the Widow

Mags, who frightened the villagers with her fierce appearance and brusque manner, but whose prickly exterior actually hid a kind and wise heart. And while the "magic" that the old woman worked with sugar, cocoa butter, and cream was purely down to her chocolatier skills, she did also have other talents— talents that went beyond making outrageously moreish fudge brownies or decadently delicious chocolate truffles.

Yes, the rumours had been true: the Widow Mags really *was* a witch. And not only that—Caitlyn had also been shocked to discover that she was the old witch's granddaughter, and to find that she herself had magic in her veins! She was a witch too.

*Or at least, I could be, if I can ever master the art of reliably working magic on cue*, Caitlyn thought ruefully.

It was certainly not something that she'd ever expected to come out of *her* life's box of chocolates. In fact, all the things that she'd always believed to belong to the realm of legends and fairytales had turned out to be true: spells and enchantments could be cast, vampires really did exist (although not quite in the way you might think!), witches did walk among us, and magic was all around if you just knew how to conjure it...

"...not from these parts, are you?"

Caitlyn came out of her thoughts to realise that the taxi driver was speaking to her. "Sorry?"

"I said—you a visitor here? When you got in at the

hospital and said you wanted to go to Tillyhenge, I thought you was a tourist stayin' in the village. Your accent... you sound a bit American but also a bit English...?"

Caitlyn gave a resigned smile. She must have answered that question a thousand times. Her strange accent always flummoxed everyone. "I was born in England, but I grew up mostly overseas—yes, some of it in the United States. So I do have a slight American accent. But I also had a British nanny and then British tutors growing up. They were very strict about me speaking the 'Queen's English' and following British pronunciation... so I suppose my accent is a bit mixed-up."

The taxi driver was practically ogling her with curiosity now. "Private tutors and a nanny? You're not royalty, are you?" he asked, only half joking.

Caitlyn shook her head, laughing. "No, definitely not! My mother just preferred to homeschool me. It was easier, especially with our lifestyle, since we were often on the road." She hesitated, then added: "My mother was a famous singer."

"Ahh... a celebrity!" said the driver, as if that explained everything.

"Yes, that's right," said Caitlyn, wondering why she was revealing all this. She was normally very careful about sharing personal information—the result of years spent trying to avoid media attention. As the adopted daughter of world-famous singer Barbara Le Fey, she had always been a prime target

3

for the paparazzi and news tabloids, especially after Barbara's unexpected death last year. It had been a relief to come to Tillyhenge, where most people did not recognise her or link her to her famous adoptive mother.

Still, the curious questions were a welcome distraction from her own troubled thoughts, so she found herself more forthcoming than usual. The taxi driver started to ask something else but stopped as a news bulletin interrupted the music on the radio. The newsreader's voice issued clearly from the speakers:

*"...authorities are still trying to establish what happened at the Cotswolds Infirmary this morning, where a bizarre case of mistaken identity seems to have taken place. Vanessa Fitzroy, the younger sister of Lord James Fitzroy, the current head of the Fitzroy estate, was brought in by ambulance and treated for a head injury. However, a strange woman was subsequently discovered in her hospital bed, and the real Vanessa Fitzroy has been found in her flat in London, where she has apparently been sleeping peacefully for the past three days. No one can explain this strange phenomenon. The hospital staff continue to insist that the bed was only left unattended briefly, and therefore there was no way the strange woman could have entered the ward without being seen. And yet they can offer no explanation as to how she came to take Vanessa Fitzroy's place in the bed. The*

*strange woman's identity remains unknown.*

*"Sources in the nearby village of Tillyhenge have suggested that this incident may be linked to the suspicious death that occurred at Huntingdon Manor, the main seat of the Fitzroy estate, only two days ago. The victim Percy Wynn—who coincidentally happened to be a friend of Vanessa Fitzroy's—was found dead in the Manor Library. He is believed to have suffered a heart attack brought on by the ingestion of a poisonous substance. Rumours amongst local residents suggest that deadly nightshade berries may have been involved, although the police have not confirmed this. However, DI Walsh of the local CID has confirmed that the police have opened a murder enquiry into the case. Neither Lord Fitzroy nor his sister, Vanessa, were available for comment.*

*"Moving on to national news, strikes by junior doctors have been escalating and are now having a severe impact on the quality of service delivered by the NHS, according to the chief executive of the National Health—"*

The taxi driver switched the radio off and caught Caitlyn's eye in the rearview mirror. "You was at the hospital, weren't you? You hear anythin' 'bout this 'mistaken identity' malarkey while you was there?"

Caitlyn wondered how the man would react if she said: *Yes, actually, that "strange woman" is my long-lost real mother.* She cleared her throat and said instead: "Um... it was all so chaotic in there. I had no idea what was going on." *Which was certainly the truth!*

"Bit creepy though, innit?" persisted the taxi driver. "I mean, it's like them stories 'bout changelings who swapped themselves into the place of a child in a family and nobody knew. You reckon there's any truth in what they're sayin', 'bout this bein' linked to that recent murder at Huntingdon Manor?"

"Er... I'm not sure."

"All sorts of odd goings-on over there, so I've heard," continued the driver with almost gleeful relish. "Wasn't there a man murdered at that masquerade ball they had at the Manor last month? And people was talkin' 'bout 'vampire attacks' on the estate earlier this year... and what 'bout them stories of a great black dog hauntin' the countryside around the estate? Me missus reckons it's the village— Tillyhenge. Says it's always had a reputation for witchcraft. If you ask me, it's that stone circle up the hill behind the village. They reckon 'ancient sites' like that are always full of black magic. Might be good for tourists, but it ain't good for the locals, I tell you!"

Caitlyn made a noncommittal sound, hoping that the man's garrulousness would mean that she wouldn't have to give any proper replies to his diatribe.

"And now I hear that the new Lord Fitzroy is actually promotin' these supernatural associations! That would've never happened in his father's day, I can tell you. Everyone said there'd be big changes when old Lord Fitzroy died and his son came back to take over the estate last year, but I reckon no one expected these crazy—"

"James—I mean, Lord Fitzroy is a very good landlord," said Caitlyn, feeling compelled to defend him. "His ideas have really helped to modernise the estate and benefit the tenants of the village and farms around. Stately homes and big estates like Huntingdon Manor have to find creative new ways to earn an income in the modern day, in order to survive, you know."

"But there must be other ways to do it, surely? Celebratin' pagan festivals and bringin' back all these old pagan traditions…" The driver made a tutting sound. "And what's this latest thing they're plannin' this weekend: a Samhain Festival on Sunday? That's practically callin' up the ghouls and demons!"

"No, it's not," said Caitlyn. "That's a complete misunderstanding! Samhain is a *harvest* festival. It was used to mark the last harvest of the year and the start of winter. Okay, it *is* also a time to honour the dead, but just as a way to remember loved ones who are no longer with us. There's nothing sinister about that."

"Don't you believe it," said the driver darkly. "This ain't like takin' some flowers to the cemetery. I heard that they're carvin' creepy faces on turnips and puttin' on pagan disguises, and there's even gonna be a bonfire—"

7

"But a lot of those things are similar to what's done for Hallowe'en! You see people dressing up in costumes and 'spooky' decorations in shops everywhere. Don't tell me you're scared of that too?"

"That's different," said the driver stubbornly. "Hallowe'en's just a silly American lark for kids and a way for the shops to make money—"

"But Hallowe'en is based on Samhain," said Caitlyn impatiently. "The Irish and Scottish immigrants took their Samhain traditions with them when they emigrated to the United States, and that's what inspired the American Hallowe'en custom. They've just adapted some things—like using pumpkins instead of turnips, because those grow better in America—but the ideas and traditions are essentially the same.

"In fact, I think it's rather clever of the Manor estate to leverage these pagan events in the calendar," continued Caitlyn. "It's just a marketing angle, that's all. It's a way to make Tillyhenge and the estate stand out from all the other places that tourists might visit in the Cotswolds. It brings business for all of the tenants on the estate and in the village. It's genius, really. I think James and his marketing team have done a great job."

The driver's eyes met hers in the rearview mirror again, bright and inquisitive. "You know Lord Fitzroy, then? You sound very familiar with him and the Manor."

"I... um... yes, he's a friend," mumbled Caitlyn,

wondering if she would ever get up the confidence to proudly announce that James was her "boyfriend".

*But is he still?* She thought miserably of the rift that seemed to have sprung up between them, all because she had dared to suggest that James's sister, Vanessa, might be involved in the suspicious death of her friend Percy. *It had been a natural conclusion to come to,* thought Caitlyn defensively. Vanessa had been acting so oddly, and there had been so much circumstantial evidence linking her to the murder... anyone would have thought that she could be guilty!

Of course, James had categorically refused to accept it. *Amazing how quickly romantic feelings go out the window when your family loyalties are threatened,* thought Caitlyn bitterly. *James wouldn't even consider my point of view! I can't believe he was angry with me for implicating Vanessa when he had no qualms about calling* my mother *a potential murderer!*

She sighed and tried to tamp down her anger. Maybe she was being unfair to James. After all, most people would struggle to accept that their naïve, spoilt younger sister could be capable of cold-blooded murder. Still, James's scornful scepticism was one reason why Caitlyn had pounced on Vanessa so gleefully when she had followed the girl in the estate grounds earlier that morning and spotted her holding Percy's dowsing pendulum. Vanessa could only have had the pendulum in her possession if she had been at the crime scene—it had seemed to provide irrefutable proof that the girl was involved in Percy's murder.

*Although... maybe I was too single-minded in trying to expose Vanessa*, Caitlyn admitted to herself, and she shuddered again at the memory. It might have been a few hours ago now, but she still felt the horror afresh each time she thought of what had happened. It had been an accident, of course: she and Vanessa had been locked in a struggle, and the other girl had lost her balance and fallen. And when she'd seen James's sister lying pale and still at the bottom of the terrace steps, with the bloody gash across her forehead, Caitlyn's heart had nearly stopped in terrified dread...

*But it's okay. Vanessa's going to be fine*, Caitlyn reminded herself hastily. The girl had been rushed straight to hospital and had since been given the all-clear. The doctors had said that it was just a mild concussion. Besides, it hadn't even really been Vanessa who suffered the head injury! That had been the shocking twist: the girl brought into hospital had somehow changed—when no one was looking—from the pretty young blonde with the big grey eyes to a strange woman with vivid red hair.

*My mother.*

Caitlyn felt her mind reel afresh at the discovery. To think that her mother Tara—the mother she had been desperately searching for—had been right under her nose the past few days, impersonating

James's younger sister!

*How* had *Tara managed to fool us all?* Caitlyn wondered. She knew that her mother had always been a particularly gifted witch, with a special talent for "glamour"—the art of disguise and transformation through magical illusion—but still, she couldn't comprehend how no one had noticed or suspected. Of course, she herself wasn't in the best position to tell. She had been abandoned by her mother as a newborn baby and had never even known the woman who had given birth to her, but surely the others...?

Caitlyn thought of James again. As landlord of the surrounding estate, which included the village of Tillyhenge, James prided himself on being perceptive and informed—and yet he, too, had been completely fooled. He had never suspected that the "Vanessa" who had arrived at the Manor a few days ago with a party of her friends was not the little sister that he had doted on since childhood. None of Vanessa's group had seemed to notice anything untoward either—even her childhood best friend, Tori, had been completely bamboozled.

"So are you over here visiting from America?" asked the taxi driver, breaking into her thoughts.

Caitlyn hastily came out of her dark musings with an effort. "Um... no, not really. I'm... er... living in Tillyhenge now."

"Is that right?" The taxi driver's eyes were bright with salacious curiosity again. Caitlyn could see that he was looking forward to having a good gossip with his wife when he got home! "But life in the village must be a comedown after the celebrity circuit, eh? Have you been to lots of red-carpet dos and fancy parties and things?" asked the driver eagerly. "What are they like?"

"Um... I've been to a few," said Caitlyn, thinking that the person he should really have been quizzing was her "cousin", Pomona—the daughter of Barbara Le Fey's equally famous actress sister.

A classic "Hollywood princess", Pomona had grown up in LA and revelled in the glamorous celebrity lifestyle. She could certainly have regaled the driver with tales of wild parties and decadent excesses—unlike Caitlyn, who, as a shy loner, had always preferred curling up at home with a book. In fact, given Pomona's love of parties and retail therapy, it had been amazing that she had accompanied Caitlyn to the depths of the English countryside and—despite the lack of good shopping!—had remained in the tiny village of Tillyhenge. It was a testament of the affection between the two girls—although Pomona's eternal fascination with magic and the paranormal might have played a part too. She had been delighted to discover Tillyhenge's witchcraft associations and had quickly made herself at home on James's estate, endearing herself to everyone with her bubbly manner and flamboyant style.

*Pomona's going to die when I tell her what happened at the hospital!* thought Caitlyn. Her cousin was at the Manor now, waiting anxiously with Vanessa's friends to hear news from the hospital, and a part of Caitlyn wanted to head there immediately. But she knew that she should go to the village first. Someone needed to tell the Widow Mags that her estranged youngest daughter had finally returned, and Caitlyn would rather that her grandmother heard the news from her than from a village gossip.

As if following her thoughts, the taxi turned off the main road and drove through some woods before emerging into a small village green.

The driver caught her eye in the rearview mirror again and said, with a grin: "Welcome back to Tillyhenge."

# CHAPTER TWO

The taxi deposited Caitlyn beside the village green and she watched it drive off with some relief. Much as she had wanted a distraction from her own tumultuous thoughts, the driver's nosy questions had been starting to get uncomfortable. She walked across the green, making for one of the cobbled lanes which would wind through the village until it reached *Bewitched by Chocolate*, the chocolate shop housed in the pretty, thatched-roof cottage at the edge of the woods.

As she walked, Caitlyn became aware of stares and whispers from the people she passed and sensed an atmosphere of tension that she had never encountered in the village before. At first, she wondered if she was imagining things. But when two of the village residents, who would normally have smiled and said hello, scurried past her without meeting her eyes, and when another resident ducked quickly into a shop instead of crossing her path, she knew that something was wrong.

There had always been a group of villagers, of course, who had hated and feared the Widow Mags. And as the old witch's granddaughter, Caitlyn had come in for her fair share of animosity too, particularly with regards to her "special relationship" with James Fitzroy. Many of the jealous local females had been unable to believe that the handsome owner of Huntingdon Manor (and one of the most eligible bachelors in England) could have chosen *her*. With her shy manner, lack of style, and pear-shaped figure, how could this interloper have trumped the far more glamorous, slim, sophisticated women that frequented James's social circles—unless she had employed some kind of black magic to bewitch him? Caitlyn knew that it was just vicious gossip and that she should ignore it, but it had been very hard to endure.

Still, over recent months, she had been heartened to see several villagers slowly abandoning their old prejudices and coming to accept and respect the Widow Mags as a member of the local community. Many had even started to patronise her chocolate shop and enjoy her handmade treats without fear. So it was incredibly disheartening to overhear malicious whispers and see those wary sidelong looks again.

*Why is everyone so hostile suddenly?* wondered Caitlyn. She knew that there had been anxiety in the village about Samhain approaching and the festival events that the Manor was planning. And the sudden, mysterious death of Vanessa's friend Percy hadn't helped things either, with many believing that the young book dealer had been hexed by the Widow Mags. Caitlyn winced as she remembered the nasty scene in the village green yesterday morning, when several villagers had formed a circle around her grandmother and pelted her with verbal abuse and rotten fruit. The situation had been diffused in the end without anyone getting hurt, but the memory of the aggressive mob gave her a chill of unease.

The cobbled path turned a corner, and Caitlyn stopped short as she nearly crashed into a woman coming in the other direction. Her heart sank. It was Vera Bottom, the unofficial leader of the "anti-witch brigade" in Tillyhenge, who seemed to spend all her spare time preaching about the evils of magic and witchcraft. Unlike many other villagers who had softened towards the Widow Mags as they got to know her, Vera seemed only to grow more paranoid and hostile. Now her eyes narrowed as she saw Caitlyn, and she took a fastidious step back, as if she might be contaminated by sheer proximity.

"What's this I hear about Lord Fitzroy's sister being turned into a changeling?" she demanded without preamble. "They say she disappeared from her hospital bed and was swapped for a strange woman. It's your doing, isn't it? You and the Widow Mags and the rest of your filthy witch family!"

"Let me pass," said Caitlyn wearily, trying to step around the woman.

Vera moved quickly to block her way. "Not until you confess what you've done," she hissed. "I know how you used black magic to get your claws into Lord Fitzroy... and now you're attacking the rest of his family too! What did you do to his sister?"

Caitlyn tried again to get around the woman, determined to keep her mouth shut and not rise to the other's baiting, but once more Vera blocked her way.

"You used witchcraft on that poor young man up at Huntingdon Manor as well, didn't you? The Manor staff have been telling us all about it. They said he was found in the Library and that he'd been trying to steal a witch's book—" Vera leaned forwards and jabbed a finger in Caitlyn's chest. "—your *grandmother's* book! And she hexed him for trying to read it."

"That's rubbish!" said Caitlyn, provoked in spite of her best intentions. "Percy died of a heart attack—you can ask the police."

"Yes, but it was no *natural* heart attack," Vera insisted. "It had been brought on by something. Don't try to deny it! He was poisoned, wasn't he?"

Caitlyn hesitated. She couldn't bring herself to tell an outright lie. "The forensic report did suggest that the heart attack might have been triggered by some kind of toxin—but it had nothing to do with the Widow Mags," she added quickly.

"*Of course* it had to do with her! Don't try to cover it up. I know what the police found in that young man's room: some Florentines from your grandmother's chocolate shop which contained chocolate-covered deadly nightshade berries!" Vera said. "It's obvious that the Widow Mags used her own chocolates to poison that young man."

"Don't be ridiculous—why on earth would she do that?" cried Caitlyn with exasperated annoyance. "The last thing anyone would do is incriminate themself by poisoning someone with chocolates from their own shop! Yes, Percy bought some Florentines from *Bewitched by Chocolate*—I sold them to him myself—but so did half a dozen other customers, and they're all fine. Besides, there weren't any deadly nightshade berries in the Florentines—that's just a stupid rumour! There were wild autumn berries like bilberries and sloe berries foraged from the woods, but nothing else."

"My sources don't lie," insisted Vera. "I have it on good authority that deadly nightshade berries were found at the Manor."

"So what? That doesn't mean that they're connected to the Widow Mags."

"Deadly nightshade is a witch's herb—everyone knows that," Vera hissed. "Belladonna. It's the perfect poison for a witch to use."

"Aww, come on! Why on earth would the Widow Mags want to harm Percy?" asked Caitlyn impatiently. "She didn't even know him!"

"Oh, she had reason," said Vera, nodding with smug certainty. "I told you: she hexed him for trying to read her book. Don't try to deny it. We all saw Inspector Walsh questioning your grandmother out on the village green yesterday. He showed her a page torn from the book—it was the page that poor young man was clutching in his hand when he was found dead. And I heard the Widow Mags identify the writing on that page as hers. So it *was* her book!" she said triumphantly. "And it was no normal book either. It was one of those—what d'you call it— 'witch's *grimoires*', wasn't it?"

Caitlyn had always marvelled at the speed of the village grapevine, but for the first time, she really feared its power. How on earth had Vera managed to learn so much in such a short time?

"So what if it was?" she said, trying to sound offhand.

"Do you think I'm a fool?" snarled Vera. "I know what a *grimoire* is! It's a 'book of spells', where the witch keeps all her wicked knowledge. It's an evil book, and that's why that young man was killed—"

"I'm not listening to this rubbish any more," said Caitlyn, trying to shove Vera aside. "Please move and let me pass."

"Don't touch me!" cried Vera shrilly, jumping back and whipping something out of her pocket, which she waved wildly in front of her. "I... I'm not afraid of you, witch! I have p-protection now! You... you cannot h-harm me!"

Caitlyn squinted at the item that Vera was brandishing in her face. It looked like a small bouquet of dried herbs and flowers, tied together with twine. A sharp, pungent aroma filled the air.

"*Vervain, trefoil, Saint John's wort, dill... Hinder witches of their will,*" chanted Vera, manically waving the herbs in front of her. "*Vervain, trefoil, Saint John's wort, dill... Hinder witches of their will!*"

"Oh, for heaven's sake—!" said Caitlyn, rolling her eyes. "Vera, you do realise that you're in the twenty-first century?"

"Do not mock me, you demon hussy!" cried Vera, waving the bunch of herbs at Caitlyn again. "You may try to pretend that there is no devilry here, but I know the truth! And I have help now. Yes! We have someone on our side who knows how to use magic too, and who can give us guidance and protection. We are not powerless in defending ourselves and our homes against your evil influence any more!"

Caitlyn's hands curled into fists. For a moment, she was so tempted to use her powers—to cast a spell on this hateful woman, show her *real* magic, and watch her squirm. Then she forced herself to take a deep breath and unclench her hands. If there was one lesson that had been drummed into her since arriving in Tillyhenge, it was the importance of keeping a low profile, of keeping their witch abilities a secret. No matter the provocation, you never retaliated with magic unless you had no choice. Besides, she knew that scaring Vera with a spell might have felt temporarily satisfying, but in the end, it would only have made things worse, deepening the woman's fear and hatred.

So she stood still and said nothing as Vera stabbed a forefinger in her direction and hissed: "Just you wait! We're going to destroy you and your whole family. We will cleanse Tillyhenge of your black magic!"

Whirling, she stalked away. Caitlyn stared after her for a moment, then she sighed and continued along the cobbled path, trying her best to push the unpleasant episode from her mind.

As she neared *Bewitched by Chocolate*, Caitlyn's thoughts returned to her mother's unexpected reappearance. She began to feel nervous, wondering how she should broach the subject of Tara to the Widow Mags. The old witch had never been easy to talk to, and when it came to the subject of her estranged youngest daughter, she was even more prickly than usual. Caitlyn knew that Tara had done something terrible before she'd run away— something unforgivable, which was why her name was never even mentioned any more. But the Widow Mags would never talk about what had happened, and Caitlyn remained confused and frustrated. Now she hoped that, with her mother finally back, her grandmother might not be able to avoid the subject and might finally give her some answers.

*But first I have to break the news*, thought Caitlyn with a gulp. For a cowardly moment, she wished that she *had* let the village grapevine deliver the bombshell—or that the Widow Mags had actually

21

seen through Tara's disguise and had already guessed the truth. Then she, Caitlyn, wouldn't have to be "the messenger". But Tara had cleverly never ventured anywhere near the chocolate shop, so the Widow Mags had never had any opportunity to expose her. In any case, the old witch might not have recognised her anyway. The Widow Mags could have been as thoroughly duped by Tara's glamour magic as everyone else.

*No, wait, there was one person who wasn't completely fooled: Viktor.* Caitlyn smiled with affection as she thought of her "vampire uncle". Even if he was over six hundred years old and looked like a doddery, decrepit old man in an ancient, dusty suit, Viktor's senses had been sharper than anyone else's. In fact, hadn't he tried to warn her when she'd spoken to him right before going to the hospital that morning? Caitlyn flashed back to the conversation with Viktor...

*"I just hope Vanessa is going to be okay, that it's just a light injury like Pomona said. I couldn't bear it if they find something really wrong with her."*

*"Hmm..."* Viktor stroked his knobbly chin. *"Reminds me of my last holiday in Transylvania, when I went to find my favourite cârciumă and it was gone. There was a new café or bistro or whatever they call it these days there instead, and it was in the same place and had the same view... and it did feel familiar somehow... and yet it was completely wrong!"* He

jutted his bottom lip out indignantly. "Dreadful palincă they served too. Nothing like the old cârciumă— nobody makes plum liqueurs like the ancient Transylvanian tavernas."

Caitlyn stared at the old vampire, completely bewildered. "Viktor, what on earth are you talking about? What café? What plum liqueur? What has all this got to do with Vanessa?"

"Same thing, isn't it?" said Viktor. "Something you remember, but nothing like you recall. Especially the scent—just like the plum liqueur. The nose never lies."

*Yes, the scent.* Viktor had complained several times about smelling a familiar scent at the Manor— one that he vaguely recognised but could not place. *"Something you remember but nothing like you recall."* As someone who had originally been *Tara's* "guardian uncle", pledged to watch over her from birth, Viktor would have been one of the few who had known her mother well. His superior senses— especially in his fruit-bat form—would have discerned that the young woman calling herself "Vanessa Fitzroy" smelled distinctly familiar. *It's a shame Viktor's memory didn't quite match up to his nose, though,* thought Caitlyn ruefully. If he could have pinpointed why "Vanessa" had smelled so familiar, he might have saved them all a lot of grief and prevented a nearly fatal accident that morning!

Caitlyn came out of her thoughts to realise that she was standing in front of the Widow Mags's cottage. The front of the small stone structure had been converted into a shop with mullioned bay windows for displaying the handmade chocolate treats. Caitlyn smiled proudly as she looked through the glass panes and caught a glimpse of the Samhain-themed display that she had helped to create: a luxurious smorgasbord of handcrafted bonbons, truffles infused with autumn spices, caramels enrobed in rich milk chocolate, pralines filled with delicate chestnut cream, and dark chocolate bars studded with toasted hazelnuts and cranberries—all surrounded by miniature pumpkins and carved turnip Jack-o'-lanterns, drifts of orange and yellow leaves, glossy red apples, and bunches of dried herbs and flowers.

Then her smile faded as she realised that beyond the window display, the interior of the shop looked dark and empty. The front door of the cottage was shut. The shop was closed.

Caitlyn frowned and glanced at her watch. It was barely midday. She had never known the Widow Mags to close the shop at this time. The old witch rarely ventured out of her cottage except for the occasional foray into the nearby woods for herbs and berries or the few necessary trips to the doctor to treat her arthritis and other ailments. She certainly wouldn't be wandering around Tillyhenge, mingling with local residents at the pub or browsing the shops on the village high street. So where was she?

The cottage was surrounded by a small garden,

tucked up against the edge of the woods which flowed up the hill behind. Caitlyn walked absently around the side of the building, wondering if there was any chance the Widow Mags might be outside in her garden...

Then she stopped, her heart giving a sickening lurch.

The wall of the cottage was covered in ugly graffiti—huge letters sprayed across the honey-coloured stone in lurid pink, neon green, and black. A series of words jumped out at her:

*"Begone sorceress!"*

*"WITCH EVIL!"*

*"Get out of our village!"*

*"SORCERY = SIN"*

*"demon hussy!"*

*"NO black magic!"*

*"end the Crone!"*

# CHAPTER THREE

Caitlyn forced her eyes away, her heart pounding. She knew graffiti was really just paint, but there was something particularly horrible about the sprayed abuse—the feeling of violation and defilement, with the naked aggression in the ugly words seeming to linger long after the attacker had gone.

Then her shock began to turn to anger. Who had done this? Her eyes drifted reluctantly back to the scrawls, and she focused on one phrase: *"demon hussy!"* Vera had used the exact same words just now, she recalled. Was Vera and her gang of vigilantes behind this?

Setting her lips angrily, Caitlyn returned to the front of the cottage. And then she noticed, for the first time, that one of the windowpanes had a large crack, as if someone had thrown a stone at it. She hadn't seen it earlier, from where she had been standing, because the light had been in the wrong direction. Now that she was closer, she was horrified to see that, in addition to the crack, there were dried food stains and splotches on some of the other windowpanes, and one slimy trail dribbling down into a pile of broken eggshells beneath the window.

Caitlyn felt anger and disgust surge through her. She wanted to hunt down the despicable group of villagers who had done this. But then a more disturbing thought intruded: *Where is the Widow Mags?* Her grandmother would never have stood by while her home was defiled like this. The fact that she wasn't here—at a time when she normally would be—caused a flicker of unease in her mind.

*Oh wait... of course! She must be with Bertha*, she told herself, smiling in relief. *How stupid of me not to think of that. Yes, Grandma must have gone to Aunt Bertha's shop. I'm sure I'll find them both there.*

Caitlyn turned towards the cobbled path that led back towards the centre of the village, but then she paused and looked back, biting her lip. The ugly words defacing the walls of the cottage seemed to scream at her, even from this distance. Shouldn't she do something to try to remove the graffiti? But what could she do? Fetch a bucket and scrubbing brush? No, that would be a waste of time. There was no way simple soap and water could remove paint from the stone walls. Could she paint over the words perhaps? Wasn't that how people normally dealt with graffiti in big cities? But she would need to find paint, rollers, ladders, and all manner of other equipment. Besides, it would take hours, and she just didn't have the time. What's more... her eyes lingered over the soft honey-coloured limestone of the Widow Mag's cottage, the quintessential feature of iconic Cotswold dwellings, and she shuddered at the thought of artificial paint plastered over the natural beauty of the stone.

Then a thought struck her: *Aren't I supposed to be a witch?* Couldn't she simply use magic to remove the graffiti? Warming to the idea, she recalled excitedly that the Widow Mags had taught her several House-Proud spells. They were just simple incantations to help with domestic cleaning and tidying chores, but surely the principle was the same? After all, the House-Proud spells were designed to clean away unwanted dirt and mess, so if she could just redirect them to the graffiti...

Caitlyn looked back at the defaced stone walls, suddenly assailed by a wave of doubt. This wasn't like mopping up some spilled cream or wiping up melted chocolate. Did she have enough magical ability to do it?

*I have to try*, she told herself. *Even if it probably won't work.* Feeling self-conscious, she closed her eyes and dredged her memory, trying to recall the spells that her grandmother had taught her. She blurted out the first one that came to her head:

> *"Whisk and whoosh, broom so bright,*
> *Sweep away this sorry sight.*
> *From dust to dawn, clean and clear,*

*Make this mess now disappear!"*

As the last word left her lips, a broom propped against the garden shed quivered, then sprang to life with a jerk. Caitlyn watched with a mix of hope and disbelief as the broom shuffled across the cobblestones towards the cottage walls, but instead of attacking the graffiti, it began zealously sweeping the fallen leaves and dirt on the path in front of the cottage. It whirled around, sending a small cloud of dust into the air, and then, to Caitlyn's horror, turned towards her and began attacking her ankles with fervour.

"Hey! No... wait... not me!" Caitlyn protested. The broom swished urgently at her feet as if she were part of the mess it needed to clean. "Stop it! Go away! Shoo!"

She hopped around on one foot, trying to ward off the broom with flustered hands. It was like trying to calm an overeager puppy who had twitching straw bristles instead of a slobbery tongue. Finally, she managed to grab the handle of the broom and mutter the Undo spell. Instantly, the broom went limp in her hands.

Caitlyn breathed a sigh of relief and propped the broom back against the side of the shed, then looked at the graffiti on the wall once more. Did she dare try again? She tried to recall another spell—something that might work better. Wait... wasn't there one about wiping away blemishes? Closing her eyes,

Caitlyn delved into her memory once more, trying to remember the words. Then she whispered them slowly, hesitantly:

*"Shine and shimmer, gleam and glow,*
*Banish blight and let it go.*
*Polish high, polish low,*
*Wipe away each blemish so!"*

She opened her eyes and looked nervously around. No broom, bucket, mop, or other cleaning equipment seemed to be attacking her. *Whew.* She glanced at the cottage and smiled in surprise and pleasure as she saw that the windows, previously covered in food stains, were now wiped clean, the glass panes sparkling. Feeling a glimmer of hope, she lifted her gaze to the graffiti on the walls. Her smile faltered and she stared in horror. The graffiti, too, was now sparkling, the ugly words looking luminous, the paint transformed so that they glittered like neon lights.

"Noooo..." groaned Caitlyn.

The offensive words seemed to taunt her even more now, their glowing outlines turning the cottage walls into a grotesque billboard. This was the last thing she needed. Instead of erasing the graffiti, all she had done was give the abuse even more of a spotlight!

"Why did I ever think I could work magic?" she muttered to herself. "I knew I couldn't do it."

Then she paused as another memory flashed in her mind—another time when she had given up in frustration after struggling to work a magical spell. The echo of the Widow Mags's voice came to her now:

*"When you start something intending to fail, that is what happens... The difficulty isn't learning to do the spell. The difficulty is believing you can. Magic only works if you really believe."*

Caitlyn took a deep breath and let it out slowly, then turned to look at the graffiti again. With new determination, she closed her eyes and searched her memory once more. There was another House-Proud spell that she had been taught: something-something... *"by water's flow"*... and *"wash away the stain"*... no, *"wash away what should not show"*... yes, that's it...

Caitlyn opened her eyes and looked straight at the graffiti, focusing not just on the words, but on the malicious intent that had been behind them. Then, slowly but firmly, she began to recite the spell:

*"By mop and cloth, by water's flow,*
*Wash away what should not show.*
*Let kindness reign, each mark restrain,*
*Clear each blot, leave no stain."*

There was a pause. Caitlyn kept her eyes on the graffiti, her heart beating fast. The paint shimmered, then slowly began to dissolve and disappear, as if being gently wiped away by an invisible hand. Caitlyn watched, transfixed, as each letter, each word of hate, was cleansed away, leaving the stone wall clean and unblemished.

She let out the breath she didn't know she had been holding, her whole body trembling with a mixture jubilation and relief. *I did it!* She laughed out loud, feeling suddenly exhilarated with the sense of success and achievement. Whirling, she hurried away from the cottage, following the cobbled lane back towards the centre of the village. She couldn't wait to tell her aunt and her grandmother about what she had achieved!

She practically ran all the way back to the village green and then down a lane leading off the village high street, to where another quaint stone cottage had been converted into a shop. The sign above the door read *"Herbal Enchantments"* and the window display showed an eclectic collection of organic soy candles, goat's milk soap, natural loofah sponges, herbal teas, essential oils, tinctures, and more. But Caitlyn barely glanced at the display as she rushed up to the front door—only to stop short in dismay as she realised that this, too, was locked.

She stepped back, surprise and confusion creasing her brow as she looked up at the closed shop. *Herbal Enchantments* belonged to her aunt Bertha—her mother's older (and much calmer, more down to earth) sister. Bertha was the gentle maternal figure that Caitlyn had craved all her life, and her aunt's soothing presence had always been a wonderful balm against any adversity and turmoil. Since arriving in Tillyhenge, Caitlyn had come to rely on Bertha as always being there, gentle and comforting. Now, the dark, empty shop felt like a slap in the face.

Caitlyn bit her lip, feeling the niggle of worry grow into a profound unease. She had been so sure that she would find the Widow Mags here with her aunt, and now she felt completely at a loss. *Where is Bertha? Where is Grandma? And what about Evie?* wondered Caitlyn, thinking of Bertha's daughter—her "English cousin" Evie: a sweet, bashful eighteen-year-old who felt like the younger sister she'd never had. It was the weekend, and Evie would normally be helping her mother in the shop, but she, too, seemed to be missing.

Suddenly, Vera's voice, thick with venom, echoed in her mind: *"We're going to destroy you and your whole family. We will cleanse Tillyhenge of your black magic!"*

Caitlyn swallowed hard, trying to stifle a flare of panic. In spite of her best efforts, her imagination began to run wild. *Oh my God—what have the villagers done to them?* Images of historical witch trials and angry village mobs flashed through her mind, even though she kept reminding herself that such torture and persecutions had ceased in the UK with the Witchcraft Act being repealed.

*Don't be silly!* she chided herself. *I'm sure they're fine. I'm sure there's a perfectly logical explanation.*

Feeling sheepish, Caitlyn remembered suddenly that she could simply call her aunt and be reassured at once. She pulled her phone out of her pocket, but a glance at the top corner of the screen made her heart sink. Tillyhenge was notorious for being a "black spot" where both phone and internet services were unpredictable and often absent. It added to the village's "spooky" reputation, although it was probably due to nothing more than an unhappy coincidence of poor network coverage in this pocket of the countryside. Caitlyn had mostly grown used to living with poor connectivity in the months she'd been in Tillyhenge, but now she felt helpless frustration as she saw the symbol for network reception showing as zero.

*Rats!* She stood for a moment, chewing her lip and considering her options. *I'll go back to Huntingdon Manor,* she decided. At least there, she would have access to better communication options, as well as support from Pomona and members of the staff if she needed to escalate the search for the Widow Mags and Bertha.

She turned to retrace her steps back to the chocolate shop. Although the official route to Huntingdon Manor involved driving out of the village, rejoining the main road which circled the dale, and entering the estate from the other side, there was a faster way: a shortcut over the hill which lay behind the village. In fact, the path started right behind *Bewitched by Chocolate,* almost from the Widow

Mags's back door, and she hurried towards it now.

It was a route that Caitlyn had walked many times, but somehow familiarity didn't seem to make it any easier, and by the time she reached the top of the steep ascent, she was out of breath and sweating profusely despite the chilly weather. She paused at the crest of the hill, panting and trying to get her breath back and took in the 360-degree view which unfolded before her.

The sky might have been grey and the weak autumn sun obscured by banks of clouds, but the panorama was still spectacular: the quintessential "rolling hills" and drystone walls of the Cotswolds countryside stretching out in all directions, looking like something straight out of a tourist calendar. And down on the other side of the hill, nestling in formal landscaped gardens like a setting straight out of a Regency romance, stood Huntingdon Manor. It looked so idyllic in the pale autumn light that it was hard to imagine a violent murder could have been committed there two nights ago.

Tearing her eyes away from the view, Caitlyn glanced at the other end of the hilltop where a circle of standing stones stood bathed in the hazy afternoon sunshine. This eerie collection of sarsen boulders was Tillyhenge's main claim to fame and the biggest draw for tourists who stopped in the village. Supposedly the misshapen forms of ancient warriors, frozen by magic but ready to awaken one day, the circle was also supposed to conceal a doorway to the

Otherworld. Tourists loved these legends and eagerly climbed the hill to view the standing stones and to test the various superstitious claims—such as being unable to count the number of stones, no matter how many times you tried. Caitlyn was sure that was just another folk myth (although she had to admit that she couldn't seem to come up with a definitive number, no matter how many times she tried to count them). Still, she couldn't deny that there *was* something about the ancient site: the stones exuded a vibe that was hard to describe but could nevertheless be felt. And right now, those eerie silhouettes did nothing to assuage her feelings of worry and panic.

*Stop it! There is nothing sinister going on. You're letting your imagination run away with you*, she chided herself.

Still, she didn't linger at the top of the hill. As soon as she'd got her breath back, she plunged down the other side, heading for the Manor house in the distance.

# CHAPTER FOUR

The gradient was much milder on the other side of the hill, sloping gently down into a sort of plateau where the main Fitzroy residence was situated, and it wasn't long before Caitlyn was hurrying up to the front steps of Huntingdon Manor.

"Mosley!" she cried as the front door opened to reveal the tall, erect figure of the Manor's butler. "Mosley, have you seen—"

She broke off as she caught sight of the figure behind Mosley: a middle-aged woman with frizzy, carroty-red hair, dressed in a voluminous purple kaftan that clashed incongruously with her sensible brown walking boots.

"Aunt Bertha!" she cried, rushing past Mosley to grab the woman's hands. "Oh, Aunt Bertha, you're all right!"

Bertha looked at her, slightly startled. "Well, of course, dear—why wouldn't I be?"

"I thought..." Caitlyn took a deep breath, suddenly

feeling very silly. Her wild imaginings seemed ludicrous now, and she felt her cheeks redden as she said: "Um... I got a bit worried. I found the chocolate shop all shut up, you see, and nobody there. And then I went around to your shop and that was closed too. It's the middle of the day and you don't normally shut at this time, so I started wondering if... well, never mind."

Bertha smiled at her. "Things have been so chaotic in the last few days, and the Manor's marketing team really need help with last-minute preparations for the Samhain Festival, so I offered to come and lend a hand. Ronnie, the head chef at the Coach House restaurant, had also been wanting Mother to come and advise him on the new chocolate creations for the dessert menu... so I thought I might as well bring her with me and kill two birds with one stone. The shops will be fine if they're closed for a day."

She paused and looked at Caitlyn curiously. "But I should be asking *you* how everything is! I heard the dreadful news about James's sister this morning... apparently, she had an accident? And there was also a report of a strange woman being found in her hospital bed? But Mosley just informed me that he received a phone call from Vanessa—the 'real' Vanessa, that is—and she is actually in London!" Bertha shook her head in bewilderment. "What on earth is going on? You've just come back from the hospital, haven't you? What happened there? Who is this strange woman who has taken Vanessa's place?"

"Er..." Caitlyn glanced sideways at Mosley, who was hovering unobtrusively behind them. She knew that the butler could be trusted to be discreet—he took his butler duties and expectations *very* seriously—but would his loyalties extend to embracing magic? Mosley seemed to sense her unease because he coughed politely and said:

"Would you like some refreshments while you discuss matters? I can have some tea brought to the private parlour here." He indicated a doorway next to them which gave onto a lovely room adorned with intricate wainscoting and damask curtains.

"Thanks, Mosley, that would be wonderful," said Caitlyn, giving him a grateful look.

As soon as they were alone in the parlour, Bertha looked at her niece expectantly. Caitlyn hesitated, wondering how to say it, then decided to just plunge in.

"Aunt Bertha, that strange woman in Vanessa's hospital bed..." She took a deep breath. "She's my mother—your sister—Tara."

Her aunt looked at her blankly.

"And yes, the real Vanessa is still in London," Caitlyn hurried on. "The girl we knew as 'Vanessa' was actually Tara in glamour all along. She took Vanessa's place, and it was she who arrived here on Thursday night with Vanessa's friends. But when Tara—as 'Vanessa'—had that fall and hit her head, it must have broken the glamour spell. She reverted to her real appearance, and the real Vanessa in London also woke up."

"So... so Tara's been here the whole time?" Bertha said incredulously.

Caitlyn nodded. "You were the one who told me that 'glamour magic' is one of her most powerful talents," she reminded her aunt. "I suppose it was easy for her to fool us. In any case, as James's sister, she wouldn't have had very much to do with you or the Widow Mags—or anyone else who might have known her before—so she was fairly safe from detailed scrutiny."

"I can't believe it..." murmured Bertha, looking dazed.

"We knew she was here at the masquerade ball last month: she was caught on the security footage. And you said you thought she was still in the vicinity—you said you could sense it, remember?"

Bertha gave her a wry look. "Well, I didn't 'sense it' very well if I never realised that she was impersonating James's sister! The thing I don't understand is: why?"

"I think you can guess why," said Caitlyn. "Tara was searching for the *grimoire*, wasn't she? She must have somehow got information that it was hidden here, somewhere, in the Manor. So by impersonating James's sister, she could get access to all parts of the Manor and spend enough time here to search thoroughly. But as it turned out, because Percy had the dowsing pendulum, he found the *grimoire* first.

He uncovered it in the Library on the first night they arrived. And whoever murdered him must have taken the *grimoire*."

Caitlyn looked pleadingly at Bertha. "Please, Aunt Bertha—you have to tell me what happened all those years ago! I know Tara was the one who stole the *grimoire* from the Widow Mags originally. You can't hide that from me any more. Why did she want it? And how did she lose it?" She grabbed her aunt's hand as Bertha pressed her lips together. "No, don't clam up again! Please! We know Tara is here. She's involved somehow in this recent murder... and the *grimoire* is at the heart of everything. Please, Aunt Bertha—something strange and bad is going on. You *have* to tell me what you know!"

Bertha hesitated for a long moment, her expression conflicted. Caitlyn held her breath. In the past, whenever she'd asked her aunt about her mother, she had hit a wall. The Widow Mags had always cut in and forbade Bertha from talking; or if the Widow Mags hadn't been there, the unspoken taboo had hung in the air, staying Bertha's tongue. In fact, the only time Bertha had defied the old witch and spoken about Tara was when she and Caitlyn had been visiting a commune together, away from Tillyhenge and the Widow Mags's domineering presence. But even then, Bertha hadn't revealed very much, other than that she had been away from home when her wild, rebellious, younger sister had run away after clashing with their mother. Now, Caitlyn looked at her aunt and hoped fervently that Bertha would finally be able to ignore the Widow Mags's edict and reveal what she knew.

Bertha avoided her eyes, gazing out the window for several minutes before finally looking back at Caitlyn again. She sighed, her shoulders slumping. Then she took a deep breath and began talking:

"You know Tara had an incredible natural ability with magic—in a way, I suppose one could call her a 'witch prodigy'. Even when she was just a toddler, she seemed able to conjure spells and enchantments purely by instinct, without any formal training." Bertha gave a small reminiscent smile. "The problem was, she was also terribly wild and headstrong—and of course, you know how autocratic Mother can be. The two of them clashed constantly, especially as Tara grew into her teens. She was always doing things to defy Mother or deliberately challenge her."

Bertha sighed. "I did try to keep the peace when I was still at home—not that Tara listened to me much. There was a big age gap between us, and we were so different in personality that we could never really relate to each other. I don't think Tara ever saw me as a friend—she certainly never confided in me. But still, I did what I could, and I think my efforts did help."

"But then you left to live in a commune," said Caitlyn, remembering what her aunt had told her before.

"Yes, that's right. Just before Tara turned

seventeen. It was the one time in my life that I did something crazy and impulsive!" said Bertha, chuckling. "And it was a wonderful adventure... I met Evie's father... I discovered my passion for herbalism, my true calling... I spread my wings..." Her eyes took on a wistful expression, and her voice faded away for a moment, before she gave herself a slight shake and said, in a brisk voice more like her usual self: "But it did mean that things got much worse between Mother and Tara because I wasn't there to act as a buffer between them any more.

"Besides, Tara had become dreadfully cocky by then. Maybe it was just typical teenage arrogance— although I have to say, Evie is about the same age now that Tara was then, and she doesn't seem to have any of that same smug confidence," Bertha observed. "Tara was completely different to Evie, though. She was so sure, so proud of her own abilities. She thought she knew everything there was to know about magic and witchcraft. She *hated* it whenever Mother told her that she wasn't mature enough or experienced enough to learn certain spells—and the thing she was most resentful about was the *grimoire*. The more Mother wouldn't let her look at it, the more she wanted to."

"But I don't understand—I thought the Widow Mags's *grimoire* was just a book of her best chocolate recipes. Why does it matter so much if Tara looks at it?" asked Caitlyn.

"Oh no, there were more than just chocolate

recipes in there. Yes, Mother did record her best recipes for magical chocolate creations, but there were other spells in there too, by other witches," Bertha explained. "You see, a *grimoire* isn't just a collection of spell recipes—it is more like a witch's private journal. Our own personal 'book of shadows', where we record our most valuable thoughts and learnings. Mother's *grimoire* was probably her most precious personal possession. It had been passed down to her from her mother and grandmother before her—and all the other witches in our line, so their collective wisdom is written in there as well."

"So it would have been passed down to you and Tara eventually?" asked Caitlyn.

"Yes, I suppose so—although I have to admit, I have always been more herbalist than witch," said Bertha with a sheepish smile. "Oh, I can conjure magic and cast spells, of course, but it is not where my natural talent lies. What fascinates me is the 'hidden magic' found in herbs themselves—the intrinsic power of nature which can be simply unlocked with a mortar and pestle, without having to resort to charms and incantations. So I have to confess, I have never made much effort to develop my witch powers beyond the basic spells and charms. Tara, on the other hand... well, she revelled in learning Higher Magic and Advanced Witchcraft and even wanted to dabble in Dark Magic. She had the kind of ambition that I never had and a thirst for magical knowledge that was almost akin to an addiction."

"So you think Tara would have been the one to receive the *grimoire* eventually because she would have appreciated it more?"

"Yes, she certainly would have merited it more than me," said Bertha without rancour. "The problem was that Tara didn't want to wait—she felt that she was entitled to it already, because even at seventeen, she was already more powerful than most witches. But for one thing, Mother wanted Tara to *earn* the right to the *grimoire*, by showing herself worthy. And for another... well, for all Tara's advanced talents, Mother didn't think she was mature enough to take on the responsibility of the knowledge."

Caitlyn frowned. "What knowledge?"

"The knowledge contained within the *grimoire*. It might only look like a slim volume on the outside, but that is because a Compression Charm has been applied between the covers to contain the vast amount of knowledge within. It has been passed down through the centuries, and countless witches have added to its pages, each with their own area of expertise. All witches are born with special talents and interests in one area, you see, and they develop their magical abilities in that direction. Mine is working with herbs, Mother's is working with chocolate... Well, one of our ancestors was a witch named Moritha who had an affinity for working with Dark Magic. She recorded many of her most powerful spells in the *grimoire*." Bertha gave a humourless laugh. "You can imagine the incredible allure that had for Tara when she found out!"

"Isn't Dark Magic supposed to be bad?" asked Caitlyn. "I know Grandma has said many times that she won't invoke it."

Bertha nodded. "Yes, it comes with great danger and a great price to pay. It is not something most witches are willing to risk. But it also has incredible potential. There is no power like that which comes with Dark Magic. It can alter reality, raise the dead, curse entire bloodlines, turn back time, and more..." She gave a slight shiver. "Of course, the 'danger' just made it even more attractive to Tara. I think she began to imagine herself as a successor to Moritha; to be able to master Dark Magic and make it do her bidding. And the *grimoire* held the key to that. So Tara became really obsessed with it, with trying to get access to it."

"If Tara was such a powerful witch, I'm surprised she didn't just use some spell to sneakily read the *grimoire*," commented Caitlyn.

"There's more to witchcraft than just having the natural ability," said Bertha with asperity. "You have to harness magic and channel it in the right way. Tara might have had a lot of raw talent, but she was still no match for Mother's greater wisdom and experience. I know she was continually stumped by the complex lock spell that Mother had cast over the *grimoire*. And of course, the more Tara challenged her, the more Mother dug her heels in—and vice versa. That's the real problem, you know," she said with a sad smile. "They are too *much* alike in personality, both so proud and stubborn, and neither willing to give an inch."

"But I asked Grandma, that night we tried to find the *grimoire* in her bedroom, and she told me that it's gone," said Caitlyn. "So did Tara finally manage to break the lock spell and steal it? Is that why she disappeared?"

Bertha gave a helpless shrug. "I think so, but I can't tell you for sure. As you know, I was in that commune up in Scotland at the time, and I was too focused on other things for a while to pay much attention to what was happening at home. When I heard that Tara had disappeared, I assumed that she'd just stormed off and run away from home in a fit of temper again. She'd done it a few times before, you see, but she'd usually return after she'd calmed down."

"But she didn't return this time," said Caitlyn.

Bertha shook her head sadly. "When I realised that this time was different, I tried to ask Mother about what had happened, but all she would say was that Tara had betrayed us all. I never understood what she meant by that. I knew that Tara had done something dreadful, something that had hurt Mother terribly, but I didn't tie it to the *grimoire* since I didn't realise it was missing until several months later. When I did notice that it was gone and tried to ask Mother about it again, she just wouldn't talk about it. And it's been like that ever since. Now, she won't even mention Tara's name any more.

"But that doesn't mean that she has forgotten her," Bertha added quickly, seeing Caitlyn's expression. "You mustn't think too badly of your grandmother, Caitlyn. I know it seems cold and harsh of her to shun Tara like this, but it's not because she doesn't care. She does still love Tara."

Caitlyn made a disbelieving noise. "She doesn't act like it. You said she won't even mention my mother's name."

Bertha sighed and said gently, "People are complicated, dear. Sometimes, they are a hostage to their own pride. And you know how your grandmother never wants to admit that she can be hurt and vulnerable. Mother has been holding on to her anger and bitterness for so long now, I think it has become part of her identity. She can't let it go. She has to cling to it, to keep herself walled off, because otherwise it would mean admitting that she's hurt by Tara's betrayal and refusal to come home."

# CHAPTER FIVE

"Um… excuse me?"

Caitlyn and Bertha looked up in surprise to see a woman sporting a smart trouser suit and a sleek brunette bob stick her head through the parlour doorway. It was Lisa, the Manor's marketing coordinator, clutching a folder brimming with leaflets and documents about the Samhain Festival. She gave them a harassed, apologetic smile.

"I'm so sorry to interrupt, but I really need to speak to you urgently, Bertha."

Bertha glanced guiltily at her watch. "Oh yes, I was supposed to meet some staff members at your office, wasn't I?"

"Yes, I've organised a group to go out on the estate with you and help you gather some more material to replace the bonfire wood that has been stolen—"

Bertha rose from the sofa, looking flustered. "I'm sorry, I *was* on my way, but I just needed to speak to my niece here first about something important."

"No, it's all right. It's not that," said Lisa quickly. "I'm... I'm having trouble with the staff and the volunteers from the village as well. Apparently, the lady who is renting the converted barn on the estate—Miss Lockwood—well, she has been telling them all sorts of things about Samhain, and they've become quite agitated."

"What sorts of things?" asked Bertha, looking annoyed.

"Well... things like this year's Samhain falls on a particularly ominous date, so we're being watched by unseen eyes all the time and any act of preparing for the festival, no matter how small, could invite a witch's curse. I was told that even certain words spoken during the preparations, in casual conversation, could serve as unknowing incantations of black magic—"

"That's ridiculous!" said Bertha irritably. "I've never heard such a load of superstitious twaddle in my life!"

Lisa pulled a face. "It seems that Miss Lockwood is very persuasive. Many of the staff seem genuinely frightened now, and they're refusing to take part in the bonfire collection—or indeed in any other preparation for the festival! I just can't afford a walkout like this now! The festival is less than twenty-four hours away, and there are still so many last-minute preparations... Can you come and speak to them again, please? I'm sure you could calm them."

"Of course," said Bertha with alacrity. Then she looked at Caitlyn. "I'm sorry, dear. You don't mind if we talk more later, do you?"

Caitlyn bit her lip. She was desperate to pump her aunt for more information about Tara, but Lisa looked so harassed that she felt too churlish to continue monopolising Bertha's attention.

"No, of course not," she said, rising as well. "I should probably go and find Pomona anyway."

But as Caitlyn left the room, she paused uncertainly. She knew she should really find Pomona and the other guests—they'd be dying to hear her first-hand account of what had happened at the hospital—but she also felt like she needed a moment to herself. Her head was spinning from all that Bertha had told her, and she wanted some quiet time to mull over things.

Turning decisively, she made her way to one of the side doors of the Manor and stepped outside for some fresh air. As she wandered into the large open space at the rear of the grounds, however, she was startled to find several of the Manor staff rushing past her. They all seemed to be heading for the old coach house, which had recently been converted into a gastropub restaurant—part of James's efforts to modernise the estate. The restaurant was not yet open for lunch, but although there were no customers, a large crowd of estate workers had gathered outside the building.

Curious, Caitlyn joined the throng and tried to

figure out what all the fuss was about. All she could hear were animated voices around her saying:

"Did you hear? She's really going to do it!"

"I'll believe it when I see it."

"Do you think it's true?"

"Wouldn't want to get too close, if you ask me. Don't want to get hexed by mistake."

Caitlyn turned to a young man in overalls—one of the junior gardeners—and asked: "What's going on?"

"It's that old woman from the chocolate shop," he said excitedly, barely glancing at her. All his attention was focused on trying to see over the heads in front of them. "They say she's come to see Ronnie the head chef, and she's going to demonstrate magic!"

"I told ya she's a witch!" said a woman next to him, nodding emphatically. "Always knew those chocolates of hers were bewitched."

*What?* Caitlyn couldn't believe her ears. Surely the Widow Mags wasn't really going to work magic for an audience? What about all the dictates that had been impressed on her since she'd arrived in Tillyhenge, about always keeping a low profile and never exposing her magical abilities unnecessarily in public?

She began to push her way through the bodies in front of her, saying: "Sorry... excuse me... excuse me..."

Given everyone's equal eagerness to get into the restaurant, she probably wouldn't have got far if it weren't for the fact that some of the staff members recognised her and instantly jerked aside, enabling her to pass. Whether this was due to respect or fear, Caitlyn didn't know and didn't care. She was just pleased to be able to squeeze through the crowd and make her way to the large commercial kitchen at the rear of the restaurant. Wriggling through the bodies, she emerged at last at the front of the crowd and found herself beholding a large semicircle of people gathered around a stainless-steel workbench in the centre of the room.

An old woman stood behind the bench, next to the stovetop. Her wild grey hair was pulled back in a messy bun, and her hunched figure was draped in a long black dress, accompanied by a black shawl. She looked almost like a storybook witch come to life, with her strong, hooked nose, fierce eyebrows, and flashing dark eyes, and the impression was accentuated by her hands, which emerged from the long sleeves of her dress, gnarled with arthritis, her fingers curved like claws.

The crowd stared at her with a mix of curiosity and trepidation. They seemed almost afraid to look at her and yet simultaneously unable to tear their gazes away. Some of them had seen the Widow Mags in the village, some had even ventured into her chocolate shop, and all had heard the rumours about her being a witch—but despite the fervent gossip, none had ever actually seen her perform magic.

Now it seemed that was all about to change.

Everyone watched with bated breath as the Widow Mags turned to the burly head chef hovering deferentially beside her and said a few quiet words, somehow seeming to dwarf him despite barely reaching his shoulder. Then she turned back to face the crowd, and a hush instantly descended across the room.

"Are... are you going to show us magic?" blurted a woman in the crowd.

The corners of the Widow Mags's mouth flickered into a smile. "Watch and you'll see."

Then she raised her arms. The crowd drew in an audible breath and several people flinched involuntarily. Everyone watched, riveted, as the old witch reached out and began stirring a dark mixture in a large bowl suspended over a cast-iron pot of boiling water. Whispers and murmurs rippled through the crowd as everyone craned their necks to see better.

"What is it?"

"What's she doing?"

"Is she stirrin' a cauldron or summat?"

"No, you daft bugger, she's stirring a bowl *above* the cauldron."

"Is she castin' a spell?"

"It ain't right!" hissed an angry voice next to Caitlyn.

She turned to see a sullen-looking young man in a white uniform scowling at the old witch. It was Neil, one of the kitchen assistants, who was notorious for being stubbornly superstitious and paranoid about witchcraft. He had always been one of the most hostile of the Manor staff, and he eyed the Widow Mags now with fear and loathing.

"Filthy old crone! I can't believe they're lettin' 'er do this!" he muttered.

Several others in the crowd heard him, and Caitlyn noticed their brows also creasing in consternation. Neil's unease was infecting those around him. In fact, as the flickering flames beneath the pot cast an eerie glow on the Widow Mags's face, and a plume of steam began rising from the pot, people edged back as if a spell might leap straight out of the mixture and ambush them.

Then a rich, heady aroma began to fill the room— sweet and tantalising, luxurious and earthy, with a nutty undertone and a velvety decadence.

*Chocolate.*

Caitlyn chuckled suddenly. The mixture was chocolate! The Widow Mags was melting chocolate! All around her, as the seductive fragrance permeated the room, others were coming to the same realisation. Caitlyn saw people inhale, their eyes brightening and their bodies relaxing as sighs of pleasure escaped their lips. A sense of warmth and comfort stole over the room, like a cosy blanket on a chilly evening, and the crowd's apprehension began to melt like the chocolate in the Widow Mags's skilled hands.

"Why are you all smilin'?" demanded Neil, eyeing

the people around him. "Are you daft? Can't you see you're bein' bewitched?"

"No, Neil," said a woman next to him "It's just chocolate in the bowl, see? Can't you smell it?" She inhaled deeply. "Mmm… that smells *so* scrumptious!"

Neil eyed the bowl suspiciously. "That ain't just chocolate. She's put you under a spell, made you blind so you can't see her witch's brew."

"You're an absolute twit, Neil," said the woman, laughing.

Neil flushed angrily. "Get stuffed, you dim cow! You're the one who—"

"Neil!" the head chef cut in. "That's enough!"

Under his boss's stern gaze, Neil subsided, although his simmering resentment was still obvious as he turned back to the Widow Mags with narrowed eyes. Everyone watched as the old witch cooled the melted chocolate slightly, then raised the temperature once again, her wrinkled face set in lines of calm concentration.

Caitlyn had watched her grandmother do this procedure many times: the art of tempering chocolate, which was crucial to achieving the glossy sheen and perfect snap that were hallmarks of fine chocolate. Still, she never failed to be mesmerised by the old witch's fluid, assured movements. It was almost hypnotic. And it seemed that she wasn't the only one. All around her, she could see members of the crowd looking spellbound as the Widow Mags masterfully manipulated the molten chocolate.

Finally, when the dark mixture was thick and glossy, the Widow Mags dipped a slender spatula into the bowl and, with a practiced flick of her wrist, swirled some molten chocolate onto the marble slab in front of her. Her hands might have been gnarled with arthritis, but they were still surprisingly dexterous, and they moved with a graceful, almost ceremonial precision. The chocolate flowed out like satin, forming elegant, sinuous patterns which hardened on the cool marble into dainty curlicues and intricate spirals.

It looked so simple, so easy, but Caitlyn knew, from frustrating personal experience, that it took great skill to wield the spatula so deftly. Her own attempts at making chocolate swirls had mostly resulted in ugly chocolate blobs, no matter how much she tried to imitate the Widow Mags's movements! A murmur began rising from the crowd, but Caitlyn heard whispers of admiration rather than hushed tones of fear. People surged closer to the workbench, their earlier apprehension replaced by awe and fascination, as they watched the Widow Mags create each miniature masterpiece.

The old witch paused and glanced up, catching the eye of the woman standing next to Neil. "Would you like to try?" she asked, holding out the spatula.

The woman squeaked in delight. "Ooh! Can I?"

Without waiting for an answer, she hurried over to the workbench and grabbed the spatula from the old witch, then dipped it eagerly into the bowl of melted chocolate. Biting her lip in concentration, she lifted the spatula and attempted to mimic the Widow Mags's flicking movement to transfer the dripping chocolate onto the marble slab. Unfortunately, she put too much force into the gesture and the glossy brown mixture splattered across the room, with a large dollop landing on Neil's face.

"Agghhh!" he cried, clawing at his cheeks as if he had been splashed by acid.

"Calm down, Neil..."

"It's just chocolate!"

"Neil—you're all right."

As several people attempted to soothe him, Neil lowered his hands from his face, his tongue darting out involuntarily to taste a smear of chocolate near his lips. Caitlyn saw a mixture of surprise, relief, and embarrassment flood his eyes.

"Bloody hell, Neil—you're a right wuss, aren't you?" said a burly man behind him, clapping a hand on his shoulder. He guffawed. "Getting all hot and bothered over a bit o' chocolate!"

The crowd roared with laughter and Neil flushed dark red. He clenched his fists, his lips shaking, then he turned and shoved people aside, storming out of the kitchen. An excited hubbub filled the room on his departure, only subsiding when Ronnie the head chef clapped his hands.

"All right, folks—show's over," he said. "The Widow Mags and I have to discuss the next season's menu now. You lot can get back to work."

Slowly, the crowd began to disperse. Caitlyn hesitated as people milled past her. She needed to tell the Widow Mags about Tara's reappearance but— glancing back at the workbench, where the old witch was deep in consultation with the head chef—she realised that she couldn't broach the subject now. She would have to find another chance to speak to the Widow Mags and break the news to her in private. Sighing, she turned and followed the others out of the kitchen.

# CHAPTER SIX

Caitlyn smiled inwardly as she followed the rest of the staff out of the restaurant, all whist listening to the chatter around her. Everyone was talking animatedly, their faces bright and beaming, like excited children leaving a funfair after a thrilling ride. Several were marvelling at the old witch's chocolate artistry while others were even talking of visiting *Bewitched by Chocolate* to sample the Widow Mags's treats for themselves.

It was ironic, really. The crowd had come expecting to see a demonstration of dark sorcery, and what they saw *was* the Widow Mags conjuring magic—just not the kind they had expected. It was the "magic" created when skill and passion came together, the magic of the age-old craft of chocolate-making honed to perfection. Caitlyn felt a warm glow of pride as she overheard several staff members talk of the old witch with new admiration and respect. In a place once filled with fear, her grandmother had conjured awe and appreciation, bewitching people simply through a display of skill and knowledge.

She stepped out of the restaurant, still enjoying the buzz of excitement around her, and began walking back towards the Manor house. But as she passed the corner of the coach house building, she was stopped short by the sight of Neil lurking behind a tree at the side of the restaurant. She frowned. *What's he doing?*

She went closer, treading softly on the leaf-covered ground, and saw that Neil was deep in conversation with someone else, partially hidden behind the tree trunk. She shifted direction, approaching from a different angle and ducking under the arching branches of a large rhododendron bush so that she wouldn't be seen. Her eyes widened as the figure behind the tree came into view and she recognised the tall, red-haired woman.

It was Leandra Lockwood, a London academic who had recently taken early retirement and moved to the Cotswolds. Leandra had rented one of the converted outbuildings on the Fitzroy estate as temporary accommodation whilst she looked for a more permanent abode, and she had made quite an impression in the village and on the estate in the few short weeks since her arrival. In a way, it was hardly surprising, since the woman had a penchant for the melodramatic, sweeping around in flowing black velvet dresses and silver medallion necklaces. And despite previously being a professor in the relatively obscure field of "Comparative Religion and Esoteric Philosophy", Leandra was no shy, reserved scholar. In fact, she had the dramatic flair and charisma of an actor and often behaved more like a self-important celebrity than a stuffy academic retiring to a quiet life in the English countryside.

So perhaps it was no surprise that the local residents had been dazzled by her. Still, Caitlyn had been bemused by the villagers' acceptance of Leandra, given that the woman talked openly about magic. Of course, Leandra couched her pursuit in different terms, claiming that she was different from the common witch who dabbled in potions and hexes. Instead, she boasted of elevated magical powers and divination skills drawn from her deeper understanding of ancient wisdoms and rituals; she even espoused a higher purpose of protecting others from evil spirits and black magic. It was obvious, though, to anyone with genuine magical insight that she was talking nothing but mystical mumbo-jumbo, and it had been galling to watch the locals lap up her grandiose falsehoods.

*I can't believe that I actually thought she was my mother for a while*, thought Caitlyn with an inner grimace as she eyed the woman. She had been led astray by a series of coincidences which had seemed to support the idea, even though her gut instinct had rejected the assumption. *Thank God, it wasn't Leandra in the end*, she thought fervently. Whatever the woman in hospital turned out to be like, it couldn't be as bad as having that patronising, sanctimonious harpy as her mother!

Then Caitlyn's ears perked up as she caught the tail-end of what Leandra was saying to Neil:

"...you were right to protect yourself. Witches are skilled at deploying black magic on unsuspecting victims."

Neil looked torn. "But... but it really *was* chocolate. I... I got a taste. It was bloody good too," he said with grudging admiration. "Maybe I was wrong... maybe she wasn't doin' magic after all... maybe she really *was* just showin' how to make chocolate decorations—"

"Fool!" hissed Leandra. "That's exactly how witches deceive you and lure you in, Neil. They hide the extraordinary in the ordinary, weaving a false sense of security around you so that you have no idea of the danger you are in until it is too late. You need to remain on your guard—and you need to warn the others."

"They don't believe me," said Neil sullenly, reddening again with remembered humiliation. "They *laughed* at me and called me a twit!"

"The laughter will soon be wiped from their faces," said Leandra with a grim nod. "They don't realise how precarious their position is; how thin the veil is between the worlds right now. Evil spirits and black magic lurk everywhere, unseen, waiting to claim victims. One misstep is all it takes! People should be taking greater care than ever—and instead, they are playing with fire, hosting this sham of a festival."

"You mean—the Samhain Festival here at the Manor?"

Leandra nodded, her mouth twisting bitterly. "They could have had my guidance; they could have benefited from my expertise, my knowledge of mystical rituals and esoteric practices. But instead, they chose to snub me." She made an angry noise. "Well, they dismiss me at their peril. When you toy with forces you don't understand, especially during Samhain, you invite calamity."

Neil looked at her uneasily. "Are you sayin' summin bad's goin' to happen?"

"Not if you know how to protect yourself," said Leandra quickly. She reached into a small pouch at her side and, with a dramatic flourish, pulled out a small bundle of herbs bound by a length of twine. There were sprigs of clover-shaped leaves accompanied by tiny globe-like blooms, bushy stems with bright yellow flowers, slender, spiky clusters of purple, and long stems with feathery leaves and dense yellow umbels. Their delicate colours seemed to glow, even in the dim shade under the trees, and a sweet, grassy scent—redolent of lemon and aniseed—wafted across to Caitlyn.

"This," Leandra declared, holding it out to Neil, "will protect you from any witchcraft."

"What is it?" asked Neil, staring at the item with wonder.

"A herb charm. It's made with vervain, dill, trefoil,

and St John's wort, bound anti-clockwise around a sliver of iron, the traditional deterrent against malevolent magic."

Neil stretched his hand out to grasp the charm, but Leandra whisked it out of his reach. "Ah-ah... this one is mine. But I can make you another. For a price, of course."

"How much?" asked Neil, eyeing the charm hungrily.

"Why don't you come to my barn tonight, just as the moon is rising? We can discuss more then. And bring any friends who value their protection too."

Neil shifted his weight: "Er... look, I don't have much money—"

Leandra gave him a coy smile: "Price isn't always counted in coin. True protection requires a more... personal investment."

"What d'you mean—"

Leandra cut him off: "I'll explain all tonight. All you have to do is turn up. A small price to pay for peace of mind, wouldn't you say? After all, what value can you place on your soul's protection against the dark forces that lurk in the shadows of Samhain?"

Caitlyn could watch silently no longer. She might have been a shy, quiet bookworm, but she also possessed a temper to match the flaming red tresses on her head when she was roused. Now, bristling with indignation and disgust, she shoved a branch aside and stepped out from behind the rhododendron bush to confront Leandra. As she marched forwards, however, she stepped on a dead twig which snapped with a loud crack, causing Neil to whirl around. He muttered a curse when he saw her and rushed away, leaving the two women alone.

"What are you doing, Leandra?" demanded Caitlyn without preamble. "How can you talk such rubbish?"

Leandra's eyes narrowed. "I didn't think you'd be the type to spy on others, Miss Le Fey."

Caitlyn ignored the dig. "You have no right to go around spreading lies like that—"

"They are not lies," said Leandra. "Everything I said, everything I warned Neil of, is true."

"You're just scaremongering and you know it!" said Caitlyn. "It's bad enough that some of the staff and villagers are nervous and superstitious without you making them even more paranoid." She gestured to the herb charm in Leandra's hand. "You're exploiting people's fears just so you can sell them stuff. You act like some great academic, but you're really nothing more than a scammer peddling fake charms!"

Leandra stiffened, but all she said, with lofty disdain, was: "Everyone has the right to protect themselves."

Her cool, dismissive manner made Caitlyn even more angry. She had thought that Leandra would show some shame or sheepish embarrassment at least, but the other woman seemed completely unrepentant. Leandra was undoing all the goodwill the Widow Mags had just fostered, undermining the progress her grandmother had just made with the staff!

"Protect themselves from what?" Caitlyn demanded. "For heaven's sake, Leandra, this is really no different to a celebration of May Morning or Midsummer's Eve—"

"If you think that, then you're an even bigger fool than I expected. Samhain is an altogether different beast to those other pagan celebrations, and we need to do everything we can to ward off the harmful influence of witchcraft and black magic during this time. The decision to stage a 'Samhain Festival' here at the Manor makes it even more important, and yet there seems to be a complete disregard for the necessary protocols to maintain the integrity of the event!" said Leandra in scandalised tones. "The Samhain bonfire, for instance—it should not be built here, in the Manor grounds, like a cheap tourist gimmick. It should be built and lit in the centre of the stone circle," she said, gesturing in the direction of the hill in the distance. "That is an ancient landmark of great mystical importance, a place where ley lines intersect and strong magic persists. The bonfire should be there!"

Caitlyn looked at her askance. "Leandra, these bonfires are just symbolic—you do know that? They're just a bit of fun, really; an old-fashioned tradition that was part of a pagan harvest festival.

They're not really meant to serve any serious purpose."

"That's where you're wrong!" said Leandra. "If the correct rituals are not performed to protect the local residents and their families, it could have disastrous consequences. The bonfire *must* be properly built, made of ritually consecrated firewood, taken from trees known for their magical powers, and laid with the correct tri-layer symbolism. Ash on the bottom, hawthorn in the middle, and rowan on top. It's the only way for the bonfire to have the necessary protective properties!" Leandra crossed her arms, adding sourly, "I did offer Lisa my skills as an adviser to oversee the Samhain Festival, but she foolishly declined. She thinks your aunt is more than qualified to guide them." She snorted in disgusted disbelief. "Bertha is nothing but a herbal shop owner! What does she know about magic practices and ceremonies? She has no real grounding in mythological traditions, folklore, and ancient wisdoms like I do."

*No, Bertha is a real witch—she doesn't need to spend years studying magic in textbooks*, thought Caitlyn dryly. Still, Leandra's passionate tirade was making her wonder if the retired academic wasn't maliciously spreading superstitious rumours after all—maybe the woman really did believe in her own gobbledygook!

"Bertha knows what she's doing," she said, trying to adopt a diplomatic tone. "She's perfectly familiar with the magical symbolism of trees and how to construct a traditional Samhain bonfire."

"She scoffed at my insistence that the rowan wood must be sourced from a dual-trunked tree," Leandra retorted. "Rowan is especially important because it is a gateway tree, you know. It's a mediator between the living and the dead, and since Samhain is a time when the veil between the worlds is particularly thin, it's crucial to find a rowan with a dual trunk to highlight the meeting of the two realms during this time. By ignoring such a key requirement, Bertha is putting everyone at great jeopardy!" She leaned forwards, her eyes bulging. "And there is more. The villagers have been telling me that there is talk of animal sacrifice—"

"*What?*" Caitlyn burst out laughing. "That's the most ridiculous thing I've ever heard! It's just the village gossips spreading hysterical rumours—I can't believe you actually swallowed it!"

"It is not just a rumour. I heard that one of the dairy farmers is preparing a bull to take part in the Festival."

Caitlyn rolled her eyes. "Yes, but not for sacrifice! One of the ancient Samhain traditions was driving livestock between two bonfires to cleanse and protect them. Lisa thought it would be fun to re-enact that. It should be very entertaining to watch, especially for the children. It's been one of the promoted highlights that's attracted a lot of interest from both tourists and locals."

Leandra looked annoyed to have the wind taken out of her sails. "Even if that were true... it is crazy to bring a bull to a place where there are children about."

"Oh, you don't know Ferdinand," said Caitlyn, smiling fondly as she thought of the enormous black bull. "He's the most gorgeous gentle giant you could ever meet. He's incredibly placid and sweet-natured, and he loves people. There'll be no danger."

As if on cue, there was a loud "*MOOO!*" and they both turned to see a group of people congregating beside the lane which led from the front of the estate, almost like a crowd awaiting a parade. People were talking and pointing with interest, and for a moment, it was hard to see what was at the centre of attention. Then, as two people stepped aside to reveal a gap, an enormous black horned beast came into view.

A wide smile spread across Caitlyn's face. "Ferdinand!"

# CHAPTER SEVEN

Caitlyn hurried over to the huge black bull that was being led into the Manor's rear yard and laughed in delight as he stretched his thick neck towards her. He thrust a soft velvety muzzle into her hand, making her giggle as his whiskers tickled her palm, and Caitlyn felt her heart melt as it always did when she looked into the bull's face.

Ferdinand had huge limpid black eyes with ridiculously long eyelashes and a pale pink, velvety nose—a combo that somehow made him look adorably "cute" despite his huge muscular body. And for all his enormous size and strength, Ferdinand was "a lover, not a fighter"—just like the famous children's storybook bull that he was named after. In fact, he had been the laughingstock of the village for a while when his soft nature had caused him to be bullied by his own herd of cows. His owner Jeremy Bottom, who owned a dairy farm on the outskirts of Tillyhenge, had despaired of ever turning him into a successful stud bull, for Ferdinand had been hand-raised by humans after being abandoned by his mother as a calf and seemed to want nothing more than pats and cuddles.

Luckily, a mishap with a "love potion" stolen from the Widow Mags's pantry meant that Ferdinand was given an inadvertent chance to win the cows' hearts, and he went from lonely days moping in a corner of his field to finally being embraced by his herd of bovine ladies.

Now, everyone was excitedly awaiting the arrival of some "Ferdinand babies" in the spring, and the gentle bull was gaining a new legion of fans as the mascot for Jeremy's recently launched educational farm experiences. Children and adults alike adored him, social media fan pages had been set up in his honour, and people came from far and wide to see him at the dairy farm. Despite his newfound celebrity status, however, Ferdinand had remained as soppy and sweet-natured as ever—and Caitlyn passed by his field whenever she could to enjoy some bovine cuddles and give him a few carrot and apple treats. Now, Ferdinand lowered his massive head and nuzzled enquiringly at her pocket.

"Sorry, sweetie," said Caitlyn. "I don't have anything for you today."

Ferdinand lifted his head and laid it gently on her shoulder, causing Caitlyn to stagger under its weight. He mooed softly and looked up at her, for all the world as if asking for a hug. Caitlyn laughed and obligingly put one arm around his neck, reaching up with her other hand to scratch him behind his ears as Ferdinand swished his tail happily.

"I see you're still falling for the big muppet," chuckled the middle-aged man in gumboots and green overalls who was holding the rope attached to the bull's head harness.

Caitlyn smiled into Jeremy Bottom's tanned, weather-beaten face. The widowed dairy farmer was one of her favourite people in Tillyhenge. Unlike his sister, Vera, who launched vitriolic attacks on the Widow Mags at every opportunity, Jeremy scoffed at the witchcraft gossip and refused to pander to his sister's bigotry. He and his teenage son, Chris, were one of the few who had always treated the old witch and her family with warmth and respect, and Caitlyn felt her spirits lift as she reminded herself that many of the estate staff and villagers *did* share Jeremy's more tolerant attitude.

"I'll always be Ferdinand's number one fan," Caitlyn told him with a chuckle. "Although I'll probably have to get in line after this Samhain Festival! I'm sure half the country will be in love with him after people see him perform the bonfire ritual."

"Aye, that's why we're here," said Jeremy. "I brought Ferdinand to take a walk around and get used to the place, so that he's ready for his big moment tomorrow." He gestured to an empty space at the other end of the yard. "'Course, it would be better if we could do a practice run around the bonfire pile, but I heard that someone's stolen all the wood that had been collected?"

Caitlyn sighed. "Yes, Bertha was really furious about that. She'd spent ages gathering the wood. It was all stacked and ready to go. But then, yesterday morning, it was gone. Someone must have taken it in the night."

Jeremy frowned. "You think it's some kind o' sabotage?"

"I don't know. I'm wondering if it might be connected to all the... er... witch-bashing going on in Tillyhenge—you know, like the graffiti on the Widow Mags's cottage."

Jeremy's frown deepened. "What graffiti?"

Quickly, Caitlyn told him about the state of the chocolate shop that morning and the ugly words of abuse sprayed all over the Widow Mags's cottage walls.

"There's no call for behaviour like that," said Jeremy in disgust. "When I find out who did it, I'm going to give 'em a piece o' my mind, I can tell you! I'll ask Chris—see if some o' his mates know anything about it."

"Do you think some of Chris's friends might be responsible?"

"They're not bad lads," said Jeremy quickly. "But they listen to the wrong folk and they're easy to lead off track, you know? Like a bunch o' sheep—all you need is a yappy sheepdog to push 'em in the wrong direction. And there's been plenty anti-witch talk in the village recently." His face darkened. "I'm ashamed to say that my own sister is one o' the worst. Always rabbiting on about ending witchcraft in Tillyhenge. Thank goodness Chris has more sense than to listen to her nonsense."

"Yes, Chris is great," said Caitlyn warmly. "He often stops by the chocolate shop to ask if we need a hand with anything."

"Aye, he's a good lad, Chris. Got into a fight with his best mate last week, actually, 'cos Steve was badmouthing Bertha's girl, Evie." Jeremy pulled a face. "Steve's older brother Neil works here at the Manor, and he's been filling Steve's head with all sorts o' rubbish about evil spirits at Samhain and witches bringing black magic... Really, what Neil needs is a good clip round the ear to bring him to his senses." He heaved an exasperated sigh, then said, in a brisk tone: "Anyway, I'll send a couple o' my men round to give the cottage a lick o' paint. That way, at least you won't have to look at them nasty words."

"Oh, thanks!" Caitlyn gave him a grateful smile. "But actually... er... I've already taken care of the graffiti. But thanks for the offer. That's really nice of you, Jeremy."

The dairy farmer shrugged. "It's no more than what's right. I reckon people around here have forgotten how to behave like decent folk—"

"*MOOO...*" said Ferdinand suddenly, catching Caitlyn by surprise and nearly knocking her off her feet as he gently butted her chest.

She staggered, laughing. "Are you complaining about being ignored? All right, sweetie..."

She reached out and rubbed the bull's rump affectionately. As she did so, she noticed a figure lurking on his other side. It was Leandra. Caitlyn had momentarily forgotten about the woman.

Jeremy gave Leandra a friendly smile. "You can come closer. Ferdinand is very friendly."

Leandra hesitated, then approached warily, eyeing the bull with a mixture of curiosity and revulsion. "You know, in many cultures, bulls are omens of misfortune—especially black ones," she said. "They're associated with conflict and death."

Jeremy gave an incredulous laugh. "You're not serious, miss!"

"I am," said Leandra, looking down her nose at him. "I wouldn't expect a farmer like you to understand. But in my old London post as Professor of Comparative Religion and Esoteric Philosophy, I studied all the mythological traditions, folklore, and magical practices across different societies, and I can tell you that bulls are associated with death and danger in many cultures. There's the Minotaur, of course, from Greek mythology, and the Bull of Cooley from Irish mythology—that's the beast that sparked the deadly war in the *Táin Bó Cúailnge*—and, of course, there are rural Hindu communities where they believe that seeing a black bull is considered a terrible omen of impending death."

Jeremy looked at her in bemusement, his smile

fading. "But... but those are just myths and superstitions," he protested.

"Many so-called 'myths' are based on a semblance of truth," said Leandra. "Trust me when I say that bringing a bull to the festival is an invitation to black magic. After all, everyone knows that horns are a symbol of the Devil." She gestured to the curved appendages growing out of Ferdinand's head. "Those wicked horns on your bull are a clear link to demonic presence and influence—"

Jeremy made a rude noise. "Are you winding me up? I've never heard o' such nonsense. Look, I don't know much about history and books and ancient rituals and stuff, but I know common sense and I reckon you might need to get a grip on that paranoid imagination o' yours."

Leandra flushed. "My imagination has nothing to do with it! There are real dangers lurking around us, especially now, with Samhain Eve approaching. You will rue your scoffing, farmer, if you continue to ignore the—*aaaghh!*"

Leandra yelped and recoiled as Ferdinand suddenly turned his massive head, then stretched his neck out, blowing gustily as he attempted to sniff Leandra's arm.

"He's just curious. He won't hurt you," said Jeremy. "Look, why don't you give him a pat? You'll see that he's the biggest softie—"

But Leandra wasn't listening. Scowling, she swatted at the bull. "Get away from me!"

Ferdinand looked at her quizzically, obviously puzzled at her hostile behaviour when he was used to most humans cooing in adoration when they saw him. He took another step towards Leandra and huffed softly, regarding her with big, dark eyes.

She gave him a dirty look. "Don't try it on with me. I know you're nothing but a stinking dung machine."

The bull grunted and deposited an enormous cowpat on the path.

Leandra made an outraged noise. "You think that's funny, do you?"

"It's just natural behaviour," said Jeremy in a patient voice. "He doesn't mean anything bad by it. Cows defecate every couple o' hours."

"He's disgusting," said Leandra, eyeing Ferdinand with contempt. She made a kicking motion with one foot. "Get away from me, you filthy brute!"

"Hey! There's no call for that," said Jeremy sharply.

Caitlyn started forwards, indignant words on her own lips as well, but before she could say anything, Ferdinand suddenly thrust his whiskery muzzle up to Leandra's face and slurped her cheek with his thick, fleshy tongue.

"*MOO...?*" said the bull said hopefully.

Leandra shrieked, manically wiping her cheek where a trail of cow drool still clung to her skin, then stumbled backwards and stepped straight into the steaming cowpat on the path. There was a horrible squelching sound and a putrid smell rose in the air.

Leandra gasped, jerking up the skirt of her velvet dress to stare in horror at the sloppy brown mess around her ankles. There were sniggers from the surrounding people and Caitlyn had to bite her lip to stop a guffaw escaping as she watched Leandra hop around on one foot, frantically trying to scrape her shoe clean on a clump of grass.

"You... you bewitched the bull to do that on purpose!" Leandra spluttered, pointing an accusing finger at Caitlyn.

"Don't be ridiculous," gasped Caitlyn, trying not to laugh. "That's just called digestion."

Leandra glared at her. Then, summoning the tattered remains of her dignity, she tried to storm grandly away—an effect that was ruined by the fact that she had to hobble, lopsided, whilst squelching wetly with each step as she disappeared in the direction of her barn. As soon as she was out of earshot, Caitlyn collapsed in giggles, clutching her stomach and leaning against Ferdinand, who stood placidly chewing the cud, completely oblivious to the uproar he'd caused.

Jeremy grinned and winked at Caitlyn. "Guess it's hard not to step in it when you're peddling that much bullsh—"

"Jeremy!"

They turned to see Lisa, the Manor's marketing coordinator, hurrying across the yard towards them, clutching a clipboard and sporting an even more frazzled expression than when Caitlyn had seen her earlier.

"Jeremy, I'm so glad you're here," she said, hastily stepping around the remains of the cowpat as she joined them. "Can I show you the route we want you to walk Ferdinand in tomorrow? And I've also had them set up a stall in the Stables for him, to save you having to take him back to the farm today and then transport him back here tomorrow. I'd like you to take a look at that and make sure it's okay for him."

"Oh aye," said Jeremy equably. He gave Caitlyn another wink, then grasped Ferdinand's head halter and gave it a gentle tug. "Come along, you big wally."

Caitlyn stood and watched, smiling, as the enormous beast lumbered off, walking placidly between Jeremy and Lisa. She felt suddenly lighter and more carefree. It was as if a weight had been lifted off her chest, as if that bout of laughter had chased all the anger and worry, frustrations and tensions of that morning away. Feeling ready to face whatever the rest of the day would bring, she turned and headed back into the Manor house.

# CHAPTER EIGHT

"Holy guacamole! Vanessa was Tara? I mean, Tara was Vanessa?" Pomona's expression was so shocked and bewildered, it was almost comical. "So your mom was, like, impersonating James's sister this whole time?"

"Hush! Keep your voice down," Caitlyn said, glancing warily around.

She had pulled her cousin aside as soon as she had found Pomona and had made sure that they were in a quiet corner of the Manor before recounting what had happened at the hospital. Still, there were always staff about in the daytime, and she wasn't confident about their privacy. Of course, gossip travelled fast on the estate, so Caitlyn knew that it wouldn't be long before the news of Vanessa's bizarre "disappearance" from the hospital and "reappearance" in London would be all over the Manor and the village. Nevertheless, she didn't want to add more fuel to the rumours than necessary.

"Man, there've been so many different stories going around all morning, I didn't know *what* to believe," said Pomona, making an effort to lower her voice. "I mean, we all heard Mosley freaking out when that call came from London, and everyone was shocked to hear that Vanessa was *there* instead of the hospital. The staff were all, like, talking about witchcraft and black magic..." She chuckled suddenly. "Actually, I think most of them were more freaked out at seeing Mosley lose his cool than anything else. It was like seeing the sun going around the moon or something! He even had to sit down while Mrs Pruett gave him a stiff whisky—can you believe it? I've never seen Mosley sit down once in all the months that I've known him!"

Caitlyn gave a small smile. She, too, found it hard to imagine the Manor's impeccably proper butler not standing with his usual erect posture. "He didn't believe all the talk of witchcraft and magic, did he?"

"Nah, I don't think so. I mean, I didn't believe it myself. I just thought... you know... maybe there was some kind of weird mix-up or something. Like, maybe the ambulance took her to London by mistake... I never thought that Vanessa could have been in London all along, and that the girl who *was* here and looked exactly like her wasn't actually James's sister!" Pomona shook her head in disbelief. "Whatever I thought you were gonna tell me, I wasn't expecting *that*!"

"Me neither. You can't imagine how I felt when

that doctor pulled the curtain back and I saw my mother lying there," said Caitlyn, swallowing hard at the memory.

Pomona threw her arms around her and hugged her tight. "Omigod, Caitlyn, you must have been through hell the last couple of hours!"

Caitlyn buried her face in the other girl's shoulder and let out a sigh, feeling suddenly so thankful that her cousin was there. Pomona was a classic Californian beauty, all tanned brown limbs, blue eyes, and big blonde hair, with generous curves that she liked to flaunt in glamorous, revealing outfits. She was loud where Caitlyn was quiet, bold where Caitlyn was shy, and reckless where Caitlyn was cautious. And yet, despite their completely opposite personalities, the two girls had been best friends since childhood. When Caitlyn had discovered that she was adopted and that Pomona wasn't really her cousin by blood, it hadn't changed their feelings for each other. They would always be "family" through bonds that were stronger than shared genes.

Now, she hugged Pomona back, then took a deep breath and straightened. She gave her cousin a weak smile. "I think the thing I just can't get my head around is how no one suspected. I mean, James didn't notice anything, Vanessa's friends didn't notice anything—"

"That's the power of glamour magic," said Pomona, nodding sagely. "See, it's more than just a physical disguise—it's, like, an entire illusion of suggestion. You know, sort of like hypnosis. So you make others believe exactly what you want them to see."

"Yeah, Bertha did tell me that glamour magic was one of Tara's strongest talents," Caitlyn recalled. "I wonder why it stopped working, though? I mean, why did Tara revert to her own self?"

"Maybe she didn't mean to. Maybe it was the blow to her head. The spell must have, like, weakened, and so Tara couldn't maintain the glamour façade anymore. And that's why Vanessa woke up!" Pomona said, snapping her fingers. "I'll bet Tara put Vanessa into some kind of 'magical coma'—you know, to keep James's sister safely out of the way while she was impersonating her—but when Tara got knocked on the head, the magic on Vanessa weakened too." She looked at Caitlyn worriedly. "Is she going to be okay? Your mom, I mean."

Caitlyn nodded. "The doctor said she's going to be fine. Apparently, her scan just showed a mild concussion. He was a bit puzzled, though, about why her symptoms didn't quite match. She seems much more groggy and confused than she should be—"

"Maybe it's the magic," Pomona suggested. "Maybe the strain of maintaining the glamour spell could have, like, magnified the effect of the concussion. Did you ask the doctor about that?"

Caitlyn gave a sardonic laugh. "Pomie, the whole A&E went into total uproar when they realised that the woman in Vanessa Fitzroy's bed had completely changed into another person. No one could think of a logical reason. Can you imagine if I'd started rambling about 'glamour magic' and 'magical comas'? They'd probably have carted me off to the Psychiatric ward for assessment!"

"What about James? He must have believed you."

"I didn't really get a chance to talk to him properly," said Caitlyn, her face clouding as she remembered the scene. "He sort of realised what had happened, of course, when he got the call from Mosley about the real Vanessa being in London, and then when he saw Tara in the bed. And he knew about glamour magic spells from what had happened at the masquerade ball. So I think he must have put two and two together. He did try to placate the hospital staff with some story about mistaken identity, but Dr Gupta—that's the doctor who had been looking after Vanessa—wouldn't buy it. He insisted on calling the police. Luckily, it was Inspector Walsh who showed up, and James was able to take him aside to talk to him."

Pomona pulled a face. "Inspector Walsh? That old sceptic is never gonna believe in glamour magic!"

"Yeah, but you know he has a lot of respect for James. Whatever James said seemed to satisfy the inspector and he helped to calm the hospital people down." Caitlyn took a deep breath. "He's arresting Tara though."

"*What?*"

Caitlyn nodded grimly. "She's still the top suspect

for Daniel Tremaine's murder, remember? Ever since she was identified in that security footage from the masquerade ball, the police have had an arrest warrant out for her."

"Jeez... so Walsh took her to jail?" said Pomona, aghast.

"No, not yet. She has to remain in hospital overnight for observation for her head injury, but Inspector Walsh had her moved into a private room with a guard." Caitlyn sighed. "But yes, once she's released from hospital tomorrow, they'll be taking her into custody."

"Have you spoken to her?"

Caitlyn shook her head helplessly. "They wouldn't let me in to see her without police permission, and I didn't get a chance to speak to Inspector Walsh. I tried, but it was impossible with all the chaos going on. And James was still dealing with the hospital authorities too—it looked like he was going to be a while—so in the end, I just decided that I might as well come back first. I needed to let the Widow Mags and Bertha know about Tara anyway."

Pomona's eyes widened. "How did they take it?"

"Well, I haven't had a chance to tell the Widow Mags yet. She's still in a meeting with the head chef in the Coach House restaurant. But I've told Bertha. She *was* pretty shocked, although..." Caitlyn furrowed her brow. "...at the same time, she didn't seem that surprised. She told me that ever since Tara ran away twenty-two years ago, she'd been using divination tools to try to find her. So she'd already sensed that Tara was close by, somewhere on the estate."

"Shame her divination tools didn't tell her that Tara was disguised as James's sister," said Pomona dryly. "Hey, speaking of divination tools—there are all these rumours going around that you were yelling something about a 'dowsing pendulum' when you and Vanessa were wrestling with each other at the top of the stairs this morning. What was *that* all about?"

Caitlyn gave her cousin an apologetic look. "Oh God, Pomie, I never got the chance to tell you what happened after you left me to go and look for that elf pouch thingy—"

"It's not an 'elf pouch thingy'," said Pomona indignantly. "It's called an Ælfpoca and it's a magical elf pouch ready to hold anything of any size." She patted her pocket. "I've got it right here, actually. I was right: there *was* one in the old Lord Fitzroy's occult collection. It looks so cute—I can't wait to use it!"

Caitlyn tried to hide her sceptical smile; Pomona's blind faith in all things magical and supernatural had always bemused her, ever since they were little girls. While she was *still* struggling to accept the reality of magic, despite all the things she'd seen and experienced since arriving in Tillyhenge, Pomona seemed to have no such problems. Her cousin had happily embraced the paranormal as easily as if she'd been born a witch herself. Sometimes, Caitlyn wished she could be more like Pomona. She laughed to herself—actually, most of the time, she wished she could be more like Pomona. Then she would be confident and gorgeous, always knowing what to say, how to flirt, and what to wear despite her big hips...

Pulling her thoughts back to the present, she said: "Yes, well, anyway, while you were off getting the Ælfpoca, I was left standing there with the garden hose—"

"Hang on, hang on... don't forget it's got a name!" said Pomona, grinning. "We've named it Hosey Houdini, remember?"

"We're not seriously going to call it that, are we?"

"Why not? It's the perfect name for a bewitched garden hose who's a great escape artist!" giggled Pomona.

"The 'escape artist' part is certainly true," said Caitlyn, pulling a face. "Okay, as I was saying: I was standing there in the gardens, waiting for you, with... with Hosey Houdini, and then all of a sudden, I saw Vanessa coming around the corner of the house, straight towards me. I panicked. I was worried that if she saw the garden hose, she would freak out and—"

"Actually, she probably wouldn't have 'cos she was really Tara," Pomona reminded her. "She's probably seen far weirder things than a bewitched garden hose who thinks that it's a giant cuddly python!"

"Yes, well, I didn't realise *then* that she was really Tara," said Caitlyn, shaking her head with reluctant admiration. "She was so good at maintaining her front. I mean, she was startled to see me, but she instantly recovered and came up with a cover story about sneaking out for a cigarette because she didn't want James to know that she was smoking."

"Ahh... playing up the naughty, rebellious younger sister stereotype," said Pomona, nodding. "Clever."

"Yes, except that her lie got her into trouble because when she tried to light her cigarette, Hosey Houdini got all agitated and started squirting water everywhere, trying to put it out."

Pomona gave a shout of laughter. "No way! Are you serious?"

Caitlyn nodded wryly. "We both got completely drenched... and I couldn't explain why this garden hose, which wasn't connected to anything, was gushing out water!"

"So what did you say?"

"Nothing, really. I just mumbled something, but she didn't seem that interested anyway. She just wanted to change into dry clothes. So we both went inside—"

"What? You just left Hosey Houdini out there?" said Pomona in dismay. "No wonder he got away again!"

"I had no choice, Pomie! Vanessa—I mean, Tara—was insisting that we go inside to change, and I couldn't think of a good reason *not* to go with her. It would have looked really odd. I was literally dripping wet. But I thought if I changed really quickly and went back out again—"

Pomona groaned and clapped a hand to her forehead. "Don't tell me... Hosey Houdini had slithered off by the time you went back."

"Yes." Caitlyn sighed. "He was gone."

"Caitlyn!" Pomona made a frustrated noise. "We'd been searching for that freakin' thing for ages! We'll never find him again now."

"No, no, Pomie—I did find him again! I haven't told you the rest of the story. Listen... so I started searching the gardens for Hosey Houdini and then guess what I saw? Vanessa on the garden path right ahead of me! And she was still wearing her wet clothes, which meant that she hadn't gone to her room to change at all. It was all a ploy to get me out of the way. As soon as I'd gone into my room, she must have run straight back out again."

"Huh? But why?"

"Because she hadn't really sneaked out for a cigarette," Caitlyn explained eagerly. "Like I said, that was just a cover story. She had actually been searching for something... using Percy's dowsing pendulum."

"Do you mean it was the same pendulum that you saw Percy holding in the Library the night he was murdered? The one he used to find the Widow Mags's *grimoire*?"

"Yes! The exact same one! I saw 'Vanessa'—I mean, Tara—holding the pendulum in her hand as she was walking in front of me. And I realised that she must have been holding it when she came around the corner of the house originally. I remember that she was looking down at something in her hand. She shoved it into her pocket as soon as she saw me and then pretended that it was a cigarette. But it must have been the dowsing pendulum! She was following its movements and using it to try to locate something."

"Locate what?"

"I think she was searching for the *grimoire*," said Caitlyn. Quickly, she recounted what Bertha had told her about Tara's obsession with the Widow Mags's magical journal.

"Wait a minute... wait a minute..." Pomona clutched her head. "I'm totally confused now. If Tara was the one who stole the *grimoire* from the Widow Mags ages ago, then why is *she* searching for it now? She should have it in her possession already."

Caitlyn shrugged. "Maybe she lost it herself since or... or maybe it was taken from her and now she's trying to get it back."

"But Percy found the *grimoire* in the Manor Library," Pomona pointed out. "So are you saying that James's father—the old Lord Fitzroy—took the *grimoire* from Tara? How? Why? And why didn't she just come here and take it back ages ago? Why wait until now?"

"I don't know! I'm just guessing here, okay?"

"Okay, okay... no need to get your panties in a bunch," said Pomona, holding her hands up defensively.

"Sorry." Caitlyn gave her cousin a contrite look and softened her tone. "Nothing makes sense to me either, Pomie. I'm just trying to piece things together based on the little I know." She thought a moment, then said: "Maybe Tara didn't realise that the *grimoire* was here in the Library until recently. I mean, it *was* concealed inside another book, wasn't it? So it could have been hidden in the Library for years without anybody knowing. It was only because Percy had that dowsing pendulum that he found it so easily."

"So..." Pomona furrowed her brow. "If Percy had the pendulum on the night of the murder... and now Vanessa—I mean, Tara—has the pendulum, then that means that she must have been there in the Library with Percy the night he was murdered! It's the only way she could have gotten hold of the pendulum."

Caitlyn shifted uncomfortably. It was the same conclusion she had come to herself when she'd seen "Vanessa" walking ahead of her, holding the dangling pendulum on its chain. At the time, it had seemed like irrevocable proof of the girl's involvement in Percy's murder, and although a part of her had been dismayed by the implications for James's sister, another part had been elated at the breakthrough in the case.

But now that she knew that "Vanessa" had actually been Tara all along, that changed everything. Suddenly, it meant that her own mother was linked to Percy's suspicious death—and that her own mother was possibly the murderer.

# CHAPTER NINE

A discreet cough sounded behind them, and they turned to see Mosley standing at a distance, eyeing them hesitantly.

"I beg your pardon, madam, but his Lordship has just returned from the hospital and he was searching for you—"

"Oh, James is back?" Caitlyn felt her spirits instantly lift. "Where is he?"

"His Lordship is in the Morning Room with Miss Vanessa's friends." Mosley turned to lead the way. "I am just about to serve a light lunch. Perhaps you would care to join them?"

As they followed the butler to the other wing of the Manor house, Caitlyn thought to herself that she was secretly glad James had returned to the Manor and rejoined Vanessa's friends before she had. They would have had wanted to know every juicy detail of what had happened at the hospital that morning, and she hadn't relished having to decide which censored version to recount. She was selfishly relieved that James would have countered their questions first. When they arrived in the Morning Room, however, Caitlyn found that Vanessa's friends weren't the only ones who wanted their questions answered. James hadn't come back from the hospital alone: Detective Inspector Walsh of the local CID had returned with him and seemed to be conducting some kind of interrogation.

"...want each and every one of you to go through your movements again on the night of the murder, but this time, it will be done with corroboration from others in the group," he was saying grimly as Caitlyn and Pomona entered the room. He glanced up and looked pleased as he saw them. "Ah! Perfect timing. You may join the others in recounting your movements too, Miss Le Fey and Miss Sinclair."

He gestured for them to join the group at the table, where Vanessa's friends sat, plates of food untouched in front of them. Caitlyn glanced at them surreptitiously as she moved to take her seat. She flashed back suddenly to the first time she'd met the group, only two days ago: Tori Fanshawe-Drury, Vanessa's best friend from childhood, with her snooty manner and ever-present smirk; Benedict Danby, Vanessa's still friendly ex-boyfriend with his suave good looks and cocky charm; and Katya Novik, newcomer to this Sloane set, with her model figure and exotic beauty...

Caitlyn had been completely over-awed by their

stylish looks when she first met them and daunted by their easy confidence—the kind of natural arrogance that often came to those born to wealth and privilege. Now, however, she was surprised to find that she no longer felt so intimidated. It was as if she could suddenly see past their veneer of sophistication to the reality beneath: Tori was scowling and chewing the corner of a fingernail, Katya's face was pale, with huge undereye shadows that her expertly applied make-up couldn't hide, and Benedict's muscled physique could not belie the way his leg jiggled nervously beneath the table. They were all making a deliberate attempt to look relaxed and nonchalant but there was a distinct atmosphere of apprehension in the room.

"Inspector, is this really necessary?" James Fitzroy spoke up from his position by the windows.

The handsome owner of Huntingdon Manor looked tired as well, his aristocratic features shadowed by fatigue and his tall figure rigid with tension. Caitlyn felt her heart go out to him. What a dreadful time James must have had in the last twelve hours! What should have been a romantic evening together last night had ended in a fight between them. They had parted on terrible terms, and she wondered if James had had as bad a night's sleep as she had. Then, first thing this morning, he had been confronted with the shock of his sister's accident and injury—followed by the even greater shock of discovering that the young woman they had rushed to hospital wasn't even his sister!

Now, he looked jaded and weary—so unlike his usually genial self—and Caitlyn wished that she could rush over and throw her arms around him. But although James had softened towards her whilst they were waiting together at the hospital that morning, she knew that a rift still lay between them. *He* was still angry at her for daring to suggest that his younger sister could be involved in a murder, whilst *she* still hadn't forgiven him for being so stubbornly defensive about his own sister and yet so quick to accuse *her* mother of murder.

Caitlyn felt the bitter twist of irony. Somehow, she had always thought that it would be her "witch" background or the fact that she looked nothing like the sophisticated beauties of his social circle that would keep her and James apart. She had never expected that it was their loyalties to their respective families that would come between them.

"With all due respect, your Lordship, I am still conducting a murder investigation, and as such must question any and all who may provide information on the case," said Inspector Walsh, his voice polite but firm. He turned back to the group and said: "Right... Miss Novik, perhaps you'd like to begin?"

Katya sat up straighter and glanced nervously around, then said in a slightly breathless voice: "We... we arrived on Thursday night, and we had dinner in the Dining Room. I was very tired so after dinner I went up to bed early, before the others."

Inspector Walsh glanced down at his notes. "And I understand that after the discovery of Mr Wynn's body, you were one of the last to arrive in the Library. Is that right?"

"I was sleeping very deeply when the murder happened, so that is why I didn't hear everybody downstairs—"

Tori snorted.

Inspector Walsh turned to her. "Yes? Is there something you would like to add, Miss Fanshawe-Drury?"

Tori considered a moment, then said, with spiteful satisfaction, "I hate to be the one to say it, but Katya is lying. I popped into her room to get something, just before Percy's body was discovered, and her bed was empty. She wasn't sleeping at all—"

"*You* are the liar," cried Katya. "I was there, in my bed!"

"Watch who you're calling a liar," Tori snapped.

"You are just making up stories to cover up for yourself! You are trying to frame me, so that no one will find out what *you* were doing—"

"Me? I was chatting with Ness in my room until we heard the commotion from downstairs," said Tori with a smirk. "I've got nothing to hide."

"You always like to think you are superior to everyone else, when you are nothing but a jealous fat *suka*!" spat Katya.

"What did you call me?" Tori snarled.

"Ladies...! Ladies...!" said Inspector Walsh, holding his hands up.

The two girls subsided, glaring at each other.

The inspector turned to Tori. "Is there anyone who can vouch for your movements that night, Miss Fanshawe-Drury?"

Tori hesitated. "Well... as I said, James's sister Ness—Vanessa—was chatting with me in my room, so she can—"

"No, she can't!" cut in Katya. "Because it was not really Vanessa who was sitting with you, was it? It was some other woman, pretending to be her. The real Vanessa has been in London all this time. So there is nobody to back up your alibi either!"

Tori looked annoyed, but before she could reply, Inspector Walsh said hastily: "Thank you, ladies. Now, I would like to hear Mr Danby's account of his movements," he said, turning to Benedict. "I believe you were the last person to see Mr Wynn alive, weren't you?"

Benedict shifted uncomfortably in his seat, his leg jiggling harder than ever. "Yeah, I was. We had a nightcap together in the Library before going up to bed. You can ask Mosley—he saw us leaving the Library and going upstairs together," he said, nodding at the butler who was standing discreetly at the back of the room.

Inspector Walsh glanced at the butler and inclined his head, then said: "And how did Mr Wynn seem to you when you left him?"

"He... he was fine," said Benedict. "I said goodnight to Perce at his bedroom door and then went to my own room, where I went to bed. Like Katya, I was sleeping when they found the body."

Inspector Walsh turned to Pomona. "Now, Miss Sinclair, can you tell me again how you and Miss Le Fey found Percy Wynn's body that night?"

"Oh sure. We were, like, hanging out in my room, and then we decided to go down to the Library 'cos Caitlyn wanted to show me this special book she'd found there. They'd turned off all the main lights downstairs so the Library was kinda dark and we had to, like, grope around. Caitlyn nearly tripped over Nibs, actually—that's her kitten—he was playing in the Library. He's got this new game where he hides and then jumps out and attacks your ankles. It's really cute but also kinda annoying..." Pomona giggled, then broke off as she saw Inspector Walsh's face. "Yeah, well, anyway, so we went over to the bookcase where Caitlyn had seen the special book earlier and we found Percy lying on the floor, next to the bookcase." Pomona pulled a face. "It was pretty obvious that he was dead."

Inspector Walsh turned to Caitlyn. "Do you have anything to add to that account, Miss Le Fey? Did you notice anything that Miss Sinclair hasn't mentioned?"

"N-no... it's just as Pomona described," Caitlyn replied.

Except that wasn't true. She *had* noticed

something else: a presence in the Library, even though no one could be seen. In fact, she had been sure that she felt someone brush past her as she walked past the bookshelves. And she had smelled a lingering fragrance in the air. But what could she have said? That an invisible person wearing perfume had hurried past her as they stepped into the Library? She doubted that Inspector Walsh would been overly impressed if she'd started recounting such a story!

Pomona looked at the inspector. "Were you hoping that we'd noticed belladonna berries rolling around on the floor next to Percy?" she asked in a half-joking tone.

"In actual fact..." Inspector Walsh cleared his throat. "I have just received new information from the forensic pathologist. The full results of the toxicology report have just come back, and it seems that Mr Wynn did not have any significant levels of atropine or other similar alkaloids in his system."

Caitlyn looked at the inspector in surprise. "Those are the chemicals found in the belladonna plant!"

"Yes."

Benedict leaned forwards, frowning. "So what are you saying? That Percy *wasn't* poisoned after all?"

Inspector Walsh shook his head. "On the contrary. Mr Wynn may not have had any atropine in his system, but the report did show unusually high levels of caffeine."

"*Caffeine?*"

Benedict went pale and his eyes darted to the cup next to his plate as if he expected it to jump up and attack him.

Tori gave a bark of laughter. "Caffeine? I've never heard of anyone dying from a caffeine overdose."

"You would not in most circumstances," Inspector Walsh admitted. "However, following the autopsy, it has emerged that Percy Wynn had an undiagnosed genetic condition called hypertrophic cardiomyopathy."

"Percy had a heart condition? At twenty-six?" said Pomona disbelievingly.

"But he was so thin!" said Katya.

Inspector Walsh gave a shrug. "Hypertrophic cardiomyopathy is a genetic condition. In fact, it is one of most common inherited cardiac disorders, and you can find it in slim, healthy young people. They're often not even aware they have the condition—there are no obvious symptoms. In Percy Wynn's case, the condition would have made him unusually sensitive to stimulants like caffeine, which increase heart rate and blood pressure. In other words, what would have just made you and me thirsty and jittery could have proven fatal for him. The high levels detected in Mr Wynn's body would have put him at increased risk of a heart attack. Then—if he had been subjected to any additional stressor—it could have triggered a sudden cardiac death."

"Are you suggesting that Percy died from an accidental overdose of caffeine?" James spoke up, frowning. "That it wasn't murder after all?"

"Oh no, there was definitely malicious intent," said Inspector Walsh grimly. "I don't believe Mr Wynn could have had that much caffeine in his system naturally. The question is, who gave him the overdose and how did they do it?" He paused, his eyes scanning the room, lingering on each one of them before adding: "I imagine the meal you had together earlier that evening would have been a good opportunity."

There was silence in the room as the implication of what he was saying sank in.

"That's preposterous!" cried Benedict angrily. "You're basically suggesting that one of us poisoned Percy at dinner!"

"Maybe it was the chocolates from that shop in Tillyhenge," said Tori, shooting a meaningful look at Caitlyn. "We were passing those around at the end of the meal, remember? It would have been easy to conceal the taste of caffeine in a chocolate truffle. Come to that, isn't dark chocolate itself full of caffeine because of the high percentage of cacao?"

"No, it's not," retorted Caitlyn. "It's got caffeine, yes, but only a small amount—a lot less than a cup of coffee! Besides, it's a stupid idea: even if one of the truffles *had* been doctored, how would the poisoner have known which chocolate truffle Percy would have chosen from the box? Someone else could have taken the poisoned one."

"That is a fair point, Miss Le Fey," said Inspector

Walsh. "Whoever administered the caffeine overdose would have had to make sure that it was in something specifically for the victim's consumption only. And I have to admit that Mr Wynn's heart condition muddies the waters slightly. Unlike the usual poisoning scenario, where death occurs fairly soon after the fatal dose, in this case, Mr Wynn could have had high levels of caffeine in his system for several hours before something tipped him over the edge. This makes it much harder to pinpoint when the murderer might have poisoned him."

He turned back to James. "I understand that the Samhain Festival will be taking place in the grounds tomorrow and that staff will be busy preparing for the event. However, in view of these new developments, I feel that it is vital to continue the investigation without any interruptions. I will need to have my men conduct further searches at the Manor and re-examine all possible evidence."

"Certainly, Inspector," said James. "We won't be using the Library in the Festival events so that will remain sealed as a crime scene and, of course, you're free to search any part of the Manor you wish."

There was an uneasy shift amongst Vanessa's friends, and for a moment, Caitlyn thought one of them would object to having police officers search their rooms again. She remembered Benedict complaining about being treated like "common criminals" the first time—but although he looked militant, he didn't say anything.

"Good," said Inspector Walsh, nodding with satisfaction. "Well, I will keep you abreast of any developments on the case, Lord Fitzroy."

"I won't be here this afternoon and evening," said James. "I'm driving down to London straight after lunch to fetch my sister and will probably stay the night. But Ness and I should be back at the Manor by tomorrow morning. And in the meantime, you can always reach me on my phone."

"I'll come to London with you!" exclaimed Tori, springing up. "I know Ness will be in a total flap, wondering what the hell is going on. She'll feel a lot better if I'm there."

"Me too! I will come as well!" said Katya brightly. "I know Ness's favourite coffee spots and all the other things she likes. Plus, there's a sale in Harrods right now. Ness loves to go shopping with me and I'm sure some retail therapy will help her recover."

"She doesn't need *you* to do anything with her," hissed Tori, narrowing her eyes at Katya.

"Who are you to say what she needs?" demanded Katya.

"I'm her oldest friend," said Tori tightly. "I know Ness better than anybody!"

"Obviously not well enough to know when she was replaced by someone else," Katya shot back in a snide tone.

"You effing cow!" cried Tori, flushing. "Just because you prance about in your tacky outfits and think you're God's gift doesn't mean you have the faintest clue about real friendship! Why don't you just stick to what you're best at—plastering your shallow life all over social media and fishing for likes from random strangers?"

"How dare you!" cried Katya shrilly.

*"Ahem."*

The two girls broke off and turned to look at Inspector Walsh.

"Before you get too excited planning your London activities, may I remind you that you are all still suspects in a murder investigation," he said, glowering at them. "And as such, you are required to remain at Huntingdon Manor until I give you permission to leave. So aside from Lord Fitzroy, no one will be going to London this afternoon."

The pronouncement fell on the room like a drenching rain shower, and everyone deflated. Inspector Walsh gave a satisfied nod and turned to leave, only pausing to shoot a stern look at Tori and Katya:

"I appreciate that it will be challenging to be cooped up here together, but I hope I can trust you ladies to behave yourselves?" he said. "I may spend most of my time on murder investigations, but I am not above arresting people for disorderly behaviour. You would do well to remember that. Good day."

# CHAPTER TEN

Caitlyn ran out of the Morning Room and chased after the inspector as he marched down the hallway.

"Wait! Inspector Walsh!"

The CID detective paused and turned around, raising his eyebrows slightly. "Yes, Miss Le Fey?"

"I... I wanted to ask you... about Tara—the woman you've got in custody at the hospital..." She took a deep breath. "Would it be possible for me to see her? Please?"

Inspector Walsh frowned. "I'm sorry. That woman is under arrest for the murder of government agent Daniel Tremaine, and she is also a prime suspect in the current murder investigation. It would be highly irregular and against protocol—"

"She's my mother," blurted Caitlyn.

"Your mother?" Inspector Walsh was taken aback.

Caitlyn looked at him pleadingly. "Please... I don't know if anyone has told you but I...I was found as an abandoned baby and adopted by the American singer, Barbara Le Fey. I only learned this myself when my adoptive mother died earlier this year. That's why I came back to England—to find my real family."

"I... er... *did* know that the Widow Mags is your grandmother," said Inspector Walsh, looking slightly discomfited at this discussion of personal background.

"Yes, it was incredible luck that I should come to Tillyhenge and find the Widow Mags's chocolate shop and then that she happened to be my grandmother! Or maybe it wasn't luck—maybe it was meant to be," said Caitlyn with a small smile. "You know, like magical destiny."

Inspector Walsh looked even more uncomfortable. The grizzled old CID detective was notoriously dogmatic and down to earth, with unconcealed scepticism for anything to do with the occult and the paranormal. Despite the many strange things that had occurred in Tillyhenge in the past few months, he was yet to be convinced that "magic" was somehow involved.

"So I found part of my family," Caitlyn hurried on. "But there was still my mother: I could never find any information about her or why she abandoned me. The Widow Mags wouldn't talk about her at all. And now she's here! Please, Inspector, I've been searching for my real mother for so long and now I've finally found her! I just want a chance to talk to her, to finally meet her. Just a few minutes... *please?*"

Inspector Walsh hesitated for a long moment, then finally he gave a sigh. "Very well. I will speak to my constable at the hospital and let him know that you may see her later this afternoon. But only for a few minutes, mind—"

"Oh! Thank you! *Thank you!*" cried Caitlyn, nearly flinging her arms around the old detective's neck and giving him a kiss on the cheek. She restrained herself just in time.

"*Ahem...* yes... well..." Inspector Walsh gave her an ironic look. "You may not thank me yet. Don't forget that your mother is the prime suspect in two murder cases, and it is my job to arrest the guilty party. Whoever he or she may be the parent of," he reminded her.

"Yes, but... but the fact that you're here questioning everyone and searching the Manor again means that you're not really convinced my mother could be guilty, are you?" suggested Caitlyn with a hopeful look.

"It does not mean anything of the sort," said Inspector Walsh tartly. "I like to ensure I have investigated a case thoroughly before closing it. Don't forget, this woman Tara has been here at the Manor too—under the guise of Lord Fitzroy's sister—therefore any evidence that my men find may well confirm her guilt."

"Yes, but you must consider other suspects too," Caitlyn insisted. "Tara isn't the only one who could have poisoned Percy. Any of the others could have done it! And they would have had much more motive—"

She broke off as she saw the inspector's eyes focus on something behind her, and she spun around to see James stepping out into the hallway. Behind him, they could hear angry voices raised in the Morning Room.

"Is there a problem, Lord Fitzroy?" asked Inspector Walsh.

James sighed. "Your questioning has caused quite a lot of distress amongst Vanessa's friends, Inspector."

"It is regrettable but necessary, your Lordship."

James frowned. "I must confess, I don't understand why we are going through all this again when we already have a suspect in custody. The woman who is under guard at the hospital... she seems the most likely to be involved in Percy's murder."

"You have no proof of that!" Caitlyn cried.

"On the contrary, there is ample evidence that Tara—while impersonating my sister—was engaged in all sorts of suspicious behaviour," said James, his voice cold and his grey eyes hard.

Caitlyn flinched at the expression on his face. All her earlier sympathy for James evaporated. She couldn't believe that he was condemning her mother openly in front of the police.

"There... there could be all sorts of innocent explanations for her behaviour," she said quickly.

"That's not what you said when you thought it was my sister," James retorted. "You were convinced of her guilt last night. You said she seemed unusually blasé about Percy's death, you told me you found her secretly searching my study, and you even said that Viktor saw her with belladonna berries—"

"Which have nothing to do with Percy's death! Inspector Walsh said Percy was poisoned by caffeine, not belladonna."

"Yes, but why did she have those berries in her possession in the first place?" James shot back. "They are still highly poisonous and a danger to others."

"It doesn't matter—they weren't used on anyone!" argued Caitlyn. "The point is, Tara had no motive for killing Percy, whereas Vanessa *did* have a good reason to want to punish him, which is why I suspected her. She had a crush on Percy and was resentful that he didn't return her feelings. Plus, she has a history of assault—"

"My sister never assaulted anyone," snapped James.

"Then what do you call what she did to that poor girl who bought the pony she wanted?" demanded Caitlyn. "You're the one who told me that story. You told me Vanessa spiked the girl's drink to get back at her—"

"With a pickling agent!" said James impatiently. "Yes, it made the drink taste unpleasant, but it was hardly a fatal poison!"

"It's still a pattern of behaviour," insisted Caitlyn.

"And does your mother not have a 'pattern of behaviour'?" asked James scathingly. "Are you forgetting that she very likely murdered a man at the Mabon Ball? And if we're talking about motives, there is one staring you in the face: the *grimoire*—the magical book of spells that once belonged to the Widow Mags, and which was hidden in the Manor Library and discovered by Percy. You yourself told Inspector Walsh that you thought the *grimoire* was the reason for the murder. And you yourself told me that the *grimoire* could be the very reason for Tara's estrangement from your family. If she was willing to forsake her family for the *grimoire* once, she could easily murder someone to get her hands on it again!"

Caitlyn reeled back as if James's harsh words were physical blows. She felt a terrible sense of betrayal. How could he use her own words against her like that? James had said that he loved her—so wasn't he supposed to be unquestioningly on her side? And yet here he was, tearing her defence of Tara apart, believing the worst of her mother without even giving her the benefit of the doubt.

Inspector Walsh looked extremely uncomfortable. "Er... perhaps it would be better if I left you two to discuss things in private," he said, backing away. "I'll be in touch, Lord Fitzroy—"

"No, wait, Inspector," said James, holding up a hand. "I'd like a word with you before you go."

Inspector Walsh waited. James said nothing,

turning instead to give Caitlyn a pointed look. She flushed angrily. James had never asked her to leave an audience with the inspector before. Despite her being a civilian with no special standing, in the past James had always insisted that she had his total confidence and was to be accorded the same respect and privileges by the police. And yet, now he was making it very clear that she was not to be included.

Trembling with hurt and humiliation, Caitlyn whirled and hurried away down the corridor before they could see the angry tears in her eyes. Behind her, she could hear the murmur of the men's voices, with Inspector Walsh saying: *"...an injured young woman is unlikely to present security issues..."* and then James's deep baritone fading away: *"...not to underestimate her... require specific methods..."* Indignation flared in her breast again. James's distrust of her mother was so obvious and mortifying. *He's treating her like a common criminal!* she thought furiously.

Caitlyn didn't realise that she had rushed outside until she tripped and found herself falling headlong to the muddy ground. Sitting up slowly, she pushed her hair out of her eyes and looked around, trying to get her bearings. She realised that she must have run unseeing out of the front door of the Manor and was now in the landscaped gardens. In fact, she was sitting on the path which joined the driveway at the front of the estate to the large yard and outbuildings at the rear—the same path that Jeremy had brought

Ferdinand along earlier that day. The memory of the bull's "digestive performance" had Caitlyn hastily scrambling to her feet and twisting anxiously around to examine her backside.

Thankfully, she had fallen on a drift of dead leaves, which had not only cushioned her fall but also protected her from any direct contact with the ground. She breathed a sigh of relief and straightened. The next moment, she almost fell over again as something large and furry rammed into the back of her knees.

"*Oof!*" exclaimed Caitlyn, staggering forwards and flailing her arms wildly to keep her balance.

She lost the fight and tumbled forwards onto the ground again, although this time she managed to roll over quickly and sit back up cross-legged. There was a flurry of movement next to her, and then she felt her face being repeatedly swiped by something that felt like slobbery sandpaper.

"Bran!" Caitlyn groaned, laughing in spite of herself as she wrestled with James's English mastiff. The dog was enthusiastically trying to demonstrate his love for her with his huge wet tongue whilst simultaneously trying to climb into her lap. "No... no... you can't sit on my lap... you're too big," she protested. "Get off... good boy, come on... *oof!* You're squashing me! Get off!"

Finally, the mastiff stopped trying to park his rump on her lap, deciding instead to lean against her. She sagged sideways under his weight but valiantly propped him up, reaching out to rub his furry chest. For a moment, there was nothing but the sound of Bran's contented panting and the soft *thump-thump-thump* of his tail on the ground. Caitlyn laid her head against his warm body and was surprised to find that she felt better. Somehow, just being in Bran's calm presence, hugging him close, and stroking his soft fur had made the hurt, anger, and confusion slowly seep away.

The mastiff turned his huge head and thrust his cold, wet nose into her hand, whining softly.

Caitlyn straightened and looked at him. "What is it, boy?"

Bran whined again and bent to sniff around her ankles. Then he got up and began circling her, whining all the while.

"What's the matter, Bran?" Caitlyn looked at him, mystified. What did the dog want?

# CHAPTER ELEVEN

Caitlyn rose to her feet and dusted herself off, all while watching Bran in puzzlement. The English mastiff was pacing agitatedly around her, completely unlike his usual placid self. Then she had a sudden idea. "Is it Nibs? Are you looking for Nibs?"

At the sound of the kitten's name, the mastiff stopped, as if transfixed, then began wagging his tail wildly.

"You're wondering where Nibs is, aren't you?"

Bran whined again, more urgently this time.

Caitlyn sighed. "I don't know where he is, sweetie," she said, suddenly remembering guiltily that when she'd got up that morning, she had been determined to find Nibs. Unfortunately, what had started out as a simple search for the missing kitten had ended up with her confronting "Vanessa" about Percy's murder, and then, what with the accident and the rush to the hospital, followed by the shock of finding Tara, Nibs had been all but forgotten.

Now, Caitlyn felt all her previous worries about the kitten come rushing back. She hadn't seen Nibs since yesterday afternoon, when she and Pomona had been eavesdropping outside Leandra's converted barn. The kitten had mischievously climbed up onto the kitchen windowsill and been spotted by Leandra, who had reached out, scooped him up, and taken him in. Not wanting to alert Leandra to their eavesdropping, she and Pomona had stolen away, planning to return to get the kitten later.

But when Caitlyn had returned to the barn in the evening, she had been dismayed to find no sign of Nibs anywhere. And she had been completely taken aback when Leandra had insisted that she had released the kitten outside her house and had not seen him since.

*Maybe Leandra was lying after all*, thought Caitlyn. She had given the woman the benefit of the doubt, especially since Leandra had seemed to graciously allow her to search the entire barn, but now she wondered if that had been a clever ruse—a "double bluff", if you will. After all, if Leandra had known that Nibs was safely hidden somewhere that couldn't be discovered by a cursory search, then making the offer would have cost her nothing. Instead, it had earned trust and dispelled any suspicions directed towards her.

*She was clever*, thought Caitlyn grimly. Still, she couldn't understand why Leandra would have wanted to hide the fact that she'd taken the kitten.

For that matter, why would she have wanted Nibs in the first place? He was not an expensive purebred cat or rare breed; he was nothing but a little moggie kitten that Caitlyn had found in the woods near the Widow Mags's cottage and rescued from drowning in a disused quarry. Even if Leandra had somehow fallen madly in love with Nibs and wanted to keep him for herself as a pet—it would still have made no sense. She couldn't keep a kitten hidden in the barn forever. Nibs wasn't a piece of jewellery or a stolen antique that she could hide in a cupboard; he was a living kitten, and someone would eventually see him or discover his presence...

Caitlyn sighed. The whole thing was a mystery. She wished that she could go to James, tell him everything, and share her worries; they would discuss things together and come up with a plan of action. In the past, she would have gone unhesitatingly to him, but now, with the chasm that had opened up between them, James seemed completely remote and unapproachable. She felt suddenly very alone.

*What should I do?* she wondered. *Should I try breaking into the barn and searching for Nibs again?* Leandra had already caught her breaking in once— there would be no easy excuse a second time. Of course, she could confront Leandra again, but she knew that the woman would simply deny all knowledge of the kitten once more.

*I wish there was something I could do to make*

*Leandra tell the truth,* thought Caitlyn wistfully. *Like... taking one of the House-Proud spells that the Widow Mags taught me and retooling it—just like I did with the graffiti—to make Leandra confess.*

But she knew that using magic to force others to surrender against their will was straying into the realms of Dark Magic, and that wasn't something that the Widow Mags or Bertha were ever likely to teach her.

Then an insidious little voice in her head whispered: *the grimoire... Bertha said that Dark Magic could "alter reality, raise the dead, curse entire bloodlines, turn back time, and more"... Moritha's forbidden spells recorded inside the Widow Mags's grimoire could definitely teach you how to wield all those abilities...*

Suddenly, Caitlyn understood why her mother would have wanted the *grimoire* so badly. There was so much power in those pages! The thought was both terrifying... and incredibly thrilling.

*Imagine what I could do!* thought Caitlyn with giddy elation. She thought of all the injustices she'd had to endure in the past, all the times she had to stand and watch helplessly whilst others were bullied or maligned or misunderstood. The memory of Leandra's smug, supercilious face flashed across her mind, and Caitlyn felt all her earlier anger and disgust return. It wasn't right that Leandra should be liked, even respected, by the villagers, when the woman talked incessantly of spirits and black magic—whilst the Widow Mags was feared and hated, despite doing nothing more esoteric than making delicious chocolates! It wasn't right that Leandra should be able to go around encouraging silly rumours and undermining Bertha's efforts to reassure the Manor staff! It wasn't right that Leandra should be able to kidnap Nibs and then blithely lie to cover it up!

*I could force her to tell me the truth about Nibs,* thought Caitlyn with grim pleasure. *I could humiliate Leandra in front of all the Manor staff and villagers, punish her for scaremongering everyone with false rumours about witches and Samhain! I could compel the stupid, superstitious villagers like Neil and Vera Bottom to love witches and celebrate witchcraft! I could even make James change his mind about my mother! Force him to apologise for badmouthing her, and induce him to defend her—*

The rasp of a warm tongue on her chin brought Caitlyn out of her thoughts with a gasp. She blinked and looked around, breathing heavily, as if she had been running. She found Bran standing next to her, his head cocked to one side and an expression of worried bewilderment on his baggy face. He whined softly and stretched up, trying to lick her face again.

"Oh Bran..." Caitlyn bent and put her arms around the mastiff, hugging him close and savouring once again the solid warmth of his furry body and the slow, calming thuds of his heartbeat.

Then she straightened and put a hand to her

temple. She felt groggy, as if she had just woken up from a dream. A very disturbing dream. She was shocked at how quickly the voice which had been an insidious whisper in the corner of her mind had suddenly turned into a roaring screech, demanding vengeance and power and retribution... Was that what the temptation from Dark Magic did?

Shivering, she pushed the lingering echo of those thoughts away and tried to focus on her original quandary. *Pomona*, she thought suddenly. She couldn't talk to James, but she could still talk to Pomona! Maybe her cousin would have a good idea of how to find Nibs.

Feeling heartened, Caitlyn turned and began to walk back towards the Manor with Bran at her heels. She hadn't gone several steps, however, when she came across Old Palmer, the Manor's head gardener, squatting next to a row of rosebushes. The gruff old man ruled his empire of junior horticultural assistants with an iron trowel and spent most of his time patrolling his cherished flowerbeds with a zeal akin to that of a territorial Rottweiler. But Caitlyn knew that his bark was worse than his bite. In fact, it was a running joke amongst the Manor staff that Old Palmer frequently threatened dire consequences for Nibs ("that bloody cat!") digging in his rose beds but lavished pats and cuddles on the kitten when he thought nobody was looking.

The thought made Caitlyn call out and ask: "Hello! You haven't seen Nibs, have you?"

The head gardener rose to stand and shook his head. "Naw, not since yesterday mornin'. Thought he'd just gone back to stay at the chocolate shop with you, like he does from time to time. You lost the little mite?"

Caitlyn hesitated. She knew that Old Palmer would instantly rally to search for the kitten if she asked, but what could she say? "*I think that woman who is renting the converted barn has kidnapped Nibs and is holding him hostage, hidden somewhere in her barn*"? It sounded completely ludicrous! Yet how else could she explain the mystery of Nibs's disappearance and Leandra's lies about not seeing him?

"Um... I hope not," she said at last, trying to make light of the situation with a smile. "I just haven't been able to find Nibs since... er... yesterday evening. I'm sure he's probably just run off and is up to mischief somewhere. They say kittens get more adventurous and start exploring further in their territory as they get older, don't they?"

"Yar, likely he's just spreading his wings," agreed Old Palmer, although Caitlyn could see worry beginning to furrow his brow. "I'll keep an eye out for the little mite and ask the juniors to do the same."

"Thanks," said Caitlyn appreciatively. "I know you must be really busy with the preparations for the Samhain Festival."

The old gardener made an impatient noise. "Wouldn't be so busy if I didn't have to deal with the young 'uns losing their tools and claiming it's a curse!"

"What do you mean?"

"Been having my lads come and tell me that their things disappeared when they turned their backs. A couple are even blaming witchcraft! Said their stuff had been 'magicked' away by a Samhain curse. Pah! Magic curse my foot," snorted Old Palmer. "Their own carelessness, more like. Brains like rusty sieves, the lot of 'em. I'm sure they just left the tools somewhere and forgot."

"I'm sure you're right," agreed Caitlyn quickly. "There have been a lot of silly rumours and superstitions going around, just because—" She broke off as she suddenly spied a familiar figure in the distance: a grey-haired old woman dressed all in black, hobbling slowly with the aid of a gnarled walking stick. She was being accompanied by the head chef of the Coach House restaurant.

With a hasty "Excuse me—I must speak to the Widow Mags!", Caitlyn left Bran with the old gardener and hurried over to intercept her grandmother.

# CHAPTER TWELVE

Caitlyn arrived just in time to hear the old witch saying tartly:

"...told you, I can walk by myself. There's no need for you to walk me the few steps to the Manor house!"

"Oh no, it is my pleasure to escort you," said Ronnie gallantly. He put a solicitous hand under her elbow. "The ground can be slippery at this time of year, especially with the recent rains, and you wouldn't want to slip at your age—"

"At my age?" The Widow Mags stopped and swung around to glare at him.

"Er... well... you know..." The head chef looked like someone who just realised that they'd stepped into a nest of snakes.

Taking pity on him, Caitlyn hastily intervened. "Hello! I'm glad I caught you, Grandma—there's something I wanted to tell you."

"Ah, yes... wonderful... well, I'll leave you two to your chat," said Ronnie, beating a hasty retreat back to the restaurant.

The Widow Mags looked at Caitlyn questioningly. "Yes?"

"Oh... um..." Faced now with the old witch's direct gaze, Caitlyn found herself losing her nerve. She hadn't had time to rehearse how she would tell her grandmother about Tara, and she wished she had thought things through first before blurting out her intentions.

"Well, get on with it, child! What did you want to tell me?"

There was no easy way to do it. Caitlyn took a deep breath and said: "Tara's back... you know, my mother... your... your daughter—"

"Yes, I know who Tara is," said the Widow Mags tartly. "And I already know that she was seen in the local area recently. The police showed me that camera footage from the masquerade ball."

"Yes... no... I mean, that's not what I mean... I know about the footage from the ball, but I wasn't talking about that... I meant 'now'. Tara's back now. Here, I mean. She's here..." Caitlyn stammered, getting more tongue-tied the more she tried to explain things. She took another deep breath, trying to marshal her thoughts, then said in a rush:

"Tara's at the hospital. I saw her this morning. She was using glamour magic to impersonate James's sister, but there was an accident and she hit her head, and I think the glamour spell must have broken because she suddenly became herself again and they found her in Vanessa's bed, and I was there too and I saw her and... and..." She ran out of breath.

The Widow Mags stared at her silently for a minute, and Caitlyn saw a myriad emotions chase themselves across the old witch's face: surprise, confusion, joy, regret, uncertainty...

Then the Widow Mags turned with a flick of her black skirts and continued walking towards the Manor house. Caitlyn stared disbelievingly for a moment, then ran after the old witch.

"Did you hear what I just said?" she asked, panting. "Tara's at the hospital; she was pretending to be James's sister and—"

"Yes, I heard you," growled the Widow Mags, not slowing her steps.

"Well... aren't you going to say anything?" demanded Caitlyn, struggling to keep up with the old witch's surprisingly quick hobble. "It's your daughter! She's finally back after twenty-two years! Don't you want to see her? Don't you want to know what happened?"

"I know what happened," snapped the Widow Mags. "My own daughter lied and betrayed me; she stole the most personal, valuable possession that could belong to a witch and gave it to the enemy."

"To the... enemy?" said Caitlyn, startled. "What do you mean?"

The Widow Mags compressed her lips and Caitlyn's heart sank, knowing that the old witch was going to refuse to answer again. She opened her mouth to protest but before she could say anything, they heard the hubbub of voices. Turning, she saw a large group of people coming out of the rear of the Manor and instantly recognised the plump figure in the lead, clad in a flowing purple kaftan, grey wool shawl, and sensible walking boots: it was Bertha. Her aunt was accompanied by Lisa, Pomona, and Vanessa's three friends. Trailing behind them were several members of the Manor staff, and from the expressions on their faces and the way they were muttering amongst themselves, they didn't look happy to be there. As they approached, Caitlyn heard her aunt saying to Lisa:

"...it's really not necessary, Lisa. Honestly, I'll be fine just by myself, and Pomona and Vanessa's friends have offered to come along. If the staff feel uncomfortable about helping with the bonfire, there's no need to force the issue—"

"No, I insist," said Lisa, folding her arms. "I won't pander to their ridiculous superstitions. It's part of their duties and it's important that they take part in the Samhain Festival preparations. Lord Fitzroy was unequivocal about that. Besides, surely having more hands would mean that you find all the necessary wood faster?"

Bertha cast a doubtful look at the scowling faces around her, then gave the other woman a weak smile. "Well, yes, I suppose. It's always good to have extra help but..." She sighed, then said in a brisker tone: "All right. Thank you. We'll start on the north side of the outbuildings and make our way through the woods at the edge of the grounds. Hopefully, we should be able to find the necessary firewood there, without having to venture further out into the estate."

Bertha stopped as she caught sight of them. "Oh!" She looked anxiously at the Widow Mags. "I'm afraid we're just off to collect some more wood for the bonfires, Mother, so I'll be a while. Will you be all right waiting in the Manor until I get back—?"

"Or we could arrange a lovely guestroom for you, madam, so you can stay the night, instead of having to go back to Tillyhenge—since you'll be coming back to the Manor again tomorrow anyway for the Samhain Festival," suggested Lisa, smiling at the old witch. "It seems silly to do all this to-ing and fro-ing."

"No, thank you. I would like to return to my cottage," said the Widow Mags firmly.

"Oh. Well, in that case, I can run you back," offered Lisa. "That way you won't have to wait for Bertha."

"Thanks, Lisa, that's very kind of you," said Bertha gratefully. She turned to Caitlyn. "How about you, dear? Will you join us? Good. And you haven't seen Evie, have you? She came to the Manor with your grandmother and me this morning and was supposed to help with the bonfire wood collection too, but I don't know where she's disappeared to."

Caitlyn shook her head. "Sorry, I haven't seen her."

"If I should see your daughter, madam, I will be sure to direct her to your whereabouts," came Mosley's voice, and they turned to see that the butler had come out of the Manor house as well.

"Thanks, Mosley," said Bertha. "Well, I suppose we'd better get going."

She nodded farewell and set off. The Manor staff dawdled, obviously still hoping to get out of the outing, but with Lisa standing there, staring at them pointedly, they had no choice but to follow Bertha as well. Vanessa's friends exchanged looks. They didn't look particularly enthusiastic about the outing either.

"This is pants!" muttered Tori. "I didn't come up from London just to traipse around out here in the cold and damp, collecting bloody firewood. I think I'm just going to go back to my room and take a nap."

"Er... my apologies, Miss Fanshawe-Drury, but that was the reason I came out. I regret to inform you that a plumber will require access to your bedrooms at present. Unfortunately, there is a severe blockage in the kitchen drainage system, and the water supply will need to be switched off while the plumber examines the pipes for the cause of the issue," said Mosley apologetically.

"What?" said Benedict, incensed. "You mean some sodding plumber is going to be clumping all over our rooms, leaving oil and gunk everywhere?"

"Oh no, sir, I shall personally supervise the proceedings and ensure that none of your personal belongings are affected in any way," Mosley assured him. He looked hopefully at the girls. "A spot of outdoor exercise would be extremely beneficial, if I may say so, madam, and it would minimise the inconvenience to your person as, by the time you return, your rooms will be available once again."

Tori gave an exaggerated, long-suffering sigh, then stalked off after Bertha. Katya followed suit and, after hesitating a moment, Benedict also followed in their wake, still looking annoyed.

"Uh... maybe I'd better go up and tidy my room a bit," Pomona said to Mosley. "'Cos... um... my bathroom is kind of... like... er, not super-neat—"

"You mean it looks like a bomb site," said Caitlyn, chuckling. She turned to Mosley. "You'd better have the plumber tied to a lifeline if he goes into Pomona's room—it might take him a week to find his way out again!"

The butler remained poker-faced. "That won't be necessary, madam. As it happens, the plumber will focus his attention primarily on the pipes around Miss Fanshawe-Drury's room and Mr Danby's room, as they are situated above the Manor kitchen. There should be no need to disturb your private quarters."

"Okay, cool." Pomona turned back to Caitlyn. Grinning, she linked her arm through Caitlyn's and said: "Hey, this kinda feels like we're on a school trip, huh? Like we should all be holding hands and walking in single file."

She started walking, then stopped, tugging on

Caitlyn's arm as the latter remained where she was. "C'mon! What are you waiting for?"

Caitlyn hesitated, looking back at the Widow Mags, who was walking away with Lisa. She bit her lip in frustration. She wanted to chase after her grandmother and demand answers about Tara, but she knew she couldn't with the Manor's marketing coordinator there. *Another opportunity lost... again!*

"Caitlyn? Are you okay?"

Caitlyn sighed. She would have to try to speak to the Widow Mags again later. "Yes, fine. Sorry, just wool-gathering..."

"Well, you're gathering the wrong thing," said Pomona with a cheeky grin. "C'mon! We'd better hurry if we want to catch up with the others."

Caitlyn cast a last chagrined look at the Widow Mags's retreating back, then turned to follow Pomona into the woods.

# CHAPTER THIRTEEN

They walked briskly in the crisp autumn air, their breaths mingling in great clouds of steam. A pale sun had made an appearance in the sky, but its weak rays cast little warmth and Caitlyn realised belatedly that, in her headlong rush out of the Manor house, she had forgotten to put on a jacket. Thankfully, the steady pace set by Bertha meant that she was soon fairly warm from the vigorous exercise—and from the flushed faces around her, it looked like the others felt the same.

In fact, the fresh air and exertion seemed to invigorate everyone, and a sense of camaraderie began to grow. Caitlyn saw Bertha listening avidly as Benedict regaled her with stories of priceless antique spice jars and apothecary containers that his father's company had sold. And even Tori and Katya seemed to have called some sort of truce and were walking side by side, chatting amicably. Only the Manor staff remained silent and apart, bringing up the rear of the group. Caitlyn could sense their gazes boring into her back, and she had to resist the urge to look back. She knew that Lisa had meant well, but she wished that the woman hadn't insisted on them joining in.

"Man, I wish they hadn't come," complained Pomona, echoing Caitlyn's thoughts as she glanced over her shoulder and made a face. "Talk about being a total buzzkill! I mean, seriously, they're, like, getting a break from their duties and boring routines. They should be grateful that they're getting to enjoy some fresh air and scenery—"

"Pomie, I'm really worried about Nibs," said Caitlyn, cutting into her cousin's diatribe. "I still can't find him, and I don't think he's just out exploring somewhere. I'm sure he's in Leandra's barn, but she flat-out denied that she has him when I asked her."

"Did you tell her that we *saw* her pick up the little fuzzball from her windowsill?"

"Well, no," Caitlyn admitted. "Because that would have meant admitting that we were eavesdropping outside her window. But even if I *had* told her that, she could still lie about keeping Nibs hidden somewhere. You can't force someone to admit something if they don't want to."

Pomona got a gleam in her eye. "Oh yes, you can if you have the right magical tools—"

"Oh God, you don't mean Evie's Truth Nougat, do you?" said Caitlyn with a groan. "That was a total disaster when we tried it."

"No, no, I mean a spell. There must be spells that can, like, get into people's minds and make them do what you want them to—"

"We can't use those kinds of spells! You know what the Widow Mags said: witchcraft shouldn't be used to force people into actions against their will. That's straying into Dark Magic."

Pomona harrumphed. "Who cares if it is? You know what your problem is? You guys are too nice and ethical. I'll bet if Leandra could use Dark Magic, she wouldn't be worrying about, like, what's 'right' and what 'shouldn't be done'. I've been telling you all along that she's sketchy, but you wouldn't listen to me."

"Hey—you're the one who said I was overreacting about Nibs!" said Caitlyn.

Pomona held up her hands. "Okay, so maybe I was wrong! It's just... it's a weird thing for her to lie about, you know? I mean, not that the little squirt isn't cute and all, but why would she want some random kitten?"

"Well, Leandra did seem very interested in Nibs the first time she met him, down at the chocolate shop," said Caitlyn, remembering. "She seemed to be fascinated by the fact that he wasn't growing, that he seemed to be stuck in time, forever a baby cat."

Pomona looked thoughtful for a moment. "You know, there's a lot of power associated with things that never age, things that remain forever pure and unchanged..."

"What do you mean?"

"Well, like alicorn, for example. People used to go nuts trying to get their hands on that stuff."

"Ali-what?"

"Alicorn—you know, unicorn horn! It's supposed to have the power to purify water, heal sickness, neutralise poison... you name it. All because it comes from the unicorn, which is a magical creature that is eternally pure and immortal. The same for mistletoe," Pomona continued enthusiastically. "In Celtic mythology, it's considered really sacred and magical because it remains green even in winter so it's, like, defying the 'seasonal death' that happens to other plants. It's linked to eternal life, and it was an essential ingredient in rituals for healing and fertility."

"So you think Leandra has taken Nibs because she thinks he has some kind of magical power?"

Pomona shrugged. "It's as good a guess as any. I mean, that woman is always jabbering about proper Samhain rituals and stuff—maybe she thinks Nibs is an essential ingredient for something she's planning."

"Ingredient?" Caitlyn shuddered. "Ugh, don't say that! It makes me think of animal sacrifices." She bit her lip, feeling even more anxious. "We need to find Nibs. But I just don't know how—I was sure I heard him crying when I was at Leandra's barn, but I couldn't find him, even when she let me search the whole place."

"Did you check inside all the cupboards and stuff?"

"Yeah, I opened every cupboard, drawer, box, chest, and bag that I could see. He wasn't in any of those places."

"Maybe she's hiding him using magic," said Pomona.

"Leandra doesn't have any magic—she's not a real witch!" said Caitlyn irritably. "She's just an arrogant, pompous know-it-all who thinks she's an expert because she spent years poring over textbooks on the occult, but in fact, she knows nothing about real magic."

"It doesn't matter—it's what she *thinks* she knows," Pomona pointed out. "It's like all those people on the internet who don't really know anything about medicine and aren't real doctors, right? But they're still going around giving dangerous advice to others, telling them to eat stupid things or do crazy stuff, just 'cos they *think* they know what they're doing."

Caitlyn started to reply but was interrupted by Bertha stopping ahead of them and turning around to address the group.

"We should be able to find the firewood we're looking for in there," Bertha said, indicating the woods in front of them. "Remember, we're looking specifically for hawthorn, ash, and rowan trees. Ash trees are the tall ones, with branches that point upwards and they'll probably have dropped a lot of their leaves by now... there, you can see a young ash silhouetted against the sky. See how smooth the bark is? Although they're not all smooth like that—the older ones have more wrinkles and fissures."

She turned and pointed at a lower tree that was so gnarled and twisted, it looked like something straight out of a fairytale illustration. "Hawthorns are easy to spot by their big red berries and by their very gnarled and thorny branches. You shouldn't have any trouble finding those. And as for rowan, that has red berries too but it won't be thorny and gnarled—that's how you can tell it apart from hawthorn trees. It has a smooth, greyish trunk as well, and the leaves will probably have turned orange and red by now—"

"Shouldn't we be looking for a dual-trunk rowan?" Katya spoke up. "Leandra says it's vital to find a rowan tree like that in order to build the Samhain bonfire correctly. You need the symbolism from the twin symmetry to represent the meeting of the two realms during Samhain."

Bertha compressed her lips. "We can certainly try to find a rowan tree that has a divided trunk, but there's no written rule that says it is essential for a Samhain bonfire. Rowan is already known as a 'gateway tree'—it's a mediator between the living and the dead. So just having the rowan wood as part of the bonfire itself will be ample symbolism." She turned back to the rest of the group. "Remember: collect any fallen branches first. We want to take what is freely given by Nature as much as possible.

Then after that, remove only the smaller branches, so we don't weaken the tree."

"What about ritualistic pruning?" Katya spoke up again. "Shouldn't you be taking only those branches growing in a westerly direction? Leandra says that's vital because if you're not taking branches in line with the setting sun—which symbolises endings—then you won't be building a bonfire that will protect us from the dead which return during Samhain."

Caitlyn noticed the staff members look at each other uneasily and draw closer together.

Bertha gave Katya an impatient look. "That's utter nonsense. We will certainly try to harvest as prudently as possible, taking only those branches which have either already weakened or have been naturally shed by the tree—but there is no need to adhere to such ridiculous superstitions."

"They're not ridiculous superstitions!" cried Katya, her colour high. "They're important principles which you're ignoring because you know nothing about the proper aspects of Samhain ritual! I wish Leandra was here—*she* should be the one leading this collection, not you!"

Caitlyn began to feel irritated with Katya as she saw the Manor staff nod and murmur in agreement, and several began to shift restlessly. The girl's persistent questioning was undermining Bertha's authority and stoking dissent among the already-nervous staff. Her aunt, however, remained calm and ignored the girl's outburst. Instead, she gestured to the woods again and said:

"If we begin now and all chip in, we should be done in less than two hours and you'll all be back in the warm with a nice hot drink."

The words worked better than any magic spell. Tori and Benedict immediately marched off towards a nearby copse of trees, whilst Pomona hurried to accompany Bertha into the woods. Even the hesitant Manor staff members turned towards the trees with alacrity and began searching for branches to collect. Caitlyn followed Katya as she reluctantly headed towards the trees as well. The other girl was scowling and muttering angrily as she joined her friends.

"...if Leandra knew about this, she'd have a fit! You can't just gloss over the rituals; they're steeped in history for a reason. Leandra has said many times that ignoring Samhain traditions is asking for trouble. We ought to be following her expertise, not just—"

"Oh, stop whingeing," Tori said, rolling her eyes. "No one cares about your stupid Samhain rituals!"

"How do you know so much about what this Leandra woman said anyway?" asked Benedict, looking at Katya curiously.

Tori turned to the girl as well. "Yeah—who is she? How do you know her?"

Caitlyn glanced at Katya. She knew that Katya had lied to the police about her alibi: the girl hadn't been asleep, as she had insisted to Inspector Walsh. She had in fact sneaked out to see Leandra on the night of Percy's murder. Caitlyn had overheard all this herself when she had inadvertently seen Katya going furtively to Leandra's barn yesterday and eavesdropped on their conversation. It had been clear that the two were old acquaintances, and she watched Katya curiously now, wondering what the girl would reveal.

"I... er..." Katya looked flustered, not meeting her friends' eyes. "I... um... just bumped into Ms Lockwood here on the estate and got chatting to her. She's... she's very interesting and knowledgeable about all things to do with magic and the occult—"

"Oh God, enough said," groaned Tori. "Don't tell me, she's another of those hippy-dippy, incense-waving types who thinks they're some celestial goddess communing with the ancient spirits of the compost heap."

Benedict sniggered and even Caitlyn had to make an effort not to laugh. She had to admit that whilst Tori could be a snooty cow, her acerbic tongue could also be very amusing. Leaving them arguing, Caitlyn turned away and wandered deeper into the woods, her thoughts still on Katya and Leandra. *Could they be involved in Percy's murder?* she wondered. It was tempting to jump to conclusions, especially given her dislike of Leandra, but she knew in her heart that just because Katya had lied about her alibi didn't mean that she—or Leandra—had to be guilty. True, Katya had seemed in awe of the older woman and was completely submissive to her. And Leandra had given the girl instructions to find out more about the police investigation. But that could all have been due to salacious curiosity and not necessarily a more sinister reason.

*Leandra was*—is—*very interested in the grimoire, though,* Caitlyn mused. Of course, that in itself was hardly surprising, given the retired academic's obsession with the occult. Still... Caitlyn thought back to the way Leandra's eyes had gleamed as she talked of the *grimoire*, then she recalled Pomona's theories about Nibs's potential value in magical workings and felt a sense of disquiet.

A bird swooped past, bringing her out of her thoughts, and she realised that she had drifted away from the main group. She could still hear voices through the forest, but she couldn't see anyone through the trees. It gave the illusion of being completely alone and, as Caitlyn began walking again, she found that there was something wonderfully peaceful about the almost-otherworldly solitude. The fallen leaves crunched underfoot, occasionally stirring up in swirling drifts of crimson, amber, and gold, and the air was thick with the earthy scents of damp soil mixed with the faint, sweet aroma of decay.

It was chilly, though, and now that she was no longer marching vigorously, Caitlyn began to feel the cold. She rubbed her hands against her arms and began to actively search for firewood, hoping that the endeavour would warm her up. Soon she was immersed in the task, gazing up at the trees or scanning the forest ground for any fallen branches of the right type, carefully picking several up and tucking them into the growing bundle under her arm. There was a soothing rhythm to the activity, and she didn't realise how engrossed she was until she was startled by the sharp, echoing call of a jay and glanced up.

Caitlyn looked around, suddenly realising that she could no longer hear faint voices around her. How far had she strayed from the group? Something rustled in the undergrowth behind her and she jumped, then chided herself for her silly nerves. It was probably just a squirrel or a fox going about its business. Still, glancing down at the hefty bundle of branches in her arms, Caitlyn decided that she had gathered enough. She turned to retrace her steps, but she had barely started walking when she paused again.

*Are those voices?* She strained her ears. Yes, she could hear voices coming through the trees on her left. Perhaps she hadn't strayed as far from the others as she'd thought. Quickening her steps, she hurried towards the source of the sound. As she got closer, however, she was surprised to hear feminine giggling. It certainly didn't sound like anyone in her group!

A moment later, she stepped out into a small clearing and came upon her young cousin Evie standing beside a large rowan tree. Next to her was

Jeremy Bottom's teenage son Chris, and they were talking and laughing together as they plucked branches from the tree and added them to a pile at their feet.

Caitlyn recalled Bertha wondering earlier where her daughter had gone, and now she smiled to herself. Evie had obviously used the firewood collection as an excuse for a private excursion into the woods with her secret crush! Still, it was lovely to see her shy young cousin so happy. With her frizzy, carroty-red hair and thin, lanky figure, Evie was usually nervous and self-conscious in public; she had certainly never imagined that Chris, with his blond good looks and status as the local teenage heartthrob, could ever prefer her company to that of the pretty, "popular" girls at school. It was heartwarming to see her blossom under his gallant attention.

Caitlyn was just wondering whether to join them or leave Evie to her romantic rendezvous when the peace was rudely shattered by a shrill voice. The next moment, a middle-aged woman came charging out of the trees on the other side of the clearing. She was brandishing something in one hand as she ran straight at Evie, and she raised her arm menacingly as she yelled:

"You filthy witch girl! I'm not going to let you get away with it!"

# CHAPTER FOURTEEN

The two teenagers jerked up in shock, and Chris sprang instinctively in front of Evie, shielding her with his body. Then he did a double take as he recognised the woman confronting them.

"Aunt Vera!" Chris gaped at her. "What are you doing here?"

"I followed you—what do you think?" hissed Vera Bottom. "I knew you'd gone off again with that brazen daughter of Bertha's. How could you, Chris? I've told you time and time again to stay away from her. She's hexing you, trying to corrupt you!" She whirled on Evie. "And you... you thought you'd got away with it, didn't you? You thought you could manipulate and corrupt Chris with your vile witchcraft and turn him against his own!"

Evie recoiled, her face pinched and scared. "No, no, I... I'm not—"

"Don't try to lie!" snarled Vera. "I know all about you and your kind. Conniving, two-faced hussies, all of you! Your grandmother, your mother, that cousin of yours who's come from America and seduced Lord Fitzroy with her spells... and you're the same! Don't think I don't know what you've done. You've used black magic to bewitch my nephew and—"

"Evie hasn't done anything to me!" Chris protested. "We're just friends, that's all. She asked if I wanted to help her collect some wood for the Samhain bonfire and I said yes."

"Samhain is a witch's festival!" Vera spat the words out as if they were poison. "It is a pagan tradition, full of evil and black magic."

"N-no, it's not. You've got it wrong," said Evie in a small voice. "It's just a community event, a chance for people to get together and have a bit of fun—"

"Fun?" Vera's voice became even shriller. "There are dangers lurking behind every shadow at this time of year, malevolent forces waiting to ambush you, curses, plagues, and misfortune... and you dare to talk about 'fun'? Don't try to pretend that it's all just harmless entertainment. Do you think you can hide behind that 'innocent little girl' act? You don't fool me, you witch hussy!"

She thrust her hand forwards and waved something in Evie's face. It was a small bouquet of dried herbs and flowers, tied together with twine, and Caitlyn recognised it as the herb charm that Vera had brandished at her in Tillyhenge that morning.

"*Vervain, trefoil, Saint John's wort, dill... Hinder witches of their will*," chanted Vera manically.

145

"*Vervain, trefoil, Saint John's wort, dill... Hinder witches of their will!*"

*Oh God, not this again*, thought Caitlyn, rolling her eyes. *The woman is completely bonkers.*

Evie, however, didn't see the humour in the situation. She stumbled backwards, trying to get away from the swishing herbs in her face. She put a hand up defensively, and as she did so, the rowan branch that she was clutching caught the afternoon light. Vera gasped when she saw the bright red rowan berries.

"Belladonna!" she screeched. "From the deadly nightshade plant. That's a witch's herb! You're trying to poison my nephew!"

"No, no—those are rowan berries," said Chris, holding up a branch himself. "See? Belladonna berries are black; rowan berries are red."

But his aunt wasn't listening. Her eyes looked crazed now, her face contorted with rage, and she launched herself at Evie, who stood frozen like a deer caught in the headlights.

"I won't allow it! You and your cursed family, spreading your witch-evil through the village and binding my brother and nephew with your filthy black magic!" Vera shrieked at Evie, raising a hand as if to strike her.

Caitlyn gasped and rushed across the clearing towards them, but Chris was faster.

"Stop!" He grabbed his aunt's wrist, twisting her arm away, and stared at her with a mixture of disbelief and horror. "What are you *doing,* Aunt Vera?"

Vera glared at her nephew, her expression unrepentant. "Teaching that witch hussy a lesson she deserves!" she snapped. "Let me go, Chris."

Chris hesitated, looking torn. Caitlyn could see the emotions chase themselves across his face—indignation and disgust warring with the forces of family loyalty and guilt at not obeying his aunt. Finally, he reluctantly released his grip. But as Vera wrenched her hand back, he said to her:

"Don't try to hit Evie again or I'll... I'll report you to the police for assault."

Vera gasped in outrage. "You'll what?"

"I mean it," said Chris, his jaw set.

"How could you?" she said furiously. "Turn on your own family? For a witch?"

"It's not about family. It's about what's right," said Chris doggedly. "You're just attacking Evie for no reason. She hasn't done anything wrong. She doesn't do black magic or hexes or... or whatever you think. It's all in your head, Aunt Vera!"

Next to him, Evie squirmed and looked anguished. Caitlyn felt her heart go out to her young cousin. She remembered being in this same position with James not that long ago, listening to him defend her and being terrified that the man she loved would recoil from her when he found out that she was a witch after all. James hadn't... but would Chris, if Evie ever found the courage to confess the truth to him?

Vera was still trying to sway her nephew. She put a hand on his arm and said urgently: "You don't realise what you're saying, Chris. You're defending her because she's bewitched you! Can't you see? She's using magic spells to manipulate you. I'm trying to protect you from—"

She broke off as they heard a noise through the trees, and the next moment, a group of people burst into the clearing: Bertha, Pomona, and Vanessa's friends, with the Manor staff trailing after them. They had obviously been attracted by the raised voices and had come to see what the commotion was.

"Evie!" cried Bertha, stopping short as she saw her daughter. "What on earth is going on?"

"Oh Mum...!" Evie ran to her mother's side, her face pale with relief.

Vera drew in a sharp breath as she saw Bertha, and her eyes seemed to grow even more wild. But before she could launch into another tirade, Bertha thrust a hand into her pocket and pulled out a small sachet. Swiftly, she opened it and shook a mixture of dried herbs onto one palm, then closed her fingers and squeezed. Caitlyn caught a whiff of lavender mixed with the sweet spice of chamomile, overlaid with the slightly camphorous, woody scent of mugwort. Bertha opened her hand again and, with a flick of her wrist, flung the crushed herbs in Vera's direction. At the same time, she murmured a soft incantation:

*"Ventis pacis, herbis adfero calma!"*

The crushed herbs rose in the air, lifted by an unseen breeze, then swirled towards Vera and enveloped her like a fragrant mist.

"What—? Where—?" Vera looked around in confusion, groping wildly in front of her face. Then she took a breath and seemed to freeze, her body rigid. The next moment, she exhaled, her body going limp, her face muscles smoothing and relaxing, all the fury fading from her eyes.

It all happened so quickly that hardly anyone saw what happened. The Manor staff, who had all congregated behind Bertha, certainly hadn't seen her actions, and they were now exchanging mystified looks, puzzled as to why Vera had changed so suddenly from screaming harpy to mellow matron.

Caitlyn gave her aunt an admiring glance. She had to admit that she had secretly always been a bit scornful of Bertha's preference for the gentle power of herbs over the mystical charms and showy spells of "proper" magic. But now, she found herself incredibly impressed by how quickly Bertha had sized up the situation, swiftly but effectively calmed Vera down, and defused the conflict—all without any confrontation.

Vera blinked and looked around, disoriented. "What... what am I doing here?"

Bertha started to answer, but Pomona jumped in first, saying brightly: "Hey Vera! Don't you remember? You came to help collect wood for the Samhain bonfire."

"I... I did?" Vera stared at her disbelievingly.

Everyone else gawked at Pomona as well, completely bemused, but the American girl grinned widely, undaunted.

"Oh yeah, you were, like, so awesome," she continued blithely. "When Bertha asked if anyone from the village would volunteer, you jumped up right away... and you even offered to organise foot massages for everyone after the walk, so we could all soothe our weary feet... and get the village ladies to knit cosy hats for us so our ears wouldn't get cold—"

"Laying it on a bit thick, Pomie," Caitlyn muttered to her cousin.

Pomona ignored her. She was enjoying herself. "And you know what? You even told us you knew where this perfect rowan tree was growing, right in the middle of the woods..." She pointed to the tree next to them. "Ta da! You brought us right to the tree—"

But here, Pomona's cheeky ploy backfired. Vera's face suddenly puckered, and the befuddled expression left her eyes.

"Rowan tree?" she shuddered. "I would never go near one of those if I could help it! They're associated with magic and witchcraft. They attract evil spirits and bring omens of doom—"

"No, no, you've got it completely upside down," said Bertha, exasperated. "Rowan trees are associated with magic, it's true, but as a *protector* against malevolent witchcraft. The wood and leaves are often used in protective charms, and the berries are wonderful in traditional remedies for all sorts of ailments. People even plant rowan trees in their garden, to protect their homes and families from evil spirits and misfortune." She gestured to the tree. "That's why using rowan wood in the Samhain bonfire is encouraged—it is believed that burning the wood will release the protective energies into the air around us."

Vera looked unconvinced. "Well, in that case, we shouldn't be touching the tree at all. That's inviting bad luck!"

"Yeah, the rowan protects us from witches and evil spirits," one of the Manor staff spoke up. "My grandma told me about this farmer who cut down a rowan tree and his whole family was struck down by a curse."

Bertha gave a weary sigh. "We're not cutting the tree down—we're simply removing a few branches. It's no different to you removing some berries or twigs to use as a protective charm or talisman. Now, shall we just gather what we need, so we can start heading back to the warmth and a nice cup of tea?"

There was a rumble of muttering among the staff, but most of them were mollified by Bertha's calm, matter-of-fact manner. Vera, however, still looked unconvinced, and she stood to one side, watching warily, as the others began to pluck twigs and branches from the rowan tree. Caitlyn noticed for the first time that it was a dual-trunk tree, its grey-brown trunk displaying almost perfect symmetry in the way it formed a "Y" that stretched upwards and disappeared into the canopy covered with clusters of scarlet berries. *Well, at least Leandra won't have anything to complain about here*, she thought wryly as she approached the tree herself.

But she had barely reached up to snap off her first twig when she heard a commotion around the other side of the tree. She peered around to find Benedict and Chris both pulling on a branch which they were struggling to extricate from the canopy.

"There's... something... stuck in here... I think..." puffed Chris, tugging hard at the end of the branch.

The next moment, it came loose, causing him to reel backwards. The entire section broke away and a tangle of branches crashed to the ground, followed by a shower of leaves and red berries. Benedict staggered back, cursing in surprise, and several other people jumped in alarm as an angry, high-pitched squeaking filled the air.

"It's a demon!" screamed one of the Manor staff. "It's a Samhain spirit come to get us!"

# CHAPTER FIFTEEN

A hubbub of frightened voices rose from the group, and people began to push and shove, smacking into each other as they tried to get away.

"Stop! STOP! There's no demon!" shouted Chris.

His young baritone cut through the uproar and tempered the panic. People paused, hovering uncertainly, and watched as Benedict cautiously approached the clump of branches that had landed on the ground. Curiosity got the better of everyone, and they all slowly copied his example. Together, they peered down at the furry brown shape lodged in the midst of the branches. It was about the size of a small cat, with big black eyes, pointed ears, a round fuzzy belly, and long leathery wings that stretched from its tiny clawed hands to its feet. It was also emitting a series of indignant squeaks, sounding for all the world as if it were telling them off.

"Bloody hell... it's just a bat!" laughed Benedict.

"Never seen no bat look like that," said one of the

Manor staff nervously.

"Bats are witches' familiars," said Vera, eyeing the little creature with loathing. "They're omens of death and misfortune, and they'll attack you so they can tangle in your hair and make a nest—"

"What a load of tosh! Bats aren't witches' familiars," said Bertha impatiently. "That's an old wives' tale. Just because they are nocturnal and only come out in the dark, they've been completely misunderstood. And as for that ludicrous nonsense about the hair—"

"This one is unnatural!" insisted Vera, pointing at the bat. "Look at those ears! He looks more like a fox with wings."

"It's a *fruit* bat," said Chris suddenly. "I've seen 'em on YouTube. They also call them 'flying foxes' 'cos they have big pointy ears like foxes. They're all over Australia, apparently."

"Australia? What is it doing here in the Cotswolds?" asked Tori.

"It's really cute," cooed Katya, bending close to the bat and reaching out as if to pat its head.

The fruit bat glared at her and emitted another series of affronted squeaks.

*Oh my God, it's Viktor*, thought Caitlyn, groaning inwardly as she recognised her vampire uncle in his bat form. She glanced at Bertha and Evie and saw that they, too, had realised the real identity of the little creature and were wondering how to shield Viktor from discovery. But before they could do anything, Benedict suddenly lunged at the ground.

"Gotcha!" he yelled, pouncing on the fruit bat.

Unfortunately, he overestimated his own abilities. The little creature moved faster than him, giving an outraged screech and jerking sideways, evading Benedict's hands at the last moment. Then, still squeaking indignantly, it began flopping along the ground, flapping its wings awkwardly, trying to take off.

"My hair! It's after my hair!" Vera shrieked and began waving her hands wildly around her head.

Her hysterical actions seemed to infect the others, causing the Manor staff to scream and scatter, clawing at their hair too. Even Katya and Tori hastily backed away, their eyes wide and wary.

"Don't worry... he won't hurt you!" Caitlyn shouted, trying to make herself heard above the din. She could see Bertha doing the same, but it was a wasted effort. No one was listening.

Changing tack, Caitlyn turned and tried to catch the fruit bat herself, chasing after it and trying to scoop it up. To her frustration, it dodged her hands too and continued flopping along the ground, its squeaks sounding more and more like the querulous rantings of a grumpy old man. Then Caitlyn saw its shape begin to wobble and stretch...

*No, no, no!* she thought in horror. *Viktor can't transform now!*

The last thing they needed was Vera and the Manor staff witnessing the old vampire shapeshift back into his human form. It would confirm every superstitious fear they had about Samhain and probably lead to a revolt on the estate! Caitlyn looked desperately at Bertha for help, but her aunt was on the other side of the clearing, trying to call people back. She turned, searching for Evie and Pomona. The two girls were hurrying towards her, with Pomona brandishing something she had scooped up from the ground.

"Hey! Look what I found! It's Bertha's herb sachet—she must have dropped it." Pomona thrust it at Caitlyn. "Quick! Do that spell to make everyone calm down!"

Caitlyn drew back. "I don't know how—"

"I do!" cried Evie, seizing the pouch eagerly.

"Hang on, do you know the spell? Have you done it before?" asked Caitlyn.

"No, but I've seen Mum do it lots of times—I'm sure it's easy!"

"Wait, Evie—" Caitlyn put a restraining hand on the younger girl's arm. Much as she loved her younger cousin, she was the first to admit that Evie's witch skills were woefully lacking. The younger girl's misguided attempts at working magic had got them into dire straits more than once; even the bewitched garden hose that was currently slithering around the estate was the result of one of Evie's spells gone wrong! Now, Caitlyn said urgently: "I don't think it's a good idea—"

Too late. Evie had already shaken a large mound

of herbs onto her palm and was now clenching her fist, crushing them with her fingers. Then she flung them out into the clearing.

"*Ventis pacis...* er... *herbis...* um... *adfero cantus!*" she chanted, screwing up her face.

Caitlyn held her breath. Across the clearing, people suddenly stopped running and screaming as the magical breeze carried the crushed herbs over their heads and swirled around their faces. They froze in place, their eyes wide as they inhaled the herbal mist. There was a collective sigh. Then everyone puffed out their chests, threw their arms wide, and began to sing opera.

"*O sole mio...!*" trilled a Manor gardener.

"*Fiiii-garo! Figaro! Figaro! Fiiii-garo!*" roared Vera.

"*La-la-la-la-la-la-LAAA!*" warbled a maid.

Even Vanessa's friends had been affected. Tori and Katya were leaning their heads together, singing in harmony, whilst Benedict clutched his chest dramatically, bellowing: "*Nessun dorma! Nessun doooorma!*"

Pomona whooped with laughter. "Oh man! This is the funniest thing I've ever seen!"

Bertha marched over to them, exasperated. "What have you girls done?" she demanded.

"We were just trying to help," said Caitlyn quickly.

"I used your calming herb mixture, Mum," Evie explained. "I was sure I chanted the spell exactly as you did!"

Bertha gave a long-suffering sigh. "I said: '*adfero*

*calma'* not *'adfero cantus'!"* She turned to face the group of singing people. The din was almost deafening now, as everyone tried to outdo each other with soaring arias and flamboyant solos. Raising her arms, Bertha called out: *"Quietis numo!"*

Instantly, everyone stopped singing. They stood, looking around at each other, with bewildered expressions on their faces.

"Wh-what happened?"

"...we were collecting firewood..."

"Where are we?"

"...something in the rowan tree..."

"A bat! There was that weird bat!"

They all turned to look at the base of the rowan tree. But there was no sign of the fruit bat any more. Instead, a stooped old man with a sunken mouth and rheumy eyes stood in its place, busily dusting off his ancient black suit and eyeing them all peevishly.

"...really, the indignities I have had to endure today! It is outside of enough!" he said, bristling. "First in the billiard room this morning with *that* great oaf—" Viktor pointed at Benedict. "—shoving things on my head, *then* the hysterical carrying-on at breakfast when I was looking for my fangs in the muesli container—" Viktor whirled to glare accusingly at Katya. "—and now this! Yanked out of a tree just when one has found a cosy spot to have a nap. It is insupportable, I tell you—"

"It's that crazy old git who was hanging upside down from Katya's bedroom ceiling," said Tori with a scornful laugh. "Really, somebody needs to take him back to his nursing home."

"Nursing home? *Nursing home?*" Viktor spluttered, going purple in the face. "How dare you! I'll have you know that vampires can live for thousands of years, and at six hundred and thirty-four, I have barely reached my prime. In fact, as a member of the Megachiroptera Order—that is, those of us who shapeshift into fruit bats—I am blessed with great vitality due to my strict fruitarian diet. I also—"

"Did he say 'vampire'?" cried Vera, and several Manor staff members began murmuring in alarm.

"Er—no, no! He said *'umpire'*," said Caitlyn quickly. "Umpire... as in cricket, you know? Viktor loves cricket and... er..." She faltered under their hard gazes and elbowed Pomona to help her.

The American girl yelped in surprise. "*Ow!* Uh... yeah... cricket! Awesome English game where you, like..." Pomona made a vague swinging motion with one arm. "... um, pitch the ball and... uh... try to get a strike and a homerun—"

"No, Pomie, that's baseball!" hissed Caitlyn.

"What's the difference?" Pomona hissed back. "It's all hitting a ball with a bat."

"Eh? What's that? Who said I love cricket?" demanded Viktor, cupping his ear. "Bloody tedious game, especially when you're playing with banshees," he grumbled. "Terrible umpires, constantly wailing over disputed calls and then vanishing between innings to haunt some distant moor... and don't get me started on werewolves! I played a match once during a full moon and the wicketkeeper kept transforming and trying to eat our batsman—"

"Yes, well... anyway!" cut in Caitlyn hastily. "That's great, Viktor... great story... you've always got such a wonderful imagination." She forced a laugh as everyone stared at Viktor, googly-eyed. "Now... um... why don't you pop back to the Manor and see what they've got for tea, hmm?" She leaned close to Viktor's ear. "I heard that Mrs Pruett is baking apple and date scones today—"

"Apple and date, eh?" Viktor's eyes lit up and he smacked his lips. "Well, that certainly merits a look."

He turned and loped off through the woods, the tails of his black suit flapping in the wind behind him. Caitlyn breathed a silent sigh of relief and stole a look at the rest of the group. They were standing, staring at the place where Viktor had been, with their mouths slightly open.

"Who was that?" Vera demanded, recovering at last.

"Seen him around the estate sometimes," said one of the Manor gardeners. "Some poor old sod who's lost his marbles, likely."

"I always thought he was a relative of Lord Fitzroy's," said Chris Bottom thoughtfully. "He seems to go wherever he likes at the Manor and has really made himself at home."

*You can say that again*, thought Caitlyn, inwardly

rolling her eyes.

"Yes, I've seen him around the Manor as well," one of the maids spoke up. "Especially when I was dusting in the Library. Actually, I... I thought I saw him hanging from the corner of the ceiling once..." She glanced around with an embarrassed expression and added hurriedly, "But I must have been wrong."

*No, you probably weren't*, thought Caitlyn. Still, she was grateful that people seemed to have come up with a mundane explanation for Viktor's constant presence around the estate, and even more grateful when Bertha distracted everyone's attention by saying:

"Well, I think we've gathered enough rowan wood." She surveyed the piles of branches at their feet with satisfaction. "Combined with the ash and hawthorn wood that we've already gathered, this should be more than ample to make up two substantial bonfires. Now, Chris, if you and Benedict can help me separate them into smaller sections and tie them up with this..." She held out a roll of green twine. "We can each carry a bundle back."

A short time later, armed with a bundle of wood each, they set off again. There was a palpable sense of relief as the Manor house came into sight in the distance. Everyone quickened their steps, and the atmosphere became almost celebratory as they marched along, carrying their bundles.

"I hope Mosley's got tea waiting," said Tori with relish. "I could murder a scone—What?" she said as

Benedict shot her a dirty look. "For heaven's sake, Benedict, are you *still* touchy about me using the 'm' word? Look, I'm sorry Percy got himself killed, but it's done, okay? Moping and crying all the time isn't going to bring him back. Neither is tiptoeing around the subject—"

"The poor sod only died the day before yesterday, in case you'd forgotten," said Benedict through clenched teeth.

"No, I hadn't forgotten. It seems to be the only thing anyone can talk about around here," said Tori sourly. "*Excuse me* for trying to move on a bit."

"Hey, Ben—we're all pretty bummed out about Percy," said Pomona, giving him a sympathetic look.

"If you ask me, some of us are making *too* big a deal out of it," said Tori, shooting Benedict a sly look. "It makes you wonder what the real reason is behind all the handwringing. You know, '*the lady doth protest too much*' and all that."

Benedict swore. "You're a real cow, Tori, you know that?" he snarled. "Just because I'm showing some normal compassion and decency about Percy's death, you're now accusing me of having sinister intentions? Why the hell would I want to kill Percy?"

Before Tori or anyone else could reply, he stormed off, his long strides taking him back towards the Manor faster than any of them. Katya gave Tori a disgusted look and quickened her steps as well, hurrying to catch up to Chris and Evie, who were walking ahead of them. Pomona tugged Caitlyn's arm, urging her to walk faster as well.

Caitlyn glanced out of the corner of her eye and saw Tori shrug and continue strolling along by herself, as if completely indifferent. But she wondered what the other girl really felt about the snub and felt an unexpected stab of pity for her.

As if reading her mind, Pomona said under her breath: "Don't feel sorry for Tori. She brought it on herself. I mean, can't she ever open her mouth and say something *nice* for once? Beats me what Vanessa sees in her."

"She's probably totally different with Vanessa."

"Yeah, well, lucky Vanessa." Pomona made a face, then she looked ahead at the Manor house again and let out a gusty sigh. "I never thought I'd find myself saying this, but—*man!*—I really need a nice cup of English tea!"

# CHAPTER SIXTEEN

The light was starting to fade, and the wind seemed to have become colder, with a dampness in the air that promised rain again that night. Caitlyn shivered and rubbed her arms briskly, wishing again that she had thought to put on her jacket before running out earlier. She breathed a sigh of relief when they finally stepped into the warmth of the Manor house.

They had all deposited their bundles of firewood in a pile, under shelter by the stable yard, and now the staff members hurried away, still muttering amongst themselves. The rest of them were welcomed by Mosley, who hastened to lead them to the Conservatory, where hot drinks and freshly baked treats were waiting. But when Caitlyn made to follow the others, Pomona put a hand on her arm and held her back.

"Hey..." She gave Caitlyn a serious look. "I didn't want to ask in front of the others earlier, but is something going on between you and James? He looked kind of pissed when he came to tell us goodbye earlier, and when I asked him where you were, he just mumbled something and got in his car and drove off to London."

Caitlyn hesitated, the feelings of anger and betrayal rushing back. She was suddenly glad to have someone to share her grievances with.

"Yes, we... we sort of had a fight," she admitted. "But it was all James's fault! He was being so horrible about my mother. He practically accused Tara of being Percy's murderer in front of Inspector Walsh. I mean, just because I mentioned some suspicious things that happened when Tara was impersonating Vanessa—"

"Well, you gotta admit, you yourself were pretty convinced that there was enough evidence when you thought she was Vanessa."

"No, I wasn't. I... I was still considering all angles," said Caitlyn quickly, irritated that Pomona was pointing out the same thing that James had. "And anyway, even if Tara did act suspiciously when she was impersonating Vanessa, there might have been perfectly innocent reasons for her behaviour. But James wouldn't even consider it! He just kept insisting that she *had* to be guilty."

"You can't really blame the guy for thinking that, given—"

"Hey, are you on my side or his?" demanded Caitlyn.

Pomona threw her hands up. "It's not about taking sides! I mean, of course I'm on your side, honey, but... well... the thing is, Caitlyn, you *are* a bit... uh... *sensitive* when it comes to your mom, you know. I mean, I'm not saying that you're overreacting," she said hastily as Caitlyn bristled. "But just that... well... maybe you're not able to think very clearly where your mom's concerned—"

"I can think fine," said Caitlyn curtly. "James is the one who's being prejudiced and unreasonable. Like... he kept going on about the belladonna berries but Percy wasn't even poisoned by belladonna anyway! So it's totally irrelevant if Viktor happened to see Tara with some berries. As for the other things... well, there could be all sorts of reasons why Tara was snooping in James's study. And all sorts of reasons why she lied about her alibi. And... and I might have been wrong about smelling her perfume in the Library that night. You said yourself that you can't accuse someone of being at a crime scene just because you think you smelled their perfume there—"

"But it's not just those things," Pomona cut in. "There's also the dowsing pendulum."

"The dowsing pendulum?"

"Yeah, you told me that you saw 'Vanessa'—that is, your mom, Tara—holding it when you were following her this morning. You told me that she was searching for something using the pendulum. But that pendulum belonged to Percy, right? So how did your mom end up with it?" She gave Caitlyn a sideways look, then said in a tentative voice: "Like I said when we were talking earlier, Tara could have only gotten the pendulum if she was in the Library with Percy on the night he was killed."

Caitlyn was silent, her heart sinking. She knew that Pomona was right, but she didn't want to face it. "It... it just means that Tara was there at the crime scene. It doesn't necessarily mean that she was the murderer," she protested weakly.

She could see the scepticism in Pomona's eyes and her spirits sank even further. If her cousin was so quick to believe her mother's guilt, there was no hope of James, the police, or anyone else being less judgemental.

"Honey, I know she's your mom and all that, but... well, the whole thing does look pretty sketchy," said Pomona gently. "I mean, it's like what happened at the masquerade ball, isn't it? The security camera footage showed that Tara was the only person who went into the Portrait Gallery right before Daniel Tremaine was found dead. So she was at *that* crime scene at the time of the murder as well." Pomona hesitated, then added: "Once might be a coincidence, but twice...?"

Caitlyn gave a sharp shake of her head. "My mother isn't a murderer."

"Caitlyn—"

"I don't care what it looks like!" Caitlyn snapped. "I'm sure there's a good reason for Tara being at both crime scenes. We just don't know about it yet. Maybe it's something to do with my father."

"Your dad?" Pomona looked surprised. "But you don't even know who he is—"

"I do now. I found a photo of him."

"You *what*? When did this happen?"

"Sorry, Pomie—I meant to tell you. It's just that so many things happened so quickly..." Hurriedly, Caitlyn recounted how she had stumbled across the secret compartment in a drawer in Leandra's study during her search for Nibs and described the photo she had found amongst the hidden documents.

"I thought it was James at first," said Caitlyn with a small smile. "James looks a lot like his father."

"Huh? Wait a minute, wait a minute... I thought you said you found a photo of *your* dad."

"I did. But there was another man in the photo who caught my eye first—because he looked so much like James. Then I realised that it couldn't be James because the photo was so old."

"You mean, it was the old Lord Fitzroy?"

Caitlyn nodded. "When he was a lot younger. Like, twenty years ago maybe. And he was standing next to a much younger man who looked—oh, Pomie, if you saw the picture, you'd know what I mean! He had my eyes. I mean, I've got *his* eyes. I'm sure it was him. My father."

"Holy guacamole... so your dad was a friend of James's dad?"

Caitlyn was thoughtful. "Maybe not a friend in the

normal social sense. He was a lot younger than the old Lord Fitzroy, and the way they were standing together... there was a sense of deference, like the old Lord Fitzroy was his boss... or... or his teacher."

"His teacher?" Pomona frowned.

"More like his mentor," Caitlyn amended. "I think my father was like a... a younger 'colleague' that the old Lord Fitzroy was mentoring."

"Mentoring in what? How to be British aristocracy?" joked Pomona.

Caitlyn took a deep breath. "Mentoring in how to be a witch hunter."

Pomona stared at her. "You're kidding, right?"

"No, listen, Pomie—remember that story that James told me? About that summer when he was a young boy and came to stay at the Manor... and the young man who was also here at the time, working with the old Lord Fitzroy?"

"Oh yeah... he was the guy who played with James and taught him all sorts of cool stuff."

"Yes, that's him. And one day, when they were playing a game, this young man created a fake ancient scroll by writing some rune symbols on a piece of parchment paper."

"Yeah, I remember. That piece of parchment you found in the Portrait Gallery a couple of months ago..." Pomona frowned. "But I thought James said the symbols on that parchment were just made-up mumbo-jumbo? He checked with some rune experts at Oxford University or something, right?"

"Yes, they weren't real rune symbols. But they looked very similar to the symbols on my necklace," said Caitlyn, putting one hand up to touch the runestone threaded on a ribbon which she always wore around her neck. "This young man *must* have seen my necklace to have been able to base his 'fake runes' on it. Which means that he must have known my mother, since this necklace used to belong to her. It was the only thing she left with me when I was abandoned—well, the only thing they found on me, at any rate."

"And," she continued excitedly, "when I showed James the photograph last night, he confirmed that it's him! The young man in the photo is the same as the one who was staying at the Manor that summer— the same one who made up those 'fake runes' for his game. James could only remember the young man's first name: it was 'Noah'. But it's definitely him."

"O-kay…" said Pomona slowly. "So we know your dad's name might have been 'Noah'. Great. But I don't see what that's got to do with Tara and what's happening now."

"Well, don't you see? It could all be connected! I don't think Tara ran away just because of the *grimoire*—I think it had something to do with Noah too. What if…" Caitlyn paused, marshalling her thoughts. James had been dismissive when she'd suggested this theory, but she felt a growing certainty that she was right. She looked at Pomona earnestly:

"Listen, we know that the Fitzroy ancestors were members of a secret society of witch hunters, which was formed in the seventeenth century during the time of King James I, right? You're the one who told me about the witch trials across Britain, because of King James's fear of witchcraft and magic."

"Yeah, but not everyone agreed with the King's ideas," Pomona reminded her. "A lot of people thought the dude was nuts."

"But the ones who didn't—the ministers in Parliament, who secretly agreed with the King but couldn't support his crusade publicly—they would have seen magic as a threat. It was a dangerous weapon that they couldn't use themselves, so it had to be destroyed. So... they formed a secret society! With members who shared the King's fear of magic and supported his crusade to destroy witches."

"Yeah, okay, that would have been the perfect way to recruit noblemen to their cause," Pomona agreed.

"Exactly! And we know that this secret society is still around," continued Caitlyn. "In fact, Daniel Tremaine admitted to being a member—"

"Wasn't that jerk trying to brainwash James into becoming a witch hunter too?"

"Yes, I think that was one of the reasons Tremaine came to Huntingdon Manor and got himself invited to the masquerade ball. He wanted to try to recruit James back 'into the fold'. The Society was angry that the old Lord Fitzroy had failed his duty. It had always been part of the Fitzroy family heritage, you know, that the heir to the estate was groomed to pledge allegiance to the Crown and join the fight against witches and magic."

"But James's dad never told him about it," Pomona mused. "Why?"

"I don't know why. Maybe the old Lord Fitzroy become disillusioned or something... anyway, whatever the reason, he left the Society and made sure that his son didn't follow in his footsteps."

Pomona laughed suddenly. "'Didn't follow in his footsteps?' James didn't just reject their cause—he actually fell in love with you: a *witch!* Man, that must have ticked them off! No wonder that creep Gerald Hopkins tried to turn him against you. And Daniel Tremaine—I'll bet he would have tried to poison James's mind against you too, if he hadn't gotten himself murdered." Then she sobered. "But I still don't get what this has to do with your dad and with Tara?"

"Well, think about it, Pomie: the old Lord Fitzroy was still a member of the Society at the time. And this young man, who knew an awful lot about the paranormal—James told me that Noah was always telling him stories about witches and monsters and magic and vampires—well, he was here being mentored by the old Lord Fitzroy. But James's father didn't work in an office or a company! So what kind of 'colleague' could Noah have been?"

"You mean—he was also a member of this secret witch-hunter society?"

Caitlyn nodded. "Yes, or you could say 'agent' if you like. After all, that's what Daniel Tremaine called himself: an agent of the British government. It just so happened that he worked for a covert branch of the government. And I think Noah did too. He came to Huntingdon Manor to train with a much older, more experienced agent: the old Lord Fitzroy."

"And then he met your mother Tara," said Pomona, shaking her head. "Jeez..."

"Yes, the timing would fit perfectly," said Caitlyn, warming to her theory. "Noah was here just at the time my mother would have been around sixteen or seventeen years old. With the Manor so close to the village, they could easily have met and fallen in love. And if Noah was a 'witch hunter', he would have been the *worst* kind of person for my mother to fall in love with! Maybe that's what the Widow Mags meant when she said that Tara had *'betrayed us all'—* apparently, that's what she told Bertha after my mother disappeared."

"So you think that's why your mother ran away? To be with Noah?"

"I don't know—I think it's definitely part of the reason. I also think it's part of the reason why the Widow Mags won't talk about Tara any more or even mention her name."

Pomona pulled a face. "That's a bit harsh, isn't it? I mean, who disowns a daughter just because she fell in love with the 'wrong' kind of person?"

"But it happens all the time, Pomie!" cried Caitlyn.

"There are so many examples of it throughout history and it's happening even now, in modern times. There are always stories in the news about horrible family tragedies that happen when a daughter or son falls in love with someone from the 'wrong' religion or background. Haven't you read about those awful 'honour killings' in Pakistan and India? And then there's the Amish and Jehovah's Witnesses. I've heard that if their sons or daughters marry someone outside their faith, they're completely cut off from their family and the community—"

"But that's freakin' extreme. Those are, like, really special groups," protested Pomona.

"Being a witch is similar," said Caitlyn in a small voice. "We keep to ourselves, we're different from others, and we have a special way of life that most people don't understand or believe in." She paused, then added pensively: "In fact, you can imagine how horrified the Widow Mags felt when she discovered that her own daughter was with a witch hunter: the very kind of man who had been responsible for centuries of persecution of witches, of torturing them and killing them—"

"But wait, Noah himself hadn't done any of that."

Caitlyn shrugged. "I don't think she would have seen it like that. It was what he represented, what he belonged to. Like being from the wrong religion."

Pomona shook her head. "I just can't believe it! I mean, okay, the Widow Mags can get pretty grouchy and all that, but inside, she's wise and kind. She'd never disown her daughter just because Tara fell in love with the 'wrong' man!"

Caitlyn sighed. "Maybe you're right. But I still think that my father is mixed up in this somehow."

"What *I* want to know is: why does *Leandra* have a photo of your dad?" said Pomona.

"It might not have been hers," said Caitlyn thoughtfully. "It was in an envelope with the name 'Carla Dowlenook' written on it."

"Who's Carla Dowlenook?"

Caitlyn gave a helpless shrug. "I have no idea. I've never heard the name before."

"So you think this 'Carla' gave Leandra the envelope with the photo?"

"Or Leandra stole it from her. There were lots of other documents in that secret compartment as well—official-looking documents. But again, I don't know if they were Leandra's personal things or... or something she'd stolen."

"Jeez, there are so many mysteries here, I'm losing track," groaned Pomona, clutching her head. "There's Percy's murder, your mom's disappearance all those years ago and her return now, your dad's background, Leandra's weird behaviour with Nibs and her connection to your dad, the missing *grimoire*... not to mention Daniel Tremaine's murder at the masquerade ball, which is *still* unsolved—"

"Well, maybe I'll get the answers to some of those things at last," said Caitlyn. "Inspector Walsh has given me permission to go and see Tara. I'm heading to the hospital in a minute."

"Holy guacamole! Really? You're gonna see your mom?" Pomona squeezed her hand. "Are you okay?"

"What do you mean?"

"Well... you've been, like, searching for her *forever*! It must be really weird to think about walking in and saying: 'Hi Mom.'"

Caitlyn gave a shaky laugh. "Yes, I suppose so. To be honest, so much has happened since she was 'found' at the hospital this morning that I haven't really had the chance to digest it properly. And..." She looked down, fiddling with her runestone necklace. "Well, it's all so different from how I imagined it would be, Pomie. I have so many questions but... I'm not even sure I want to know the answers now."

"Oh, honey..." Pomona threw her arms around Caitlyn in a hug. "Listen, whatever Tara says and whatever you find out, you gotta remember that it's okay. You can be your own person. You're not defined by your mom."

"What's that supposed to mean?"

Pomona shrugged. "I just don't want you to be disappointed."

Caitlyn drew back. "Oh. So you're like James too. You've all judged my mother and written her off already, when you don't even know her—"

"Hey, it's not like that! I'm not ganging up with James against your mom, okay?" protested Pomona. "But you gotta admit: you've built Tara up in your mind and... well, I just don't know if the reality will be what you think." She grabbed Caitlyn's hand and squeezed it. "You gotta remember that *you* are awesome, no matter what."

Caitlyn looked at her cousin in bewilderment. "Er... thanks. But I don't understand why—"

"Well, you're hanging on to this thing of finding your mom and getting all the answers about your past... blah-blah-blah.... It's like you think once you meet her, your life will become perfect, and you'll suddenly transform into all the things you want to be. Like cool and confident and—" She shot a mischievous look at Caitlyn's hips. "—have a smaller booty—"

"I do not think that!"

"Yeah, you do. Secretly. Inside. You think finding your mother is gonna fix everything and somehow, like, define you. But you're freakin' awesome as you are, Caitlyn!" said Pomona passionately. "I mean, sure, it's great finding your mom at last and getting to know her, but you don't need her to know who you are. You are your own person."

Caitlyn stared at the other girl in surprise. She knew that people often dismissed Pomona as a vapid social butterfly, a good-time party girl with nothing more than fun, fashion, and flirtation on her mind. But she had always known that beneath the sassy attitude, flamboyant style, and irreverent manners, there was a thoughtful, caring core to her cousin that many didn't see. Still, it was startling to hear Pomona speak so seriously and earnestly, instead of joking and making light of the situation.

"Thanks, Pomie," she said at last, smiling affectionately. "It's really sweet of you to say all that... but I'm sure you're worrying for nothing. I'm sure Tara isn't as bad as you all think."

# CHAPTER SEVENTEEN

The hospital was still busy, but Caitlyn was more familiar with the layout now and quickly found her way to the private room which Tara had been moved to. She'd half expected to see several policemen on guard outside the room, but there was only a young constable in uniform who touched his cap as she approached.

"Miss Le Fey? Inspector Walsh said you're allowed to see the patient for ten minutes."

"Thank you." Caitlyn paused outside the closed door, suddenly confronted by the enormity of what she was about to do.

As she had said to Pomona, so many things had happened, one after the other, that she hadn't really had the time to process anything properly. Now, it finally hit her that she was going to meet her mother face to face at last. This was the moment she had been waiting for, the one thing she had dreamt of more than anything else since discovering that she

was adopted. She should have been dashing
headlong into the room—instead, she was standing
there, paralysed by a rush of nerves.

*How should I act? What should I say?* It was crazy,
but Caitlyn suddenly found that she had to fight a
strong urge to run away.

"Is everything all right, miss?"

Caitlyn started and glanced at the constable, who
was watching her with quizzical concern. "Er... yes,
fine."

She took a deep breath and let it out slowly. Then
she did it again. It took her three attempts before she
finally found the courage to turn the doorknob and
step into the room.

Her first thought was that Tara looked much,
much younger than she had expected. She hadn't
really been looking properly when Dr Gupta had
pulled the cubicle curtains back in the ward that
morning and revealed her mother sleeping. The
shock had made everything a blur. But now she
could observe that the woman on the bed in front of
her looked far younger than her supposed forty
years. In fact, she looked barely older than Caitlyn
herself, which made it even harder to grasp the
reality that this was her *mother*.

As if reading her mind, Tara said in a droll tone:
"I suppose I'm not what you were expecting."

Caitlyn flushed and looked down, aware that she
had been staring.

"You can come closer," said Tara with an impish

smile. "I won't bite."

Slowly, Caitlyn approached the bed where Tara was sitting, propped up with pillows. Her mother was not classically beautiful, but there was something strikingly attractive about her, with her high cheekbones and brown eyes that seemed to glow with a dark intensity. Her hair fell in lush waves to her shoulders and, without the glamour magic to give it a blonde sheen, Caitlyn could see that it was the same brilliant shade of red as her own. But beyond that, she struggled to see anything of herself in this enigmatic young woman. She didn't have that arrogant tilt of the head, that bold spark in the eyes, or the confident assurance in the voice.

It all added to the overwhelming sense of dissonance. It was as if Caitlyn were sleepwalking in a dream where everything was completely wrong: the sky was down, the earth was up, the grass was blue, the sun was black, fish walked on land and birds flew in the ocean... and most of all, this woman who looked like a defiant teenager was somehow supposed to be her mother.

Not only did the young woman not look like a mother, but she didn't act like one either. Caitlyn didn't really know what she had expected, but— based on all the emotional reunions she had seen on TV and in movies—a part of her *had* imagined tearful hugs, loving exchanges, and tender words of regret. Instead, Tara was regarding her more with analytical curiosity than motherly tenderness and made no move to reach out for an embrace.

"How come... how come you look so young?" blurted Caitlyn at last. It was not the first thing she'd expected to say to her mother, but it was the only thing that sprang to her head.

Tara waved a hand carelessly. "Oh, it's the side effect of being trapped in a liminal space for so long."

"Liminal space?" Caitlyn furrowed her brow. She recalled Leandra Lockwood talking about liminal spaces when the woman was speculating about why Nibs wouldn't grow: *"They're well-known in folklore and mythology... almost every culture has similar stories... an in-between realm... where time moves differently compared to the human world... and if you get caught there, you may find that time stands still..."*

"Yes, a place between the worlds. That's where I've been all these years... until you returned to England, actually," said Tara. "Your return broke the spell and enabled me to leave the Cloistered Crones."

"The Cloistered Crones?"

"Are you going to repeat everything I say like a parrot?" asked Tara, looking amused. "The Cloistered Crones are old witches who have decided to retreat from our world and renounce all earthly bonds. They dwell in a liminal space—a Cloistered Coven that is surrounded by powerful magic—and there they will remain until the end of time, devoting themselves to the study of ancient *grimoires* and higher forms of witchery, as well as tending to a repository of magical herbs and creatures. They are also the unrivalled mistresses of Protective Magic, and anyone who is given sanctuary by them cannot be hunted." She gave Caitlyn a curious look. "Haven't you heard of them? All witches grow up hearing stories about the Cloistered Crones. Any witch who is being truly hunted can call to the Crones for help and protection—in fact, it's whispered that many of the witches who were burnt at the stake during the witch trials in the fifteenth century were saved by Crone magic before the flames could consume them. But there was a price to their protection: those witches couldn't remain in this world—they had to live out their days in the Cloistered Coven. That's why they were presumed to be dead, burnt by the fire, because no one ever saw them again... Ahh, but I keep forgetting that you weren't raised a witch, were you?"

Caitlyn shook her head slowly, still trying to process everything that Tara was telling her. "No. I never realised that I was descended from witches until a few months ago, when I arrived in Tillyhenge. In fact, I only found out that I was adopted when Barbara Le Fey—my adoptive mother—passed away earlier this year. Her lawyer told me at her funeral." She paused, remembering the shock of that day. "I'd always felt like I didn't really belong, but I thought it was just me imagining things... then it turned out that Barbara had found me by the roadside as a newborn baby when she was visiting the Cotswolds during a tour of the UK, and she decided to adopt me and take me back to the States. I think it was something she did on a whim, because lots of celebrities were adopting babies at the time. Maybe that's why she always seemed so distant—oh, she was very good to me, and she gave me every luxury—but I always felt that she treated me more like a pet than a child."

"She didn't do it on a whim," said Tara. "Although it certainly helped that it was a trend in Hollywood at the time for lots of stars to adopt babies. No, *I* put the idea in her head. With a spell."

"*You* did?"

"Yes, I picked Barbara Le Fey especially because I knew that, as a global star with her wealth and status, she'd be able to bypass a lot of the usual bureaucracy for adoption and take you away more easily. I engineered the whole thing," said Tara, looking proud of herself. "I wanted a way to get you out of the country, out of the reach of the Society's agents."

"The... Society?" said Caitlyn. "This is the secret society of witch hunters that the old Lord Fitzroy belonged to, isn't it?"

Tara's expression hardened. "Yes. The secret organisation set up by ministers of King James I to hunt down witches and destroy magic. I never knew their official name. They just called themselves agents of the Society."

Caitlyn felt like her head was spinning. There was so much new information coming at her, all at once. She had so many things to ask, so many things she didn't understand, but one burning question, above all else, hovered on her lips.

"Why... why did you abandon me?" she asked in a trembling voice.

Tara heaved an impatient sigh. "I didn't *abandon* you. I sent you to a safer place. The agents were coming after us, and I was still weak from the birth. My magic powers were almost non-existent, so it seemed like the best option."

"Why didn't you take me back to the Widow Mags? To Bertha? Couldn't they have helped to protect me?"

At the mention of her family, Tara's face closed. "I don't need their help," she said curtly. "Besides, they couldn't have done anything anyway. Not against agents of the Society."

"How do you know?" argued Caitlyn. "If you never even asked, how would you have known what they could have done to help? The Widow Mags is a powerful witch. I'm sure she could have figured out a way to—"

"I wasn't asking Mother for anything!" snapped Tara, suddenly sounding exactly like a petulant seventeen-year-old. "Besides, I knew what I was doing. I could have stayed one step ahead of the agents, even with my diminished powers, if it hadn't been for you, this newborn baby, dragging me down!"

Caitlyn drew back, hurt. Tara saw her face and her expression softened in remorse. "Sorry, that came out wrong. It wasn't that I didn't want you, but... well, you were so tiny and helpless, and you made *me* helpless too—and I didn't like that. I wasn't used to being helpless! I was used to be able to do anything, and suddenly, here I was, nothing more than a pathetic girl with a wailing baby..."

She sighed and looked away. There was a long silence. Finally, Tara cleared her throat and said, not meeting Caitlyn's eyes:

"Look, I... I suppose I just wasn't really ready to become a mother at seventeen. And I never realised how a growing baby would sap not only your strength but also your magic. My powers diminished with every month of the pregnancy, and by the time you were born, I could barely do the simplest of spells! It was awful, demeaning, humiliating, terrifying! I had been a powerful witch—perhaps one of the most powerful witches of all time. I could do things at seventeen that other witches took a lifetime to master. I *knew* I was destined for great things... and then I got pregnant."

Caitlyn was silent. She knew that Tara was trying to explain, maybe even apologise—in a typically teenage, unintentionally thoughtless way!—for having failed to live up to any "motherly expectations". But it still hurt.

"So you never wanted me," she said in a small voice.

Tara shifted uncomfortably in the bed. "That's not really true. I mean, getting pregnant was an accident, but then once it happened..." Her face softened even more, her eyes taking on a faraway expression. "Noah told me that he would take care of me, that we would be a family. He said it didn't matter that I was a witch—that he loved me anyway and wanted to marry me."

"Noah... my father?" said Caitlyn breathlessly.

Tara gave a wistful smile. "He adored you, you know, from the moment he laid eyes on you. He said you were the most beautiful, most perfect thing he had ever seen." She tilted her head, eyeing Caitlyn with unexpected tenderness. "And I see a lot of Noah in you. You have his kindness, his compassion."

Caitlyn wrapped her arms around herself, feeling her wounded heart soothed by the words. "Is he... where is he?"

Tara looked away. "He's dead."

Caitlyn caught her breath. Somehow, she had already known the answer, and yet the words still hit her like a bodily blow.

"How... how did he die?"

Tara turned back to meet Caitlyn's eyes, her own burning with bitterness. "He died trying to protect you and me from the Society. We had been in hiding, but they discovered our trail and came after us. I had just given birth a day ago and was still weak from the ordeal. Noah told me that he would lead the agents away so that I could take you and get to safety, and then he would come to find us later. But what we hadn't expected was that they would send agents after me and the baby as well. We thought that they would just concentrate their efforts on Noah since he had the *grimoire*."

"Oh, the *grimoire!*" Caitlyn had almost forgotten about the book of spells and its central role in this past tragedy. "*Why* did you steal it from the Widow Mags?"

"It wasn't really stealing—it would have been mine eventually," said Tara, scowling. "If Mother had just let me have access to the book, if she had *trusted* me! But no, she thought I was a silly teenage girl with romantic ideas, and that Noah was using me so that the Society could get their hands on the *grimoire* and destroy it—"

"But maybe she was right—not about Noah, of course," said Caitlyn hastily. "But the Society has always hated witches and wanted to destroy everything to do with magic. How could you possibly trust them?"

Tara's eyes flashed angrily. "You sound just like Mother. Completely stuck in the past, completely close-minded. She could never see that there was a chance for change, a chance to create a world where witches didn't have to hide themselves all the time, to end centuries of persecution and oppression!"

Tara leaned forwards, clenching a fist. "But Noah could see that different future, just like I did. In fact, he was the one who first told me his dream: to convince his superiors that witches didn't have to be destroyed, that witches could work together with the Society. And I had the power to unite all the covens— after all, I had magic skills and abilities well beyond any witch my age. They would have had to listen to me! I could have become High Sorceress and represented my people in our partnership with agents of the Crown, and to fight those who want to use magic for evil." Tara's eyes were shining now, her voice shaking with fervour. "Don't you see? It would have been the most amazing achievement in history—it would have been a chance to *rewrite* history!"

Caitlyn couldn't help thinking that it all sounded very naïve—not to mention incredibly arrogant. Bertha had certainly been right about Tara's sense of cocksure confidence! The dissonance hit her again as she realised how worldly-wise and cynical she felt compared to this brash teenager who was supposed to be her mother.

"What?" demanded Tara, glowering at her. "Are you laughing at me?"

"No, I just... well, I think it was a bit naïve," said Caitlyn. "I mean, even if you and Noah had genuinely believed in this 'brave new world' where witches and the British government could work together to use magic for the common good... well, how do you know his superiors in the Society genuinely believed that too? *Noah* might not have been using you, but they could have been using *him*. They could have let him think that they shared his ideals, but behind his back, they could have been planning to destroy the *grimoire* all along. And destroy you too." She looked at Tara, who remained silent. "It's true, isn't it?

Otherwise, why would you have ended up on the run, trying to escape the Society's agents?"

Tara pursed her lips angrily, looking like a sulky teenager who had been proven wrong but still didn't want to admit it. "Noah and I weren't naïve," she said doggedly. "It all went wrong—but it doesn't mean that we weren't right to imagine that we could change things."

In spite of herself, Caitlyn found that she was touched by the words and the simple ferocity with which Tara said them. No, she couldn't blame her parents for dreaming, for wanting to change the world. And maybe her mother was right: even if you failed, it didn't mean that it wasn't worth trying. It was all too easy to retreat, like the Widow Mags, into defensive isolation, to wall yourself off with old prejudices and fears... but maybe life couldn't be lived as a perpetual attempt to preserve the status quo. Maybe there was a joy and fulfilment in embracing change, and new realms of possibility that were worth all the potential risks and heartache...

"What happened to the *grimoire* in the end?" she asked softly. "I assume that the Society agents never managed to get their hands on it, since it ended up in the Fitzroy Library and was hidden for decades."

Tara shrugged helplessly. "I don't know. I never saw Noah again after we separated. He had told me to go to Huntingdon Manor in the Cotswolds—he said that his old mentor Lord Fitzroy had withdrawn from the Society and would be sympathetic to our cause.

He would help to protect us. But after we separated, I realised quite quickly that I was still being followed, and I knew that I could never reach the estate in time." She clenched her jaw. "I was so *angry* and *frustrated* that my powers were so weak! I managed to conjure enough magic to cast a spell so that Barbara Le Fey's driver would take a detour and drive her past the very spot where I had left you by the roadside, just outside Tillyhenge. But I knew that wasn't enough. I needed something more powerful—something that would ensure that you were taken safely out of the country, away from the Society's influence."

Tara looked back and met Caitlyn's eyes. "Then I remembered the stories I'd been told as a little girl about the Cloistered Crones. I had no idea if they really existed or if they were just old witches' tales, but I was desperate. I was willing to try anything. So I invoked them... and they answered! They offered me sanctuary—and a powerful protection spell for you—if I forsook this world and joined their Cloistered Coven, remaining there for as long as their spell kept you safe."

"But... I might never have returned to England and found my way back to Tillyhenge. So you could have been trapped there, in that liminal space, forever," said Caitlyn, slightly horrified as she suddenly imagined herself being confronted with the same prospect.

"I had no choice. It seemed to be the only way to

keep you safe and—" Tara broke off, looking uncharacteristically awkward and embarrassed. "Well... I was your mother," she said gruffly at last, in a way that suddenly reminded Caitlyn of the Widow Mags.

She stared at the young woman in front of her as she struggled with the conflicting emotions churning inside her. It was true that she had been terribly hurt by Tara's aloofness and dismissive account of the pregnancy. The "wonderful, moving mother-daughter reunion" that she had dreamt of for so long had been a bitter disappointment. But now, as she realised what Tara had done to keep her safe, she felt unexpectedly moved. Tara may not have shown any of the conventional displays of maternal affection— she didn't offer gushing words or sentimental gestures—and she would probably never behave in the way conventionally expected to show "motherly love". Yet in another way, she had made a far greater sacrifice. Caitlyn tried to imagine herself giving up the chance of being with the man she loved, of never seeing her family again or any of the people and places that were dear to her, of losing the chance to live a full life here on Earth... She winced just thinking of it. And yet that was exactly what Tara had done, despite only being seventeen—and for a baby that she hadn't really wanted or been ready to have in the first place.

Caitlyn let out the breath that she didn't know she had been holding, her whole body slackening with a newfound, unexpected calm. It was as if an unseen weight had lifted off her chest and she could breathe properly for the first time.

She hadn't been abandoned—she *had* been loved; she *had* been cherished.

It might not have been in the clichéd way that everyone expected, but she *was* loved, nonetheless. And it was ironic how keen Tara was to set herself apart from her own mother, when she was far more like the Widow Mags than she realised or cared to admit. Beneath their prickly exteriors, their blunt tongues, and their proud, aloof manners, both her grandmother and mother had a fierce generosity of spirit—and a hidden capacity for great tenderness and devotion.

# CHAPTER EIGHTEEN

"Well, anyway!" said Tara in a brisk voice, looking embarrassed and obviously keen to change the subject. "So... yes, I never knew what happened to the *grimoire*. I knew that the Society never got their hands on it because when I finally returned to this world, I used magic to infiltrate their inner circle, and I quickly found out that they were still searching for Mother's *grimoire*. Most of the agents who had been hunting me and Noah were no longer alive. Gerald Hopkins was one of the last, and the Society silenced him before I could speak to him—"

"So he *was* murdered!" cried Caitlyn. "In hospital, where they found him dead in his bed."

"Yes, he was murdered—by Daniel Tremaine," said Tara. She gave a self-satisfied smile. "But I took care of Tremaine."

"You mean... you killed him?" asked Caitlyn, her heart sinking. "The security cameras caught you going into the Portrait Gallery that night at the masquerade ball, right before Daniel Tremaine's body was found. Did you murder him?"

"I had no choice. It was self-defence. Do you think he would have let me live, knowing that I was a witch?"

"But you didn't have to kill him!" cried Caitlyn. "You could have used magic to incapacitate him or disarm him or... or—"

"Don't be a fool," said Tara scornfully. "If I had only weakened him temporarily and let him go that day, he would have been free to continue his foul work for the Society. I was doing it to protect *you* as much as anything else."

"Me?" Caitlyn stared at her.

"Yes, didn't you know that Tremaine was trying to recruit James Fitzroy back into the fold? He wanted James to take up his father's mantle as one of the Society's key members and continue the Fitzroy legacy that his father had abandoned. Tremaine was already trying to poison James against you, and he knew all the mind tricks, how to creep under a person's moral defences, how to coerce them without them realising—"

"James would never have fallen for his tricks!" insisted Caitlyn. "You don't know James. He's always fair and compassionate... and even after he found out that the Widow Mags was really a witch, he still supported her and defended her. He hates the bigotry that's being spread by some of the villagers in Tillyhenge. He would never have succumbed to

Tremaine's witch-hunter propaganda—"

"Really?" said Tara, raising a mocking eyebrow. "What, are you telling me that James Fitzroy has *never* been prejudiced, has *never* let his personal loyalties affect his judgement?"

Caitlyn shifted uncomfortably, thinking of her last fight with James and how angry she had felt about his double standards for his family versus hers. It was true: he *had* been convinced that Tara was guilty and he'd been completely unwilling to listen to any counterarguments.

*But he turned out to be right, didn't he?* a little voice whispered in her head. *Tara* was *guilty; she had killed Daniel Tremaine, just like James had maintained...*

Caitlyn pushed the thought away. Still, her stomach clenched in dread as she looked her mother in the eye and asked: "What about Percy... did you murder him too?"

"No, of course I didn't murder him," said Tara irritably. "What would I do that for? I needed that boy to find the *grimoire*! I'd guessed that Noah had somehow managed to send the *grimoire* to the old Lord Fitzroy for safekeeping, before the Society's agents could find him, and so it had to be hidden somewhere on the estate. But it could have been anywhere—in the Manor, in the grounds, in the woods, in the village—and the chances of me finding it just by randomly searching..." She made a face. "Then I happened across a magazine article about

Percy and his shop of rare books, all supposedly found with the help of a dowsing pendulum that he had inherited." Tara's eyes gleamed. "I knew that was what I needed to find the *grimoire*. And how fortunate that he should happen to be friends with Vanessa Fitzroy, James's younger sister—it was almost as if it were meant to be!"

"Did you impersonate Vanessa so you could ask Percy to look for the *grimoire*?" asked Caitlyn.

"No, that would have been too obvious. But I did drop hints about the *grimoire*, knowing that Percy wouldn't be able to resist searching for it while he was here at the Manor. That first night, when I heard Benedict come upstairs without him, I wondered if Percy had remained in the Library to search for the book. So I decided to go down and join him. But when I walked in, I found him lying on the floor, dead. I didn't know then that he had already found the *grimoire*—it was only later, when I heard the rumours around the estate about the torn page in his hand, that I realised. But I *did* see Percy's dowsing pendulum on the floor next to him, and I managed to pick it up just before I heard you and Pomona come into the Library."

"So I was right when I thought that there was a presence in the Library that night—it was you!" cried Caitlyn. "I was sure I felt someone brush past me, and I smelled your perfume—that is, Vanessa's perfume that you were wearing—but I never saw anyone—"

"Invisibility Aura Charm," said Tara, waving a hand carelessly. "It's a simple spell if you know how. It's an advanced form of glamour magic, really: you're simply bewitching people to see you as blending seamlessly into the environment around you, so that you are essentially 'invisible' to them."

Caitlyn frowned. "But... if you weren't involved in Percy's death, then what were you doing with those deadly nightshade berries? I know belladonna isn't what poisoned Percy—the police found that it was actually an overdose of caffeine—but I still don't understand why you had those berries. Viktor saw you with them on the night you arrived at the Manor."

"Oh, the berries were for the Nocturne Sight spell. You know the juice of belladonna dilates the pupils, don't you? That's how the plant got its name: because women used to squeeze juice from the berries into their eyes and make their eyes look bigger, which they thought made them look more beautiful. Stupid and dangerous, of course, but—" Tara gave her a wink. "—it's totally different when magic is involved! If used in the Nocturne Sight spell, belladonna juice isn't poisonous at all and can dilate your pupils and enable you to see in the dark."

"Oh. So you used them that night you went down to the Library?"

Tara nodded. "The Invisibility Aura Charm might have hidden me from sight, but I would have still revealed myself if I had to use a light to see. With the belladonna juice, I could go anywhere in the Manor, even in total darkness, without having to worry."

"But you still didn't see who murdered Percy?" Caitlyn pressed.

"No, I told you, he was already dead when I got there."

"What about when you left the Library? Did you see anyone in the vicinity outside?"

"No—oh wait, I did see one of the girls through a window. Katya. She was running towards the house from the direction of the rear outbuildings."

"Yeah, Katya had sneaked out to see Leandra Lockwood." Caitlyn paused thoughtfully. "She did lie about her alibi... but I don't think she's Percy's murderer. For one thing, whoever it was who killed Percy obviously took the *grimoire* as well, but Pomona and I overheard Katya talking to Leandra and it's clear that they don't have it. They're searching for it too, just like everyone else."

"I know the *grimoire* is still on the estate," said Tara, gritting her teeth. "The dowsing pendulum kept indicating that it was near. In fact, I was *so close* to finding it this morning when I was outside in the gardens! After you drenched me with that stupid garden hose, I managed to give you the slip and go back outside with the pendulum, and it led me to the terrace outside the Ballroom. I'm sure it was there, somewhere, on the terrace." She cast Caitlyn a peevish look. "I might have found the *grimoire* already if it hadn't been for you jumping on me. In fact, I wouldn't be stuck here in a hospital, under arrest, if it weren't for you!"

Caitlyn bit back the sharp retort that sprang to her lips, reminding herself that she was still, essentially, dealing with a truculent seventeen-year-old.

"If you had confided in me and let me know who you really were, there wouldn't have been any misunderstanding," she said as calmly as she could. "Why didn't you? I could have helped you—"

"I didn't need anyone's help," said Tara loftily. "I knew what I was doing, and I would've been able to manage fine by myself."

Caitlyn had a sudden flashback to the first day she had arrived in Tillyhenge and walked into the Widow Mags's chocolate shop. She had startled her grandmother, who had dropped some cocoa beans on the floor, and when she had bent down to help pick up the scattered beans, instead of thanks, she had been treated to a snarled *"I can manage!"* from the old witch.

Now, as she looked at Tara, she remembered Bertha saying: *"That's the real problem, you know... They are too much alike in personality, both so proud and stubborn, and neither willing to give an inch."*

She sighed and reminded herself that this was her mother. Making a supreme effort, she offered Tara a conciliatory smile and said, "Look, what's done is done. We might as well focus on what to do going forwards—"

"It's obvious," said Tara impatiently. "You have to help me escape."

"Well, I *have* been talking to James and Inspector Walsh and trying to persuade them that you're innocent. If I can get them to at least release you on bail, then—"

"No, it's no use going through official channels. You're wasting your time. First of all, even if they can't hold me for Percy, they can still keep me in custody for Daniel Tremaine's murder. And secondly, even if they somehow agree, it could take days— weeks!—with the bureaucracy and lawyers. No, the only way is to simply break out."

"Break out?" Caitlyn looked at her blankly.

"Yes, you have to release me and help me escape police custody."

Caitlyn glanced over her shoulder at the shut door of the room, fervently hoping that the constable outside couldn't hear their conversation!

"But... I don't understand. Why do you need my help to do that?" she asked her mother. "I thought... well, surely with your powers, you could easily use magic to escape if you wanted to?"

"The concussion seems to have sapped some of my powers," said Tara irritably. "It should be temporary, though, and I should regain my full abilities within a few hours. But even when I do, I won't be able to work any magic... because of *this*."

She pulled the blankets back and thrust a leg out, brandishing her bare ankle. Caitlyn looked down. At first, she thought that she was looking at an ankle bracelet—then she realised that this wasn't the dainty foot accessory often found for sale around tourist beaches. No, this looked much more rustic: a length of ancient twine braided into a loop which encircled Tara's ankle, and then dangling from that— like a gigantic charm—was what looked like a huge tangle of knotted twine. *No, wait, not a random tangle*, thought Caitlyn, looking closer. There was a complex symmetry to the loops and twists, with an intricate pattern emerging that pointed at a deliberate design. Nestled amongst the knots were tiny shards of iron and clusters of dried rowan berries. Caitlyn frowned. The object looked vaguely familiar, but despite racking her brains, she couldn't remember where she had seen a similar item before.

"What is it?" she asked Tara at last.

"It's a witch knot," Tara replied, her face twisted in revulsion. "It was one of the tools used by witch hunters in the fifteenth century to bind witches and prevent them from using magic to free themselves and escape."

Caitlyn stared at the lattice of knots next to her mother's ankle. "But why do you—"

"That old detective inspector must have put it on me while I was still semi-conscious," said Tara, scowling. "He obviously found out that I'm a witch and knew that human locks and handcuffs wouldn't be able to contain me once I regained my magical abilities, so he decided to use a witch knot."

Caitlyn shook her head "No, that can't be right. Inspector Walsh is a total sceptic. He doesn't believe in magic at all, and he would never have thought of—"

She broke off. No, Inspector Walsh might not have thought of containing Tara's witch power, but there was someone else who would have. Someone, moreover, whose family had a past association with witch hunters and who would have had access to a private collection of occult objects that would have contained a witch knot...

*James.*

The realisation hit Caitlyn like a physical blow. She looked up to see Tara watching her.

"It was James, wasn't it?" her mother asked, her lips curling back in disgust. "He told the old inspector to use the witch knot on me. In fact, now that I think about it, I remember seeing one in the old Lord Fitzroy's occult collection."

*Yes, that's why it seems so familiar*, thought Caitlyn. She had seen one very like it on that first night when Vanessa (or rather, Tara impersonating Vanessa) and her friends had arrived at Huntingdon Manor. The whole group had gone up to view the old Lord Fitzroy's occult collection in the Portrait Gallery, and she recalled Benedict and Pomona admiring some items in a glass display case. The witch knot had been there amongst them.

Still, she didn't want to believe it. "No, James would never... He wouldn't... He knows how abhorrent the witch-hunting practices were. He would never use one of their tools himself!"

"Are you sure you know him as well as you think you do?" Tara raised an eyebrow.

Caitlyn swallowed. She remembered how James had told Inspector Walsh that he wanted a private word before leaving for London, and how he had pointedly waited for her to leave them alone. She was suddenly back in that corridor of the Manor, walking away from the men and hearing their voices behind her, with the inspector saying: *"...an injured young woman is unlikely to present security issues..."* And then James had replied: *"...not to underestimate her... require specific methods..."*

*Specific methods.* Caitlyn felt sick. Had James gone behind her back and given the police this cruel device to hold her mother captive? A horrible sense of betrayal swamped her. *How could he?* she thought furiously. She couldn't believe that James, of all people, could sanction a device that had been used to hunt and torture witches. She had always believed him to be on *their* side—

*RAP-RAP-RAP!*

Caitlyn jumped and hunched instinctively as the door opened a crack and the constable peered in.

"Miss Le Fey? I'm sorry, but Inspector Walsh did say that you were only to be allowed ten minutes and... er..." he glanced down at his wrist apologetically. "It's already been fifteen."

Tara grabbed Caitlyn's hand and squeezed hard.

"No, you can't go yet!" she hissed under her breath. "I haven't finished telling you how to release me—"

"Um... er..." Caitlyn struggled to maintain her composure as she turned to face the young constable. "Can we have five more minutes? Please?" she said, looking at him pleadingly.

He hesitated. "But the guv'nor said—"

"Please..." Caitlyn opened her eyes very wide and let her voice tremble slightly. "Just five minutes!"

He caved, no match for a pair of beseeching eyes in a pretty face. "I... all right. But only five more minutes."

He shut the door, leaving them alone again. Instantly, Caitlyn flung herself on the witch knot, trying desperately to prise the taut loops apart with her fingernails.

"It's no use," said Tara, jerking her foot away irritably. "The magic is too strong. The only person who can untie a witch knot is the person who fastened it in the first place. You're wasting your time."

"Maybe I can use a counter-spell—"

"No, there's no time to faff around. You have to listen to me," said Tara sharply. "There is one other way to release a witch from the binding magic of a witch knot and that is to cut it loose with a rowan-thorn blade."

"A what?"

"It's a magical blade crafted from the highest thorn of a hawthorn tree combined with the branch of a dual-trunk rowan tree for the handle. Once consecrated by a spell, such a blade will hold a unique power: the ability to cut through any enchantment or magical bond, including a witch knot." Tara leaned forwards, speaking urgently. "You have to find such a blade and bring it back here, tonight, while I'm still in the hospital. It will be much harder for you to get close to me once they transfer me to the police station tomorrow."

"How am I supposed to find a blade like that?" cried Caitlyn. "I have no idea where to even *begin* looking—"

"The old Lord Fitzroy's occult collection, obviously!" said Tara impatiently. "The witch knot probably came from there, so a rowan-thorn blade is likely to be there too. You just need to go back to the Manor, sneak up to the Portrait Gallery, and search in there—then come back here tonight, after midnight, when the wards will be quiet and empty."

"I... I can't!" said Caitlyn as the enormity of what Tara was asking hit her. "You want me to lie and steal and effectively help a murder suspect break out from police custody—"

"It's the only way!" Tara insisted. "You know they will never release me—do you want your mother to be captured and imprisoned forever?"

"It... it wouldn't be forever," said Caitlyn weakly. "I would find a way to get you out on bail. And once your case goes to trial, I would make sure that you have the best lawyers. There is no proof that you killed Percy, and we can say that Daniel Tremaine was self-defence—"

"*NO!*" Tara looked at her fiercely. "Once they have me in their clutches, they will never let me go. They will use any means to keep me imprisoned—"

"Inspector Walsh isn't like that. He might not believe in magic, but he's a decent policeman and a good man. He would never hold you without reason."

"You fool, do you think your plodding provincial detective can do anything once the British secret service step in?" demanded Tara. "The Society has agents everywhere, and once they find out about me, they will make sure that I am moved to their custody. I will be locked up and hidden away, maybe even tortured—"

"No, that won't happen!" cried Caitlyn, recoiling from the picture that Tara's words were painting. "James would never let that happen—"

"James Fitzroy comes from a family of witch hunters!" snarled Tara. "Do you really think you can trust him?"

"I—"

There was a sharp knock on the door, and the constable's voice, sounding sharper this time, said: "Miss Le Fey? You really must leave now, otherwise I will be forced to escort you out."

Caitlyn rose from the bed, her eyes panicked.

"Will you be able to live with yourself, knowing that you condemned your mother to suffer at the hands of witch hunters?" asked Tara in an urgent whisper. "I gave up everything to save you once, Caitlyn. Now I need you to help me."

Caitlyn licked dry lips. "I don't know if I can find the blade... and what if something goes wrong and we're caught trying to escape—"

"Once the witch knot is severed, I'll be able to use some magic again. Enough to get us out of here without anyone knowing. They'll just come in the morning and find the bed empty. It'll all be fine if you just do as I say." Tara caught her hand and looked her straight in the eye. "You have to trust me."

"Why should I?" cried Caitlyn wildly.

Tara gave a slow smile. "Because I'm your mother."

# CHAPTER NINETEEN

Caitlyn arrived back at Huntingdon Manor in a state of numb shock and anguish. She had spent the whole trip back agonising over what she should do and still hadn't come up with an answer. She couldn't bear the thought of letting Tara down, of not doing enough to save her own mother—and yet at the same time, she knew that what Tara was asking her to do was wrong, and she couldn't shake off the feelings of guilt and unease.

She sighed as she climbed the steps to the Manor's front door, wishing desperately that there was someone she could turn to, someone she could share her dilemma with. James would have been the first person she would've run to in the past, but he seemed completely unapproachable now. She was still simmering with anger at his betrayal over the witch knot, and she didn't dare trust him any more. As for Pomona, her usual confidante in everything... even her cousin seemed an uncertain ally now. She recalled the way Pomona had defended James and how her cousin had echoed his doubts about Tara's innocence... no, she didn't dare trust Pomona either.

So who was left? Evie? Her aunt Bertha? The Widow Mags? It wasn't fair to put this on Evie's young shoulders, and anyway, Caitlyn doubted that her shy, inexperienced cousin would be able to counsel her much. As for her aunt and her grandmother... Caitlyn hesitated. Even if they agreed with her in believing Tara's innocence, would they approve of helping Tara escape in this way? Or would they try to prevent her from returning to the hospital that night? Caitlyn bit her lip. If there was any chance she was going to do it at all, she couldn't take the risk of anyone stopping her...

"Caitlyn! You're back! How was it? What was she like?"

Caitlyn blinked and realised that Pomona rather than Mosley had opened the front door.

"Come in, come in!" said Pomona without waiting for her to answer. She grabbed Caitlyn's arm and yanked her inside, then propelled her down the hallway and into the first empty room that they came across. As Caitlyn dropped down on the plushily upholstered sofa, she looked around and realised that they were in the same small parlour that she had been sitting in with Bertha that morning, talking about Tara. It seemed like a lifetime ago now.

"The others are all in the Conservatory, but I wanted to talk to you in private first," said Pomona.

She looked at Caitlyn avidly. "So? What happened? What was it like meeting your mom at last?"

"It was... it was weird, more than anything else," confessed Caitlyn. "Partly because Tara looks like a seventeen-year-old; she talks like a seventeen-year-old—well, she *is* a seventeen-year-old! She hasn't aged since the day she left me by the roadside, because she's been trapped in a liminal space this whole time."

Pomona's eyes were round. "Holy guacamole! Are you kidding me? She was in a 'liminal space'? So, it's true that time stops in there, huh? I've, like, read about them, of course, but I never imagined that they could really exist! Omigod, that is so awesome! Do you think if I just hop in and out every year, it could stop me getting old? I mean, I don't mind getting a *bit* older, but not more than, like, thirty-two, you know, before all the really bad wrinkles set in and your boobs start sagging and—"

"Pomie!"

"Oh... yeah... right. Your mom. Sorry, keep going."

Caitlyn pulled an exasperated face. Still, a smile tugged at the corners of her lips, and she was surprised to find that she felt better. Somehow, her cousin could always lift her spirits, even in the darkest moments. *Maybe I can tell Pomona everything*, she thought with sudden yearning. *Surely she would understand? Surely she would help me?*

"Well, go on!" urged Pomona. "Tell me more about

this liminal space!"

Caitlyn hesitated a moment longer, then pushed her anguished thoughts aside and continued with her story. She recounted Tara's entire tale, from the romance with Noah and their shared idealistic dreams to their betrayal by the Society, Tara's ruse to get her newborn baby safely out of England, and finally her pact with the Cloistered Crones, giving up a life in this world in return for sanctuary and protection—at least until the spell was broken by Caitlyn's return to Tillyhenge. Pomona listened open-mouthed, and when it was finished, she flopped backwards onto the sofa cushions, gobsmacked.

"Man!" she said, shaking her head. "That is, like, the most amazing story I've ever heard! I mean, can you imagine if it was made into a movie?" She grinned and slanted Caitlyn a sideways look. "Who would you get to play *you*?"

"Pomie!" said Caitlyn, exasperated.

"Okay, okay...!" Her cousin put her hands up. "You've gotta admit, though—it's an incredible story. And at least we know the answers to a lot of our questions now." She looked at Caitlyn, concerned. "So what happens to your mom now?"

"Well, she's being transferred from the hospital tomorrow into custody at the police station," said Caitlyn cautiously.

"How are the police gonna keep her in a cell? Won't she just, like, use magic to break out?"

Caitlyn hesitated, once again wondering if she

dared to trust her cousin. If she told Pomona about the witch knot—and if her cousin didn't agree with helping Tara escape—then she would have forfeited her chance to rescue her mother. On the other hand, if she just didn't mention the witch knot, Pomona would be none the wiser.

"Um... I think the concussion is still affecting Tara's witch abilities," she said at last. After all, that wasn't really a lie. "I don't think she'll regain her full magic powers for a while." She paused, then heaved an exaggerated sigh and said, watching Pomona surreptitiously, "I wish there was a way she didn't have to remain in police custody."

Pomona shrugged. "Well, she's got to face the charges sooner or later, right? Better to get it over with. Don't worry, I'll call my lawyer back in LA and make sure that she gets the best representation available here. We know your mom's not involved in Percy's murder and... and maybe if she confesses to Daniel Tremaine's murder on the grounds of, like, 'diminished responsibility' due to a freaked-out mental state or self-defence or whatever, then they might drop the murder charge or reduce the sentence."

"Yes, I suppose so," said Caitlyn, trying to hide her disappointment that Pomona hadn't immediately suggested a mission to rescue Tara instead. She had been right not to trust her cousin after all.

"In the meantime, if we focus on finding the *grimoire*, that should help her, right?" said Pomona.

"'Cos if we can show that someone else has it—that they were likely the person who murdered Percy to get their hands on it—then that indirectly proves Tara's innocence." She gave Caitlyn a smug smile. "And you know what? You're not the only one who's found answers. I did some detective work too while you were gone."

"What do you mean?"

Pomona looked like the proverbial cat who had got the cream. She leaned forwards and said in a melodramatic voice: "I found out Leandra Lockwood's secret!"

"What secret?"

"I've been doing some research online into her background. She lied about why she moved to the Cotswolds: she didn't just decide to retire early from her professor job—she was fired!"

"Fired?"

"Yeah, the official press releases were full of these polite statements, trying to put a positive spin on things. You know, like—" Pomona put on a smooth, newsreader voice: "—*Ms Lockwood has decided to take early retirement and the college wishes her well—blah-blah-blah...*" She reverted back to her own voice. "But when you start digging deeper, there was a bunch of stuff on social media and in the tabloid papers which said that Leandra was actually asked to leave by the college because of some kind of scandal. Apparently, the parents of one of her students accused her of brainwashing their daughter and—" Pomona made exaggerated air quotes with her fingers. "—'leading her into dark occult practices'. There were no names mentioned, but how much d'you wanna bet that this 'student' was Katya? I mean, aren't Eastern Europeans, like, pretty religious?"

"Well, it's a huge area with millions of different people," Caitlyn demurred. "I don't know if you can generalise—"

"Okay, but they're mostly Christian, right?"

"Orthodox Christian, I think—"

"Exactly! Can you imagine how Katya's parents would have felt when they found out that their precious daughter was being encouraged by Leandra to dabble in witchcraft? And her dad is some kind of trading tycoon, right? I'll bet he's rich and powerful enough to put the screws on the college and make them force Leandra out.

"And that would explain why Katya lied about her alibi for the night of the murder," Pomona continued blithely. "If she's still in contact with Leandra and sneaking out to see her, then she wouldn't want to admit that, just in case it gets back to her parents. In fact, she mentioned that on the day we were eavesdropping through the window of Leandra's barn—remember? Leandra was chewing her out for sneaking out to the barn the night before, and Katya said something like..." Pomona screwed her face up in an effort to remember. "'...out here, away from London, my parents will never know'—you see? It all fits perfectly!"

"Okay," said Caitlyn cautiously. "Well, this might explain Katya and Leandra's connection, but I don't see how that relates to Percy's murder—"

"It proves that Leandra was using Katya to find the *grimoire!*"

Caitlyn frowned. "That's a bit of a leap."

"It all fits!" Pomona insisted. "Leandra is obsessed with magic and witchcraft, right? She's spent her whole life studying the occult, and she likes to show off that she's the top expert on magical rituals and mystical customs and blah-blah-blah—but at the end of the day, she's not a witch, is she? All she can really do is spout stuff that she reads in textbooks. And I'll bet that really burns her up inside. I'll bet she's desperate to belong to the magical world that she's so obsessed with." Pomona sighed and added, in a more charitable tone: "I mean, I can kind of relate. I've always been fascinated by magic and the paranormal, and I'd give anything to have been born a witch like *you.*"

"If anyone deserves to be a witch, it's you, Pomie," said Caitlyn warmly. "I mean, honestly, you put me to shame with the amount of stuff you know about magic and myths and legends and the occult."

"Aww, thanks," said Pomona, grinning and making a mock-curtsy. "So yeah, what if Leandra believes that the *grimoire* could give her the ability to become a *real* witch? Someone capable of *working* magic and not just a pathetic academic who can only


216

*read* about magic in books."

"But we've always been told that witches are born, not made," Caitlyn protested. "Even if Leandra got hold of the *grimoire* and recited its spells, it would be of no use. Nothing would happen if she doesn't have the innate ability to work magic—"

"But she might be able to *gain* it temporarily!" said Pomona. "Don't you remember? Evie told us about a chocolate philtre that was created by the Widow Mags as her own Samhain Gourmet Glory entry when *she* was a young witch. Evie said that if a witch drank this philtre, it could boost her powers. Even someone who didn't know they were a witch might suddenly find that they could work magic because the philtre awakened the abilities dormant within them. What if Leandra somehow found out about the existence of this chocolate philtre—don't you think she would give anything to get her hands on it? And the recipe for it is in the Widow Mags's *grimoire*!"

Caitlyn started to argue, then stopped. Pomona was right. She had completely forgotten how this had all started: with Evie's desire to enter this year's Samhain Gourmet Glory competition for witches across Britain. Her young cousin had been so despondent and frustrated when her own attempts at creating a magical Truth Nougat had continually resulted in disastrous flops, and she had spoken wistfully of this chocolate philtre. The hunt had been on for the Widow Mags's *grimoire* ever since.

"But wait... you'd still need *some* kind of

connection to the magical realm," Caitlyn reminded Pomona. "Evie told us that the chocolate philtre wouldn't work on just anybody—it has to be someone with latent magical ability inside them. And I don't think Leandra is descended from witches, however much she'd like to think that."

"No, but maybe she found a workaround," said Pomona thoughtfully. She snapped her fingers. "Hey! Maybe that's why she kidnapped Nibs!"

Caitlyn looked at the American girl quizzically. "What? I'm lost."

"Listen, it's well-known that witches have familiars, right?"

"You mean like a cat or a toad? I thought they were basically like witches' pets."

"No, not just pets! They're supposed to help in working magic and to serve as a bridge between the witch and the supernatural world. That's why people are so scared of them, see? And if you had a creature that was *extra* special—like, say, something that would never age or grow old... well, maybe Leandra thinks that would be extra useful for someone like her." Pomona nodded excitedly. "Yes, she might not have the natural birthright of magic, but maybe she thinks she can use Nibs as a... a bridge to the magic realm, so the chocolate philtre can still work on her as if she were a born witch."

"That all seems a bit far-fetched," said Caitlyn. "You don't know any of this for sure; you're just making it up—"

"No, I'm not! It's based on fact! Well, okay, not 'fact' exactly, but there are loads of stories of people who have been obsessed with finding objects or creatures of great purity, because they believed that it would give them certain powers. Like... remember what I told you about unicorn horn? Well, all the kings and queens and other nobility in Medieval and Renaissance times were nuts about it. The House of Medici, for example. They hired spies and informants across Europe and commissioned secret expeditions to search for unicorns, all because they thought the purity of the horn would protect them from assassination.

"And Hitler!" continued Pomona, warming to her subject. "He was, like, *totally* obsessed with the occult, and also with 'pure' things, right? Well, one of the things that he was desperate to find was the Spear of Destiny—the embodiment of purity and sacrifice—because there was this legend that said whoever possessed the spear would hold the fate of the world in their hands. I mean, he made half the Nazi army run around searching for this thing: there were special task forces to raid museums and sacred sites, and whole sections of the SS just to oversee archaeological digs—"

"Leandra isn't Hitler."

"No, but I'll bet you anything that she wants power just like he did: the power to do magic."

Caitlyn swallowed. She didn't want to admit it, but she had a bad feeling that Pomona was right.

# CHAPTER TWENTY

Caitlyn glanced over her shoulder as she hurried down the corridor, checking to make sure that no one was following her. Dinner had been an ordeal. She had sat and made polite conversation with Pomona, Tori, Benedict, and Katya, all whilst itching to sneak away. When the group finally retired to the Drawing Room for chocolates and port, she had quickly made an excuse about needing to fetch a cardigan from her room and hurried away. She was fairly sure that no one had seen her furtively make her way to the rear of the Manor and head up the old servants' staircase, instead of taking the main staircase in the front hall. Still, she didn't want to take any chances.

She paused at a turn in the corridor and peered around the corner, checking to see if there were any Manor staff about. Thankfully, at this time of the evening, the maids were unlikely to be going about their duties, and in any case, this rear upper wing of the Manor was usually deserted. Satisfied that the coast was clear, Caitlyn hurried down the darkened hallway to a familiar oak door covered with iron studs. She tried the heavy brass handle, relieved to find the door unlocked. She could have used magic to gain access, but it would have taken more time. The heavy door swung open on silent hinges and Caitlyn stepped into the Portrait Gallery, a long room which ran the length of the Manor house, filled with oil portraits of the Fitzroy ancestors... and with cabinets displaying the old Lord Fitzroy's occult collection.

Groping along the wall, Caitlyn found the main switch and illuminated the row of chandeliers that hung from the ceiling. Their soft glow brought light to the room but also seemed to make shadows loom larger, especially amongst the cluster of furniture draped in white sheets occupying the far side of the gallery. As usual, she felt a sense of eerie unease envelop her, and she had to fight the urge to glance at the oil paintings of the Fitzroy ancestors to see if their eyes were following her. It was silly—she had been in the Portrait Gallery often enough now to know that the "creepy vibe" was probably just the result of her overactive imagination. Still, she hurried across to the shrouded white forms, keen to get her task over with so that she could leave as soon as possible.

Quickly, she found the display case that Benedict and Pomona had been poring over on the first night the group arrived. Pulling the sheet back, she peered down through the glass pane. Her eyes ran over the Greek astrolabe, the alchemy set with alembic and crucible, the Victorian skeleton clock, the antique scrying mirror... and then paused at the dusty gap next to the sixteenth-century witch bottle. That gap was where the witch knot had lain.

If she had been clinging to a vain hope that James hadn't betrayed her after all, that the witch knot around Tara's ankle hadn't come from the Fitzroy collection, the gap in front of her silenced all doubts. In her mind, the echo of Katya's voice talking about the witch knot that first night resounded: "...*when you tie a specific sequence of knots, while chanting a special incantation, you can bind a witch in place and drain her of her magical abilities, making her powerless.*"

James had known that and had used the knowledge against her family. Caitlyn gritted her teeth, feeling the surge of outrage again. Her mother was right: she couldn't trust James. She couldn't let him dictate and control her—or her family. If she had been still unsure about what to do, now her anger hardened that uncertainty into bitter resolve. She would return to the hospital tonight and set her mother free.

But to do that, she needed a rowan-thorn blade. *Where am I going to find that?* Caitlyn wondered despairingly. She looked around the gallery. Tara had been convinced a blade could be found amongst the artefacts in the collection. There was nothing resembling what her mother had described in the display case in front of her. She turned to the cabinet next to her and was just about to lift the sheet that covered it when she heard a heavy thumping noise that was coming from the corridor outside and growing louder.

Caitlyn remembered suddenly that she had left the gallery door wide open. Berating herself for her stupidity, she turned to go back and shut it. But in her haste, she caught her foot in a fold of the white sheet she was holding. She tripped, lurching sideways, and flailed her arms, trying frantically to regain her balance. But it was no use. The next moment, she crashed to the floor and lay face down in a tangled heap between the cabinets.

*Thump-thump-thump-thump...*

Someone had come into the Portrait Gallery. Caitlyn struggled to push herself up into a sitting position, but she had barely risen to her elbows when someone shoved her head down again with a furry hand.

*Wait a minute... "furry hand"?*

Caitlyn turned her head sideways, then let out an exasperated laugh as two enormous paws came into view. She realised that the "hand" was in fact a huge muzzle which had been thrust eagerly into the back of her head. Now she felt a cold, moist nose snuffing next to her cheek, and a slobbery tongue began licking her face.

"Ugh... Bran, stop!" she cried, struggling to sit up

whilst pushing the English mastiff's head away from her.

Bran wagged his tail, obviously thinking that this was a new kind of game, and tried to climb into her lap.

"No... noo... euw... no," spluttered Caitlyn, scrambling to her feet to get away from the dog's slurping tongue. "I love you too, Bran, but no licking... uggh... no licking!"

"WOOF!" he barked, his jowls wobbling comically. He bounced a couple of times—the room almost shook—and then dropped into a play bow. "WOOF! WOOF!"

"*Hush!* Shhh! You have to keep quiet!"

The mastiff looked at Caitlyn, his droopy eyes quizzical, then he brightened and reached down to seize one end of the white sheet in his mouth. He shook the sheet vigorously from side to side as if it were a giant rag-toy.

"Hey! No, don't do that!" cried Caitlyn, grabbing the other end of the sheet and trying to tug it out of the dog's mouth.

Bran's baggy face lifted in delight. This was his favourite game. "*GRRRR!*" he growled joyfully, jerking his head and throwing all his weight back as he yanked against the sheet. "*GRRR—RRRRR!*"

"Stop it, Bran! Let go!" panted Caitlyn, wrestling with the mastiff. "I said: LET GO—"

"Caitlyn? What on earth are you doing here?"

Caitlyn gasped and spun around, clutching the

white sheet to her like someone clutching a towel to their naked body.

James stood in the doorway of the Portrait Gallery with a young woman hovering behind him.

"J-James!" she stammered, trying not to sound guilty. "I... you startled me."

Bran finally abandoned his newfound sheet toy and lumbered over to his master, his tail wagging. James came slowly into the room, absent-mindedly patting the English mastiff.

"I thought Bran was just mucking around when he kept trying to get me to follow him... but no, he was obviously coming to find you." He glanced at the uncovered cabinets next to Caitlyn and then at the sheet in her hands. "What are you doing?"

"I... um..." Caitlyn groped frantically for an excuse—any excuse. "Er... I was looking to see if there might be a... a Lantern Carving Set in your father's collection. You know, to carve the turnips for Samhain... um... I heard Bertha talking about such sets existing in the Middle Ages with... er... special knives and scoops to use on the turnips. I thought it might be nice to have one on display during the Festival tomorrow. You know, for... for educational purposes."

"A Lantern Carving Set? I've never heard of such a thing," said James. "As far as I'm aware, people just used ordinary knives or kitchen tools to hollow out the turnips and beets and carve faces in them."

"Er... I thought you'd gone to London?" asked

Caitlyn, trying to change the subject.

"I did. Traffic was surprisingly good, and the journey down was much quicker than I'd thought it would take." He gestured towards the girl still hovering in the gallery doorway. "Ness felt fine, and she was impatient to join her friends, so we decided not to stay the night in London after all but to come straight back instead. We made great time on the motorway and arrived about ten minutes ago. I've just been hearing all about your bonfire wood outing from the others in the Conservatory... Oh, I beg your pardon—I should have introduced you: this is my sister, Ness."

He didn't say *"the real Ness"* but it hung, implicit, in the air between them, and Caitlyn saw James's mouth compress into a thin line. So, he was still angry about Tara's impersonation.

"Hi... you must be Caitlyn," said Vanessa, looking at Caitlyn with friendly curiosity.

"Hi." Caitlyn offered the girl a shy smile, wondering why she was still hovering in the doorway.

Vanessa noticed her looking and hurriedly stepped into the room, coming over to join them. "Sorry... old habits die hard. I used to be terrified of this room when I was a little girl and hated coming in here. This place always gives me the willies."

Tara's "Vanessa" hadn't displayed any qualms about coming into the Portrait Gallery. In hindsight, so many of the signs were there if they had only known to look. In fact, Caitlyn recalled James commenting on his "sister's" unusual indifference when the group had come up here on their first night at the Manor, but he had accepted Tara's quick explanation of changing with age without question.

Vanessa gave her a sheepish smile. "You probably think I'm silly—"

"Oh no, not at all. I feel the same," said Caitlyn, warming towards James's sister.

Vanessa beamed at her, and Caitlyn had an uncomfortable flashback to the moment she had first been introduced to the "fake" Vanessa. That girl, too, had flicked her long blonde hair back with easy grace and smiled at her with great warmth and charm, and it was jarring to realise that she had been fooled by Tara's glamour magic all along.

It was almost like a mental and emotional violation—not to mention the actual physical violation that Vanessa herself had suffered, being forced into a magical coma to keep her out of the way. Caitlyn was sure that Tara hadn't done it with genuine malice, but it was still nonetheless a thoughtless, cruel gesture by a ruthless seventeen-year-old bent on achieving her own goals, without consideration to others. Caitlyn stole a glance at James and suddenly felt a flash of understanding for what he must be going through. How did he feel, looking at his sister now and remembering how he had been tricked and lied to? For a moment, she could almost sympathise with his anger and hostility towards her mother...

Then she hardened her heart. *That still doesn't give him the right to use the witch knot on her,* she thought grimly.

Oblivious to her dark thoughts, Vanessa glanced at the uncovered cabinets and asked cheerfully: "Are you into magic? My dad was completely obsessed with it, you know. Witches and spirits and hexes and all that stuff. That's why he had all these creepy things in the cabinets here."

"Er..." Caitlyn tried for an honest but diplomatic response. "Well... I suppose everyone is fascinated by magic in some way, aren't they?"

"Not me," said Vanessa with a laugh. "I mean, I dabbled a bit in horoscopes and tarot cards when I was at school, but I was never that interested in witchcraft and vampires and all the other supernatural stuff like the other girls." She glanced at James and grinned. "Unlike my big brother. Did you know that James used to secretly wish that he was a wizard?"

James reddened. "That was a long time ago," he said. "I was just a young boy."

"Yes, but I remember you used to talk about it even in your teens," insisted Vanessa. "And that summer that Mother took us to a village fête near Stonehenge—there was an old woman there with a fortune-telling tent, remember? Everyone said that she was a witch and could use divination to see the future." She giggled. "You got so excited when she looked into her Dark Mirror and told you that one day, you would meet a beautiful witch and marry her."

"*Ahem...* yes, well," said James, clearing his throat and avoiding Caitlyn's eyes. "It was just a bit of fun. Everyone knows that fortune-tellers at carnivals and fairs are just entertainers who invent random predictions for amusement. Similar to the slips of paper found in fortune cookies. One doesn't really take it seriously."

"*You* took it seriously," said Vanessa with a teasing look. "You told me—"

"Shall we rejoin the others downstairs?" said James hurriedly, turning to lead the way out of the Portrait Gallery.

Vanessa gave Caitlyn a wink, then called to Bran and skipped out into the corridor with the mastiff lumbering happily at her heels. Caitlyn glanced at the cabinets in chagrin, but with James waiting pointedly, she had no choice but to re-drape the sheets and follow him out of the Portrait Gallery.

Caitlyn watched as Vanessa chattered happily to her brother whilst they made their way back downstairs. Now that she had met the real Vanessa, the difference between her and Tara's impersonation seemed blindingly obvious. True, the two girls looked exactly alike, and Tara had even managed to capture Vanessa's childlike sweetness and bubbly manner, but there was a subtle difference that couldn't be disguised. It was especially apparent in Vanessa's open, candid face, her blue eyes clear and without guile—whereas even the best glamour magic hadn't been able to hide the gleam of strategic cunning and careless arrogance that had lingered in Tara's eyes when she had been impersonating James's sister.

When they reached the Drawing Room, Vanessa hurried in to rejoin her friends, but James put a hand out to hold Caitlyn back when she would have followed suit.

"Caitlyn... wait... can I talk to you for a moment?"

She turned to look at him expectantly.

James shifted his weight, looking uncharacteristically awkward, then said in a rush: "I... I wanted to apologise... for what I said before I left for London. You know, when we were talking to Inspector Walsh."

Caitlyn blinked in surprise. She started to speak, but James held a hand up.

"No, please...let me finish. I shouldn't have jumped down your throat like that. I suppose I lashed out because I was so angry about what had happened to Ness. I think it was the over-protective, big-brother instinct kicking in," he said with a rueful expression. "And maybe... maybe I was also angry with myself for not seeing the truth earlier. I mean, looking at Ness now, I just don't understand how I didn't notice the difference." He shook his head in baffled disbelief. "How did I not know my own sister?"

Caitlyn felt herself softening towards him. "I can understand," she said gently. "I mean, I was thinking something similar myself, and I'm not even her brother."

James gave her a grateful look. "Yes, but that's no excuse to take it out on you. And..." He hesitated. "And I shouldn't have said those things about your mother. I'm sorry."

Caitlyn swallowed, not knowing how to respond. "I suppose we're both a bit touchy where our families are concerned," she said grudgingly at last.

"Yes... and Caitlyn, there's something else," said James, looking like he was struggling to find the words. "I... er... I was worried about how the police would be able to handle Tara. You know, because of her abilities with magic. So... um... well, I suggested to Inspector Walsh that it might be prudent to use a certain... er... medieval device which is rumoured to have the power to constrain witches." He paused, giving her a shamefaced look. "I gave him the witch knot from my father's occult collection to help him detain Tara and keep her under guard. I'm sorry—I know you'll be upset hearing this. I had no intention of hurting you or Tara. It was just... I thought it was for the best."

Caitlyn stared at him. She hadn't expected James to admit to the witch knot and she was touched by his remorseful manner. The fact that he had confessed to her, himself, without prompting, went a long way to soothing her hurt and anger. And he clearly hated having lied to her and gone behind her back. *Everyone makes mistakes*, she reminded herself. James had realised how wrong he was and was apologising—wasn't that enough to forgive him?

She smiled, feeling her heart lifting. She didn't want to be angry with James, didn't want to keep fighting with him. She wanted to return to that old easy camaraderie and intimacy that they shared. And she felt a rush of relief as she realised that she wouldn't have to make the difficult decision now about whether to help free Tara tonight.

"Thank you for telling me," she said, looking up at James warmly. "It's okay. I think I can understand why you did it. But you can just call Inspector Walsh now and ask him to take the witch knot off, can't you?"

James hesitated, then he sighed and said: "I can't, Caitlyn. You have to realise that. Tara is too powerful. The police would have no way to keep her in custody if her powers aren't checked—"

Caitlyn pulled back. "I can't believe you're saying that! You're helping to deliberately keep my mother incarcerated and—"

"Caitlyn, she's a suspect in a murder investigation. Two, in fact," said James, starting to look irritated. "Have you forgotten that? Tara has to be subjected to justice, just like everyone else. She can't have *carte blanche* to commit crimes without facing the consequences just because she's your mother!"

"She's innocent! She—" Caitlyn caught herself as she suddenly remembered that her mother was, in fact, *not* completely innocent. Tara *had* confessed to killing Daniel Tremaine (and had shown very little remorse for doing so!). "I mean, even if Tara *had* done anything, there would have been good reasons. She was probably forced to, for... for self-defence or something like that," she amended.

"And I'll make sure that the police are aware of that. If things do progress to a trial, I will personally ensure that your mother is given the best defence to refute the charges," James promised. "Even if it is proven that she is involved in either of the murders, there are all sorts of mitigating factors that can be called into play to dismiss the charge or at least reduce the sentence."

It was an echo of what Pomona had said and what she herself had suggested to Tara. A part of Caitlyn desperately wanted to agree with James. It would be so nice just to hand things over to him and let go of all the angst and responsibility. But then the memory of Tara's voice rang in her mind:

*"Once they have me in their clutches, they will never let me go. They will use any means to keep me imprisoned... The Society has agents everywhere... they will make sure that I am moved to their custody. I will be locked up and hidden away, maybe even tortured..."*

Caitlyn flinched mentally at the image. She felt horribly torn. What should she do?

Her anguish and confusion must have shown on her face because James said earnestly: "I'm not trying to persecute your mother, Caitlyn. You have to believe me! I want to see her exonerated as much as you do, and I promise I will do everything I can to make sure that the charges against her are dropped. But you know Tara is a loose cannon. If she is allowed free, there's no telling what she might do. She has shown herself to be ruthless and completely reckless when it comes to achieving her own ends—and with her magic powers, she could cause untold chaos. The witch knot is to protect her—and everyone around her—as much as anything else."

He caught her hand and brought it to his chest, tucking it close to his heart. "Caitlyn—please, you have to trust me."

# PART TWO

# CHAPTER TWENTY-ONE

Caitlyn stood at her bedroom window and stared out into the darkness as she listened to the distant chimes of the grandfather clock in the front hall downstairs: ...*Seven... Eight... Nine... Ten... Eleven... Twelve...* Midnight.

She turned and began to pace the room, her thoughts bouncing nervously around. If she was going to help her mother break out of hospital, she didn't have much time left. There would only be a few more hours of darkness before the world began waking up. But did she really want to do this? Despite her earlier outrage, her resolve was weakening. James's "confession" to her had changed everything. And a part of her—a part she didn't really want to acknowledge—knew that he was right: Tara *was* headstrong and impetuous, pursuing her own agenda with a ruthless determination that could be devastating to others. Setting her free could be careless at best, criminally dangerous at worst...

*But she is my mother*, thought Caitlyn, her mind churning with emotion. *And she gave up everything for me once. Don't I owe her this in return?*

*Besides, it could also be the fastest way to find the grimoire*, she reasoned, trying to take a calm, logical approach. If Pomona was right about Leandra's agenda, then the retired academic was holding Nibs to use him in her schemes. But if she, Caitlyn, had the *grimoire*, then she would have power on her side: she would be able to expose Leandra and rescue the kitten. It would also be a way to flush out Percy's real murderer. Finding the *grimoire* was the key to everything.

*And Tara is my best hope of finding that book.* Her mother was already fixated on retrieving the Widow Mags's book of spells, so it made sense to combine forces with her. And with Tara's magic skills, they would have a strong advantage, even if they no longer had Percy's dowsing pendulum.

As for James's concerns about Tara's unpredictability...? *It'll be fine. I'll just keep an eye on her and make sure that she doesn't get into trouble.*

Before she could agonise more about it or change her mind, Caitlyn slipped on some shoes and grabbed the oversized wool cardigan slung over the foot of her bed before hurrying from the room. She crept down the corridor, making her way as quietly as possible from the guest bedroom wing to the rear of the Manor. Very soon, she was facing the metal-studded oak door of the Portrait Gallery once more.

Taking a deep breath, she turned the brass handle and pushed the heavy door open, as always surprised not to be met with the horror-movie-clichéd creak of the hinges. The air was cold and still, and the gallery looked even more forbidding than it had done earlier. Caitlyn had to steel herself to step inside and walk over to the group of white shrouded shapes on the far side.

Quickly, she found the display case that she had been about to examine earlier, just before Bran had interrupted her. She lifted the sheet and peered down through the dusty glass panes at the contents within...

There was nothing resembling a rowan-thorn blade.

She yanked the sheet off the next cabinet standing alongside. Again, nothing.

Nor was there anything in the next one. Nor the next one.

Soon, she had exhausted every one of the cabinets and display cases clustered together in that corner of the gallery and had drawn a blank.

Starting to feel frantic, Caitlyn re-draped the sheets and looked around. She spied another cabinet that was set apart from the others, standing by the wall beside the tall arched windows. She hurried over and lifted the sheet to peek underneath, then sighed in disappointment as she saw that the shelves were filled with books: rows and rows of leather-bound volumes and nothing more.

She dropped the sheet back into place and straightened up, biting her lip. What was she going to do? How could she rescue Tara if she couldn't find a rowan-thorn blade to sever the witch knot? She was about to return to the original group of cabinets when movement in the corner of her eye caught her attention. She turned back to the window and realised that it was something outside: a black shape moving erratically across the night sky. She strained her eyes to see better, but the moon was obscured by clouds, making it impossible to make out any details. All she could see was a dark form, weaving from side to side, its outline merging with the great darkness beyond every few moments, before sharpening into silhouette against the dim night sky once more, so that it seemed to appear and disappear with the blink of an eye.

Unbidden, the echo of Leandra's voice, ominous with foreboding, rang in her head: *"...Samhain is a time of great danger! It's the time when the veil between the living and the dead is at its thinnest, and evil and malevolent spirits will be walking the Earth, searching for unwary victims..."*

In spite of herself, Caitlyn felt a shiver slide down her spine as she watched the shape loom bigger and bigger. *It's coming closer*, she realised, backing away from the window. *Oh my God, is it attacking m—?*

*BANG!*

Caitlyn jumped and instinctively ducked, throwing her hands over her head and hunching her body. She braced herself for pain, shock, injury... but when nothing happened, she raised her head in bewilderment. She stared at the window in front of her, which was empty except for a big blurry smudge in the centre. Then her gaze dropped to the dark shape huddled at the base of the window. As her eyes acclimatised, she realised that she was looking at the round mound of a small furry belly, two pointed ears above a little foxy face, and long leathery wings sagging on either side. It was a fuzzy brown fruit bat lying half-stunned on the window ledge.

Caitlyn groaned silently. *Not an evil Samhain spirit after all,* she thought wryly. Marching up to the window, she wrestled with the catch before managing to heave it open—just a small amount, but enough to reach through the gap, grab the fruit bat, and gently drag it into the room.

"Viktor!" she whispered, cradling the little fruit bat in her arms. "Viktor, can you hear me? Are you all okay?"

The fruit bat blinked stupidly at her for a moment, then began making garbled squeaks interspersed with what sounded like hiccups. He also smelled oddly of cinnamon and orange.

"Ssh! You'll wake everyone up!" Caitlyn admonished. "I can't understand you when you're in your bat form, Viktor."

The little bat gave a grumpy squeak, then it shook itself and hopped out of Caitlyn's hands onto the ground, where its form began to wobble and blur. A few minutes later, a balding old man in a dusty black suit stood swaying in front of her.

"Viktor, are you all right?" asked Caitlyn in concern, putting out a hand to steady him. "You smacked into the glass pretty hard. Maybe you should get some medical attention—"

"Eh? Nonsense!" said the old vampire, lifting his fists into a classic boxer's stance and bouncing up and down on his rickety knees. "Just a small—*hic!*—miscalculation mid-flight, that is all. I am fighting fit!" He threw a jab with his right fist and toppled over.

"Viktor!" cried Caitlyn in alarm, bending down to help the old vampire.

"I'm fine, I'm fine... don't fuss," said Viktor irritably as Caitlyn set him back on his feet.

Then she reeled backwards at the alcoholic fumes coming off him. "Viktor, are you drunk?" she said suspiciously.

"Certainly not!" said the old man indignantly. "Vampires do not get drunk. We merely—*hic*—become slightly merry."

"Well, why do you smell like you fell into a vat of brandy then?" demanded Caitlyn.

"It was a barrel of mulled wine, to be precise," said Viktor. "And I didn't *fall* in, young lady. I was merely—*hic!*—perching at the edge for a taste..." He shut his eyes and raised his nose, inhaling deeply in memory. "Ahh, nothing like hot mulled wine: that spicy cinnamon sweetness, those tangy orange flavours, the piquant fragrance of star anise, the warm glide of liquor down your throat..."

"Viktor?" said Caitlyn after a minute. The old vampire seemed to have drifted off to sleep standing up.

He awoke with a snort. "Eh? Where was I?"

"You were telling me how you fell into a barrel of mulled wine," said Caitlyn dryly.

"I didn't fall." He glowered at her. "Vampires have exemplary balance. I was startled by that Pruett woman coming into the kitchen and shrieking like a banshee. Actually, she sounded worse than a banshee. Banshees are quite musical, you know, whereas she was—"

"Viktor!" Caitlyn had to resist the urge to shake the old vampire. "Never mind banshees! What *happened*?"

"Yes, all right, all right. Young people... always so impatient," grumbled Viktor. "As I was saying, I was ambushed whilst I was enjoying a sample of the mulled wine, and although I deployed instant defensive reflexes, I was ultimately walloped by a tea towel and—*hic!*—knocked into the barrel. Nasty things, tea-towels, I tell you. Especially when they're wielded by a shrieking human female. Nevertheless, I managed to climb valiantly out of the barrel and take off through the kitchen window—no mean feat, I tell you, when the place was full of females screaming about bats and their hair." He harrumphed. "Well, it was difficult flying with soggy wings, and anyway—*hic!*—I was feeling in need of a kip, so I decided to go and find my usual corner in the Library." He pointed to their feet, indicating the floor below, where the Manor's Library was situated, directly underneath the Portrait Gallery. "I was aiming for one of the Library windows just now. Slight miscalculation, that's all."

"Did you—" Caitlyn broke off as she heard the distant chime of the grandfather clock again. It was striking 1 a.m. She swore under her breath. Viktor's arrival had completely distracted her from her original task. Now an hour had passed, and she still hadn't found a rowan-thorn blade. How was she ever going to free Tara?

She turned back to the old vampire. "Viktor, listen—do you know what a rowan-thorn blade looks like? I need to find one urgently."

"Eh? Why would you need that?"

"It's a long story." Caitlyn hesitated, then on an impulse told the old vampire about Tara's impersonation, her unmasking, and her imprisonment by the police, as well as the plan to release her. When she finished, she braced herself for a disapproving lecture or an attempt to dissuade her from her plan, but Viktor merely said:

"I knew there was something odd about that girl. Did I—*hic!*—not tell you that she smelled funny?"

Caitlyn gave him an exasperated look. "Yes, but that could have meant all sorts of things. How was I to know that you meant she was someone in a glamour disguise rather someone with bad BO? Anyway, never mind all that now. I just need to find this rowan-thorn blade." She gestured to the white-draped cabinets behind them. "I've been looking and looking but I just can't see anything like it. But maybe I missed it, and you can—"

"Why are you searching when you can simply fashion one yourself?" asked Viktor.

"What do you mean?"

"'Tis no difficult feat to make a rowan-thorn blade. You simply find yourself a twig from a dual-trunk rowan tree and—*hic!*—a thorn plucked from the highest branch of a hawthorn tree and bind them together using hair from a true witch."

"That's it?" said Caitlyn in disbelief. "But I thought this was some special magical blade that can cut through all enchantments—"

"It is, but its power comes not from fancy design or elaborate construction. It arises from the latent forces of its inherent components and from infusing the blade with intention."

"Oh." Caitlyn digested this for a moment, then she brightened. "The bonfire wood that we collected! That was from a dual-trunk rowan." She turned towards the Portrait Gallery door. "Come on! We'll go down to the pile by the stable yard and get a twig from there."

"And *I* shall fetch you a hawthorn thorn," said Viktor, puffing his chest out importantly as he followed her. "I can easily find a suitable hawthorn tree and reach the highest—*hic!*—branch by flying in my bat form."

"Er... are you sure that's a good idea?" asked Caitlyn, looking at him askance. "I mean, you shouldn't drive when you're drunk, so I imagine it would be the same with flyin—"

"I told you, vampires do not get drunk," said Viktor loftily, then he walked straight into the Portrait Gallery door. "OUCH! Who put that door there?" he demanded.

Caitlyn sighed. *Great*, she thought. *I'm heading off to break a suspect out of police custody, armed with nothing but a few twigs and a drunk old vampire. Wonderful.*

# CHAPTER TWENTY-TWO

As it was, Viktor surprised her. He shapeshifted into his fruit-bat form as soon as they stepped out of the Manor and took off before Caitlyn could protest further. And by the time she had found the pile of bonfire wood and extracted an appropriately sized rowan twig for the handle, the little fruit bat was back, carrying something in his tiny claws. He hovered above Caitlyn for a moment, his leathery wings beating a rush of air that stirred her hair, before flopping awkwardly down on the ground, landing on his face.

"Ow!" grumbled Viktor as he sat up—back in human form a few minutes later—and rubbed his head.

Caitlyn bent to pick up the dropped thorn from the ground and held it gingerly up to the light. It was only about an inch in length but thin and viciously sharp at the tip. She placed it next to the end of the rowan twig, then wondered how she would bind the two together.

"You need a strand of your hair," said Viktor, watching her.

"How do I know if I'm a 'true witch'?" whispered Caitlyn.

"It is true if you believe it," said the old vampire.

Caitlyn took a deep breath and reached up to grope along her crown. Selecting a long strand of hair, she gave a sharp yank, wincing as she felt the pinch on her scalp. Lowering her hand, she stared at the long, thin filament that gleamed fiery red, even in the faint light. Then she carefully began wrapping it around one end of the thorn before looping it around the other end of the rowan twig, around and over and behind and back, looping and crisscrossing as firmly as she could, until both were pulled tight together. At the end, she was left with a short section of hair, and she stared at it, wondering what to do. If she didn't secure it somehow, the hair strand would simply unravel again.

"How am I going to knot this?" she murmured.

"With magic, of course," said Viktor. "Hasn't Mags taught you any Intention Knotting spells?"

Caitlyn racked her memory. "I don't think so."

Viktor scratched his head. "What about Elemental Sealing? Or Natural Affinity Bonding?"

Caitlyn shook her head.

"What kind of magic *have* you learnt, then?" asked Viktor tetchily.

"Mostly just culinary enchantments for chocolate-making or domestic spells for household chores," said Caitlyn with a rueful shrug.

"Harrumph. Well, chocolate isn't going to help us much now, is it?"

Caitlyn looked down at the makeshift blade in her hands, then looked back up, struck by an idea. "Why not? I can cover the binding in chocolate, can't I?"

"Eh?"

"Look, I'll show you..." Caitlyn focused on the loops and twists in front of her, concentrating all her will onto the hair strand, then she shut her eyes and imagined a thick coating of rich milk chocolate enveloping the strands, fixing them rigidly in place. When she opened her eyes, she gave a whoop of glee. "It worked! Look—it worked!"

She thrust the rowan-thorn blade at Viktor, turning it over to show him the middle where the thorn and twig were joined by what looked like several thick bands of chocolate. Smiling proudly, Caitlyn carefully tucked the blade into the big outer pocket of her oversized wool cardigan and then, giving Viktor a quick wave of thanks, she hurried towards the front of the Manor, where Pomona's car was parked. She had borrowed the keys from her cousin earlier, for her visit to the hospital, and was glad that she hadn't returned them yet.

As Caitlyn slipped into the driver's seat, she was startled to see the passenger door open, and the next moment, Viktor climbed laboriously into the car next to her.

"Viktor, what are you doing?"

"Accompanying you, of course."

"What? No, you can't—"

"You will need protection as you embark on your quest, and who better to guard your wellbeing than your own guardian uncle?"

"Viktor, I'm not going on a quest," said Caitlyn with long-suffering patience. "I'm going to sneak into a hospital and you'd just get in the way—"

Viktor bristled. "I'll have you know that I was infiltrating enemy lairs and breaching fortified castles long before you were born, young lady! We vampires are masters of shadowy stratagems and clandestine manoeuvres!"

Caitlyn opened her mouth to argue, then paused, thinking hard. Maybe it wouldn't be a bad idea to let Viktor tag along. After all, the old vampire *had* saved the day several times in the past and his ability to fly could come in very useful. And, if she was honest with herself, she appreciated the company. It would be nice not to feel so alone in this haphazard crusade, and unlike James or Pomona, Viktor wouldn't judge or try to interfere with her plans to rescue her mother.

"Okay, you can come," she told Viktor. "But you've got to keep quiet and stay with me. No running off the minute you smell a fruit salad or see a fruit hamper in someone's cubicle!"

"I do not behave in such an unprincipled manner," said Viktor, looking affronted. "Just because I am a fruitarian does not mean I have no control over my appetites."

"Hmm... past experience does not support that," muttered Caitlyn under her breath.

"Eh?"

"Never mind," she sighed, starting the engine and praying that the sound of the motor would not awaken anyone in the Manor house.

They made good time to the hospital, and after parking the car, Caitlyn led the way to the entrance. She paused behind a bush, eyeing the double doors. There didn't seem to be a security guard stationed outside but that didn't mean that there wouldn't be someone in a nearby security office, monitoring the CCTV cameras. And at this time of the night, with visiting hours over, she was sure that anyone not in uniform would be noticed and detained.

As she was pondering this, Caitlyn noticed a distinguished-looking middle-aged man hurrying towards the entrance. He looked slightly dishevelled, like someone who had dressed in a hurry, and he was talking urgently on his mobile phone as he approached the double doors. His voice drifted across in the cold night air:

"...just got here and will be up in the ward in five minutes. Just keep her comfortable until I arrive. Administer oxygen but don't intubate or administer any IV fluids until I've had a chance to assess her..."

His voice faded away. Caitlyn watched him step inside and disappear from view. She turned to Viktor.

"That's it, Viktor! You're old—er, I mean older. You look like you could be a consultant surgeon or something like that. We just need you to pretend that you're a doctor who's been called in for an emergency. That way, you can walk right in."

"Eh?"

"Just walk very quickly and importantly through the front door and talk into this while you're doing that," instructed Caitlyn, handing Viktor her mobile phone.

The old vampire stared at the device as if it might bite him.

"Here... put it up to your ear," said Caitlyn, taking his hand and positioning the phone next to his ear for him.

"And what will you do?" Viktor asked.

"I... I'll just act like I'm with you. Hopefully no one will pay me much attention if I keep my head down."

She spun the old vampire around and propelled him in front of her towards the entrance.

"Now start talking as if you're a doctor," she hissed.

Viktor eyed the phone doubtfully, then began tottering towards the double doors, saying in a loud, quavering voice: "*Ahem*, yes, Nurse? Have you procured the leeches yet? Upon my examination, should the humours be imbalanced, we may have to resort to bloodletting to relieve the excess—"

"Leeches?" Caitlyn spluttered, hurrying to keep pace with him. "What are you on about?"

Viktor gave her a huffy look. "I'm masquerading as a physician, as you instructed."

"Yes, but no one uses—" Caitlyn broke off with a sigh. They would draw more attention standing here arguing. It was the lesser of two evils to just keep walking and let Viktor continue. "Never mind."

She ducked her head and tried to walk as inconspicuously as possible as they hurried through the double doors whilst Viktor continued blithely into the phone: "Furthermore, ensure that the apothecary has supplied us with sufficient quantities of laudanum and tincture of opium for the pain..."

Caitlyn hurried them through the main hospital foyer and paused at last beside a large potted palm, breathing a sigh of relief as no one rushed out of a nearby security office to stop them. It looked like her ploy had worked. She glanced quickly around, wrinkling her nose at the faint smell of antiseptic that always seemed to permeate hospitals. The foyer was completely empty at this time of the night, the reception desk unmanned.

"Come on," she whispered to Viktor. Trying not to look furtive, she turned and began leading the way down the maze of corridors to the ward at the rear of the hospital where Tara was being kept.

# CHAPTER TWENTY-THREE

A few minutes later, they arrived by the nurse's station, where a single preoccupied nurse sat with her head bent over paperwork. In the office behind her, Caitlyn could hear the murmur of female voices, and drifting out from across the ward were the sounds of various beeping monitors, but otherwise the place was hushed and quiet.

Beckoning Viktor to follow her, Caitlyn slipped past the nurse's station and tiptoed down the corridor that led to Tara's private room. She paused beside a trolley piled high with bed linen and towels and peered around it; she could see the young constable sitting on a chair positioned next to Tara's bedroom door.

"We need to distract him somehow, otherwise we'll never be able to get into the room," she whispered to Viktor.

"Ah, I shall simply use my vampire powers of hypnosis and send him into the deepest slumber," said Viktor, starting down the corridor.

"No, wait!" Caitlyn hissed, grabbing his arm and yanking him back behind the trolley. "Viktor, the last time you tried that, you put yourself to sleep instead!"

"I was not sleeping—I was merely resting my eyes," said the old vampire indignantly. "However, if you do not think hypnosis is appropriate, I can create some vampire mist instead to obscure and confuse him."

"No, I don't—" Caitlyn broke off, her eyes darting to the end of the corridor, beyond Tara's room, where another door was visible—a door with a bright green "Emergency Exit" sign above it. "Actually, that could work! Can you make the mist come out from beneath that door there?" She pointed.

Viktor squinted down the length of the corridor. "Certainly, I can direct the mist wherever you want, in any form you want: a whisper of haze, a veil of vapour, a blanket of white, a tsunami of—"

"Uh... no, no, just some wisps coming from beneath that door would be fine," said Caitlyn hastily. "And can you make them quite dense, so that they look like smoke?"

The old vampire nodded and stretched out a hand, waving his bony fingers. Slowly, from the gap at the base of the fire exit door, white tendrils of mist began to rise, seeping out and curling upwards, looking exactly like smoke escaping from a fire. Caitlyn held her breath and watched the young constable. It took him a minute to notice the mist, then he sat upright in his chair, his eyes fixed on the curling white plumes which were rising and filling the end of the corridor.

With an exclamation, the constable sprang up and hurried towards the fire exit. Caitlyn saw him sniffing loudly, looking confused, as he obviously couldn't smell any smoke. Still, the presence of the mist was enough to make him push open the fire exit and wander out into the stairwell to investigate.

As soon as the door shut behind him, Caitlyn sprang out from behind the trolley and started towards Tara's room door. "Come on, Viktor! Now's our chance!"

She ran pell-mell down the corridor, skidding to a stop outside Tara's door and yanking the doorknob open. She rushed inside to find her mother sitting up, wide awake, in bed.

Tara gave a satisfied smile as she saw Caitlyn. "I was wondering when you'd get here."

Caitlyn stopped short, slightly piqued. *Does Tara take my obedience for granted? She sounds like she never doubted that she would be rescued... does she think I'll just blindly do whatever she asks?* Then Caitlyn thrust the thoughts aside; there was no time for recriminations now. They might only have a few minutes before the constable returned.

Hurrying over to the bed, she said: "Hi... er... Mum..."—then trailed off awkwardly. It felt somehow wrong to call the seventeen-year-old girl in front of her "Mum".

"Why don't you just call me 'Tara'? 'Mum' sounds so old—ugh!" said Tara, wrinkling her nose and shuddering. Then she looked at Caitlyn expectantly. "Well, did you get it?"

Caitlyn nodded, fishing the rowan-thorn blade out of her pocket and holding it out proudly. "I had to make it myself, but it should still work."

"Ah! Good on you," said Tara with an approving nod, and Caitlyn felt herself glow. She might have felt weird calling this teenage girl "Mum", but she still revelled in the feeling that her mother was proud of her.

She turned to the witch knot attached to Tara's bare ankle and hesitantly placed the thorn against the knot, unsure what to do. Was she supposed to saw against it?

"You need to press the blade down on the centre of the witch knot and focus your intention," instructed Tara.

Caitlyn gripped the rowan-twig handle tighter and did as her mother said, leaning forward and putting her weight into the blade. But something wasn't quite right: her hand kept slipping and sliding on the rowan twig, and when she pressed down, she felt the thorn wobble. What was going on? She lifted one hand from the handle, then looked in horror at the dark brown streaks coating her palm.

"Oh no," she whispered as she realised that the chocolate that she had used to bind the hair strand was melting from the warmth and pressure of her hand gripping the rowan handle. And the harder she pressed, the faster the chocolate melted!

"You used *chocolate* to bind the blade?" said Tara incredulously.

"I'm sorry—it was the only spell I knew," said Caitlyn, her cheeks reddening.

Tara gave an impatient sigh. "Never mind. Just focus on the blade. The binding might still hold long enough for you to sever the knot."

Caitlyn gritted her teeth and reapplied herself to the task. The handle wobbled in her grip, the rough bark slipping beneath her fingers, and the thorn blade tilted precariously to one side, but she continued pressing down on the witch knot, trying to focus all her will to break the bond with the point of the thorn. Then, just when she thought the strand of hair would unravel completely, she felt a sudden release of pressure, and the witch knot fell onto the bed, the loop attaching it to Tara's ankle severed.

"I did it!" cried Caitlyn, jubilant.

Tara didn't answer. She was rotating her ankle experimentally, then setting it gingerly on the ground as she stood up from the bed. She stumbled for a few steps, then regained her footing and hurried to the door.

"Come on!" she hissed to Caitlyn. "We have to get out of here. Is the constable still there?" She opened the door a crack and peered outside. Then she gave a laugh. "I don't believe it. Is that Viktor?"

Caitlyn realised suddenly that the old vampire hadn't followed her into the room. As she joined Tara at the door, she saw why. Viktor was standing valiantly on guard outside the door, swaying slightly with his scrawny arms akimbo as he blocked access to the room with his body. Feeling a rush of affection for the old vampire, Caitlyn was about to step out when Tara caught her arm and stopped her. Her mother jerked her head towards the fire exit, which was opening to reveal the young constable returning. He stepped back into the corridor, then stopped short as he saw Viktor.

"Who are you?" he blurted.

"I am Count Viktor Konstantin—*hic!*—Alexandru Benedikto Dracul, of the Megachiroptera Order," said Viktor, attempting to make a sweeping bow and toppling over in the process.

"Whoa!" cried the constable, rushing forwards to grab the old vampire. "Are you all right, sir? Er... which ward are you from? Have you wandered away from your bed? Here, let me call a nurse—"

"Nurse? I do not need a nurse!" said Viktor, brushing the young man's hands off. "I'll have you know, I am an Ancient Guardian Protector, skilled in subterfuge and combat, and I am in prime condition! In any case, even if I were to sustain an injury, it would be of no consequence. With my vampiric regenerative abilities, I would heal within a few days at the most."

"Your... your what?" said the young constable,

completely bewildered.

Tara made an amused noise as she watched the scene through the gap. "I see that the doddery old bat hasn't changed at all. He used to drive me bonkers, following me everywhere, insisting that he was my 'guardian uncle' and needed to protect my honour."

"Viktor always calls himself my 'guardian uncle' too," said Caitlyn. "I've always wondered what he meant by that. I mean, I know vampires are 'Ancient Guardians' with a duty to protect the vulnerable and keep order in the magical realms—"

Tara gave a huff of contempt. "Is he still wittering on about that old code of honour thingy? No one follows those ancient beliefs anymore! He's probably the only one who still cares."

"I think it's quite nice that Viktor does," said Caitlyn staunchly. "But is he really my uncle? How can he be your uncle too?"

"Well, not 'uncle' in the usual sense. I suppose he's really more like a godfather. And the reason he's assigned himself to you is because I asked him to watch over you, if you ever returned to Tillyhenge."

"Oh...in the letter you left him," Caitlyn said, remembering what Viktor had told her before. Twenty-two years ago, he had returned to England after an extended stay in Transylvania to find Tara missing, with no explanation other than a letter announcing that she had become a young mother, an appeal to watch over the baby, and instructions not to search for her.

She opened her mouth to ask more, but Tara cut her off impatiently "We're wasting time talking." She shut the door and turned away from it. "Come on, while Viktor keeps him occupied, we can go out the window."

"Wait—we can't just leave him," protested Caitlyn.

"He'll be fine," said Tara with a dismissive wave. "That old fruit-sucker has got himself out of similar predicaments before. Besides, he won't thank you for worrying about him."

Caitlyn frowned as she followed her mother to the window. "Yes, but old people say things sometimes because they're too proud to admit any weakness. It doesn't mean that they don't need looking after. You can't just abandon them—"

"Who said anything about abandoning?" said Tara, rolling her eyes. "Stop being so melodramatic. Look, Viktor is providing us with the perfect opportunity to escape. You'd be insulting his efforts if you didn't take it."

She looked down at her hands, flexing her fingers experimentally, then flicked a finger at the windowsill and whispered: *"Open wide, path provide!"*

Instantly, the sash lifted, presenting them with a wide opening leading into the hospital grounds. Tara grinned, pleased to see her magic powers returning. Then she ducked her head and climbed through without a backwards glance. Caitlyn hesitated, throwing an agonised look back at the door of the room, through which she could still hear Viktor's quavering voice arguing with the constable. Whatever Tara might have said, it felt wrong just leaving the old vampire without even letting him know...

Then Caitlyn turned resolutely towards the window. No, her mother was right: while he might have looked like a decrepit old man, Viktor wasn't helpless. *In fact, he'd been looking after himself for six-hundred-odd years before I arrived in Tillyhenge,* Caitlyn reminded herself. *And it's certainly true that he's been in numerous battles with supernatural creatures. So he should be able to extricate himself from the hospital without problem.* In the meantime, she couldn't let Tara out of her sight, so she had no choice, really, but to follow her mother.

Swallowing her misgivings, Caitlyn ducked her head and climbed out through the window.

# CHAPTER TWENTY-FOUR

Caitlyn stood up on the other side of the window and looked quickly around for Tara. Her mother was already several feet away, standing in the shadow of a large holly shrub as she surveyed the area and decided on her next move. Caitlyn hurried over to join her.

"Listen," she said breathlessly to Tara. "The police will start searching for you as soon as they've discovered that you're gone. I think the best thing would be if you lie low for a while—at least until the Samhain Festival is over. You can come back to the Manor with me and hide in my room. Then we can think about how to—"

"Hide in your room?" said Tara scornfully. "Don't be ridiculous! I don't hide. Do you think I'm going to sit in your room, twiddling my thumbs? What do you take me for? I'm going to find the *grimoire*." She held her hands out in front of her and flexed her fingers again, smiling with smug anticipation. "And once my powers are fully restored, no one will be able to stop me."

Caitlyn looked at her mother nervously. Suddenly, she felt like someone who had seen a beautiful, powerful tiger trapped in a cage and had been so moved by its plight that all she had been able to focus on was releasing it from captivity. But now that it was "free", she was beginning to realise that she had a huge, killer cat prowling loose on her hands and no idea how to contain it.

"The first thing we need to do is retrieve the dowsing pendulum," continued Tara, oblivious to her daughter's growing unease. "That's still the best way to find the *grimoire*. I must have dropped the pendulum when I fell down the terrace stairs. What happened to it after I was brought to hospital?"

"I... I don't know," said Caitlyn, trying to gather her thoughts. "I think James or Mosley or one of the staff might have picked it up. They've probably handed it over to the police."

"Then that's where we'll need to go first," said Tara. "With the two of us, it should be easy. I can immobilise all the officers while you search the station—or wait! I could use an *Impello* hex to make them lock themselves up in the cells!" She gave a gleeful chuckle. "That should be fun to watch. And it would free us both up so we can search more quickly."

"Wait, what?" said Caitlyn, taking a step back. "You want me to help you raid the police station? No,

I can't!"

"Why? Are you scared?" taunted Tara.

"It's not about having the courage!" said Caitlyn hotly. "It's about what's 'right'. It was bad enough helping you escape tonight; I'm not going to rob the police station or assault any officers!"

Tara rolled her eyes. "For Goddess's sake, stop being so histrionic! We're not going to 'assault' them. It'll just be a little hex—a bit of magical coaxing in the right direction, that's all. I can add an *Oblivio* spell as well, afterwards. That will wipe their memories so that they don't remember anything and won't be 'traumatised'." She made air quotes with her fingers, then asked mockingly: "Is that *caring* enough for your sensibilities?"

"What? That's even worse," said Caitlyn, appalled. "That would be like people who are victims of the date-rape drug, who not only have to deal with the violation but also with the gap in their memory—"

"What are you on about?" said Tara irritably. "Nobody is raping anybody!"

"You shouldn't be using an *Impello* hex at all," said Caitlyn. "It's completely wrong and unnecessary! There are other ways to get things done without resorting to that kind of magic."

"You seriously sound just like Mother," said Tara, scowling. "Anyone would think that I was suggesting I make the officers commit *hara-kiri*! What is your problem with using a bit of Dark Magic? People are forced into doing things against their will all the time.

They'll get over it."

"You can't seriously mean that!" cried Caitlyn, aghast. "Dark Magic is to be avoided at all costs—"

Tara made a rude noise. "I can see that you've been completely brainwashed by Mother and her sanctimonious standards. Just because Dark Magic is incredibly powerful and *could* be used for harm doesn't mean that it should be banned altogether! That's a completely stupid, narrow-minded attitude. It's not all black and white. Besides, the fact that it can be dangerous is all the more reason we should learn the forbidden spells and how to use them properly."

"No," said Caitlyn firmly, feeling weirdly like a parent talking to recalcitrant teenager. "We're not going to the police station and we're not hexing anybody."

Tara glared at her, then folded her arms and turned away. *Is she going to sulk now?* wondered Caitlyn in exasperation. She was about to argue further when Tara sighed and turned back to her, a contrite expression on her face.

"You're right," she said, looking slightly sheepish. "I'm sorry—I got a bit carried away." She gave Caitlyn a rueful look. "I'm not a very good role model, am I?"

Caitlyn felt a rush of relief and sympathy for her mother. She recalled the way she herself had felt in the Manor gardens earlier that day, when she had felt an overwhelming temptation to use the forbidden knowledge in the *grimoire* to punish others. The power of Dark Magic had a seductive allure, and she could understand and empathise with Tara.

"No, it's okay. I know how frustrated you must feel," she said, smiling at her mother.

"Actually, I'm feeling dizzy more than frustrated," confessed Tara, putting a hand up to her head.

"Dizzy?" Caitlyn looked at her mother in concern. "That might be a side effect of your concussion. Maybe you shouldn't be up and walking around so soon." She caught Tara's arm to steady her as the other woman swayed slightly.

"I... I think I'll sit down," murmured Tara, lowering herself to the ground and leaning against a rock at the base of the holly shrub.

Caitlyn looked at her mother worriedly. It was hard to tell in the shadow of the large shrub, but Tara did look pale. She glanced around, wondering what to do if Tara needed medical assistance. Returning to the hospital would mean that all their escape efforts would have been in vain!

"I'll be all right," Tara said in a faint voice, as if sensing her worry. "I just need a moment... Actually, do you see any dandelions around?"

"Dandelions?" said Caitlyn, looking at her mother quizzically.

Tara nodded. "I always remember Bertha saying that dandelion root is fantastic. It's used as a remedy for all sorts of things: it detoxifies your body, acts as a diuretic, and even controls blood sugar and inflammation. So maybe it might help my dizziness as well? The diuretic effect might help reduce the pressure or swelling in my head." She made as if to get up. "They're weeds, aren't they? So there should be a few growing around here. If we can find some—"

"No, you stay here," said Caitlyn, pushing her mother back down. "I don't think you should move until your dizziness clears up. I'll go and search. I'll be right back," she promised.

She scurried away, keeping to the shadows and trying to avoid any open spaces where she might be caught by security cameras. As she moved, she scanned the ground, looking for the familiar narrow, jagged-edged leaves and tall flower stalks of the dandelion. *It's a weed... haven't I seen it growing everywhere in the cracks at the edge of the pavement?* she mused, veering towards a concrete path.

Then she spotted one: a basal rosette of bright green toothed leaves crowned with a cluster of stalks carrying the iconic, white, fluffy seedheads. She hurried over to yank the plant up, struggling for several minutes with its stubborn tap root before finally pulling it out of the ground. Then she rushed back to where she'd left Tara.

"Here, I got one!" she said triumphantly as she rounded the holly shrub. "I hope it's—"

She broke off and stared stupidly at the empty space where Tara had been sitting. Then she scanned the surrounding area as she tried to make sense of things. There was no sign of her mother anywhere. She frowned. *Where is she? Has she gone to search for dandelions herself too?*

"Tara?" she called in a hushed voice. "Mum?"

The only reply she got was the soft murmur of wind rustling through the nearby trees. A horrible suspicion began to nag at Caitlyn, but she pushed the thought away. Instead, she started to walk in expanding circles around the holly bush, calling softly for Tara and peering into the darkness around her. Finally, after several minutes of fruitless searching, she had to admit defeat.

The dandelion dropped from her limp fingers as Caitlyn felt the truth hit her in the face. Her mother had tricked her: Tara had feigned an attack of dizziness and concocted those lies about the dandelion benefits so that she could sneak away while Caitlyn was busy searching for the weed. She had taken advantage of Caitlyn's concern for her wellbeing, knowing exactly how to manipulate her daughter and tug at her heartstrings. The whole thing was slick and clever, and Caitlyn felt like a complete fool. *How could I have been so gullible?* she thought angrily. What hurt even more, though, was the sting of betrayal—the thought that her own mother had been ruthless enough to use Caitlyn's compassionate nature against her.

A rustle in the bushes behind her interrupted her agonised thoughts, and she whirled around, raising her arms blindly to defend herself. Then she sagged in relief as she saw the stooped old man in the dusty black suit that stood there.

"Ahh, here you are. I would have found you sooner, but that young constable was quite a nuisance to shake off—"

"Oh Viktor!" she cried, impulsively throwing her arms around the old vampire's neck. "I'm so glad you're here!"

Viktor stumbled backwards, looking alarmed at her excessive display. "Er... yes, well, I'm pleased you're so delighted with my presence," he said, hurriedly extricating himself from her embrace. He looked beyond her. "Is Tara not with you? I had been looking forward to seeing my rapscallion witch niece again."

"No, she's gone," said Caitlyn in a shaky voice. "Viktor, she tricked me! She scared me by pretending to be ill and then sneaked away while I was rushing to get something to help her. All because she didn't like me telling her not to use Dark Magic and she wanted to get her own way!"

"Oh dear. It doesn't sound like that young lady has changed at all in twenty-two years," said Viktor in an ironic echo of Tara's scornful words about him earlier.

"But we need to find her," said Caitlyn urgently. "Tara is so reckless and ambitious and... and she doesn't seem to have many scruples. With her magic powers restored now, I'm scared of what she might do."

"Never fear," said Viktor, squaring his shoulders.

"I shall find her for you. She can't have gone far."

"But... she could have gone in any direction! And there's no moon tonight—how are you going to find her?" asked Caitlyn, not wanting to point out that, as an old man, Viktor could hardly cover much ground at speed.

He must have read her mind, though, because he said: "I shall search in my fruit-bat form, of course. The Megachiroptera are known for their fantastic night vision and olfactory senses," he continued proudly. "I can detect the faintest scent of fruit and nectar from the greatest distance—"

"Viktor, my mother isn't a plum."

"—and see with crystal clarity even in the dead of night. I have unparalleled levels of aerial endurance and prowess. I am a master of the skies!" Viktor raised both arms theatrically.

"Yes, that's great, but that's not going to help find Tara," said Caitlyn wryly.

Viktor glowered at her. "Your mother may suffer from an excess of confidence, young lady, but *you* seem to have the opposite problem! Perhaps if you cultivated some more faith in things being possible rather than *im*possible, you might enjoy more victories!"

Before Caitlyn could reply, he hunched over, his body contorting and deflating as it shrank down into his fuzzy brown fruit-bat form. Then, with a final grumpy squeak, Viktor took off, disappearing quickly into the night sky.

# CHAPTER TWENTY-FIVE

"Caitlyn! Wake up!"

Caitlyn opened bleary eyes and struggled into a sitting position against the soft, feather pillows of her bed. She blinked and put a hand up to shield her eyes from the morning light which streamed into the room as Pomona yanked back the curtains. Her cousin whirled and hurried back to the bed.

"You've got to get up, Caitlyn!"

"Wh-why?" she mumbled, rubbing her eyes. "What's happened?"

"Your mother's escaped—that's what's happened!"

Instantly, Caitlyn was wide awake, her grogginess dissipating like mist in the sun. The events of the night before came rushing back to her, and she felt the familiar sense of panic and betrayal wash over her again as she remembered Tara's trickery. *No...* For one wild moment, she held on to the desperate hope that the whole thing had been a vivid dream, a nightmare scenario dreamt up by her overactive imagination, but one look at Pomona's face and she knew that everything she remembered was true.

"Caitlyn! Did you hear what I said? Your mother escaped from the hospital!"

"Y-yes, I heard..." Caitlyn put a hand up to her temple, which was beginning to throb. "Um... does anyone know how she escaped?"

Pomona shook her head. "The police are still investigating. The constable who had been left to guard Tara was blabbing about being distracted by a possible fire and then meeting some crazy old English count or something, but Inspector Walsh thinks that he's just making things up to cover up for his own carelessness. I'll bet what happened is that he fell asleep, and Tara just sneaked out past him. Anyway, the inspector is downstairs with James now and he'd like to speak to you."

"Oh... yes, of course," said Caitlyn, her heart hammering as she wondered how to face the police.

She climbed out of bed and reached distractedly for her robe, then froze as she caught sight of her own reflection in the mirror opposite. She looked horrendous, wan and haggard, with enormous dark circles under her bloodshot eyes. One look at her and Inspector Walsh would never believe that she had been sleeping soundly in her bed all night!

"Um... Pomona? I look absolutely awful. I don't want James to see me like this. Is there anything you can do to help me look better?" she asked, knowing that her cousin wouldn't be able to resist the chance to play with make-up.

Pomona gave a squeal of excitement. "Are you saying I can give you a makeover?"

"Well, not a full makeover," said Caitlyn hastily. "But it would be great if you could help me look a bit fresher; you know, like healthier and... er... not so tired."

"Oh sure! Nothing a bit of concealer and bronzer won't fix! Quick, go and have a shower and then I'll get to work—"

"No, there's no time for a shower," Caitlyn decided. "I'll just splash some water on my face and get changed."

Fifteen minutes later, Caitlyn gazed at her reflection in the mirror again, but this time in awe instead of horror. She was amazed at Pomona's skills: where the dark circles had been, her undereye area now looked bright and smooth, and with the help of some special eye drops, Pomona had even restored her bloodshot eyes to sparkling hazel. Her cheeks had been delicately highlighted with a creamy peach blush which complemented her milky complexion and echoed the fiery glow of her red hair. Finally, Pomona had expertly applied mascara to her lashes and shaped her eyebrows so that they lifted her face, making her instantly look much wider awake.

"Pomona, you're a magician!" gushed Caitlyn, staring at herself in wonder. "I mean, I don't even have skin like this on my best day!"

Pomona smiled with satisfaction. "Well, I'm glad that you're finally making some effort," she said. "I mean, I know James would think you looked gorgeous in, like, a potato sack, but seriously, you want to look nice for him, right?"

"Yes, Pomie," said Caitlyn, feeling slightly guilty that her cousin had no idea of the real reason for her desire to improve her appearance. She took the lip gloss that Pomona handed her and dabbed the tube on her lips, giving them a rosy glow that matched that of her cheeks. Then she stood up and surveyed herself one last time in the mirror. "Okay, I'm ready."

Downstairs, Caitlyn was glad to find Inspector Walsh with James in the privacy of the latter's study. She hadn't relished being questioned under the inquisitive gazes of Vanessa and her friends. The men rose politely as she entered, and James gave her a warm smile.

"Good morning! I hope you slept well?"

"Um... yes, really well," said Caitlyn, hurriedly pinning a bright smile to her face. She saw Inspector Walsh look at her assessingly and silently crossed her fingers that Pomona's make-up skills would stand up to the detective's scrutiny.

"Miss Le Fey... please have a seat," said Inspector Walsh, gesturing to the armchair opposite his. "I assume you've heard the news from Miss Sinclair?"

"It seems that Tara might have left the hospital without permission?" said Caitlyn, putting on a puzzled expression.

"Your mother has broken out of police custody," said Inspector Walsh bluntly. "She is essentially a fugitive on the run."

Caitlyn tried to look suitably shocked. "That's terrible!"

"Yes. It is imperative that we find her, both for her own safety and for those around her," said Inspector Walsh. He gave her a speculative look. "My constable tells me that you were with your mother a long time yesterday afternoon—well *beyond* the originally agreed period—and that you seemed deep in discussion about urgent matters."

"Well... it... it was the first time I'd met my mother properly, Inspector. We had a lot to catch-up on."

"Indeed. Including how you might help her escape?"

James shifted in his seat, frowning. "Inspector, that was uncalled for."

"With all due respect, your Lordship, I think it is a justifiable line of questioning, given that Miss Le Fey was the only person to see Tara yesterday, aside from the doctors and nurses. Furthermore, her personal relationship with the suspect makes her a likely accomplice," said Inspector Walsh evenly. He turned back to Caitlyn. "Well, Miss Le Fey? Did you have any part in your mother's vanishing act?"

Caitlyn tried to speak but her tongue felt stuck as she wrestled with her guilty conscience. "I..." She cleared her throat. "I had no idea she was going to disappear like that," she said at last, which was a semblance of the truth.

"That doesn't answer my question," said Inspector Walsh, giving her a hard look. "Did you or did you not assist your mother in getting past the police guard and absconding from the hospital premises last night?"

Caitlyn licked her lips, which suddenly felt dry despite the ample lip gloss she had applied. "I... I wasn't—"

She glanced involuntarily at James and, as their eyes met, saw sudden understanding dawn in his. Her heart skipped a beat. *He knows.* James had always been better at reading her than anyone else, and he knew that, somehow, she had been involved in her mother's escape. Caitlyn braced herself, expecting to see his face harden, his grey eyes turn cold, his expression accusing—but to her astonishment, James gave her a look of compassion.

"Inspector." He rose to his feet and came around his desk to stand by Caitlyn. "I really cannot allow you to harass Caitlyn in this manner. She is the most honest, principled person I know, and I'm sure she would never do anything unlawful or attempt to deceive the police in any way. In fact, I would personally vouch for her integrity in this matter."

Caitlyn stared at him, open-mouthed. She felt suddenly overwhelmed by emotion: a rush of love for James's compassion and understanding mingled with a wave of guilt that made her squirm in her chair. She remembered how James had warned her about Tara and how she had snapped at him... and now here he was, defending her in spite of everything. She felt like a complete worm. All she wanted at that moment was to be alone with James so she could explain everything and apologise for not trusting him. But with Inspector Walsh there, she had to swallow her passionate words. Instead, she reached out impulsively and caught his hand, squeezing it hard and giving him a heartfelt look of love and gratitude. James glanced down, then his grey eyes twinkled as he squeezed her hand back.

Inspector Walsh cleared his throat, breaking the moment between them, and said: "Again, with all due respect, your Lordship, your own personal relationship with Miss Le Fey hardly makes *your* testimony an unbiased one. However, I will accept your assurances *for now* and absolve Miss Le Fey of any involvement in her mother's disappearance—*for the moment.*"

"Thank you, Inspector," said James.

"Y-yes, thank you," Caitlyn echoed, trying to keep her turbulent emotions from showing on her face.

"In the meantime..." Inspector Walsh turned back to Caitlyn. "Anything you can tell me about your mother's possible plans would be very helpful in locating Tara as soon as possible."

Caitlyn let go of James's hand and sat up straighter. She gave a helpless shrug. "All I know is that she's looking for the Widow Mags's *grimoire.*

She's obsessed with finding it. So if you can find the book, then I'm sure you'll find her as well."

"Yes, well, my men have been continuing their efforts to find it, but there has been no sign of the book anywhere," said Inspector Walsh testily.

"What about the murderer?" asked Caitlyn. "Have you made any progress on that? Because whoever killed Percy is likely to have taken the *grimoire* so—"

"I'm well aware of that, Miss Le Fey. And we are continuing our investigation on the case. We now know that Percy was poisoned by a caffeine overdose and not belladonna, as originally thought. Caffeine poisoning is rare, but it *is* a substance that is present in a variety of foods, drinks, exercise supplements, and over-the-counter medications for instant energy boost and weight loss. This is both a good thing and a bad thing, depending on your point of view: good because it means that anyone could have easily obtained the 'murder weapon', so to speak, but bad for the same reason, since it widens the field of suspects—"

"Wait—did you say weight-loss pills?" Caitlyn interrupted him.

"Yes, that's right. People take them because the pills supposedly increase your metabolism and fat-burning," said Inspector Walsh, his tone making it very clear what he thought of such beliefs. "It's extremely popular amongst models and those in the fashion industry, although there *have* been several documented cases of adverse effects. In fact, just last year, a model in London collapsed during Fashion Week due to complications from excessive use of caffeine-based weight-loss supplements..."

Caitlyn tuned the detective out as she thought furiously. So far, she had been reluctant to "name and shame" Katya to the police out of respect for the girl's privacy, but now she wondered if she had been naïve to think that the girl wasn't involved in Percy's murder. After all, as a part-time model and fashionista, Katya would be ideally placed to get hold of such weight-loss pills. And given Percy's infatuation with her, there would have been plenty of opportunity for her to slip him an overdose.

As for motive... *Maybe Pomona is right after all and Leandra is behind everything*, thought Caitlyn. *She certainly has some kind of hold over Katya and could easily get the girl to do anything for her, including poison Percy and steal the* grimoire. *Except...* Caitlyn frowned as her theory began to wobble. *...how would Leandra have known about the* grimoire *in the first place, to instruct Katya to steal it? Percy only found it in the afternoon on the day they arrived, and he'd had no chance to tell Katya about his discovery before she sneaked out to see Leandra that night. So how could Katya have planned to poison Percy to steal the* grimoire, *if she didn't even know he had found it in the first place?*

"Miss Le Fey?"

Caitlyn started. "Sorry," she said quickly. "I was just thinking..." She took a deep breath. "Inspector, there is something I haven't told you. It's about Katya Novik. Tori was right: she did lie about her alibi."

Inspector Walsh raised his eyebrows. Caitlyn quickly told him about eavesdropping outside the barn window and learning about Katya's clandestine outing to see Leandra Lockwood on the night of the murder, plus what Pomona had found out about the retired academic's background and her undue influence over the girl.

"I'm sorry I didn't mention this before," she said as she concluded. "I wasn't sure there was any connection to the murder and I... I guess I didn't really want to be a 'tattletale' and get Katya into trouble with her parents, if this was just... I mean, it's her personal affair who she wants to be friends with," she said awkwardly. "But when you mentioned weight-loss pills just now—well, Katya is a part-time model and she's very slim..."

Inspector Walsh inclined his head. "Yes, I'm aware of Ms Lockwood's background and the scandal surrounding her dismissal from a certain London college, as well as her controversial relationship with Miss Novik. And yes, I knew the latter lied about her alibi and was in fact visiting Ms Lockwood at her barn, instead of sleeping in her bed as she'd claimed." He smiled at the expression on Caitlyn's face and said dryly, "Did you think that the police were having a kip this whole time, Miss Le Fey? It may not sound as exciting as witch books and magic spells, I grant you, but nothing beats good old-fashioned detective work to solve a case."

Caitlyn gave him a contrite look. "I'm sorry, Inspector. I didn't mean to imply.... it's just that you seemed very dismissive of the other suspects the last time we spoke."

"I simply do not like to jump to conclusions before facts are established and corroborated," said the old detective tartly. "But in any case, Miss Novik and Ms Lockwood *can* both be dismissed as suspects. I have an eyewitness—one of the stableboys who happened to be staying overnight to look after a horse with colic—and he has provided them both with an alibi. As you know, the stable courtyard is right next to the barn where Ms Lockwood is staying. The stableboy saw Ms Lockwood open the door to Miss Novik at half past eleven that night and also saw the latter come out of the barn again—alone—at around quarter past midnight and return to the Manor. Those times mean that there is no way either of them could have been involved in Mr Wynn's murder, since he was still seen alive and well *after* Miss Novik had already left the Manor, and his body was found well before she returned."

Caitlyn sat back, digesting this. It looked like Pomona's conviction that Leandra was behind Percy's murder was wrong. But if neither Leandra nor Katya were involved, then who was? The two women had had the best motive; the rest of Vanessa's friends seemed even less likely as suspects. Tori might have been smug and unpleasant, but she had no reason to harm Percy or any personal interest in the *grimoire*; Benedict might have had some interest in the book's value as an antique, but he also had no reason to kill Percy and, in fact, seemed to be the only one in the group to really mourn their friend.

Inspector Walsh had obviously read her mind because he said: "You can see, Miss Le Fey, why suspicion should fall on your mother. None of the remaining suspects have a strong motive, whereas *she* had a very strong motive for attacking Mr Wynn that night: to seize the *grimoire*. Furthermore, she had the perfect opportunity—we know that Miss Fanshawe-Drury had provided a false alibi for her because she thought that Tara was actually her best friend, due to her... er... disguise. And as for means— well, your mother could easily have obtained caffeine powder or supplements from any number of sources."

"But Tara *didn't* murder Percy!" Caitlyn insisted. "She went down to the Library that night, yes, but she says that Percy was already dead when she arrived. She found his body on the floor next to the bookshelf, and no one else was in the Library with him. And the *grimoire* was already gone. The murderer must have taken it. In fact, that's the best proof that she *didn't* do it!" she said earnestly. "If my mother *had* killed Percy, she would already have the *grimoire*, wouldn't she?"

# CHAPTER TWENTY-SIX

"Caitlyn is right, Inspector," James spoke up. "The fact that Tara is still searching for the *grimoire* seems to suggest that she isn't the murderer."

"Hmm..." said Inspector Walsh. "Not necessarily. Someone else could have taken it from her possession, after she killed Percy."

"Who?" demanded Caitlyn. "There was nobody else here that night! The staff are all accounted for, and Katya was at the barn with Leandra, which only leaves Tori and Benedict, who were both upstairs—"

She broke off suddenly, her thoughts racing. At the mention of "upstairs", something Tara had said last night at the hospital came back to her. It was something which had caught her attention at the time but which she had ignored, too preoccupied with asking her mother about her own past. Now, though, she heard Tara's voice once more in her mind: *"...when I heard Benedict come* upstairs *without him, I wondered if Percy had remained in the*

*Library to search for the book. So I decided to go down and join him..."*

Caitlyn sat upright. "Inspector, what did Benedict say in his statement?" she asked.

"What do you mean?"

"Like... what did he say happened that night? He was the last person to see Percy alive, wasn't he?"

"Yes, Mr Danby and Mr Wynn were having a nightcap in the Library and went upstairs together at around a quarter to twelve. This was corroborated by the butler. So it appears that Mr Wynn must have come downstairs again and returned to the Library by himself."

"Are you sure Mosley *saw* them go up the stairs together?"

Inspector Walsh frowned. Then he turned to James and said: "Would you mind summoning the butler, sir?"

A few minutes later, Mosley stood before them, his posture so erect that he looked as if he might topple backwards.

"Yes, certainly, I saw Mr Danby and Mr Wynn retiring to bed together after their drink in the Library," he confirmed.

"But did you actually see *both* of them going up the stairs with your own eyes, Mosley?" asked Caitlyn.

The butler looked at her in surprise. "Well, yes, in a manner of speaking. That is, I saw Mr Danby at the bottom of the stairs, and I assumed that Mr Wynn was further up, around the curve of the staircase, out of sight, because Mr Danby was talking to him."

"What did he say?"

Mosley gave an apologetic cough. "Well, it has been a few days and I'm afraid my recall may not be verbatim, but I believe Mr Danby said something along the lines of: 'Wait up, Perce! You're going too fast for me'—or something like that."

"But you never actually saw Percy himself?" persisted Caitlyn.

Mosley looked chagrined. "No, madam. In actual fact, I did not."

Caitlyn turned triumphantly to Inspector Walsh. "So it could have all been an act put on by Benedict to pretend that Percy was going upstairs with him—and in fact, I think it *was* an act! You see, I just remembered Tara telling me yesterday that she had been watching and waiting, and she noticed Benedict arrive upstairs *without* Percy. She wondered what Percy was still doing alone in the Library, and that's why she went down... and then she found his body. So that means that Benedict lied: Percy never went upstairs with him—in fact, Percy was probably already dead when Benedict left him in the Library!"

Caitlyn looked eagerly at the inspector. But if she had hoped that he would spring up, congratulating her on cracking the case, she was disappointed. Inspector Walsh looked thoughtful and responded in his customary reserved fashion:

"That is a serious accusation, Miss Le Fey," he

said. "Mr Danby could simply deny that version of events and insist that Mr Wynn *did* accompany him upstairs, only returning to the Library himself later. Without evidence to support your suspicions, it would be Mr Danby's word against your mother's."

James hadn't said anything, but Caitlyn could see from the expression on his face that he was disturbed by the thought of his sister's ex-boyfriend potentially being a murderer.

"It isn't just her word against his," she argued. "There are also other things, such as easy access to the poison. Didn't you just say that caffeine is also found in exercise supplements?"

"Yes, particularly in weightlifting and muscle-building circles. It is supposed to enhance endurance and boost strength or something along those lines," said Inspector Walsh dismissively.

"Exactly!" said Caitlyn. "Benedict is really into his workouts and weight training. I've heard Tori tease him about it several times. In fact, you can tell just from looking at him that he does a lot of muscle-building. So this would fit perfectly: he could easily have had a stash of caffeine supplements with him that he could have used to kill Percy. You just have to find it! Have you searched his room?"

"My men searched all the guest rooms twice. There was nothing suspicious found in Mr Danby's room," said Inspector Walsh.

Caitlyn bit her lip. She was sure that she was right. "You need to search again," she insisted. "I'm sure there's something there. Maybe he's hidden it somewhere, like... did you check the fireplace, for instance? Maybe he's hidden something up in the chimney?"

"Miss Le Fey—my men know how to do their job," said Inspector Walsh, glowering at her. "Rest assured that they searched every nook and cranny. If there was anything hidden in Mr Danby's room, they would have found it. However, I will take your suspicions into account and will investigate Mr Danby further. In the meantime, if you can think of any additional information that might help us in finding your mother, I would appreciate you letting me know as soon as possible." He rose from his chair and gave James a respectful nod. "Good day, your Lordship."

"I'll see you out, Inspector," said James, rising as well.

Caitlyn watched them leave, feeling a bit deflated. Mosley gave her a sympathetic smile, then hurried after the other two men.

"Sir, I thought you'd be happy to know that the plumber has completed his inspection and managed to resolve the blockage in the kitchen pipes. The water supply is fully restored now and..."

His voice faded away as the men left the room. Caitlyn remained in her armchair, her brow furrowed, as she mulled over the murder case. Then she sat up suddenly as Mosley's last words registered fully in her mind. Springing up from her chair, she dashed out of the study and down the hallway, looking for the butler. She found him just as he was about to return to the Morning Room to oversee breakfast.

"Mosley! You know just now, when you were telling James about the problems with the plumbing... what was the cause of the blockage?"

"Well, if you can believe it, madam, it was a small plastic bag. It had lodged in a bend of the greywater pipes and prevented the water from flowing through freely. And—given the age of the Manor's plumbing system—the build-up of pressure caused an escalation of issues, culminating in a serious blockage."

"Yes, and this plastic bag that caused all the problems—how did it get in the pipes?"

"It is a bit of a mystery, madam. It is too large to have been flushed down any of the kitchen or pantry sinks. The plumber suspects that it may have come from the sewage pipes which carry waste from the toilets and join up with the kitchen pipes before they both empty into the main waste pipe. He thinks that it is likely to have been a visitor during one of the public tours who carelessly disposed of the bag down the toilet when they were using the public lavatories." Mosley sniffed with disapproval. "Unfortunately, they are prone to flushing all manner of things down the toilet, despite the signs specifically asking them not to place anything in the bowl except toilet paper."

"This bag... was there anything in it?"

Mosley's normally impassive features twitched

with disgust. "I must confess, I did not personally check, madam. Perhaps the plumber might have had a look out of curiosity."

"Does the plumber still have the bag?" asked Caitlyn urgently.

"I am not sure. He is still packing up in the rear courtyard, so I can enquire if you wish?"

"Actually, I'll ask him myself. Can you just take me to him, please?"

Obviously mystified by her interest in the mundane domestic matters of the Manor, but too well trained to question her curiosity, Mosley led the way to the back of the Manor and out through of the rear trade entrance to a small courtyard area where a large white van was parked. A thickset man in navy overalls was bending over in the back of the van, rearranging some tools, and he looked up at their approach. His expression changed to one of surprise as Caitlyn explained her request.

"It were just a bit o' rubbish, miss," he said. "The usual sort o' thing that people are always flushin' down the toilet."

"Yes, but have you kept the bag?" persisted Caitlyn.

"I threw it in the bin," said the plumber, nodding at the large industrial bins lining the back wall of the Manor.

Caitlyn hurried over and tried to lift one of the lids but was stopped by Mosley, looking scandalised.

"Miss Le Fey! You cannot search in there with

your bare hands! Please... allow me."

Caitlyn waited with impatience as Mosley hurried to fetch some rubber gloves and then, with fastidious care, donned the gloves, lifted the lid of the nearest bin, and began poking gingerly through the contents. Finally, the butler lifted out a small green plastic bag, the end tied with a knot.

"Is that it?" Caitlyn asked the plumber eagerly.

"Aye, that's the one."

"Quick—open it," Caitlyn said to Mosley.

The plumber looked taken aback. "Not sure if you want to be doin' that, miss," he said. "Could be all sorts o' unpleasant stuff in there. You know, soiled sanitary pads, used toilet paper—"

"No, I have a hunch it's something totally different," said Caitlyn, watching eagerly as Mosley overcame his distaste to carefully wriggle the folds of plastic loose.

The knot came undone, and he pulled the edges of the bag cautiously open. The three of them peered in. There was a large pile of fine, white powder in the bottom of the bag.

The plumber drew a sharp breath. "Bloody hell— drugs? Is that cocaine?"

"No, not cocaine," said Caitlyn, looking with satisfaction down at the contents of the bag. "I think when the police analyse it, they'll find that it's caffeine powder."

# CHAPTER TWENTY-SEVEN

Luckily, Inspector Walsh had not left the Manor yet, and Caitlyn was gratified to see the old inspector look much more impressed when she found him and told him about her discovery.

"I remembered overhearing Mosley talking about the plumbing problems yesterday afternoon, just as we were setting out to collect the bonfire wood," Caitlyn explained. "He was apologising to Vanessa's friends about the water supply being interrupted, and the plumber needing access to their private ensuite bathrooms. Benedict's, in particular, because it is directly above the kitchen. I remember Benedict seemed especially agitated by the whole thing. I didn't think much of it at the time—I thought he was just annoyed at the inconvenience—but just now, when Mosley mentioned it again, I suddenly realised that Benedict was afraid of what the plumber might find! And when Mosley told me about the plastic bag, I was sure that it was Benedict who had flushed it down the toilet to get rid of evidence. That also explains why your men didn't find anything hidden in his room."

"Hmm... well, it is a plausible scenario, Miss Le Fey," conceded Inspector Walsh. He indicated the green plastic bag, now securely zipped into a large evidence bag. "It all rests on whether this bag really does contain caffeine powder."

"Do you have anything with you that can confirm that? Like, special tests?" asked Caitlyn hopefully.

Inspector Walsh shook his head. "We have presumptive tests for initial identification in the field, but those kits are designed to identify controlled substances, such as certain drugs—they wouldn't provide any conclusive information about a legal substance like caffeine powder. For that, I would have to send it to a forensic laboratory with special equipment to do a thorough analysis to determine its exact chemical composition."

"Oh." Caitlyn sagged with disappointment. "But... that could take days."

Inspector Walsh gave her an unexpected smile. "Yes, but there is another tool, used by all the best detectives. Come with me."

Puzzled, Caitlyn obediently followed as he led the way to the Morning Room where Vanessa and her friends, together with Pomona, were gathered, busily helping themselves from the lavish breakfast buffet. The group looked up curiously as they entered, and Pomona sidled over to Caitlyn.

"What's going on?" she asked under her breath.

"I'm not sure, Pomie. We may have found some evidence that points to Percy's murderer, but Inspector Walsh seems to be following another hunch—" She broke off as Vanessa came forwards and spoke to the detective.

"Inspector, are you looking for my brother?" she asked. "I think James is with Lisa the marketing coordinator. They're having a last-minute meeting about the Samhain Festival that's supposed to take place this afternoon."

"No, as a matter of fact, I was hoping to speak to your friend, Mr Danby," said Inspector Walsh.

"Me?" said Benedict, attempting to look nonchalantly surprised, although Caitlyn noticed that his fingers clenched around his fork.

"Yes, I would appreciate it if you could answer some further questions," said Inspector Walsh.

"Of course, what would you like to ask me?" asked Benedict, rising with exaggerated casualness and strolling over to join them by the door.

"Perhaps you'd like to go somewhere more private?" suggested Inspector Walsh, gesturing to the hallway outside.

Benedict stole a glance at his friends, who were all watching with puzzled concern, and gave a forced laugh. "You make it sound as if I have something to hide, Inspector! No, go ahead and ask me anything you like."

"Very well. It seems that the plumber has just

discovered the cause of the recent blockage in the Manor's kitchen, and the culprit is a plastic bag that the plumber believes was flushed down the toilet— probably from one of the guest bedrooms upstairs."

"And? What has that got to do with me?" asked Benedict, making a valiant effort to look indifferent.

"It has to do with you because I have a feeling you know exactly what is in that bag, sir."

Benedict gave another forced laugh. "Sorry, digging around in the sewage is not one of my hobbies."

Inspector Walsh ignored the attempt at humour and continued: "My men have established that you placed a large order online for a supplement powder with an extremely high concentration of caffeine."

"That was for my workouts!" said Benedict quickly. "It's not a crime to take caffeine supplements before training. 'Pre-workouts', we call 'em. Everyone who's serious about weightlifting takes them."

"And everyone who is serious about committing murder?"

"Wh... what d'you mean?" asked Benedict, licking his lips.

Inspector Walsh leaned forwards and looked Benedict in the eye. "I mean that such a supply of caffeine supplement powder would be very convenient for administering an overdose. In fact, the chemical profile of that batch is currently being analysed, and I have no doubt that it will match the sample taken from the murder victim's blood. It would have been very easy for you to dissolve some of the supplement powder in one of Mr Wynn's drinks and—"

"NO!" shouted Benedict, his face flushed. "No, it didn't happen like that! I never put anything in Percy's drinks! He was the one who took—"

He broke off, staring at them, his eyes wild and panicked. All his suaveness and self-assurance had gone. He just looked like a terrified man backed into a corner.

"It was Percy," he said dully, at last. "He was the one who approached me and asked me for tips on weight training." He glanced across the room at Tori and Katya, still sitting at the table. "He was desperate to impress Katya, you see, and he thought that maybe if he bulked up a bit, she might notice him more. He'd already had all the basic advice; he wanted to know how to go the extra mile, to really push himself. So I gave him a few tips—you know, some of the techniques used to get results faster. A couple of them are a bit controversial, I suppose, but there's nothing really illegal or dangerous."

"And was caffeine supplement powder one of these 'tips' that you passed on to Mr Wynn?"

"Yeah, I gave Percy some of my stash. Hey, I was trying to do a nice thing!" Benedict said defensively. "And caffeine is perfectly safe. Everyone I know takes a pre-workout with caffeine in it. You might get the jitters and your heart feels a bit strange for a while, but it usually settles down."

"Not in Mr Wynn's case. With his cardiac condition, even a slight margin above the recommended dosage was fatal."

"Well, how was I to know that the stupid bugger would take an overdose?" cried Benedict angrily. "I even warned him not to go over the recommended dose. I said 200 to 300 milligrams max, no more—people often think a higher dose is better but it's not true: you don't build muscle any faster. But Percy must have ignored what I said. When we went to the Library that night, I did notice that he seemed a bit odd and twitchy. He must have taken some of the supplement powder upstairs in his room before coming down for dinner. But you know, I didn't think too much about it. I mean, it wasn't as if he was acting ill! If anything, he seemed more energetic than usual, and he was really excited about something. Then, after we'd had a couple of whiskies in the Library, he told me that he'd found a 'witch's spell book' and that he was planning to show it to Katya—"

"Percy was going to show me the *grimoire*?" cried Katya, looking chagrined.

"He thought it would impress you, because you're into witchcraft and the occult and things like that," Benedict explained.

"And you, Mr Danby? Were *you* interested in this book?" asked Inspector Walsh.

"Well, yes," Benedict admitted. "It sounded like a valuable antique, and when Percy got it out from one of the bookshelves, I could see that it was a unique piece, probably worth tens, maybe even hundreds of thousands of pounds at auction. I tried to get a closer look at it, but Percy wouldn't let me hold it. Then I—" He faltered, looking shamefaced. "Well, I tried to snatch it from him. We ended up in a sort of tug-o-war and then he... he started gasping and clutching his chest... and the next thing I knew, he'd collapsed."

"Oh Benedict..." gasped Vanessa, covering her mouth.

"Wait a minute, wait a minute..." Pomona stepped forwards. "You're saying the whole thing was an accident?"

Benedict gave them an anguished look. "Yes, of course it was an accident! I never meant to hurt Percy, I swear! I just wanted to have a better look at the book. If he'd just given it to me, none of this would have happened!"

"Did you attempt to revive Mr Wynn?" asked Inspector Walsh.

"Of course I did!" cried Benedict. "I was going to give him CPR but then..." He shuddered at the memory. "He was just lying there, staring at the ceiling, and his eyes were empty... and I knew that he was dead."

"Why didn't you call for help?"

"I... I don't know. I lost my head, okay?" Benedict ran a shaking hand through his hair. "All I could think about was getting away from the body. So I ran out of the Library and legged it back to my room."

"The butler tells us that he heard you talking to Mr Wynn as you were going up the stairs," said Inspector Walsh, raising his eyebrows.

Benedict reddened, looking even more shamefaced. "I... er... yes, I saw Mosley hovering in the hallway just as I was running up the stairs and I thought... I don't know why, but I was suddenly terrified that he would know that I'd left Percy dead in the Library. So I... I just pretended that I was talking to Percy, who was ahead of me, up the stairs. Look, it wasn't... I didn't really plan to do that on purpose," he said weakly, aware that it must seem like a very calculated move to a detective.

"If you had no intention of hiding the death of your friend, why did you not confess everything the next morning?" asked Inspector Walsh.

"I don't know," said Benedict again, looking wretched. "I was going to, but then when I heard that it had been escalated to a murder enquiry, I suppose I just freaked out. All I could think about was the *grimoire* and how people might think that I'd killed Percy to get my hands on it."

"What happened to the *grimoire*?" asked Caitlyn. "It wasn't with Percy when we found his body."

"Yeah, I took it with me by mistake when I panicked and ran from the Library. It wasn't until I was back upstairs, in my room, that I realised I was still holding that bloody book in my hand."

"What did you do with it? Have you still got it?"

asked Caitlyn breathlessly.

Benedict shook his head. "I meant to return it to the Library the next morning, actually, but then when I came downstairs, I found that it had been sealed off as a crime scene. I was just wondering what to do when *you*—" He nodded at Caitlyn. "—came back from the village and told us that Percy's death had been escalated to a murder inquiry. Bloody hell, I *really* panicked then. I guessed that the police might search our rooms, so I knew I needed to get rid of the book fast. I managed to slip out when everyone was at lunch—"

"Oh, when you stormed off after having that fight with Tori!" said Caitlyn. "Was that just a ploy so you could sneak out?"

"No, of course not," said Benedict, shooting Tori a dirty look. "I really *was* cheesed off with Tori. She was behaving like an absolute cow. I mean, I was feeling pretty rotten about Percy, and no one else seemed to care that he'd died only the day before." He took a deep breath, composing himself. "But yes, I did also take that opportunity to slip out of the Manor with the *grimoire* so I could dispose of it."

"Dispose? Are you saying that you threw it in the dustbin?" asked Inspector Walsh sharply.

"No, I tossed it into that old well by the Coach House restaurant. I couldn't go far from the house, and I remembered seeing the well when I parked my car. It looked pretty disused, so I thought it was probably safe. No one was likely to look in there, at least for a long time, I hoped. And if it was found, then at least it wouldn't be anywhere near me."

Caitlyn's heart leapt at his words. Next to her, Pomona gave a laugh and said: "Oh man, I can't believe that we've been running all over the place searching for the *grimoire* and the darned thing has been, like, sitting in that well the whole time!"

# CHAPTER TWENTY-EIGHT

Inspector Walsh signalled to a constable who had been waiting in the hallway outside and said a few words in his ear. As the constable hurried away, the inspector turned back to Benedict and said gravely:

"You could have still come clean. If you had handed the book over to the police the morning after and explained what had happened, the whole thing could have been resolved very quickly. But your attempts to mislead Mosley and hide the death of your friend, together with your disposal of the book, all add up to make you look guilty."

"Look, I panicked, okay? I... I wasn't thinking straight. Everyone was talking about Percy being murdered for this *grimoire*... and *you* were talking about belladonna poisoning as well," Benedict reminded the inspector. "That sounded so sinister. I was worried that if I confessed to having the book in my possession, you would never believe me if I said that I hadn't done anything to Percy, that he'd just collapsed."

He sighed. "And then it got even worse when you came back this morning and started questioning us again, and you mentioned that Percy had actually been poisoned by *caffeine*, not belladonna! I suddenly remembered that I'd given him some caffeine supplement powder. And when you told us about Percy's heart condition as well, I realised what must have happened: he must have already been feeling the effects of the caffeine overdose, and then when we started wrestling over the *grimoire*... well, it must have tipped his heart over the edge." Benedict hunched his shoulders miserably. "So in a way, it *was* all my fault."

"Oh Benedict, darling... it wasn't your fault!" said Vanessa staunchly, springing up and rushing to his side. "The whole thing was a terrible accident. I'm sure now that the police know the truth, they'll take the circumstances into account...?" She looked at Inspector Walsh hopefully.

The detective inspector did not reply. Instead, he turned to the constable who had just returned to the room. The latter shook his head.

"There was nothing there, sir," said the constable. "It's empty."

Inspector Walsh turned back to look accusingly at Benedict. "My constable says there is nothing in the well. The *grimoire* isn't there."

"What d'you mean, it isn't there?" said Benedict. "It has to be there! I definitely threw it in there!"

Inspector Walsh gave him a cynical look. "This would all be a very convenient story, Mr Danby, if your real intention had been to steal the book from Mr Wynn. It is a valuable antique—you said so yourself—and this ensure that it 'disappears' until you are ready to fence it. It is a well-known technique of art and antique thieves to hide items until they are no longer 'hot' and can then be sold on the market without drawing undue attention."

"What? No, that's bollocks!" cried Benedict. "I've told you the truth! This wasn't some elaborate masterplan!"

"I'm afraid that may have to be decided in court," said Inspector Walsh. "In the meantime, I would like you to come down to the station with me to give an official statement."

Benedict turned pale. "You can't do this. My father won't allow it... he knows people... he'll get me a lawyer—"

Inspector Walsh inclined his head. "You will be entitled to your phone call and legal representation of your choice, sir." He indicated the door. "Now... if you please?"

Vanessa made a sound of protest, Katya watched with shocked eyes, and even Tori seemed lost for words for once as Benedict was escorted out of the Morning Room by the constable.

Inspector Walsh paused beside Caitlyn on the way out of the room. "As I said, Miss Le Fey, there are other tools a detective can use—and a well-executed bluff is one of the best."

She stared at him. "All those things you said: the online order of caffeine that your men found, the chemical profile analysis... they were all made up?"

Inspector Walsh gave a grim smile. "They were intelligent guesses. Sometimes you just have to convince the suspect that you have the evidence, even if you don't *yet*—their guilty conscience will do the rest."

With a nod to the others, he left the room. A few minutes later, they saw him again through the windows, escorting Benedict into a blue-and-yellow police car. Several members of the staff had gathered outside, their heads together, whispering, as they watched the police car leave. Caitlyn had no doubt that the news of Benedict's arrest would be around the entire estate and the village of Tillyhenge in a few hours.

Turning back to the room, she saw that Vanessa had sat down, looking shocked and distressed. Obviously, Tara's portrayal of a close friendship between the exes had not been a fabrication. Caitlyn wondered for a moment if she should go over and try to comfort James's sister, but a look at the protective way that Tori and Katya were huddled around their friend suggested that she probably wouldn't be welcome.

"Holy guacamole..." said Pomona, coming to join her at the window. "Do you really think Benedict could have engineered the whole thing?"

Caitlyn glanced at Vanessa again, then said, keeping her voice low: "I don't know. I suppose it *could* be true. Benedict *is* very materialistic. Remember the night they arrived—when we were all in the Portrait Gallery—how he kept talking about how much everything is worth and trying to get James to sell his father's occult collection?"

"Oh yeah! Katya got really mad and said he was obsessed with money," said Pomona, remembering. "And you know, something like the Widow Mags's *grimoire would* be worth a crazy amount 'cos it's one-of-a-kind."

"Yes, except... Benedict didn't know the *grimoire* existed until Percy showed it to him in the Library that night," Caitlyn pointed out. "Percy himself only found it earlier that day. I don't see how it could have been pre-meditated."

"Well, maybe he didn't plan it. I mean, thinking about it—even Percy himself didn't know about his weird heart condition, so how could Benedict have known about it to poison him? So yeah, it *had* to have been just a spontaneous, opportunistic thing," Pomona mused. "Maybe after Percy showed the *grimoire* to him, Benedict got greedy and decided that he wanted it. Like, maybe the death *was* an accident—but then Benedict decided to profit from that accident. He didn't *plan* it but he made the most of it."

"Mmm... maybe. That seems really cold-hearted, though, and Benedict did seem genuinely upset about Percy's death," said Caitlyn thoughtfully. "I remember thinking that he seemed to be the only one really mourning Percy, compared to the others. So maybe it did all happen exactly as he said, and he really was just a victim of bad luck and bad decisions." She sighed. "I almost feel a bit sorry for him."

"Nah, I wouldn't worry. There's no solid evidence against him, and I'm sure his rich daddy will make sure that he wriggles out of the charges," said Pomona, waving a hand. She glanced at Vanessa on the other side of the room. "You know, at least we know now why 'Vanessa' seemed so offhand before about her friend being murdered. It was 'cos she wasn't Vanessa at all—she was Tara."

Mention of her mother took Caitlyn's mind back to the *grimoire*. Benedict's confession might have solved the mystery of Percy's murder, but it still left them in the dark about the whereabouts of the Widow Mags's book of spells.

As if reading her mind, Pomona said: "If Benedict was telling the truth and he really threw the *grimoire* into the well, why isn't it still there? I mean, we were searching there yesterday morning and we never saw it when we dragged Hosey Houdini out of the well—"

"Oh my God—that's it!" cried Caitlyn.

Pomona looked at her blankly. "What's it?"

"Don't you see? That's where the *grimoire* must be: inside Hosey Houdini!" said Caitlyn excitedly.

"Okay, you're not making any sense—"

"Think, Pomona! What does Hosey Houdini think he is? What was he before?"

"You mean before he was a garden hose? He was that cute python that Evie created by mistake."

"Exactly! And what do pythons do?"

"What d'you mean—what do they do? They squeeze things and swa—" Understanding dawned on Pomona's face. "You mean... Hosey Houdini has swallowed the *grimoire*?"

"It's the only thing that makes sense! The *grimoire* was in the well, and then Hosey Houdini must have slithered in there too. Real pythons like to find places to curl up and hide, don't they? And then maybe he felt hungry or he did it out of curiosity—I don't know—but for whatever reason, he swallowed the *grimoire*. Just like a real python swallowing its prey!" Caitlyn paused for a moment, thinking. "And you know what? I've just remembered something: yesterday afternoon, when I was out in the gardens, I bumped into Old Palmer, the head gardener. He was complaining about several garden tools and things that had gone mysteriously missing recently. The junior gardeners swore that they would put their tools down for a moment and then when they turned around, the tools would be gone. They were really spooked about it and talking about a Samhain curse or something, but—"

"You're telling me that you think it was actually Hosey Houdini? That he likes munching gardening equipment?" asked Pomona, chuckling.

Caitlyn nodded. "And him swallowing the *grimoire* would explain everything else that happened yesterday morning too! When you went off to get the elf pouch thingy and I was left alone with Hosey Houdini in the gardens, Vanessa turned up—except that it wasn't *really* Vanessa, of course; it was Tara— but anyway, she was using the dowsing pendulum to search for the *grimoire* and the pendulum was leading her straight towards me. I've just realised now that it was because I was holding Hosey Houdini with the *grimoire* in his belly!"

"Do you think Tara knew—?"

"No, I don't think so. In fact, when I spoke to her at the hospital, she didn't mention the garden hose at all. She was just following the pendulum, which only gives you indications for general direction and proximity." Caitlyn paused, thinking again. "But it explains why Tara ended up on the terrace. After we both got wet and I had to leave Hosey Houdini to go and change my clothes, he slithered off again. And he must have taken himself to the Ballroom terrace, because that's where I found Tara when I eventually followed her there. She was bending over one of the half-wine barrels—you know, the ones they put there for the Samhain Festival. I think they're going to use them for the apple-bobbing games. Anyway, I'll bet that Hosey Houdini was curled up in one of those half-wine barrels—"

"Do you think he's still there now?" cut in Pomona excitedly. "C'mon! Let's go and look!"

# CHAPTER TWENTY-NINE

They made their way quickly to the Ballroom on the other side of the Manor. When they arrived, they found the place humming with activity as staff members scurried in and out of the open doors leading to the terrace, carrying trestle tables, props, and other equipment. The Ballroom itself had been transformed into a sort of autumnal wonderland, with the walls decorated with clusters of dried leaves, acorns, and pinecones, and the chandeliers festooned with garlands of ivy. Fresh hay bales covered with burlap sacks had been strategically placed around the room to provide some seating, and they were accompanied by an assortment of misshapen turnips and pumpkins, their carved faces lit by flickering candles. Outside on the terrace, several wooden trestle tables were being set up next to the stone balustrade, and Caitlyn could see Mrs Pruett and her kitchen assistants hovering around the tables, setting out platters of food.

Lisa, the Manor's marketing coordinator, was standing at the edge of the terrace, frowning down at a clipboard. There was a half-wine barrel placed by the balustrade next to her and Caitlyn hurried across to this eagerly. But when she looked down into the barrel, now filled with apples bobbing gently on the surface of the water, she was disappointed to see no sign of Hosey Houdini.

Lisa looked up with a harassed expression. "Oh, Caitlyn, I suppose you've heard the news?"

"You mean... about Vanessa?" said Caitlyn, feeling her way.

"Well, apparently she's *not* Vanessa!" cried Lisa, throwing up her hands. "The whole thing is completely bizarre. If I hadn't heard it from James himself, I would have thought that it was some kind of practical joke. Although... it *is* some kind of elaborate hoax, I hear? Or a strange case of mistaken identity? James wasn't very clear when he was telling me about it... Anyway, I was all set to cancel the Samhain Festival yesterday when we thought that Vanessa had had an accident, but now it appears that Vanessa was fine and was actually in London all along?" She shook her head in bewilderment.

"So the Festival *is* going ahead?" asked Pomona.

Lisa sighed. "Yes. James and I had an emergency meeting this morning and we agreed that it was the lesser of two evils to go ahead as planned. We've put out so much advertising and marketing, and there's been such an enthusiastic response that there will likely be tourists and local families coming from all over the country." She glanced distractedly at her watch. "They'll all be arriving in less than two hours. It's just too difficult to cancel the event at this late stage. I don't think we'd be able to get the message out to the community in time to prevent people from making the trip. And we certainly can't just put up a sign at the front gate saying that everything's been cancelled without good reason. People will be furious at the inconvenience of having come all the way, and it will be terrible for the Manor's reputation!"

"Honey, I'm sure everything will be fine," Pomona said, trying to soothe the agitated woman. "People are gonna have an awesome time at the Festival and there will be lots of good PR for the Manor."

Lisa sighed again and glanced at the activity around them. "I just hope I can get everything set up in time. Most of these things were supposed to be set up yesterday, but when we heard about Vanessa's accident, I'd planned to cancel the whole event. And then this morning, when we decided to go ahead after all, I had to do a complete U-turn and rush to get everything ready. So now we're really scrabbling to get things in place before people arrive." She paused, her face brightening. "Oh—but I heard just now that the police have arrested someone for the murder? It would be a relief to know that at least the situation with the young man who was Vanessa's friend has been resolved."

*My God, news really* does *travel fast on the Manor*

*grapevine*, thought Caitlyn. "The police have taken one of Vanessa's other friends in for questioning," she replied cautiously. "They haven't made a formal arrest."

"Ah, well, as long as there are no more dramas today," said Lisa fervently. "I just need a few more hours for this Festival to pass uneventfully and for everyone to have a good time and then go home safely!"

"Um... by the way, Lisa," said Caitlyn in a casual tone. "What happened to all the other wine barrels that were here on the terrace yesterday?"

"Oh, I decided that since we'll be serving food and refreshments out here on the terrace, we need to move the games elsewhere," Lisa replied. She indicated the wine barrel next to them. "I've left one here, but I've asked the staff to move the others further out into the grounds and spread them around in different places, so that people can come across them as they're wandering around."

"Ah, right, and... er... when you were moving the others, you didn't happen to see a garden hose, did you?" asked Caitlyn.

"A garden hose?" Lisa looked surprised. "No, I don't think so. The other barrels were all emptied before they were moved. Why do you ask?"

"Oh...um..." Caitlyn was groping for an excuse when Lisa's attention was diverted by a figure in black hobbling out onto the terrace.

It was the Widow Mags. She was accompanied by

313

Evie, who was carefully carrying a large tray upon which rested a magnificent three-tier chocolate cake, decorated with clusters of fresh figs and autumn berries and frosted with dark chocolate ganache.

"Holy guacamole, that is some cake," said Pomona, eyeing it in awe.

"Oh my goodness!" cried Lisa, rushing over to the old witch. "That looks fabulous! But James told me you were only helping to provide some chocolate truffles and bonbons—"

"I decided to do a cake as well," said the Widow Mags, waving Evie towards one of the trestle tables on the terrace. Caitlyn and Pomona hurried to help the younger girl set the enormous cake down in the centre of the table.

"This is marvellous! Thank you so much," said Lisa, beaming. "It looks absolutely scrumptious! It'll be the highlight of the Festival refreshments, I'm sure." She gave a little laugh. "In fact, I must make sure to steal a slice myself before it's all gone. I'm sure it'll all be eaten in a flash and people will be fighting over the last morsels."

"Oh, you need not worry about that," said the Widow Mags. "I have placed a Replenish Charm on it so that it will never run out. There will be enough cake for everyone."

Lisa blinked. "I... I beg your pardon?"

The Widow Mags smiled at her, then gestured to Evie again. The girl obediently cut a slice from the bottom of the cake, placed it on a plate, and handed it to Lisa.

"Oh no... I didn't mean... no, no, I wanted to save the cake for everyone to see it before we cut—" Lisa broke off, her eyes wide as she stared at the base of the three tiers, where the wedge of cake had been cut out. Slowly, the chocolate sponge and buttercream interior expanded outwards, and the edges of the ganache frosting drew together, until the gap sealed itself over and the cake looked pristine once more.

"How... how did it do that?" choked Lisa.

The Widow Mags didn't reply; she simply motioned for Lisa to taste the cake. Once the woman had tasted the first mouthful, she forgot all about the magically regenerating cake.

"*Mm...mmm!* Oh my God... this is... *mmmm...*" mumbled Lisa with her mouth full as she gobbled forkfuls of chocolate cake. "*Mmm...* unbelievable... *mm-mmm! ...so* delicious..."

"Jeez, maybe she and that cake should get a room," sniggered Pomona. She turned eagerly to Evie. "Can I have a slice too?"

Caitlyn was about to ask for a taste as well when she realised that the Widow Mags was beckoning to her. Hurrying over to her grandmother's side, she was surprised to see the old witch looking uncharacteristically timorous and ill at ease.

"I heard that you went to the hospital last night," she said gruffly.

"Yes, that's right."

"You saw her? Tara?" The old witch cleared her

throat, not meeting Caitlyn's eyes. "How is she?"

"She's... she's fine," said Caitlyn, startled. After her grandmother's apathy yesterday to the announcement of Tara's return, the last thing Caitlyn had expected was the Widow Mags to voluntarily ask after Tara's welfare. Did she care after all?

"She's still got some lingering side effects from the concussion, but overall she's very well and back to her full capabilities," she told the old witch. She paused, then added, shamefaced: "Actually, she tricked me into helping her escape police custody."

The Widow Mags gave a dry smile. "I see that Tara hasn't changed much then. She was always clever and quick to size up a situation, to exploit any weakness."

"Yes, she played on my emotions and manipulated me," Caitlyn admitted. "Is that how she managed to steal your *grimoire*? Because she tricked you as well?"

The Widow Mags sighed. "No, she could never trick me. I could always see through her schemes. But she knew other ways to get under my defences..." She was silent for a moment, then she began to talk, her voice distant: "I had known for several months, of course, that Tara was sneaking out to meet *him*. That witch hunter. An agent of the Society who had sworn to destroy all witches. She might be adept at conjuring charms and spell-crafting, but she couldn't hide the truth from me." She shook her head. "To fall in love with a witch hunter was foolish enough, but to believe his lies...! Of course, Tara would never listen to me. If I told her to go left, she would go right; if I told her to go up, she would go down—just to spite me. She wouldn't believe me when I told her that her lover would betray her. She just kept insisting that he was different—"

"But I think he really *was* different," Caitlyn protested. "Noah—my father—he wasn't like the other Society agents. He didn't want to destroy witches; he didn't fear magic. He wanted to find a way for us to all co-exist—"

The Widow Mags gave a bitter laugh. "Yes, Tara told me about their dream. A new world where witches and the British government could work together to use magic for the common good. Hah!" Then she glanced at Caitlyn, her expression softening slightly, and she said grudgingly: "Well, your father may have been different. I'll grant you that. But he was as naïve as Tara for trusting his superiors. They told him that they needed something from the sisterhood of witches as a gesture of faith, to prove our good intentions." Her voice rose in indignation. "*We* were the ones who had been persecuted for centuries, and now *we* had to prove our good intentions?"

Caitlyn winced, sympathising with the old witch's outrage. "Is that why Tara wanted the *grimoire*?" she asked, although she already knew the answer.

"Yes. She thought offering to share such a

valuable magical asset would impress the Society, and she was furious when I refused to give the *grimoire* to her. Tara may have been a gullible fool, but I certainly was not. Even if Noah had been sincere, do you really think his superiors were being honest? Do you think they would have been content with just looking at the *grimoire* and then giving it back? My *grimoire* is a book of immense magical power. The Society would have either wanted to destroy it or use it for their own ends."

Caitlyn was silent. She knew that the Widow Mags was right.

"Of course, that wasn't the only reason Tara wanted my *grimoire*," the old witch continued cynically. "She had long been obsessed with it and craved the knowledge within its pages. The fact that the Society wanted it too, simply gave her a convenient additional reason to take the book."

"Bertha told me that Tara was fascinated by the Dark Magic spells in the *grimoire*?" said Caitlyn questioningly.

"Yes, Dark Magic can be seductive in its promise of power with no boundaries," said the Widow Mags grimly. "Tara was drunk on the idea of being the most powerful witch, of revelling in her superior abilities compared to her peers..."

"Was she really that amazing?" asked Caitlyn.

The Widow Mags hesitated, then said: "It is true that Tara had an extraordinary ability to wield magic, well beyond most witches in England. But being born with more natural talent than others is not what determines greatness. Your mother thought that all she had to do was gain the knowledge that I was denying her—especially the forbidden spells of Dark Magic—and that would make her all-knowing and all-powerful. But what she never understood was that it wasn't enough to just have a gift—you needed to have the ability to direct that gift too."

The old witch gave Caitlyn a sad smile. "The sharpest knife used without skill is no better than a blunt instrument. And skill is not something that you can gain easily. Talent you can be born with, but skill you have to hone through years of practice under a multitude of challenges. It is something you need to nurture through discipline and grace and humility. I wish Tara could have understood that."

# CHAPTER THIRTY

Caitlyn was quiet and thoughtful as she and Pomona made their way slowly down the terrace steps and into the landscaped gardens. When she had been with Tara last night and listened to her account of the past, she had felt her sympathies pulled firmly in her mother's direction. It had seemed like Tara was terribly wronged, that no one had truly appreciated her, and that the Widow Mags had been unfairly harsh and close-minded. And yet now that she had heard her grandmother's side of the story, she couldn't help feeling that the old witch had good reasons for her stance too.

*Maybe they're both right... and they're both wrong,* thought Caitlyn with an inward sigh.

"Uh... Hello? Earth to Caitlyn?"

Caitlyn blinked. "Sorry, Pomie, I was miles away."

"Miles away? You were practically in another solar system," grumbled Pomona. "You haven't heard a single thing I said to you since we left the terrace."

"I'm sorry," Caitlyn said again, giving the other girl a contrite smile. "I just—"

She broke off as they rounded a corner and found Bran suddenly blocking their path. The English mastiff was pacing back and forth and whining, his wrinkly forehead even more furrowed than usual. He perked up when he saw them and bounded over, wagging his tail vigorously.

"Hey, you big lump," said Pomona with a grin. "Yeah, yeah, great to see you too... just don't slobber over me... no, don't do that—what's the matter with him?" she asked as the mastiff continued to circle them, whining anxiously.

Caitlyn shook her head in puzzlement, watching the giant dog. "I don't know. He seems to be really agitated about something."

Bran had taken a few steps away from them and was standing there, looking back at them. He whined plaintively, his eyes pleading.

"What is it, Bran?" Caitlyn walked over to lay her hand gently on his huge head.

The mastiff walked a few paces away again, then paused and looked back at her, his tail wagging hopefully.

"I think... he wants us to follow him!" said Pomona.

"Yes, I think you're right," said Caitlyn, putting a hand on the mastiff's collar as he began to move forward again.

Together, they walked alongside the mastiff as he

plodded towards the large open space behind the Manor house, which was surrounded by several outbuildings. Staff members were hurrying to and fro, carrying props, equipment, and other paraphernalia for the Festival, but Bran ploughed through them, paying no attention to people who nearly crashed into him. Caitlyn had to shout a few hasty apologies as they accompanied the mastiff across the yard whilst he walked past the Coach House restaurant, past the entrance to the stable complex, before heading determinedly for the area beyond.

This was where old workers' cottages and a number of other outbuildings had been renovated and transformed into short-term accommodation. It was one of James's successful ideas to modernise the estate and find new ways of generating income. And chief among the new dwellings was a converted barn that had been leased by Leandra Lockwood. Caitlyn had had a hunch where the dog was leading them and her suspicions proved to be correct as the mastiff lumbered up to the barn building. He dropped his nose to the ground and began to sniff earnestly, his baggy jowls trailing drool as he walked in loops and circles. Caitlyn and Pomona watched him, mystified.

"What's he doing?" asked Pomona.

"I don't know, although I can take a good guess: he's probably searching for Nibs. You know how much he adores Nibs, and he's been really agitated, poor thing, since Nibs went missing. I found him wandering out in the gardens yesterday searching for his little friend."

"I still think Nibs is in there," said Pomona, gesturing to the barn. "I told you Leandra kidnapped him and is keeping him hostage. You need to speak to her again and tell her straight up that you think she's lying and demand to know where she's keeping Nibs. In fact, *I'll* do it!" Pomona whirled and marched up to the front door of the barn.

"Wait, Pomona—"

Too late. Pomona was already rapping loudly on the door, and it swung open a moment later to reveal Leandra in a full-length, Gothic-style, velvet dress of bright emerald-green, with enormous lace-trimmed sleeves and a corseted bodice. Her eyes were heavily shadowed in shimmery black and green, her lips painted a blood-red, and her brows darkened and drawn into such high arches that she looked permanently startled. But what really made their mouths drop open were the huge, black, bat-like wings attached to Leandra's back by a leather harness and the dramatic headdress she wore, with its two black horns that curled back into wicked points high above her head.

"Yes?" she said.

"Whoa..." Pomona eyed her up and down. "Are you going off to audition for the next *Maleficent* movie?"

Leandra flushed angrily. "I have dressed as befits the occasion. It is Samhain Eve—one of the most important dates in the esoteric calendar and a celebration of ancient customs that have been observed for millennia. On such a night, steeped in tradition and ritual, we should all be honouring—"

"Uh... okay, okay," said Pomona hastily, cutting the woman off before she could start another lecture. "Listen, we've come to ask you about Nibs. You know, the little black kitten—?"

Leandra made an impatient noise. "I have already told your friend: I don't have your kitten! I put him out the front door—here—" She gestured to the doorstep. "—Friday afternoon, and I haven't seen him since."

"Now, see, I think you're lying," said Pomona baldly. "I think you're hiding Nibs somewhere and keeping him hostage."

"What? Why on earth would I want to do that?"

"'Cos you wanna use him in some stupid ritual which you think will make you a real witch."

Leandra spluttered with indignation. "That's... that's preposterous! I have no desire to become some common dabbler in petty spells and home-brewed potions—I am far better than that! I use more refined and elevated magical practices, which are tied to scholarship and expert knowledge of ancient wisdoms. Practices that demand not just a fleeting interest, but a *lifetime* of dedication. I engage in rituals passed down by the most esteemed practitioners of the arcane arts, which are completely removed from the crude practices of folk witchery..."

She paused at last, running out of air, and glared

at the two girls, panting. Caitlyn felt a stab of doubt as she looked at Leandra. Maybe the woman wasn't a clever mastermind hiding some secret strategy after all; maybe she really was just a crazy, superstitious shrew and nothing more. Surely no one could be this histrionic and deluded and still be faking it?

Pomona, however, was undeterred. "You can yell all you want. I know you're lying. You'd better hand Nibs over or I'm gonna call the animal welfare services—"

They were interrupted by a loud bark and turned to see Bran hunched over by the side of the barn, a few feet down from the door. He was pawing frantically at the ground and whining with excitement. The next moment, he began to dig in earnest, ploughing into the ground at the side of the barn with his enormous, paddle-like paws.

"Hey! Wait... what is that animal doing?" cried Leandra indignantly. "If he damages anything, I'm certainly not going to pay for it."

She followed the two girls as they rushed over to the mastiff. They had to dodge several huge clods of dirt and soil sailing through the air as they approached.

"Bran! BRAN!" shouted Caitlyn, reaching out to grab the dog's collar and pull him away from the side of the barn.

Looking down, she saw that there were deep trenches radiating out from a point at the base of the barn wall, where Bran had raked back the hard soil with his claws and unearthed a shallow hole right next to the barn's foundations. At the edge of the hole, beneath the barn wall, she could see some sturdy wood beams and realised that she was looking at the joists of a raised floor that must have been put in when the interior of the barn was modernised. Right underneath were dense batts of fluffy, dark grey material compressed into the spaces between the joists.

"What is that?" asked Pomona, bending and peering into the hole.

"It's mineral wool," said Leandra over their shoulders. "It's used for insulation."

Bran had been straining against his collar and now he nearly pulled Caitlyn off her feet as he lunged forwards and began scrabbling at the exposed foundations again, dragging out some of the mineral wool that had been tucked tightly between two of the joists.

"Bran, what are you doing?" cried Caitlyn, exasperated as she tried to wrap her hand more firmly around his collar and pull him back again. "You're going to dama—"

She stopped. Had she imagined it or had her ears caught a faint sound?

Pomona came up to her. "Man, that dog is like—"

"Shh!" Caitlyn shushed her. "Listen!"

She strained her ears and heard it again: the faint mewling of a kitten.

"It's Nibs!" she gasped, lunging for the hole herself and starting to pull at the mineral wool with her hands. "Quick! Help me!"

A few minutes later, they had unearthed a fair-sized opening in the dense insulating material, and Caitlyn peered into the dark hole.

"Nibs?" she called. "Nibs, are you there?"

"*Mew! Meeeew!*"

The next moment, something small, black, and covered in dust and fluffy fibres crawled out of the hole in the mineral wool.

"Oh, Nibs!" cried Caitlyn, scooping the kitten up and hugging him close whilst Bran bounced around them, barking in excitement.

The kitten gave a happy chirrup, then shook himself and sneezed, sending a cloud of dust and mineral-wool fibres everywhere. Other than being slightly dishevelled, he didn't look too worse for wear.

"Well, I hope that you absolve me now of any involvement in a cat-napping plot," said Leandra, looking pointedly at Pomona. "It's obvious that the stupid creature crawled under the barn floor somehow and got stuck in there."

"Uh... yeah, I guess," said Pomona reluctantly, and when Leandra turned and stomped back to the front door, she stuck her tongue out.

"Pomie!" remonstrated Caitlyn in a whisper. Luckily, Leandra went in and shut the door without a backward glance.

"Okay, so I was wrong about her kidnapping Nibs,

but I still think she's up to no good," Pomona muttered. She looked at the kitten, who was now squirming in Caitlyn's arms. "How the heck did he get under that barn floor?"

Caitlyn set the wriggling kitten down and smiled as she watched Bran cover him with slobbery licks. Then she glanced at the base of the barn wall again and noticed for the first time that there were thin, narrow gaps set at intervals along the base, just where the wall met the ground.

"Look..." She pointed these out to Pomona. "Those must be some kind of vent for airflow under the house. Maybe Nibs crawled into one of those and then got lost and trapped inside." She glanced at the closed front door and lowered her voice. "That would explain why I heard him crying when I was searching Leandra's study on Friday afternoon. I couldn't work out why he sounded like he was under her desk and yet I couldn't find him. It's because he was right underneath me, under the floorboards!"

"Are you sure Leandra couldn't have, like, kept him caged up under the floor or something?"

Caitlyn gave a laugh. "I think you need to give it up, Pomie. We were wrong about Leandra. She isn't some power-hungry witch wannabe—she really is just a pompous, pedantic academic who's a bit obsessed with the occult, and this thing with Nibs was just a weird coincidence."

Pomona jutted her bottom lip out. "I still think there's something sketchy about her. I mean, you said she was trying to scare the villagers and estate staff with stupid superstitions about Samhain and peddling those herb charms—"

"I think it strokes her ego to feel like all the villagers look up to her and think she's got power too, but I don't know if there's a sinister agenda beyond that," said Caitlyn. She bent and picked Nibs up again. "Anyway, I'm just glad we found this little monkey. Come on, we'd better take him back to the Manor right away so he can get something to eat and drink. The poor thing probably hasn't had anything for forty-eight hours."

They made their way back to the Manor and left Nibs in the warmth of the kitchen, eagerly tucking into a bowl of shredded roast chicken under the loving eye of Mrs Pruett whilst Bran sat drooling next to her. As they stepped out of the kitchen, Caitlyn started towards a side door that led out of the Manor house but stopped as Pomona caught her arm.

"Hey! Where are you going?"

Caitlyn looked at her in surprise. "To look for Hosey Houdini. We still need to find him, remember? The *grimoire* is probably in his belly and—"

"Hang on, hang on... Look, it's not that I don't want to help, but the Samhain Festival is starting in—" Pomona glanced at her watch. "—less than an hour now! And the place is already crawling with caterers and workers and members of staff. We can't start searching now. The grounds are enormous, and we have no idea where to even start looking. Why don't we just leave it until after the Festival is over? It'll only be a few more hours and the *grimoire* will be safe until then. No one except us knows that it's in Hosey Houdini's belly—and he'll probably be curled up safely in some hole somewhere."

"But—"

"C'mon," said Pomona, taking her arm firmly and leading her towards the main staircase in the front hall. "You know, Leandra was right about one thing: you gotta dress up for Samhain Eve. And they might call it fancy Celtic names over here, but it's still basically Hallowe'en, which means... COSTUMES!" She grinned at Caitlyn. "Wait until you see what I've prepared for you!"

# CHAPTER THIRTY-ONE

Caitlyn stared at her reflection in the mirror in dismay. "Pomie, I can't wear this!"

"Why not? It's *perfect*," said Pomona gleefully, reaching up to adjust the pointed black hat atop Caitlyn's head. "If anyone is entitled to wear a witch costume at the Festival today, it's *you*."

Caitlyn winced as she looked at her reflection again. She couldn't believe that Pomona had hired a traditional witch costume for her, complete with enormous cone-shaped black hat, black satin dress with ragged hems, black pointy-toed ankle boots, and—worst of all—black-and-white striped stockings!

"This... this is like some terrible joke," she said, shaking her head in distaste.

"No, it's not. It's called irony," said Pomona, looking pleased with herself. "Anyway, you haven't got anything else... unless you'd like to swap with me?"

"No thanks," said Caitlyn hastily, shuddering as she looked at Pomona's skin-tight, neon pink, leopard-print bodysuit, complete with faux cat ears and perky tail attachment. As usual, her cousin seemed to have gone for the loudest, tightest, brightest costume in the shop! Still, Pomona managed to wear it all with such panache that the overall effect was somehow "fierce and fantastic" rather than "gaudy and tacky". Not for the first time, Caitlyn wished that she had the American girl's aplomb and body confidence. Whereas she always tried to hide her pear-shaped figure in loose clothes and muted colours, Pomona happily flaunted her curves in bright shades and revealing outfits—and carried it all off with stylish flair.

Caitlyn looked back at the mirror again and decided that she had got off lucky: at least her witch dress was fairly loose, with a modestly high, Victorian-style collar.

"All right," she said wearily. "I'll wear this. I'll just have to hide from James all evening."

"Rubbish! I'm sure James will think you look adorable," said Pomona. She thrust something at Caitlyn. "Don't forget your broom!"

Caitlyn made a face but took the miniature toy broomstick with a resigned sigh. She waited as Pomona put the finishing touches to her own costume—a headband sporting two leopard-spotted furry ears, some stick-on whiskers, and a pair of shiny, black patent-leather boots—then the two girls made their way out of the Manor.

Outside, it looked like the Festival was already in full swing. The grounds around the Manor house were filled with people milling around, admiring the gardens, which had been decorated with carved pumpkins, bunches of corn husks, life-size wicker figures of mythical beasts. Fire torches were mounted on iron stands, their vivid orange flames casting a warm, inviting glow against the grey autumn sky. The heady aroma of mulled cider and warm apple tart wafted through the air, mingling with the wonderful smell of freshly baked bread—no doubt a teaser of the harvest feast Mrs Pruett and her team had laid on at the Ballroom terrace.

Towards the rear of the grounds, in the big open space next to the Coach House restaurant, a series of stalls had been set up to showcase local foods and handicrafts for sale. Next to them were several areas marked out for traditional games and activities, from tarot readings and cider-pressing demonstrations to craft tables where children and adults alike gathered eagerly to try weaving leaf garlands and making corn dollies.

The most popular game, of course, was apple-bobbing, and the air was filled with the sound of raucous laugher as people gathered around the wine barrels and attempted to lift up one of the bright red apples bobbing in the water—using just their teeth, no hands allowed!

A minute later, the laughter was drowned out by

the haunting sound of a fiddle and pipe, accompanied by the soft drumming of a tabor, playing a lively folk-dance tune. Caitlyn saw that a Morris dancing troupe dressed in Gothic black had assembled in the centre of the open space and were beginning to cavort around, the bells tied to their shins jingling as they hopped and skipped and circled through their choreographed routines.

There was something mesmerising about the harmony of their movements, and the simple rhythmic clacking that filled the air as they struck their hazel sticks against each other in time to the music. One of the dancers spun past Caitlyn, her black hat tipping aside to reveal a crop of auburn hair. It was such an unnaturally bright shade that it was obvious it had come out of a bottle. Nevertheless, the vivid colour suddenly brought Tara to mind.

*I wonder where she is*, Caitlyn thought uneasily, eying the throng of people around her. She was sure that her mother was here at the Festival where all the action was, and it was frustrating not being able to find her. But despite peering intently at the crowds around her, she couldn't spot any familiar faces. Everyone was in costume: there were white-faced ghouls and brooding Grim Reapers, fur-clad Vikings and sinister scarecrows, gawky skeletons and bandaged zombies—and lots and lots of witches in every shape, size, and variety! Suddenly, Caitlyn didn't feel so bad about her witch costume—if anything, it helped her blend in and avoid attention.

But with all the painted faces and elaborate props everywhere, it would have been challenging to recognise any friend or acquaintance, never mind a woman skilled at glamour magic. There was no hope of spotting Tara in the crowd.

Still, with what she knew about Tara's impetuous nature, Caitlyn couldn't help feeling nervous. She knew that her mother was desperate to find the *grimoire*... did she have some reckless plan in store? *What if she unleashes a Dark Magic spell? What if she hurts someone?* Guilt nagged at Caitlyn, and she wondered again if she had done the right thing in helping her mother escape the hospital. If Tara were to do anything reprehensible here at the Festival today, it would be partly her fault...

Lisa's words came back to her, and she echoed them fervently in her own mind: *"I just need a few more hours for this Festival to pass uneventfully and for everyone to have a good time and then go home safely..."*

"That apple-bobbing game looks awesome!" said Pomona, interrupting her thoughts. "C'mon, I wanna have a go!"

She trotted off towards the nearest wine barrel and Caitlyn followed, her eyes still scanning the crowd anxiously. She was soon distracted from her thoughts, however, when she arrived at the wine barrel and found Pomona struggling to nab an apple by her teeth. With her hands obediently tucked behind her back, the American girl lunged and twisted, splashing water everywhere and ducking her head under more than once as she tried to grab one of the bobbing red fruits. Caitlyn found herself laughing and whooping alongside the gathered audience, and when Pomona finally emerged, dripping wet but triumphant, with an apple clenched in her mouth, she cheered her cousin as loudly as the others around the barrel.

"Man, I'm soaked!" said Pomona with a laugh as she rejoined Caitlyn. "It was super fun, though. You gotta try it too!"

"Maybe later," Caitlyn demurred, eyeing Pomona's bedraggled state. Her cousin's bodysuit was wringing wet, and her blonde hair hung in damp tendrils around her face. "You'd better change out of that wet costume before you freeze and catch a cold."

"Aww, what a bummer," Pomona grumbled, although Caitlyn could see her start to shiver. "I've barely even worn this costume for an hour! And what am I going to wear instead?"

"You can have my witch costume," said Caitlyn quickly. "I don't mind wearing normal clothes—"

"Uh-uh! You're not getting out of it that easily!" Pomona retorted. "Don't worry—I'll cobble something fabulous from my wardrobe." She grinned. "Wait here, I'll be back in a minute."

"Why don't we meet up on the Ballroom terrace?" Caitlyn suggested. "I'm going to get a drink and we can pick up some food there too."

Pomona gave her a thumbs-up gesture, then

disappeared in the direction of the Manor's front door. Caitlyn began to make her own way through the crowd, heading for the terrace. As she walked through the throng of people, all talking, laughing, and enjoying the festivities, she found herself nodding along to the lively rhythm of the folk music and was suddenly surprised to realise that she felt happy. Cheerful, even. Pomona's fiasco with the apples had driven all the worries about Tara, James, the bewitched garden hose, and the *grimoire* from her mind... and it was lovely to feel the load lift from her shoulders.

*Maybe Pomona's right and I should just put things aside for a while,* Caitlyn thought. After all, it was true that they couldn't do much whilst the Festival was in full flow and the place was full of visitors. They could resume their search for the *grimoire* when the whole thing was over—a few more hours shouldn't make a difference.

And as for her mother... Caitlyn felt her guilt ease slightly as she realised that Benedict's confession meant that Tara was absolved of Percy's murder. And the altercation with Daniel Tremaine *could* be explained as a form of self-defence. So Tara wasn't really the dangerous fugitive that everyone painted her to be—she was just a slightly hot-tempered, over-confident seventeen-year-old who had made a few misguided decisions and crossed the line sometimes.

*And she's not going to do anything reckless here today—I'm just being silly and paranoid,* Caitlyn chided herself. After all, while Tara might not have wanted to twiddle her thumbs in Caitlyn's room, surely she would still see the value of keeping a low profile? The last thing she needed was to call attention to herself and alert the police.

*Besides, Viktor is keeping an eye on her,* Caitlyn reminded herself. *I'm sure he would jump in and stop Tara before she does anything truly dangerous. So really, I should stop worrying and just enjoy the Festival.*

Feeling much better, Caitlyn began humming to the music, smiling, and nodding at the people she passed as she made her way through the crowd. A sense of light-heartedness filled her and she was glad that Pomona had insisted that she wear a costume after all. There was a wonderful anonymity from being in disguise and blending in with the sea of "witches" around her. She wondered suddenly where James was. In spite of what she had said to Pomona, she *did* want to see him—embarrassing costume or not! She hadn't been able to spot him or Vanessa and her friends in the crowd. *Perhaps they're on the Ballroom terrace,* thought Caitlyn, quickening her steps. After all, that was where the food and drinks were.

As she rounded the side of the Manor house, Caitlyn noticed two large piles of firewood which had been carefully stacked next to each other. *Ah, the bonfire mounds,* she thought. Beside them, a small crowd of people were congregating around something, and Caitlyn's smile widened as she spied Ferdinand in the centre of the group. The enormous bull was wearing a cowbell around his neck and a headdress of pinecones, berries, and evergreen boughs tucked between his horns. He looked so sweet, with a slightly bemused expression on his gentle face and his tail swishing happily as he enjoyed the fuss and attention from his adoring fans. Caitlyn was tempted to join them, then she reminded herself that Pomona might be looking for her and continued to the Ballroom.

When she arrived and mounted the steps up to the terrace, she found it thronged with people, all eating, drinking, and talking with their mouths full. She stood on tiptoe and craned her neck, trying to see if Pomona was anywhere amongst them, but there was no sign of her cousin. Deciding to get a drink herself first, Caitlyn wove through the crowd, heading for the row of trestle tables lined up against the stone balustrade. Each was covered with a linen table cloth and displayed a smorgasbord of food items—all except the last in the row, which was reserved for drinks.

Caitlyn made her way over to the last table and surveyed the various bottles and jugs accompanied by rows of gleaming mugs and glasses. Judging by the little signs set up next to the containers, Lisa had attempted to provide a traditional selection of warm, spiced concoctions and refreshing ales and cordials, in addition to the ubiquitous tea and coffee. There were honey mead and barleywine, Damson plum cordial and fruit ales, and—Caitlyn noted with a smile—a decorative cast-iron cauldron set at the end of the table, filled with (according to the label) mulled cider: a delicious, warm, spiced apple cider, infused with cinnamon, orange peel, and cloves.

She took an empty mug and picked up the ladle in the cauldron, keen to sample some of the cider for herself. But as she peered into the cast-iron container, she was disappointed to see that it seemed to be empty, save for a few drops of amber liquid at the bottom. *What's happened to all the cider? Has everyone drunk it already?* It seemed unlikely, given the size of the cauldron and the fact that all the other drinks containers were still mostly full... Then Caitlyn noticed a spill of liquid down one side of the cauldron which pooled over the edge of the table. Curious, she leaned and looked over the end. She could see more amber liquid in a puddle on the floor, spreading sideways out of sight beneath the table.

Really puzzled now, Caitlyn lifted the linen tablecloth and bent to peer under the trestle table. It took her eyes a moment to acclimatise to the dimness beneath, then she choked back a surprised laugh as she saw the pile of green rubber coils. It was Hosey Houdini!

# CHAPTER THIRTY-TWO

Caitlyn stared at the bewitched garden hose, her mind racing. She couldn't believe that after all their searching, she had found Hosey Houdini right here, almost literally under her feet! He must have slithered out of the wine barrels before they were removed from the terrace and somehow managed to conceal himself amongst all the Festival paraphernalia that had been placed here in the past few days. It seemed a miracle that no one had noticed him. Still... what was there to notice? Unless he started moving around or lisping, Hosey Houdini looked exactly like any other run-of-the-mill garden hose. And this spot he had found, tucked away out of sight beneath the linen tablecloth of the trestle table, was the perfect hiding place.

Caitlyn straightened and glanced around, trying to decide what to do. This trestle table was at the end of the row, just a few yards from where the stone balustrade terminated at the end of the terrace.

There was a second flight of steps there, which led down to the gardens around the rear of the Manor house. If she could drag Hosey Houdini out from under the table and down those steps, she'd hopefully be able to find a quiet place, away from the Samhain festivities, where she could examine him properly.

Casting a surreptitious look over her shoulder to make sure that no one was watching, Caitlyn reached under the table and grabbed the brass connector end that was Hosey Houdini's "head". Carefully, she dragged the bewitched garden hose out from his hiding place. He made a sleepy, gurgling noise as he was lifted, but thankfully didn't wriggle or try to slither away. Caitlyn grappled with him for several moments and finally managed to heave him out from under the table. Wrapping her arms around as many coils of rubber as she could manage, she began to half drag, half hobble towards the steps at the rear of the terrace.

It was difficult going, especially as she was trying to keep her movements subdued, so as not to draw any unnecessary attention, and the rubber loops hung like a dead weight in her arms. She paused beside the baluster that marked the end of the stone balustrade and leaned gratefully against it for a moment, using the chance to get her breath back as well as to check again that no one was watching.

So far, so good. Most of the people were congregated at the other end of the terrace, and everyone seemed to be too busy eating and talking to pay her much attention. Then her gaze sharpened as she spied a big mane of glossy blonde hair amongst the heads at the other end. She craned her neck to see... yes, it was Pomona! Caitlyn hesitated—she wanted to wave and call to her cousin, but she was afraid that by doing so, she might attract too much attention from everyone else as well.

Standing on tiptoe, she tried in vain to catch Pomona's eye, but the American girl was too far away and there were too many people between them. In any case, Pomona's attention was being monopolised by an old man in an ancient black suit who was talking to her and gesticulating indignantly. *Wait a minute... is that? Yes, it's Viktor!* realised Caitlyn as she watched the old vampire argue with her cousin. She gritted her teeth in frustration. It was maddening to have two people who could help her so near and yet no way to attract their attention!

She glanced down at Hosey Houdini, wondering if she could leave him for a few moments whilst she went across the terrace to summon Viktor and Pomona, but she decided that she didn't dare risk it. What if he slithered away and disappeared again? Now that she had finally found him, she wasn't taking any chances. Frustrated, Caitlyn leaned back against the balustrade as she pondered what to do. Then she perked up as her gaze drifted out over the grounds and landed on the roof of a small wooden structure. It was peeking out from behind a section of topiarised hedge at the end of the path that led from the rear terrace stairs. *Could that be some kind of shed?* Yes, it looked like it—probably somewhere for Old Palmer and his team to store tools and supplies so that they would have them handy for this side of the gardens.

Caitlyn straightened. The shed wasn't that far away—just a few yards beyond the bottom of the steps. If she could just drag Hosey Houdini down the stairs and over there, she'd have somewhere safe to stash him whilst she ran back to get Viktor and Pomona.

Feeling cheered, she began hauling Hosey Houdini down the steps, trying not to trip on the remaining loops that dragged behind her. She managed to get to the bottom without stumbling or falling, and began half-lugging, half-dragging the bewitched garden hose down the path. He seemed to get heavier with every step, and she was panting and sweating, despite the chill autumn air, by the time she reached the shed.

Caitlyn freed one hand and groped experimentally for the door handle, relieved to find it unlocked. She pushed the door open, then leaned against the side of the shed for a moment to catch her breath. She let most of the coils slide to the ground, to give her arms a rest, but kept a firm hold on the front end of the piping.

"My... God... why are you so heavy?" gasped Caitlyn, panting. "I'm sure you didn't weigh this much before..."

Hosey Houdini stirred and lifted his brass connector head. "Ss-ssss?" he lisped sleepily.

Caitlyn coughed as a heady cloud of alcoholic fumes wafted out from the brass opening.

"I don't believe it," she muttered as the sweet smell of apple, cinnamon, and cloves, mingled with citrus and alcohol, engulfed her in a hazy fug. She thought of the empty cauldron sitting on the trestle table, then looked severely down at the sluggish garden hose. "You guzzled that whole cauldron of mulled cider, didn't you?"

As if in answer, Hosey Houdini gave a little twitch and made a gurgling noise that sounded suspiciously like a hiccup.

*Great*, thought Caitlyn. *As if things weren't complicated enough, I now have to deal with a* drunk *bewitched garden hose—*

"What are you doing?"

Caitlyn jerked round to see Vera Bottom standing behind her, watching her suspiciously. She cursed inwardly. Vera was the last person she wanted to see. She hoped the woman hadn't heard her talking to Hosey Houdini.

"Um... nothing," she said, giving Vera a breezy smile. "I just... er... saw this garden hose next to the tables on the terrace and thought I'd move it before anyone trips on it."

As Vera eyed the loops of rubber pooled around her feet, Caitlyn kept a tight grip on the brass connector head and prayed fervently that Hosey Houdini wouldn't suddenly start writhing around or "lisping" to them. She had no idea how she would explain things to a shocked Vera if that were to happen! Keen to distract the woman's attention, she blurted:

"I'm surprised to see you here, Vera. I wouldn't have thought the Festival was your cup of tea?"

Vera sniffed and said defensively: "Well, I decided that, as one of the senior residents of Tillyhenge, it was my duty to come to the Festival and see what was happening here. Of course, *I* have no interest in your wicked pagan rituals, but I need to stay informed on the depraved practices taking place on our doorstep—"

*Yeah, right,* thought Caitlyn cynically. *You're just nosy but don't want to admit it.*

"—so we can be proactive about protecting ourselves from the evil influence of black magic and witchcraft," continued Vera sanctimoniously. "Especially at this time of great danger during Samhain, when evil and malevolent spirits are everywhere."

*Oh God, not this again,* thought Caitlyn, struggling not to roll her eyes. Both Vera and Leandra sounded like a broken record, going on and on about the dangers of Samhain. Something of her thoughts must have still shown in her expression because Vera stiffened and said:

"Are you mocking me? Well, you won't be laughing

much longer! I intend to expose you and the Widow Mags and the rest of your filthy witch family, so that everyone will know the foul ways you have tried to bewitch and control us." She folded her arms and fixed Caitlyn with a defiant glare. "Know thy enemy, as they say!"

Caitlyn sighed and said wearily: "I'm not your enemy, Vera. No one is trying to bewitch you or control you or anything like that. If you could just let go of this crazy paranoia about magic and witchcraft, you would see that the Widow Mags and Bertha and Evie and me... we're just fellow villagers trying to live a quiet life in Tillyhenge."

"Liar!" hissed Vera. "Do you expect me to believe that? I'm not a fool! I've suffered at the hands of your family too many times already. Oh yes, don't think I've forgotten! That time I was forced to eat chocolate cake from the floor? And the time all the cows were hexed on Jeremy's farm? Even in the woods yesterday—you used magic on me! I know it!"

Caitlyn opened her mouth to retort, then hesitated. She couldn't deny that Vera *had* been beset by magic spells on several occasions, although more often than not, it had been the woman's own fault.

"Those weren't... it's not what you think—" she started trying to explain, but Vera cut her off.

"But I'm not scared of you now. You can't menace us anymore," she said, tilting her chin up and looking at Caitlyn smugly. "Because we have someone on our side now who also has powers of her own. Someone who truly understands the evils of witchcraft, and who can guide us on how to ward off malevolent magic."

Caitlyn suddenly recalled Vera saying something similar before. Yesterday morning, when she had bumped into the woman in the village, just after returning from the hospital, Vera had brandished the herb charm at her and cried: "*I have help now. We are not powerless in defending ourselves and our homes against your evil influence any more!*"— belatedly, she realised who Vera was talking about.

"It's Leandra, isn't it?" she asked. "She's the one telling you all this rubbish about Samhain superstitions and dangers. Vera, it's all nonsense! It's just scaremongering—"

"It's not rubbish!" said Vera, scowling at her. "Leandra used to be a professor at one of the top universities. She's spent her whole life studying witchcraft and magic; she's an expert on evil forces and how to protect against them. No one knows more than her about myth and traditions and folklore and ancient wisdoms... and she's been generously helping us, so that we—the upstanding, respectable residents of the estate—can expose you filthy witches and your black ma—"

"Aww, for goodness' sake!" said Caitlyn, starting to lose her temper. "Leandra is just brainwashing you so that she can sell you those stupid herb charms and get you to stroke her ego by treating her like some kind of mystic. You *are* a fool if you can't see how she's manipulating you!"

"She's not brainwashing us—she's showing us the truth," said Vera stubbornly. "She's even told us that if we find the Widow Mags's evil book of spells, she will help us exorcise it, so that it never has the power to hex anyone again—like that poor boy who was murdered."

"What?" said Caitlyn with incredulous scorn. "And you believed her? She's just using you to find the *grimoire* so she can gain it for herself."

"No, you're wrong," said Vera, vehemently shaking her head. "Leandra is good. She—"

She gasped and broke off as Hosey Houdini suddenly raised his brass connector head and swivelled it around like a submarine periscope.

"*Ss-ssss?*" he lisped and squirmed in Caitlyn's grasp.

Vera shrieked and jumped backwards, her eyes bulging. "Oh my God! It's... it's alive!"

"Oh no... that... that was just me," said Caitlyn, pretending to wave her end of the garden hose up and down, causing ripples to move along the length of rubber piping.

Unfortunately, that movement seemed to aggravate Hosey Houdini and he began to writhe around, his long hose body undulating and thrashing on the ground, whilst making a gurgling noise that sounded ominously like a blocked drain.

"You bewitched it the garden hose?" asked Vera in

a terrified voice.

"No, no, that's not what I meant!" said Caitlyn. "I just..."

She racked her brains, trying to come up with a plausible explanation, but before she could think of anything, Hosey Houdini gave a mighty heave and a shudder. His brass connector head made a retching sound, and then he regurgitated a puddle of amber liquid, splattering several drops onto Vera's legs.

"Aaaaghh!" she screamed, hopping around as if she had been splashed by acid. "Get it off me! Get it off me!"

"Vera, stop! Calm down! It's only mulled cider," Caitlyn said, dropping the garden hose as she put out a hand to calm the hysterical woman. "The... um... water pressure must have caused a backflow when I moved the hose."

Hosey Houdini shuddered again, a spasm rippling down the length of his long hose-body, and then, with another retching sound, he spewed out a slimy pile onto the ground.

Caitlyn stared at the glistening mess of items: a tin mug, two red apples, a candlestick, a pair of secateurs, some twigs and leaves, a garden trowel, several rocks, another garden trowel, a misshapen turnip... and a slim leather-bound volume.

*The grimoire!*

Caitlyn had to restrain herself from snatching up the book. Instead, she glanced quickly at Vera, wondering if the other woman had recognised the

Widow Mags's book of spells as well. Vera was staring down at the pile of regurgitated items with horrified disgust, but it was hard to see if she was focusing on any one object in particular. All her bravado had gone, and her hand was shaking as she pointed at the slimy pile and said in a hoarse voice:

"How... how did those things get in there? How could they all fit in a garden hose? It's black magic, isn't it? It's—"

"Oh, it's a phenomenon called a... a hydraulic backwash siphon!" Caitlyn gabbled, hastily kicking some of the twigs and leaves over the *grimoire* to cover it from view. "It happens when... er... water pressure builds up in a pipe that's been immobile for a long time and then... er... this creates a powerful suction effect, similar to... to... when you suck things up using a straw and... um... objects get caught in the pressure vacuum by accident. But once the pressure is equalised, then... er... they are expelled... Um, ask any plumber," she added with false airiness. "They see it all the time."

Vera narrowed her eyes, but something in Caitlyn's blustering explanation must have convinced her because she seemed to calm slightly. She shot another suspicious look at Hosey Houdini, who seemed to be settling down now that he had purged himself of his greedy haul. He gave a sleepy gurgle, but thankfully didn't wriggle or writhe anymore.

"Anyway!" Caitlyn continued with artificial

brightness. "I'm sure you'll be wanting to get back to the Festival. Have you checked out all the stalls and games yet? And I think they're going to light the bonfire soon—you won't want to miss that, Vera!" She gestured to the pile of items at their feet. "Why don't you go on first? I'll just clean up this mess here..."

Vera hesitated a moment longer, then, with a final scowl at Caitlyn, she stalked away. Caitlyn waited until the woman had turned a corner and was out of sight around the edge of the topiary before she relaxed, sagging against the side of the shed with a sigh of relief.

Then she looked at the pile of regurgitated items again, her heart speeding up with excitement. Dropping to a crouch, she reached in and carefully extracted the *grimoire* from the slimy pile. She had been worried that the book might have been damaged from its long immersion inside the garden hose, but to her surprise, it was completely fine, its pages dry and intact.

"What d'you expect? It's magic," she murmured, smiling to herself.

She flipped the *grimoire* open, looking reverently at the dark writing and the symbols and drawings it contained. It seemed to almost hum with magic, and she felt her fingertips tingle as she turned the pages. There was no order or organisation to the sections. It really was just like a personal journal, with recipes, spells, and other charms written at random—

352

although Caitlyn noticed that the front section was filled with the Widow Mags's distinctive spidery scrawl whereas the back contained much more faded text and arcane script that obviously came from different hands. There were runic inscriptions and ancient annotations, enigmatic glyphs, doodles, Sibylline strokes, and long complex spells that whispered of ancient curses derived from Dark Magic. Even just skimming the titles gave Caitlyn a taste of the great forbidden power hidden in these pages, and she shivered as she glimpsed the potential: necromancy, soul binding, blood magic, resurrection...

She was so engrossed in looking at the *grimoire* that she didn't hear the soft footsteps approaching until it was too late.

Something came down suddenly over her head and tightened around her shoulders. Something rough and heavy, which wrapped around her face and blinded her.

Caitlyn gasped as she felt the *grimoire* being tugged from her hands. She clenched her fingers, trying desperately to hang on to one corner of the book, but it was yanked away, and she was left flailing, trapped in a suffocating darkness.

# CHAPTER THIRTY-THREE

For a minute, panic took over, and Caitlyn fought and thrashed blindly. Soil fell into her eyes, sharp twigs jabbed at her face, and dried leaves tangled in her hair and crushed against her neck, crumbling unpleasantly down the back of her collar. Then she forced herself to calm down and take stock: she was grappling with a heavy, rough fabric that had been shoved over her head and pulled down around her body. A sack of some kind? She groped with her hands for the edge of the sack, and finally, hunched over and wriggling, she managed to pull the smothering fabric up and off her body.

She gave a gasp of relief as she freed her head and gulped in the fresh air. She saw now that she was holding a heavy burlap sack—the kind that gardeners use for hedge clippings, pruned branches, and other plant debris. Someone must have jammed it down over her head and shoulders. It had been the perfect distraction whilst they'd snatched the *grimoire.*

Angrily, she tossed the burlap sack aside and looked around, hoping to see the thief still retreating. But all she could see were the tall topiary and manicured gardens around her and, in the near distance, the terrace along the side of the Manor house. There seemed to be even more people milling on there now, but they were all busily eating, drinking, and talking—none of them were running, and none looked remotely furtive.

Caitlyn sighed with frustration, furious with herself. How could she have let the *grimoire* be taken from her like that? She should have been more careful; she should have been more on her guard! Who had attacked her? Closing her eyes, she tried to remember any details of her attacker. She hadn't seen their face—she didn't even know if they were male or female. But while she hadn't been able to see, she *had* been able to hear and smell. There had been light footsteps, so probably a woman... and a grassy fragrance... yes, a sweet liquorice-like aroma, like aniseed... plus a tangy, lemony scent...

Caitlyn opened her eyes excitedly, recalling where she had smelled those exact same scents: when she had seen Leandra Lockwood talking to Neil outside the Coach House restaurant! It had wafted across from the bundle of herbs that Leandra had been brandishing: a herb charm made of—Caitlyn dredged her memory—vervain, trefoil, St John's wort, and dill... Yes, the sweet aniseed aroma would have come from the dill and the lemony scent from the vervain!

"Caitlyn?"

She turned swiftly at Pomona's voice and smiled with relief as she saw her cousin hurrying down the path towards her, followed by Viktor several steps behind. The old vampire was struggling to keep up and called out to Caitlyn, but she barely heard him as she rushed forwards.

"Oh, Pomie!" she cried. "I had it! The *grimoire*! It was inside Hosey Houdini—we were right; he'd swallowed it, and he vomited it up—"

"Omigod, really?" Pomona grabbed her shoulders. "Where is it? Show me!"

Viktor arrived at last, wheezing and looking uncharacteristically agitated. Caitlyn turned to him worriedly.

"Viktor, are you all right? You should have told Pomona to wait for you. Here, maybe you should sit down for a moment—"

"No, no, I'm fine," said the old vampire irritably, brushing her hands away. "But that is not—"

"Where is the *grimoire*?" demanded Pomona.

Caitlyn gave her cousin a rueful look. "I haven't got it any more. While I was looking at it, someone threw a sack over my head and snatched the *grimoire* out of my hands—"

"What?" Pomona looked outraged. "Caitlyn! How could you let that happen?"

Caitlyn shrank back, surprised at her cousin's anger. "I... I'm sorry—they came up behind me and took me by surprise. But I think I know who took it,

Pomie!"

Viktor caught her arm urgently. "No, you're wrong; it's not—"

"I'm sure I'm right, Viktor!" insisted Caitlyn. "It was Leandra. I didn't see my attacker, but I smelled dill and vervain, and you know she was selling those herb charms to everyone, remember?" She turned back to Pomona. "And you're the one who said Leandra wanted the *grimoire* so that she could get her hands on the Widow Mags's chocolate philtre recipe, because she thinks it might turn her into a real witch—"

"What?" Pomona gave a scornful laugh. "Nothing can turn that pathetic poser into a witch. Leandra is nothing but a stuffy, sanctimonious cow who wouldn't know real magic if it came up and smacked her in the face!"

Caitlyn drew back, looking at her cousin uncertainly. "Er... are you okay, Pomie? You seem a bit..."

"A bit what?"

"Well, you just don't seem like yourself—"

"*That's* what I've been trying to tell you, if you would only listen to me," said Viktor in a querulous voice, glowering at her. "It's because she *isn't* herself. She is not your delightful American friend—she is your mother!"

"My... my mother...?" Caitlyn turned back to the other girl and then gasped as Pomona seemed to shimmer before her eyes, the honey-blonde locks transforming into fiery red, the full, hourglass curves narrowing into the slimmer figure of a seventeen-year-old girl. "Tara?"

"I told you not to tell anyone, Viktor," said Tara, giving the old vampire a sulky look. "You promised!"

"I did no such thing," said Viktor. "I merely agreed not to reveal your glamour disguise in the middle of the crowd on the terrace. But Caitlyn asked me to find you for her, and my promise to her comes first."

Caitlyn felt a rush of affection for the old vampire, and she gave him a grateful smile before turning back to her mother.

"Where's Pomona? What have you done with her?"

"Oh, don't worry about her," said Tara, waving a careless hand. "I've put a Petrify Charm on her. She'll be immobile for a few hours, but she'll be fine."

"*What?* How could you?"

"I needed her out of the way for a bit. It was just too good an opportunity to miss when she went up to her room to change. Glamouring myself as Pomona meant that I could move more freely around the Festival."

"You can't keep doing things like this!" said Caitlyn angrily. "You can't just go around doing things to suit yourself without thinking about how it might affect others. It's so selfish and—"

"Hey, don't lecture me," snapped Tara. "Am I the mother or are you?"

"*What?* I... you—" spluttered Caitlyn.

"Look, the important thing now is to find the

*grimoire.* You said you think Leandra took it, didn't you? Right, we need to find her. Come on!"

Tara turned and marched away without a backward glance. Caitlyn stared after her, open-mouthed. She couldn't believe the surreal exchange she'd just had. Then, as she realised that Tara was fast disappearing in the distance, she hastened after her mother. It was true that they needed to find Leandra as quickly as possible and retrieve the grimoire—the rest could wait.

She followed Tara into the main throng and saw that her mother was making a beeline for the twin mounds of bonfire wood stacked at one end of the open space. A makeshift wooden podium had been erected next to one of the piles, and Caitlyn caught sight of James, Bertha, and Lisa standing on the podium. A little distance beyond them, positioned just at the mouth of the path that led between the two bonfire stacks, stood Jeremy with Ferdinand beside him. The farmer had his hand on the bull's head halter whilst Ferdinand placidly swished his tail and chewed the cud.

People had begun sensing that something was imminent, and a crowd was gathering around the bonfires. Caitlyn could hear several calls of "Hush!" and "Quiet!" as everyone arranged themselves in a wide semicircle around the podium, their faces turned up expectantly. The loud hubbub of talk and laughter died away, replaced by a low murmur of eager anticipation.

Then there was a commotion as a tall woman in an emerald-green dress, with faux-leather wings and a black horned headdress, pushed her way up to join the others on the podium. *Leandra.* She began talking and gesticulating earnestly to James, whose bland expression, Caitlyn knew, disguised an irritation he was too polite to express. Lisa, however, wasn't so restrained, and she looked openly annoyed as she started to argue with Leandra, but before things could escalate further, Bertha spoke up. Caitlyn couldn't hear what her aunt said, but whatever it was caused James to give a reluctant nod as Leandra triumphantly took her place next to him, whilst Bertha stepped back with a good-natured shrug.

Lisa scowled and looked for a moment as if she would protest, then she glanced at the waiting crowd and sighed. Shooting Leandra a final dirty look, she stepped forwards and plastered a bright smile to her face as she lifted a microphone in her hand.

"Ladies and gentlemen, thank you ever so much for joining us at the splendid Samhain Festival here at Huntingdon Manor!" she said in an effusive voice. "As many of you are aware, celebrating Samhain is a tradition steeped in history, originating from ancient Celtic festivals. It marks the end of the harvest season and the beginning of winter—and is a time not only to give thanks for the abundance the earth has provided but also to honour our ancestors and those among our loved ones who are no longer with us.

"We sincerely hope you've enjoyed the games and activities so far, and perhaps even indulged in a little retail therapy at some of the stalls—" Lisa sent a knowing smile around the crowd and was rewarded with a wave of chuckles. "—and of course, we hope you've sampled the delectable spread of food and drink available on the terrace. And now, without further ado, I am absolutely thrilled to announce one of the Festival's event highlights. Please join me in welcoming Lord Fitzroy, who will lead us in the lighting of the Samhain bonfires!"

The crowd erupted in cheers and applause as James stepped forwards and took the microphone, looking slightly embarrassed.

"Please... do call me James. There's no need to stand on ceremony," he said, giving everyone a gracious smile. "Thank you, Lisa, for that wonderful welcome. I would like to add that, for me, Samhain is—more than anything—a time for family and community. So I am delighted that so many of you have come from far and wide to celebrate the Festival with us here at Huntingdon Manor."

The crowd whooped and cheered again, and Caitlyn felt warmed by the looks of genuine respect and affection she could see directed at James. He might have balked at the role of "lord of the manor", but since inheriting the estate and stepping into his late father's shoes last year, James had proven himself to be an inspirational leader and beloved landlord—adored as much for his lack of airs and graces as for his willingness to roll up his sleeves and "muck in" on his tenant farms whenever extra help was needed.

Now, everyone watched with excited anticipation as James turned towards Leandra and held a hand out for the beacon torch. But Leandra ignored his outstretched hand, shouldering him aside and almost whacking his head with one of her leather wings as she stepped to the front of the podium.

She held up the fire staff alight with flickering orange flames. "Behold the Ceremonial Flame!" she crowed. "A luminous beacon to guide us through the coming darkness, for Samhain is not merely a festival of fun and games—no, it is a time of great peril as the veil between worlds thins to its most fragile, exposing us all to the evils that lurk just beyond our sight! Yes, tonight we stand on the precipice of darkness as spirits walk among us, creeping at the edges of our vision—"

Lisa made an indignant movement and tried to interrupt, but Leandra ignored her, raising her voice even louder as she continued:

"—and those who dabble in black magic and witchcraft seek to beguile us with their schemes and trickery... but fear not, for *I* am here!" She spread her arms, smiling benevolently down at the bemused audience. "As a scholar who has dedicated my life to studying and observing the arcane arts, I have an unparalleled ability to understand ancient traditions and a profound knowledge of how to defend ourselves against the forces of darkness, which seek to encroach upon us. It is not a duty I take on lightly, of course." Leandra put a hand to her chest in a gesture of false modesty. "But I am glad that the wise decision was made to abandon the misguided notion of relying on quaint herbs and folklore—" She cast a disdainful glance towards Bertha. "—and to entrust *me* instead with the solemn task of guiding us this Samhain Eve. As someone who truly understands the gravity of this moment, I can help to manifest the unseen, the unheard, the unimaginable—and I will consecrate this torch now so that it ignites the bonfires with flames that soar into the night and—"

"Oh, shut up, you pompous windbag!" came a disgusted voice from the front of the crowd. A young woman with red hair that seemed to burn even brighter than the flames of the beacon torch emerged from the throng, and strode towards the podium.

Everyone froze in surprise, then a couple of people began to laugh and shout in agreement. Soon everyone was joining in, clapping and booing, obviously thinking that the interruption was all part of a comic act—akin to a pantomime gag.

Leandra scowled in outrage as the laughter and booing rose around her, her cheeks flushed with humiliation. She turned angrily to the newcomer who had mounted the steps to the podium, but she was pushed aside by Bertha, who rushed forwards crying: "T-Tara?"

# CHAPTER THIRTY-FOUR

Tara gave her elder sister a distracted smile and flicked her eyes to James, but she kept her attention on Leandra. Advancing to the front of the podium, she said to the woman:

"That was the biggest load of sanctimonious tripe I have ever heard! Who are you to lord it about like some supreme high priestess when anyone can see that you don't know the first thing about dealing with real magic?"

"How... how dare you!" spluttered Leandra, going bright red. "I won't be spoken to like that by a... a jumped-up little cow who thinks she knows better than her elders! Oh yes, I remember you—do you think I'd forgotten? You're just the same as you were all those years ago: flaunting yourself as a 'witch prodigy' when, really, you're nothing but an insufferable brat! I already held a professorship in Comparative Religion and Esoteric Philosophy before you were even born, you little harridan, and I'll have you know that I have published more papers and authored more textbooks on mythological traditions and magical practices than anyone else in Great Brit—"

"Papers? Textbooks?" Tara gave a scornful laugh. "Is that all you can do? Witter on about magic in an academic journal that nobody is ever going to read? You think that's impressive?" She leaned forwards and smiled, baring her teeth. "I'll show you what's *really* impressive..."

She pointed at the fire staff in Leandra's hands and whispered: "*Ignis extinguo!*"

The torch was snuffed out, as if blown on by an invisible giant. The crowd murmured in surprise—*Is this part of the show?* many were wondering—and there was a smattering of applause which faded to an uneasy silence as they watched Tara turn towards the two bonfire stacks.

She raised one hand in the air and snapped her fingers.

Instantly, the two piles of wood burst into flames, sending sparks up into the night sky and a gust of heat across the crowd. People gasped and stumbled backwards, putting more distance between themselves and the bonfires.

Tara gave a gleeful laugh and turned to look sarcastically at Leandra: "How's that for a '*ceremonial torch*', eh?"

Leandra had paled and jumped back just like everyone else, but now she squared her shoulders and stepped forwards again, giving Tara a disdainful look and saying in a voice that only shook slightly:

"I'm... I'm not afraid of some cheap pyrotechnics. Do you think you can scare me with those tricks?"

Below the podium, people began to relax again, and there was a tinkle of nervous laughter from the crowd, accompanied by some hesitant clapping. The audience's reaction seemed to embolden Leandra, and she thrust herself into Tara's face, saying:

"And even if that *were* real magic, I have protection—yes, that's right, I am not defenceless! I have armed myself with defensive charms and guarding talismans..." She gestured to the various chains and necklaces she was wearing around her neck. "This, a pentacle amulet made of silver... and this, a rowan-berry necklace... and this, an iron nail cross... and I have this too!" she added, reaching into the folds of her skirt and pulling out a herb charm. "And this!" She pulled another thing out of her pocket—this time, a rusty old saltshaker, which she proceeded to sprinkle manically around her.

Tara gave an incredulous laugh. "You think a bunch of herbs and a sprinkle of salt can stop me?" she sneered, raising a hand again.

Caitlyn's heart lurched. "No, no, no...!" she said, pushing frantically through the crowd to reach the podium.

"Dearie me, that girl is worse than a kraken in a teashop," muttered Viktor, trotting after her. "She can never curb her impulses..."

People turned and looked at them in surprise, the crowd's expressions sobering as they saw the genuine concern on Caitlyn's face. They stepped back hurriedly, opening a path to the podium, and Caitlyn arrived just as Bertha stepped forwards and put a hand on her younger sister's arm.

"Tara—that's enough," she said, her voice firm but calm, like a mother cutting off a toddler mid-tantrum.

Tara hesitated, her eyes flashing, and it looked for a moment as if she would lash out at Bertha too. Then, to Caitlyn's relief, she shook off her older sister's hand and took a step back. Folding her arms, Tara gave Leandra another sneering look and said:

"You're too pathetic to even bother with anyway... and you're a total hypocrite too! Acting all noble and self-righteous, when in reality you're nothing but a common thief!"

Leandra bristled. "What do you mean?"

"Don't pretend you don't know what I'm talking about! Just now, by the terrace—you assaulted my daughter and stole the *grimoire* from her."

A gasp rose from the crowd at the word "assault" and people began to look even more uncertain. James turned rapidly to search for Caitlyn, his grey eyes anxious. Then he saw her standing beneath the podium and his shoulders relaxed. He made to move towards her but was stopped by Leandra saying in outraged tones:

"I didn't assault anybody! I have no idea *what* you

are talking about. I haven't got the *grimoire*."

"Liar!" snarled Tara. "You've been scheming to get your hands on that book ever since you arrived at Huntingdon Manor. Don't deny it! You might talk about your scholarly knowledge and academic credentials... blah-blah-blah... but really, you're just a witch wannabe! You thought that if you got hold of the *grimoire*, you'd be able to learn magic. Well, good luck with that! The *grimoire* is for those who have the *real* ability to cast spells, and you're not worthy of—"

"I have more right to that *grimoire,* missy, than anyone else! Because without me, it wouldn't even exist today," hissed Leandra.

Tara stopped, momentarily nonplussed. "What do you mean?"

"*I* was the one who contacted your witch-hunter lover and told him that his superiors at the Society had lied to him, that they weren't planning to *study* the *grimoire*, as they had told him—they were planning to destroy it!" Leandra gave Tara a condescending look. "I can't believe you actually trusted the Society and thought they would support your dream of a joint witch-government alliance. Well, I suppose one can't expect much from a child like you, but I would have thought that your lover, at least, would have known better. But he was just as naïve as you were."

"Noah wasn't naïve!" cried Tara, furious tears springing to her eyes. "He was brave... and brilliant...

and he believed in a better world where witches weren't hunted and persecuted, a world where we could teach people not to fear magic and the supernatural—"

"He was an idealistic fool," said Leandra. "If *I* hadn't warned him, he would never have been able to rescue the *grimoire* in time, and you would never have been able to escape the Society and go on the run. You should be *thanking* me."

Tara frowned. "You're lying. Noah never mentioned your name. I would have remembered—"

"That's because he knew me as Carla Dowlenook," said Leandra impatiently. "An anagram of my real name. It was my alias when I started working with the Society as a consultant on occult matters. Yes, that's right: the Society wanted to have people on their side who had an understanding of magic too. And when they called me in to confirm the validity of the *grimoire*, I rejoiced at first, thinking that here, at last, was the chance to perform a definitive study of a witch's *grimoire*, a real 'book of spells'! But then, to my horror, I realised that the Society had no scholarly intentions. They didn't want to study what they did not understand—they wanted to destroy it! That's when I decided that I had to do anything I could to save the book so that it could be preserved for further study." Leandra's eyes glowed. "Think what the research and analysis of this book could mean for the field of occultism, how wonderful it would be to have this *grimoire* enshrined in a museum—"

"A museum?" said Tara indignantly. "The *grimoire* isn't a tourist attraction for the public to gawp over! It belongs to my family—it's mine by right!"

"No, it's *mine* by right, since I saved it!" retorted Leandra.

"Neither of you are entitled to the *grimoire*," said a familiar voice. "The book belongs to me."

Caitlyn whirled to see the crowd part like the Red Sea before an old woman who hobbled slowly forwards to join them. The Widow Mags might have been hunched over with age and arthritis, her skin wrinkled and her hair grey, but her dark eyes still flashed with as much fire as Tara's, and she didn't need flamboyant spells to assert her authority. Several people began to clap and cheer as the old witch walked past them, obviously still believing that this was all part of an elaborate performance.

"Mother..." said Tara, her bravado faltering for the first time. For a moment, she seemed suddenly smaller and younger, then a defiant look came over her face and she raised her chin. "I suppose you've come to lecture me."

Before the Widow Mags could reply, another voice rang out in the air, shrill and gleeful:

"None of you have any right to the *grimoire* because the book is *mine* now!"

There was a ripple of excitement in the crowd and people craned their necks, standing on tiptoe, to see who had shouted. A few even cheered again, thinking that this was an exciting new addition to the "show". Vera Bottom stepped out from the crowd, holding something above her head, and Caitlyn caught her breath as she saw that it was a slim leather-bound volume.

She cursed herself as she recalled Vera brandishing an herb charm and chanting: "*Vervain, trefoil, Saint John's wort, dill... Hinder witches of their will!*" When she had smelled the scents of vervain and dill, her mind had immediately jumped to Leandra—but she had forgotten that another woman had also been wielding herb charms; a woman who hated witches with an all-consuming passion.

Now Vera walked towards the bonfires, her expression triumphant. "Yes, *I* have your book of witch knowledge... and I'm going to destroy it, so that you don't have your evil powers anymore! The bonfires of Samhain are meant to purify and purge, aren't they?" She held up the *grimoire* towards the flames. "Well, they can cleanse Tillyhenge of your filthy magic!"

"Wait, Vera—what are you doing?" cried Jeremy Bottom, dropping Ferdinand's halter and rushing towards his sister.

"No!" gasped Leandra, jumping down from the podium and running towards the other woman. "You can't burn that book!"

"Vera, please!" cried Caitlyn, rushing towards Vera as well.

James sprang down from the podium too, his long

legs taking him quickly past the women, but as he approached, Vera screamed:

"S-stop! Get back!" She waved the *grimoire* wildly in front of her as she spun left and right, trying to face everyone surrounding her. "Don't come any closer or I'll throw it into the fire!"

# CHAPTER THIRTY-FIVE

A hushed silence fell over the crowd as everyone watched Vera in anxious bewilderment, many beginning to wonder if the scene wasn't a performance after all.

James took a slow step forwards, his hands outstretched and his voice soothing, as if talking to a frightened horse. "Vera... don't do anything rash... Why don't you give me the book—I'll keep it safe for you—and we'll go into the Manor and have a talk about all this?"

His gentle tone and calm, unthreatening manner must have cut through her rising panic. Vera wavered, her face softening and her hand beginning to lower away from the bonfire.

James gave her an understanding smile. "I know you're scared, and I know how hard it must have been for you lately... I give you my word, Vera, that I will listen to any grievances you may have and do everything in my power to make things right for you.

Just hand me that book now... and we'll go in, and I'll get Mrs Pruett to make you a nice cup of tea—"

Tara made an impatient noise from the podium and shouted: "I'll make it easy for you, you stupid shrew! Hand over that book now or I'll hex you until your eyeballs roll out the back of your head!"

"*Tara!*" said Bertha reproachfully.

Caitlyn groaned, wanting to throttle her mother. Vera had almost placed the *grimoire* into James's outstretched hands, but at Tara's words, she flinched and snatched it back, then turned determinedly towards the bonfires.

"No, no, you can't destroy that book—" gasped Leandra, launching herself forwards.

She tackled Vera, trying to wrench the *grimoire* from her grasp, but Vera fought like a caged animal, yelling and thrashing. Then—before Leandra could stop her—Vera pulled her arm free and tossed the *grimoire* straight at the fire.

Caitlyn sucked a breath in, feeling time slow down as she watched the leather-bound volume sail overhead, in a wide arc, towards the blazing flames of the nearest bonfire.

"*Nooooo!*" screeched Leandra.

"No!" shouted James

"NOOOO!" screamed Tara furiously from the podium. She flung out a hand, pointing at the flying *grimoire*, and intoned: "*IGNIS INTERCEPTUM!*"

Next to her, Caitlyn felt a sudden rush of movement, and she jerked her head around in surprise to see Viktor leaping up into the air, both arms outstretched, like a geriatric goalkeeper diving for a football. Her mouth dropped open, unable to believe that such an old man could leap so high— then she realised that Viktor was transforming in midair, his body compressing and shrinking, his arms spreading into leathery bat wings, his head morphing into that of a fuzzy brown fruit bat.

He swooped and dived for the *grimoire*, trying to grab it in his tiny claws before it fell into the fire. But just as he reached the book, a zigzag of shimmering light sliced through the air, aiming for the *grimoire* as well.

The little bat squeaked in alarm and flapped his wings wildly, attempting to swerve, but it was too late. Caitlyn screamed in horror as she saw Viktor hit by the jagged pulse of light, and the night exploded with fiery incandescence…

Then the little fruit bat plummeted from the sky.

The *grimoire* bounced sideways, thrown off-course by the shockwave from the spell, and sailed through the air to land several feet away. But Caitlyn barely spared the book a glance as she rushed to where the fruit bat lay motionless on the ground.

"Oh my God, Viktor… Viktor…?" she sobbed, picking up the limp little body and cradling it close to her chest.

Her hands shaking, Caitlyn felt desperately for a heartbeat in the small furry chest, her own heart clenching in despair as she felt nothing. "No, no…

Viktor... *please...*"

Tara appeared next to her, her eyes wide, her face a mask of dismay. "I... it was an accident," she stammered. "I didn't mean to hit Viktor... I was trying to save the *grimoire,* but he flew in so fast—"

Caitlyn ignored her mother, concentrating all her efforts on trying to find a heartbeat, a pulse, anything. Her hands moved frantically over the limp body of the fruit bat, stroking the drooping leathery wings, touching the tiny slack claws. *No, no, Viktor can't be gone! There has to be a way to revive him! Can one do CPR on a bat? Or mouth-to-mouth?*

Then Caitlyn became aware of an intense heat around her. Screams and shouts rent the air, and she looked up with shocked eyes to see that the bonfires had become twin roaring infernos, blazing with a seething ferocity that went far beyond any normal fire. The backlash from Tara's misfired spell, which had thrown the *grimoire* sideways, must have also spilled into the bonfires, supercharging them with magical force. The already-blazing flames had been whipped into a fiery maelstrom which reached out with almost demonic intent, trying to burn and consume everything in its path.

The crowd screamed and scattered, running in every direction, fuelled by pure panic. Caitlyn felt the skin on her face puckering from the searing heat, her eyes smarting and blurring. Then she felt someone grab her elbow and haul her roughly to her feet.

"Caitlyn! Come on... you can't stay there!"

It was James, his tall frame shielding her from the heat of the flames as he pulled her along with him. She clutched Viktor's limp little bat body to her chest and stumbled alongside him, running into the crowd. People were yelling and pushing, falling onto each other and lashing out in panic as fear began to turn the crush into a stampede.

Caitlyn glanced back and saw that Tara was a few steps behind them; she looked frantically around for Bertha and the Widow Mags, wanting to make sure that they were safe as well...

Then her heart nearly stopped as she saw her grandmother walking *towards* the flames. *What is she doing?* She stumbled to a stop and was about to rush towards the old witch when James caught her arm.

"Let me go!" she panted, trying to pull free. "I need to save her—"

"Wait, Caitlyn—look!" he said, pointing.

Caitlyn turned and saw that the flames were receding before the Widow Mags, like waves rearing back from an imposing rock cliff. They snapped and crackled angrily, sending out greedy tongues of fire, still trying to devour what they could, but the Widow Mags would raise a hand each time, and the flames would quiver and jerk back, as if burned, themselves.

Then Caitlyn saw Bertha and Tara pause and look at each other. With sudden purpose, they turned and walked to join their mother. Taking stances on either side of the Widow Mags, they each raised their arms and unleashed their own magic. The fire shrank back even more and began retreating.

A lump rose in Caitlyn's throat. She watched the three witches—her mother, aunt, and grandmother—working as one, melding their powers in graceful unity. It was a moment that she wanted to hold in her heart forever.

Then the scene was rudely shattered by a new round of screaming. Caitlyn jerked around at the sound of heavy hooves and frantic snorts and grunts. She gasped to see Ferdinand charging through the crowd, his eyes wild and terrified, his horns slashing left and right as he tossed his head in a frenzy. People shrieked, scrambling to get out of his way, tripping over their own feet and shoving each other haphazardly.

"Ferdinand!" came Jeremy's hoarse voice as the dairy farmer ran desperately after the bull. "Stop!"

But the bull was beyond recall, his usually placid nature completely subsumed by the primal fear of fire that blinded him to everything. He gave a guttural bellow and charged straight at a group of children who were stumbling along the path in front of him.

# CHAPTER THIRTY-SIX

James shouted in alarm and let go of Caitlyn's elbow, hurling himself at the group of children.

*"James!"* cried Caitlyn, her eyes widening in terror. There was no way he could reach the children in time without being trampled himself.

She turned to face the oncoming bull, her heart pounding. She had no time to think consciously about what to do—she could only go on instinct. She shut her eyes and reached inside herself, gathering all her will... then she projected it outwards, directly at the charging bull. She could feel Ferdinand's panic and fear, raw and pulsating, and she was almost overwhelmed by the sheer force of his frenzied terror. But she took a shaky breath and imagined it softening, melting, pooling over his body and around his feet, just like a puddle of glossy, melted chocolate...

Caitlyn opened her eyes and looked straight at the bull. He was still coming towards her, but his steps were slowing. His gallop became a faltering trot, then a lurching walk, until finally, he stopped before her, his chest heaving.

"Ferdinand...?" said Caitlyn, putting out a hand hesitantly.

The bull gave a deep bellow and tossed his head, showing the whites of his eyes, but Caitlyn held her ground.

"Shh, sweetie... it's all right," she crooned, taking a step towards him and stretching closer. "It's all right, Ferdie..." She put a tentative hand on his neck and stroked soothingly.

Ferdinand gave a great sigh, dropping his head, and nestled his quivering muzzle into the palm of her other hand. His huge body was still shuddering and shivering, and his flanks were drenched with sweat—but his eyes were no longer wild. They were dark and limpid, and he looked at her with a familiar doleful sweetness as he said: "*MOOO...*"

"Oh my God, Caitlyn—I don't know how you did it... but *thank you*," gasped Jeremy, coming up beside her and grabbing Ferdinand's head halter. He turned to the bull and put a gentle hand up to Ferdinand's head. "You big wally—what were you thinking? Thank goodness you didn't hurt anyone..."

As the farmer led Ferdinand away, Caitlyn looked anxiously around for James. She drew a breath of relief as she spotted him a few feet away, gently helping a child to his feet. Then she realised that people were no longer running and screaming, and the clamour of fear and panic was dying down. In fact, everyone seemed to be staring in the direction of the bonfires, their eyes wide with awe.

Caitlyn turned to look for herself and saw Bertha, Tara, and the Widow Mags standing in a circle around the bonfires, which had shrunk down into two smouldering piles of ash. All around her, she could hear murmurs of wonder and astonishment:

"Did you see that...?"

"It were magic, weren't it?"

"I saw her walk straight into the fire!"

"I *told* you they were witches..."

"It was amazing, I tell you—straight out of a fairy tale, that was!"

"They saved us...!"

But Caitlyn barely listened as she walked slowly towards her mother, grandmother and aunt. She was watching, her heart in her mouth, as Tara and the Widow Mags turned towards each other and faced each other properly for the first time. There was silence as they stared at each other. Two pairs of flashing dark eyes, two sets of stubborn chins, two women so alike in pride and defiance.

Then... a softening of the shoulders... a quiver of the lips...

"M-Mother?" said Tara in a gruff voice. "I... I'm sorry—"

The Widow Mags pulled her youngest daughter into her arms. Tara made a muffled sound and threw her own arms around her mother's neck, holding her tight. Bertha watched them, tears in her eyes but a smile on her lips. Nobody spoke for a long moment. Even the crowd watched with hushed respect, feeling unbearably moved by something they didn't quite understand.

At last, the Widow Mags sighed and released Tara. She stepped back and was about to speak when her eyes fell on Caitlyn, standing forlornly a few feet away, clutching the inert form of the little fruit bat in her arms.

The old witch drew in a sharp breath and said: "Viktor—?"

"You can save him, can't you?" asked Caitlyn, her eyes pleading, as the Widow Mags hurried over. She held up the limp little body. "He... he was hit by Tara's spell... but I'm sure he'll be fine... he just needs a healing charm—"

"Caitlyn," said the Widow Mags gently. "Viktor is beyond the help of any healing spell charm."

"N-no!" cried Caitlyn, her voice breaking. "No, he's not. Viktor's a vampire! He has amazing powers of regeneration—he told me so himself! He just needs a bit of help... *please...*" She gulped back a sob. "I know you can do it, Grandma... *Please!*"

The Widow Mags shook her head sadly. "He is gone, Caitlyn. There is only one way to bring Viktor back now, and that is to call him back from the dead."

"Well... you can do that, can't you?" asked Caitlyn desperately. "I know you can! You have magic powers beyond anything anyone can imagine! I've seen you conjure the most amazing things; you can do anything you set your mind to!"

The Widow Mags sighed. "Yes, I can do many things, but not this. Resurrection requires powerful spells that tap into Dark Magic, and that is a type of witchcraft which I cannot invoke... I'm sorry, but I cannot do as you ask. I cannot bring the dead back to life."

"But I can."

Caitlyn whirled to see Tara stepping forwards. Her mother looked different somehow—solemn, subdued, with her usual air of aggressive confidence missing—but her face was pale and determined.

"Tara, stop!" said Bertha, hurrying after her. "Do you realise what you're saying? Dark Magic always requires a price, and for something as powerful as a Resurrection spell, that will be more than—"

"*I* will pay the price," said Tara with a spark of her old arrogance. "I shall beset no one but myself."

She held a hand out to Caitlyn. "Take my hand and hold it tightly... and keep your other hand on Viktor's heart."

Caitlyn hesitated and Tara said, with a ghost of her familiar cocky smile: "Trust me. I'm your mother."

Slowly, Caitlyn lifted one hand and placed it in Tara's outstretched one.

"Good... now, whatever happens, *do not let go,*" said Tara. She gave Caitlyn a wink and added, low:

"I'm glad all that practice is finally going to be put to use."

Then she began to chant softly—strange syllables and intonations that Caitlyn had never heard before, rolling vowels interspersed with sharp consonants, the arcane phonemes of a powerful, forbidden spell in a language lost to time. Tara's voice rose, becoming almost a single, sonorous crescendo where each word thrummed with magic. A glow seemed to light within her. It flowed down her arm into Caitlyn's hand, and Caitlyn felt a shock of sensation that was simultaneously hot and cold, burning and tingling. The glow travelled through her and out her other arm, down to where her hand lay over the fruit bat's heart, and she caught her breath as she watched it spread over the limp little body.

For a moment, nothing happened... and then Caitlyn felt something shift in the pulse of magic flowing through her body. She looked up at her mother, alarmed, and gasped to see Tara changing before her eyes: the bloom of youth leaving her cheeks, the vigour seeping from her body. Creases appeared at the corners of her eyes, hollows under her cheeks, and the radiance of her skin dulled and faded, leaving blemishes and fine lines. Her shoulders rounded, the lithe young body stiffening and thickening, the lush mane of red hair thinning and drying.

Caitlyn cried out and recoiled, instinctively trying to pull her hand out of Tara's grasp, but her mother tightened her grip, her eyes burning with resolve. She bent her head and chanted even faster. The brilliant aura grew and grew until the incantation seemed to envelop them in a glowing bubble of magic.

And then it burst in a shower of light. Caitlyn fell back, gasping, blinded for a moment. Her mother released her hand and also staggered backwards.

"Tara... *Mum!*"

"I'm... I'm all right," said Tara, panting slightly. She waved Caitlyn away in a gesture that brought the Widow Mags vividly to mind. "I'm fine! Stop fussing!"

Behind them, they suddenly heard a tetchy voice say: "Anyone seen my fangs? Seem to have lost them mid-flight. Thought they were feeling a bit loose and jiggly this morning... Confounded garlic, that will be my third pair this year! I really need to find a better dentist."

Caitlyn whirled to see a stooped, balding old man in a dusty black suit standing where the little fruit bat had been, feeling his jaw with his long, bony fingers and grumbling to himself.

"Ohhh... *Viktor!*" she cried, throwing her arms around his neck, laughing and crying at the same time. "You're alive!"

"Eh? Of course I'm alive." Viktor fished an ancient lace handkerchief, stiff and yellowed with age, out of his jacket pocket and thrust it at Caitlyn. "What in the blazes are you blubbering for?"

# CHAPTER THIRTY-SEVEN

"Omigod, I can't believe I missed everything! You mean, like, Vera stole the *grimoire*... and Tara whipped Leandra's butt with magic... and the Widow Mags tamed a monster fire... and James saved a child's life... and you cast a spell on Ferdinand... and Tara brought Viktor back from the dead... and I missed it *all?*"

Caitlyn tried not to laugh at Pomona's woebegone face. "I'm sorry, Pomie! I wanted to come and rescue you as soon as I heard what Tara had done to you, but then things started happening so fast, one after the other, that I just didn't have the time... If it's any consolation, it's a lot nicer *hearing* about what happened than actually *being* there. Trust me, facing a charging bull or being trampled by a panicking crowd isn't as cool as it sounds. And that awful moment when I thought Viktor had been killed by the **Ignis Interceptum** spell..." She shuddered at the memory. "I never want to go through that again."

"Yeah, that sounded pretty awful," agreed Pomona, sobering. Then she brightened. "But he's fine now, right?"

"Yes, he's back to his old, crotchety, fruit-mad self," said Caitlyn with a wry smile. "He's gone off somewhere now, searching for his lost fangs, as usual."

Pomona shook her head. "You know, I wanted to be mad at Tara for hexing me, but I guess she's redeemed herself with this whole resurrection thing. I mean, if she hadn't stepped up, Viktor would have died for sure, and, jeez, talk about paying a big price!"

"I know. I just don't understand my mother sometimes," said Caitlyn, shaking her head. "She can be so arrogantly thoughtless and unprincipled and even ruthless... and yet she can offer herself up in the most selfless of sacrifices without even pausing to think. Like giving up her time in this world to protect me when I was a baby or offering her own health and youth to save Viktor."

"It's like she exists at the two extremes, with nothing in between. You kinda want to hate her... but you can't help admiring her too," said Pomona with a grin. "But, man, did she really just, like, age in front of your eyes?"

Caitlyn nodded. "It was so surreal, Pomie. Like watching a time-lapse video of someone going from teenage to menopause or something." She paused, then gave Pomona a shamefaced smile. "It sounds a bit mean saying this, but I'm selfishly glad, in a way, because now at least she looks more like my mother. It was just too weird before when my 'mother' was a teenager younger than me!"

"Where is she now? I'd really like to meet her."

"She's gone back to Tillyhenge with Bertha and the Widow Mags. They left just after the ambulance and paramedics had gone, and the visitors had all been sent home—"

"Were there a lot of injuries?" asked Pomona, aghast.

"No, thank goodness! Which is a miracle, really, considering how panicked everyone was. There were a couple of cuts, scrapes, and bruises, of course, but nothing serious. In fact, I think poor Lisa is in the worst state. She looks like she's going to have a nervous breakdown from worrying about the bad publicity for the Manor."

"It's all over social media already, isn't it?" said Pomona, making a face.

Caitlyn nodded ruefully. "Everywhere. I think I even saw a reporter and camera crew turn up just as the ambulance was leaving, so it'll be all over the standard media channels soon too."

"No wonder Bertha, Tara, and the Widow Mags wanted to sneak away. Still, I wish they stuck around. I really wanted to meet your mother," Pomona pouted.

Caitlyn gave her a soothing smile. "Don't worry, Pomie, you'll meet her soon enough. We've all been invited to *Bewitched by Chocolate* for a special dinner later at midnight—"

"Ooh, are we going to have a 'dumb supper'?" asked Pomona eagerly. "I've always wanted to attend one of those."

"What's a dumb supper?"

"Caitlyn!" Pomona rolled her eyes in exasperation. "You're, like, a disgrace as a witch! You might be able to do awesome spells and all, but you're really crap when it comes to magical knowledge. Maybe you should get some private tutoring with Leandra," she suggested with a grin.

Caitlyn groaned. "Don't even joke about that. If I never have to hear another lecture about Samhain again, it'll be too soon! Actually, I overheard the staff gossiping earlier and it seems that Leandra is packing up and going back to London."

"You mean... we're not going to enjoy any more sermons about 'correct magical procedure'?" asked Pomona, clutching her chest in an expression of mock dismay.

Caitlyn giggled, then she sobered and said, "You know, I feel a bit sorry for Leandra—"

"You're kidding!" exclaimed Pomona. "Caitlyn, that woman nearly got the *grimoire* destroyed! If she hadn't done a dumb thing like jumping on Vera, then maybe Vera wouldn't have thrown the *grimoire* into the fire and Tara wouldn't have used that freaky spell and the bonfires wouldn't have gone berserk and Viktor wouldn't have nearly gotten killed—"

"Yes, but Leandra was also the one who saved the *grimoire* in the first place, all those years ago," Caitlyn pointed out. "Without her, it would have been destroyed by the Society."

"I guess..." said Pomona grudgingly. "I still think she's a sanctimonious loudmouth who loves the sound of her own voice and thinks she's the queen of smart-ass mountain, though. And I don't care what you say—" she added, holding up a hand as Caitlyn started to protest, "—messing with people's heads and scaring them silly, just to make herself feel important, is pretty skanky."

"But maybe she really believed in what she said—"

Pomona made a rude noise. Then, dismissing the subject of Leandra with a wave of her hand, she added: "Anyway, the important thing is that the *grimoire* is safe now, right?"

Caitlyn gave a relieved sigh. "Yes. It's back where it belongs, with the Widow Mags."

Pomona chuckled. "I'll bet Tara's gonna start pestering her about it soon enough, and then they'll be butting heads again!"

"Oh God, don't say that, Pomie!" Caitlyn groaned. "I was hoping that after what happened today, and after all these years apart, things might have changed between them. Oh Pomie, I wish you could've seen that moment when they were all standing together! The Widow Mags, Bertha, and Tara, all working to fight the monster fire... It was

incredible! It gave me goosebumps watching them."
She smiled wistfully. "Surely an experience like that
would change everything? And Tara is older now,
more mature, so maybe they'll learn to get along—"

"You sure she's older on the *inside* as well as the
outside?" asked Pomona doubtfully. "Anyway, that
was in a crisis. People can be, like, their best selves
in a crisis, but once it's all over and you get back to
'real life'... I don't know... leopards don't change their
spots, right? I think you're stuck with the personality
you've got. Like, oil is oil and water is water, and the
two just don't mix. Especially when you heat things
up," she added with an impish smile. "That's when
things start spluttering and exploding in the pan!"

Caitlyn looked at Pomona in surprise. It wasn't
like her cousin to be so cynical.

"What?" said Pomona, giving a shrug. "Hey, I like
to be realistic." Then, seeing Caitlyn's crestfallen
expression, Pomona gave her a contrite look. "Oh
honey, I didn't mean to burst your bubble! Look, I
could be totally wrong. I mean, I'm *never* wrong—"
She grinned. "—but you know, there's always a first
time. Anyway, why don't you forget it all for now and
just enjoy the dumb supper tonight?"

"What *is* a dumb supper, anyway?" asked Caitlyn
curiously.

"It's, like, this old Celtic tradition on Samhain Eve.
Basically, you all sit down for a meal that honours
the dead—'cos, you know, the veil between the
worlds is supposed to be much thinner during

Samhain, and so you can communicate with departed spirits a lot easier."

"So you just sit and eat together and that's it?"

"No, you gotta eat the whole meal in silence! That's why it's called 'dumb', see? And there are also other cool rules, like laying an extra place at the table for the spirits to come and join you, and having all the cutlery positions reversed and all the crockery in black. Oh, and you gotta serve the meal back-to-front—you know, like dessert first and starters last, because doing everything backwards symbolises the spirits returning from the Otherworld to this one. I've even heard some people wear masks while they're eating, so that their identities remain secret. It's so that evil spirits can't recognise you." Pomona giggled and rubbed her hands with relish. "Oooh, I can't wait to see what we do tonight!"

She sprang up from her bed and hurried over to the wardrobe. "What are you going to wear? I think black would be good—"

"Wait, Pomie, I've just thought of something," said Caitlyn, standing up as well with some agitation. "Hosey Houdini—we've totally forgotten about him! We need to put him somewhere safe so he doesn't escape again. I just hope he's still in that shed by the terrace." She hurried over to the bedroom door. "C'mon, can you help me?"

Pomona groaned. "All I've done this whole weekend is schlep around the estate looking for that darned piece of rubber piping!"

Caitlyn gave her a teasing smile. "I thought you said he was cute and you wanted to keep him as a pet."

Still grumbling, Pomona joined her at the door. But as they were stepping out, she stopped and snapped her fingers. "Hang on! We're forgetting the Ælfpoca. Good thing I never returned it to the occult collection in the Portrait Gallery, huh?"

She hurried back into the room and rummaged in her bedside drawer, then returned with something in the palm of her hand. It was a tiny drawstring pouch made of soft deerskin, its opening secured with leather ties.

"Behold the Ælfpoca."

Caitlyn looked at it doubtfully. "That doesn't look big enough to fit a pair of earrings."

"That's the whole point! That's why it's called an 'elf pouch'. It has fairy magic so it can expand inside to fit anything, but the outside remains tiny enough to slip into your pocket. What? Don't roll your eyes at me!" Pomona said indignantly. "Jeez, Caitlyn, for a witch, you sure aren't open-minded about magic!"

Caitlyn dipped her head, chastised. "Sorry, Pomie. It's just... it sounds so improbable, like the kind of thing you read about in books as a child. You know, like Mary Poppins's carpetbag or something."

Pomona gave her a sarcastic look. "Yeah, and a garden hose that thinks it's a python is totally realistic, huh?"

"You're right," said Caitlyn, giving her a penitent

smile. "Well, I suppose we'll see if it works soon enough."

Luckily, when they arrived at the shed, they found Hosey Houdini still fast asleep.

"Thank goodness he's still here!" said Caitlyn, letting out a breath of relief. Then she thought of something and added: "You know, we should really let Inspector Walsh know that Hosey Houdini swallowed the *grimoire* and that's why his constable couldn't find it in the old well. It would back up Benedict's story and help him get off a murder charge. Although I don't know *how* we're going to explain it—I mean, Inspector Walsh is so dismissive about magic. We'll never convince him that..."

She trailed off as she realised that Pomona wasn't listening. Her cousin was bending over the bewitched garden hose, which had its brass connector end tucked under one rubber loop, like a bird tucking its head under a wing.

"Aww... he looks so cute," Pomona cooed, reaching out to stroke his rubbery coils.

Hosey Houdini raised his head sluggishly. "*Ss-sss...?*" he lisped, dribbling amber liquid from the brass connector.

"Wow, he really went to town on that mulled cider, huh?" said Pomona as the sweet aroma of cinnamon, cloves, and citrus, mixed with the heavy reek of alcohol, filled the shed.

"He guzzled the whole cauldron," said Caitlyn dryly. "But I suppose it was a hidden blessing. It kept him sleeping here instead of slithering off."

"Oh good—he'll be easier to get into the Ælfpoca if he's dopey," said Pomona, lifting the pouch in her hands. She pulled the drawstrings open and reached down to grasp one of the loops.

"*Sss-ssssss!*" said Hosey Houdini, weaving his brass connector head back and forth like a snake.

"Oh, hold still..." Pomona muttered, concentrating on trying to shove the other end of the hose into the pouch.

But it was just too large. No matter how much she tried to stretch the pouch's opening or force the end in, she just couldn't fit the hose into the soft cavity.

"If you can't even get Hosey Houdini's tail in, how are you going to fit his whole body?" asked Caitlyn, watching askance.

Pomona shot her an accusing look. "It's you. Your negativity is messing things up. Remember how the Widow Mags said magic only works if you believe? Well, your 'un-believing' is, like, jinxing things. You should be *helping* with your witch powers, not making it more difficult."

Caitlyn started to argue, then swallowed her words. Maybe Pomona was right. Her cousin's belief in the Ælfpoca might have sounded crazy, but surely it wasn't crazier than many of the other things that she'd seen since arriving in Tillyhenge? Reading glasses that flew like giant butterflies, a cauldron that stirred itself, an enchanted folly tower that could summon vampire bats—not to mention Hosey

Houdini himself, of course! A bewitched garden hose that thought it was a snake. Magic had surprised her countless times and challenged her preconceptions. Why was she still so sceptical?

Trying to quash her feelings of doubt and incredulity, Caitlyn took a deep breath, shut her eyes and prepared to summon a spell. But before she could do anything, she heard a gasp of delight and opened her eyes to see Pomona watching in wonder as the garden hose began sliding smoothly into the pouch. Coil after coil, he wound himself into the drawstring gap until, with a final flick of mulled cider droplets, he disappeared, and the leather ties pulled tight. Pomona stared down at the tiny drawstring bag in her palm, now round and full like a little pumpkin. It looked so innocuous and ordinary, with only a slight iridescent shimmer along a fold of deerskin giving its magical credentials away.

"Omigod—did you see that?" she cried, jumping up and down with excitement. "That was me! I made that happen" She squealed with elation, her face flushed. "I did it! I worked magic!"

Caitlyn looked at Pomona, dumbfounded. "You... you worked magic?"

"Yeah! I was, like, focusing really hard on the Ælfpoca, right, and imagining Hosey Houdini sliding into the opening, and then... it happened! Just like how I believed it would!" She looked at Caitlyn triumphantly. "You see? You were wrong: people don't have to be born a witch; they *can* gain magic later."

"But—"

"Oh no, wait! I have another idea!" Pomona cried. "Maybe the magic was in me all along! You said some people have latent magical ability inside them, right? Maybe I *am* a witch, but I just never realised it... you know, like how some girls don't grow their boobs until late in their teens—yeah, I'm just, like, a late developer!"

Caitlyn started to protest again, then she stopped, looking at Pomona's flushed face and shining eyes. She had never seen her cousin look so happy. *Besides*, she thought, *could Pomona be right? Could she have really worked the necessary magic for the Ælfpoca?* It was true that Caitlyn herself hadn't done anything, and the pouch had been inert and ineffectual only a few minutes ago, so the only explanation...

"Don't you think it's awesome?" said Pomona, beaming at her. "We can be witches together!"

Pushing her doubts away, Caitlyn returned her smile. "Oh Pomie... I've always said that if anyone deserves to be a witch, it's you."

"Omigod, I've gotta, like, get a whole new wardrobe to fit my new witch identity! Definitely more black. Shoes with buckles are so 'in' right now. Gotta be careful though. Don't wanna end up at the Baba Yaga end of witch style—no offence to the Widow Mags—but yeah, something way cooler, like neo-Goth, maybe, with that dark aesthetic... mmm...

black lipstick and fishnets..." Pomona's eyes glazed over as she wandered out of the shed and began walking dreamily away. "Ooh, and accessories! I've gotta get a black leather choker... and do you think they do broomsticks in hot pink...?"

# CHAPTER THIRTY-EIGHT

By the time they got to *Bewitched by Chocolate* later that evening, it was close to midnight. But despite the late hour, the Widow Mags's cottage was humming with activity. Even from the top of the lane, they could see the golden glow of light spilling out of the open door and windows and hear the hubbub of talk and laughter. Gazing at the cottage windows, Caitlyn was startled to see the silhouettes of several people milling about. She had thought that they were coming for a small family meal, but it looked like half the village had been invited!

"Holy guacamole, looks like there's a freakin' party!" whooped Pomona, quickening her steps. "Isn't that Jeremy Bottom? And there's Chris with Evie... oh, and I can see Mosley and Vanessa—man, I hope she hasn't brought those snooty friends of hers... Hey! There's that young mother from the village, the one with the little girl who was taken hostage during that garden party and then the

Widow Mags rescued her with those awesome chocolate butterflies—"

Pomona broke off, sniffing in an exaggerated manner. "Omigod, can you smell that? It's, like, the best thing I've ever smelled... in my life... ever!"

The American girl rushed ahead and disappeared through the cottage's open door. Caitlyn followed more slowly, laughing softly at her cousin's enthusiasm. It was true that the most wonderful, rich aroma of chocolate was wafting out of the cottage: dark and decadent, sweet and heavenly, with a hint of buttery caramel. It reminded her of the first time she'd arrived at the doorway of the chocolate shop and how she had stood, just like this, inhaling deeply and feeling her mouth begin to water. She could almost taste the rich, creamy confectionery melting on her tongue.

But when she walked into the cottage, the sense of déjà vu was broken. Gone was the empty shop and the dark, dusty interior with its peeling paint and faded furniture that she had encountered on her first day in Tillyhenge. Instead, she was met by gleaming glass counters, freshly painted cabinets bulging with chocolate treats, and a warm atmosphere of twinkling lights and laughter as she found herself suddenly surrounded by friendly faces.

Mingling happily with the residents of Tillyhenge were several of the Huntingdon Manor staff, including Mrs Pruett, James's PA Amy Matthews, Mosley, Lisa and the rest of the marketing team.

Everyone was sipping from glasses of elderberry wine or ginger beer and chatting merrily—except for Mosley, who stood clutching his glass, eying the room with a slightly tormented look. Caitlyn wondered at his expression; the butler almost looked as if he were longing to walk around with a tray serving drinks!

On the other side of the room, James and Vanessa were chatting to Evie and Chris, and Caitlyn was delighted to see the two girls giggling together. Vanessa might have been several years older than Evie in age, but somehow, with her childlike temperament and ingenuous manner, she seemed a perfect match for the younger girl. As Caitlyn headed towards them, their voices drifted across the room, and Caitlyn heard Vanessa say to Evie:

"Oh, you must come riding with me sometime! Don't worry, I'll teach you—it's really easy. You just need a gentle pony."

"Thanks, I'd love to!" Evie gave her a shy smile. "I just need to get my recipe for the Gourmet Glory competition finished first."

"What's that?"

"It's..." Evie glanced sideways at Chris, then took a deep breath and said: "It's an annual competition for witches to come up with their own magical recipe."

Chris's blue eyes widened and he turned to Evie, who bit her lip and stared at him anxiously. There was a long moment, then a slow smile spread across

Chris's face. He reached out quietly, out of sight of the other two, and caught one of Evie's hands, lacing their fingers together. Evie blushed bright red and looked for a moment as if she might faint. Then she broke into a tremulous smile, her face glowing with happiness.

"Can you really do magic?" asked Vanessa in a hushed voice, oblivious to what was going on between Chris and Evie. She glanced at her brother. "James told me about Caitlyn—it's so amazing! Are you a witch too?"

"Er..." Evie dragged her attention from Chris back to the other girl. She hesitated, then said with a bashful smile: "Yes, I am... although I can't seem to control magic very well. I keep messing up all my spells," she confessed in a dejected voice.

"Oh, darling, I'm sure it just takes practice. You should have seen me when I first started riding! I was bouncing around like a sack of potatoes!" Vanessa giggled. "And it took me years to win my first blue ribbon in showjumping."

"Really?" said Evie, looking at the other girl in gratitude. "Thanks. Maybe you're right—maybe I just need to practise more."

Caitlyn smiled, thrilled that Evie seemed to have found a new friend in Vanessa, whose sweet, bubbly nature would hopefully do wonders for her young cousin's confidence. She hurried to join them but she hadn't gone a few steps when she nearly tripped on something small, black, and furry attacking her ankles... followed by something huge, fawn-coloured, and furry colliding with her hip. She gasped and stumbled, just managing to regain her balance before she fell over. Turning, she found Bran the English mastiff standing before her, with a little black kitten gambolling about his feet.

"Oh...you two!" said Caitlyn with an exasperated laugh. She bent and picked up the squirming kitten, then smiled at the mastiff, who sat on his haunches with his tongue lolling out and his jowly face pulled back into an expression of doggie contentment. "You're happy to have your little friend back, aren't you, Bran?"

Bran gave a deep bark—the shelves of the cottage shook—and wagged his tail. Then, as Caitlyn set Nibs down on the floor again and the kitten scampered off, the mastiff lumbered happily across the room after his little friend, nearly mowing down two people in the process. Caitlyn chuckled, watching them for a minute, before turning back towards the group she had been heading for. But then she noticed Bertha standing in front of the counter at the rear of the shop, her forehead furrowed in a puzzled frown. She changed direction, going over to join her aunt instead.

"Aunt Bertha—is anything the matter?" she asked.

"Oh... hello dear," said Bertha, looking up distractedly from the miniature cast-iron cauldron which had been placed at one end of the counter. A rich, chocolatey aroma rose from the cauldron, but when Caitlyn glanced inside, she was surprised to see that it was empty, save for a few drops of thick, dark brown liquid which pooled around the ladle.

"I just don't understand it," said Bertha, lifting the empty ladle. "I only brought this cauldron out from the kitchen a few minutes ago and it was full of hot chocolate... but it's completely empty now! I'd forgotten the ladle, so I went back into the kitchen to fetch it, and when I came out, the cauldron was empty." She glanced around the room. "Can people have drunk all the hot chocolate in that short a time?"

Caitlyn started to reply, then paused as her eyes caught sight of a trail of dark brown liquid spilling over the lip of the cauldron and spreading across the counter to disappear over the far edge. She suddenly had a hunch, and when she leaned over the counter to peer into the space behind it, her suspicions were confirmed. Lying in a haphazard jumble in the space between the counter and the wall were several loops of green garden hose, its rubber piping liberally smeared with chocolate.

"Oh God... not again," groaned Caitlyn as the end of the hose rose suddenly, like a periscope, and gave a delicate belch, dribbling some milky chocolate from the brass connecter.

"What on earth is that?" cried Bertha, gaping at the creature.

"Aunt Bertha... meet Hosey Houdini," said Caitlyn

dryly. "He's your hot chocolate thief."

"*Ss-ssss?*" said the bewitched garden hose as he turned towards Bertha. He wriggled the other end of his long body—for all the world like a dog wagging a tail in greeting—and Bertha reached out to pat his brass connector head uncertainly.

"Ohh awesome—you found him!"

Caitlyn turned to see Pomona rushing up to them. "Pomie, I thought you said the Ælfpoca would be secure—"

"It is! I just let Hosey out for a bit. The poor thing's been cooped up in there for hours. I needed to walk him."

Caitlyn restrained the urge to roll her eyes. Then she brightened and said, "Actually, this is good timing. Bertha can help us break the enchantment and change Hosey Houdini back—"

"What? No! You can't do that!" cried Pomona.

Next to them, the garden hose gave a whimper and shrank away, its brass connector head shaking vehemently.

"Pomie, we can't leave him like this—"

"Why not? I'll look after him. I've decided to keep him as my familiar," announced Pomona grandly.

"Your... familiar?" said Bertha, looking at the American girl quizzically.

"Oh yeah, hasn't Caitlyn told you?" said Pomona, beaming. "I'm a witch! I know, I know, I might not give off the right vibe yet, but don't worry, I'm working on my look. Not totally sure what aesthetic to go for yet—by the way, Bertha, do you know if anyone does, like, designer witch hats? Anyway, I *do* know I want something 'different' for my familiar. You know, not a regular cat or toad—so Hosey Houdini is perfect! He's cute and funny and, like, totally unique... aren'tcha, buddy?" She cooed at the garden hose, who gurgled happily and coiled a rubber loop around her shoulders.

Caitlyn started to protest again but as she watched Pomona lovingly coax Hosey Houdini back into the Ælfpoca, she swallowed her words. She felt too mean parting Pomona from her newfound pet, and besides, it seemed cruel to Hosey Houdini as well (she couldn't believe she was saying this about a garden hose!) to turn him back into his original inanimate form. With a resigned shrug, she gave up and watched Pomona saunter happily away, swinging the (now full) Ælfpoca from her fingers.

"Why does Pomona think that she's a witch?" Bertha asked, looking befuddled.

Caitlyn recounted what had happened in the shed. "Do you think it could be true?" she asked as she finished. "Did Pomona really work magic? But how? I thought you had to be born a witch."

"Well, there are different ways to tap into magical ability, dear," said Bertha. "Those who are born witches can access it more easily, but that doesn't mean that others can't find it within themselves to make things happen. After all, magic—as you know— is simply the ability to create change through the force of will."

Caitlyn was silent. She was recalling how the Widow Mags had told her something similar not that long ago, when she had been dumbfounded by a woman claiming to have become pregnant through a scammer's fake "fertility spell". Now, Caitlyn heard her grandmother's voice once again:

"...A witch has a natural ability, which cannot be matched—just as there are great artists like Picasso or Van Gogh who are born with superior artistic talent that cannot be rivalled. But that does not mean that no one else can learn to paint or draw. Everyone has a degree of artistic talent, however small, and everyone can be taught to produce a simple work of art with time, determination, and practice. It is the same with magic. Those who believe can access its powers, even if they are not born a witch... In spite of—in the face of—scepticism from all around her, she held on to her faith. And that creates the most powerful magic of all."

Then she thought of Pomona, doggedly ignoring all the teasing and mockery, and wholeheartedly embracing the mythical power of the Ælfpoca.

"Are you saying that Pomona made magic happen simply because she wanted it badly enough?" she asked Bertha. "But what about Leandra Lockwood then? If all you need is to believe in magic, why isn't Leandra a witch?"

"Ah, but there's a difference," said Bertha with an ironic look. "Pomona believes in magic with a pure, childlike wonder. For her, it is enough to know that it exists, and she asks for nothing more. Leandra, on the other hand, sees magic merely as a status symbol, a tool to make her superior over others. She doesn't believe in magic for itself—but for what it can do for *her*."

Caitlyn sighed and shook her head. "I still don't understand…"

Bertha gave her a gentle smile. "You will, dear. In time." Then her demeanour turned brisk. Indicating the empty cauldron on the counter, she said: "Well, I suppose I'd better take this back to the kitchen and fill it up again."

"I can do that if you like," Caitlyn offered. She raised her nose and sniffed the air. "Mmm… I can smell all sorts of amazing things coming from the kitchen."

"Yes, we've planned a lovely menu for the dumb supper. Mother and Tara are putting the finishing touches to the dishes—well, if they don't kill each other first," said Bertha with a grimace.

"Oh?" Caitlyn cocked her ear and realised that, above the noise of the conversation, she could hear voices drifting out from the kitchen at the rear of the cottage. Raised voices. Sharp words and shrill accusations.

"I don't think they've ever been in the same room for longer than ten minutes before they started bickering," said Bertha with a sigh. "I don't know what's going to happen now that Tara is back. How are she and Mother going to live here together?"

"Well, perhaps I can help with that," said a familiar, deep baritone.

Caitlyn turned swiftly to see James standing behind them.

"I couldn't help overhearing what you were saying just now, and I think I might have a solution," he said. "As you know, Leandra Lockwood has given up her lease and is returning to London immediately. So the barn will be empty, and I'm happy to offer it to Tara for as long as she likes. Consider it an extension of this cottage." He smiled. "I was thinking it would be a nice way for Tara to be near and for you all to enjoy being together as a family, without... er... actually living in each other's pockets."

"Oh, James—really?" Caitlyn felt a rush of love towards him for such a magnanimous gesture towards a woman that he had distrusted so much. "It's incredibly generous of you! Are you sure? You'd lose the income from the holiday rental—" Then, as he waved dismissively, she stood on tiptoe to give him an impulsive peck on the cheek. "Thank you! Thank you so much!"

She was surprised to see James flush pink. She was so used to being the one who was shy about public displays of affection that it was an unexpected delight to see him blush for once.

"That's very kind of you, James, and I'm sure it will help a lot in keeping the peace," said Bertha, smiling as she watched them.

"I wonder if I should also rope off a corner of the Library as Viktor's official den," said James dryly. "He seems to have taken up residence there anyway and makes a daily habit of scaring the staff."

"Speaking of Viktor, where is he?" asked Caitlyn, scanning the room for the old vampire. "I would have thought that he would be here."

"He did say that he was coming," said Bertha absent-mindedly. "Perhaps he's just a little late." Then she gave a cry of surprise and jerked up on one foot as something pounced on her feet. They all looked down to see a familiar little ball of black fur clinging to one of Bertha's ankles.

"Nibs!" said Caitlyn in exasperation, bending to detach the kitten from her aunt's foot. "I'm sorry, this seems to be his new game—attacking people's ankles—and he's doing it to everybody."

Bertha laughed, reaching out to ruffle the kitten's fur. "Oh, it's all right. He gave me a fright, that's all. I'm sure it's something that he'll grow out of, soon enough."

"I don't know," said Caitlyn doubtfully. "I mean, Nibs seems to be remaining a kitten forever—which is not terrible, I suppose—but I do wish I could solve the mystery of why he just won't grow." She paused, thinking. "You know, about the only thing that Leandra Lockwood said to me which made some sense was that Nibs might have got trapped in a 'liminal space', where time moves differently, and so he's been affected by some kind of time-warp spell."

"Well, yes, that's what happened to Tara, dear," said Bertha. "It's why she was still seventeen when she returned to this world—" She broke off suddenly. "Actually, you know what? I just remembered something: when I was chatting to Tara earlier, she mentioned that the Cloistered Crones had a black cat living at the sanctuary who used to be a great mouser—yes, they have mice, even in liminal spaces!—and Tara said that this cat had a litter of kittens just before she left." Bertha eyed Nibs, still trying to wriggle out of Caitlyn's arms, and chuckled. "Who knows, maybe Nibs was one of that litter. Given his mischievous ways, I wouldn't be surprised if he followed Tara through the portal when she came back into our world and accidentally got 'trapped' here, unable to return home to the Cloistered Coven. Since he's a creature from a liminal space, though, he would be imbued with the time-warp enchantment, which means that he's immune to the forces of time in our world. That's why he never grows."

Caitlyn stared at her aunt. "Oh my God... you could be right..." Turning to James, she asked eagerly: "Do you remember the day we rescued Nibs?"

"How could I forget? It was the day I met you," said James with a teasing smile that made Caitlyn blush vividly.

She laughed self-consciously and hurried on with her theory. "Well, we found Nibs nearly drowning in that disused quarry which had been flooded in the recent rains. And that quarry was not far from the stone circle, which is a site known to be at the intersection of ley lines, a place of ancient magic…"

"Yes, a spot likely to be a portal to the Otherworld," Bertha finished for her.

Caitlyn nodded eagerly. "Exactly! I must ask Tara, but I'll bet that's where she re-entered our world… and where Nibs followed her through. The portal then closed, leaving him lost and wandering the forest on his own—"

They were interrupted by a diffident cough and a prim voice saying: "Excuse me, sir…"

They turned to find Mosley standing behind them, shuffling his feet and looking slightly sheepish. "Forgive the intrusion, your Lordship, but I was wondering if there might be any need for my assistance in serving the drinks?"

"Relax, Mosley," said James, giving the butler a good-natured pat on the shoulder. "You're a guest this time, and you're here to enjoy yourself. Everyone is managing fine; they can help themselves. You should take the opportunity to have a rest from your duties."

But Mosley didn't look remotely gratified at the thought of having "a rest from his duties". In fact, he looked so pained that Bertha took pity on him.

"Why don't you come and help me set the table for the supper, Mosley?" she suggested. "I haven't laid the places yet—I was just going to use a Dining

Deployment spell—but you can do it by hand instead if you prefer?"

Mosley brightened, looking as if all his Christmases had come at once. He straightened and puffed his chest out, saying importantly: "Certainly, madam—a dinner party for such a large number of guests will require astute planning and strategic placement. One needs to ensure an arrangement that is pleasing to the eye and incorporates the key principles of design and symmetry, with exact spacing to create balance and proportion." He made a distressed noise. "Had I known that my assistance would be required with the table-setting, I would have made sure to bring my Butler Stick to calibrate the individual place settings and ensure that the twenty-four-inch rule is adhered to. Guests must have ample elbow room. But I shall endeavour to achieve a similar result, if you can but spare me a ruler or tape measure? And if I may suggest—even for a rustic setting such as this—some simple table appointments would not go amiss. A freshly laundered tablecloth and a centrepiece of candles with autumnal foliage would aid greatly in stimulating the appetite—"

"Er... there's really no need for such formalities here, Mosley," said Bertha, looking slightly taken aback. "I know this is a special Samhain supper, but it's really just a very casual, family-style affair."

"Oh, but correct etiquette is essential, even in the most low-key of occasions, madam! Indeed, it is only through maintaining the customs and traditions of proper decorum that we can elevate any gathering from the mundane to the truly memorable," Mosley said earnestly. "The art of etiquette is not limited to grand balls and state dinners alone; it is a reflection of respect, consideration, and grace that should be present in every interaction, no matter how casual or modern!"

Bertha exchanged bemused looks with James and Caitlyn, then gave a helpless shrug and said to Mosley: "Well... er... if you feel so strongly about it... Come on, I'll see if I can find you a tape measure."

They disappeared through the door leading to the kitchen and had barely been gone a minute when Tara stormed out of the same door, her face flushed and her dark eyes smouldering with anger. Despite no longer resembling a seventeen-year-old, she still seemed uncannily like a recalcitrant teenager who had just had a fight with her parent.

"Your grandmother is a controlling, pigheaded, nitpicky old hag!" she fumed to Caitlyn. "I tell you, I'm going to—"

She broke off, noticing James standing next to her daughter. Raising an eyebrow, she smirked and said: "Well, darling, aren't you going to introduce me to your Prince Charming?"

"Er... this is James Fitzroy... James, this is my mother," said Caitlyn, thinking how absurd it was to be making formal introductions when the two had already lived in the same house together for days now, albeit without it being on an honest footing.

"It's a pleasure to make your acquaintance properly at last, Tara," said James rather stiffly.

Tara grinned at him. "Oh, go on, say it! I know you want to! You want to bite my head off for impersonating your baby sister. Well, I *am* really sorry to have done that—I honestly didn't mean her any harm; it was just the easiest way to gain access to the Manor and be able to move around and search for the *grimoire* freely. But I made sure to put Vanessa in a Spellbound Coma where she would have nothing but sweet dreams and wake up refreshed, with no memory of what had happened." She extended a hand to James and gave him a smile that was equal parts penitent and playful. "There! I humbly apologise and ask for your forgiveness. Friends?"

"I... er... perhaps it *would* be best if we try to forget the past and start afresh," said James, unconsciously taking her hand.

It was clear that he was not immune to Tara's cajoling and charm, and five minutes later, Caitlyn stood watching in bemusement as her mother had James laughing uproariously over a humorous account of her infamous hospital escape.

"Jeez, looks like James and your mom are best buddies already," said Pomona with a laugh as she sidled up to Caitlyn.

Caitlyn shook her head. "I know—I almost can't believe it. This time yesterday, James wanted her thrown in jail! Maybe she's cast an enchantment spell on him or something..."

"Nah, that's just your mom switching on the charm. You know, the kind of magic mere mortals can call up: it's called 'charisma'," said Pomona with a wink. She gestured to the people milling around the room. "Man, it's so awesome to see so many people here tonight, all chilled and happy and celebrating..."

Caitlyn silently agreed as she turned to look across the room as well. It was heartwarming to see those from the village and the Manor estate who had championed and supported the Widow Mags all here together. There was Terry, the owner of the village pub, who had always welcomed the Widow Mags to his establishment, and treated her with gracious respect, in spite of the hostility from the other villagers. And beside him stood Kate Jenkins and her daughter Molly. The little girl used to be terrified of the Widow Mags, but—as Pomona had described— after being saved by the old witch's quick actions and magical intervention, she now delighted in coming to the shop of her "favouritest witch" to choose chocolate treats.

Caitlyn realised suddenly that these people had become her extended family, and she felt a wonderful sense of belonging. Her gaze slid over to a group nearby, where Lisa was regaling several villagers with a story about the Festival. Standing at the edge of the group was Amy Matthews, who had escaped an abusive marriage when her husband—the Fitzroy estate's late gamekeeper—had been murdered several months ago. Caitlyn had quickly befriended Amy when she first arrived in the village, during a time when all of Tillyhenge had been gripped by the mystery of the "White Stag". She was pleased to see the pretty young widow so relaxed and happy now, compared to when Caitlyn had first met her.

"Wow, check out Amy's new haircut. She looks awesome. She, like, really came out of herself, huh?" commented Pomona, following her gaze.

"I think her new job as James's PA is really giving her confidence," said Caitlyn with a smile.

"It's not just the job," said Pomona, smirking. "It's *luuurrrve.*"

"What d'you mean?" asked Caitlyn, startled.

"Haven't you noticed the way she and Jeremy keep sneaking looks at each other?" said Pomona, nodding her head at the dairy farmer, who was standing on the other side of the group.

Caitlyn rolled her eyes. After shopping, Pomona's favourite pastime was matchmaking, and she never missed an opportunity to try to get two people together. Still, when Caitlyn turned to look again, she was surprised to see that her cousin was right: Amy and Jeremy *were* exchanging flirtatious glances when they thought nobody was looking.

"They'd make such a cute couple," said Pomona, beaming. "Amy deserves a nice man like Jeremy after her jerk of a husband, and it would be awesome for Jeremy to have someone again after being a widower for so many years. Plus, having another woman in his household might stop Vera from trying to throw her weight around and poison everyone with her toxic witch crap."

Somehow, Caitlyn doubted anything could change Vera's malicious nature. As if reading her thoughts, Jeremy detached himself from the group and came over to them.

"Been wanting to come over and say hello for a while," he said, doffing an imaginary cap at the two girls. "And actually, I wanted to apologise too."

"For what?" said Caitlyn, surprised.

"For Vera," said Jeremy, looking down and shuffling his feet. "I don't know what to say, really. I mean, I can't believe she acted the way she did! I'm right sorry, not just for today, but also for what Vera's done in the past—"

"Oh, Jeremy, there's no need to apologise," said Caitlyn quickly.

"Yeah, it's not like it's your fault," Pomona chimed in.

Jeremy sighed. "To be honest with you, I wish... I wish I could send her away. But she's got nowhere else to go and..." He paused, looking anguished. "Well... she's my sister."

Caitlyn thought suddenly of the squabbling voices she had overheard in the kitchen earlier and leaned forwards impulsively to put a hand on Jeremy's arm.

"It's all right, I understand," she said, giving him a compassionate smile. "Things can be difficult when it's 'family'. Believe me, I know."

"Yeah, you know what they say about family: can't live with 'em, can't legally sell 'em," quipped Pomona.

Jeremy chuckled. "Thanks. You've made me feel a sight better." He looked over their shoulders. "Ah... reckon we're being called in..."

They were indeed all being shepherded through the door to the rear of the cottage.

Pomona rubbed her hands with relish. "Ooh, the dumb supper is about to begin!"

# CHAPTER THIRTY-NINE

As she followed the others into the kitchen, Caitlyn wondered how on earth the Widow Mags was going to fit everyone at the rustic wooden table where they normally had their meals. But when she stepped into the kitchen, she was amazed to find that it had somehow expanded into a room almost as large as the Dining Room at Huntingdon Manor. And whilst the table in the centre was still the worn, solid oak that did daily duty as worktable, dining table, chocolate workstation, temporary storage surface, and everything in between, it had somehow stretched to four times its usual length, and its accompanying chairs had multiplied so that everyone could sit down comfortably.

Amid a chorus of "oohs" and "aahs" from the other guests, Caitlyn slowly approached the table, her eyes widening in wonder. Mosley had truly outdone himself. A black linen tablecloth had been thrown over the top of the table and clusters of glossy red apples, berries, and autumnal foliage were arranged down the centre, interspersed with flickering candles that cast a warm glow across the faces of the gathered guests. The place settings had been meticulously laid out in two opposite rows down the length of the table and consisted of a quirky assortment of mismatched crockery, scratched glasses, and tarnished cutlery alongside intricately folded, faded tea-towels that had been pressed into service as makeshift napkins.

Bowls and platters of steaming food had been laid out along the length of the table, and Caitlyn felt her stomach growl as she eyed the feast on offer. There was creamy roasted parsnip soup with thyme and sour cream, wild-mushroom tarts fragrant with herbs and garlic, a slow-cooked venison pie redolent with flaky pastry and red-wine gravy, roasted root vegetables with honey and mustard, and crisp roast potatoes sprinkled with sea salt and rosemary—plus a generous joint of succulent roast pork, marinated in cider and cooked with sage and apples, that took pride of place in the centre of the table.

And on the side counter sat several lovingly prepared desserts: an apple-and-pear crumble crowned with a crispy, buttery topping, a sticky toffee pudding oozing with toffee sauce, and—the *pièce de résistance*—a rich, moist, dark chocolate sponge cake filled with blackberry compote and decorated with chestnut-buttercream frosting. From the way several guests were hovering around the sweet dishes, it looked like many would have been quite happy to start the meal with dessert!

As people started to find their places at the table, however, Pomona made a sound of protest and cried:

"Hang on! Isn't the table set up wrong for a dumb supper? Shouldn't all the forks and knives be, like, reversed in their positions... and don't we have to walk backwards to the table?"

"Those are American traditions," growled the Widow Mags.

"Yes, I'm afraid dumb suppers over here are much simpler affairs," said Bertha, giving Pomona an apologetic smile. "I think those fun rituals and rules were invented by the American descendants of the Irish and Scottish immigrants who took the Samhain tradition over to the New World."

"Oh. So you guys don't really do anything?" said Pomona, crestfallen. "Why call it a 'dumb supper' then?"

"Well, we do eat the meal in silence—that is one tradition we uphold. And we do set an extra place and an empty chair at the head of the table, for any spirit who wishes to join us." Bertha indicated the far end of the table, where a chair sat empty before a place setting. "You see, we focus more on the 'gathering-together-of-family' aspect; we see the dumb supper simply as a symbolic sharing of the harvest with the spirits of our ancestors."

"But you can walk backwards to your chair and hold your knife and fork in the wrong hands if that makes you feel better," said Tara, giving Pomona a wink, as Vanessa and Evie giggled next to her.

Before the American girl could reply, the back door of the cottage was flung open, and Viktor tottered in, looking very dapper. His ancient black suit had been freshly pressed, his grey hair had been carefully combed across his balding pate, and he was proudly curling back his lips to show a pair of yellowed fangs as he nodded at everybody.

"Evening... evening all... apologies for the tardy arrival... Took forever to find my confounded fangs, but I did locate them at last—" Viktor paused by the kitchen counter, transfixed by the desserts. "Ahh! Apple-and-pear crumble—my favourite!" He bent over the dish, nearly poking his long nose into the crumble topping as he inhaled appreciatively.

"Viktor! Get your bony beak out of my crumble!" snapped the Widow Mags.

The old vampire jerked upright, looking affronted. "I was only having a sniff," he said huffily.

"Greedy old fruit bat!" muttered the Widow Mags.

"Crabby old crone!" Viktor shot back, glowering at her.

*Oh God, not them as well*, thought Caitlyn with an inwards groan. Hastily, she tried to change the subject:

"Viktor! I'm so glad to see you. I was getting worried that you might miss the supper."

"Well, I would have got here sooner had I not been waylaid by that infernal female asking a million questions about the fire," said Viktor tetchily.

Lisa looked up sharply. "What female? Where was this? At the Manor?"

"Yes, young lady with a peculiar speaking trumpet, stopping anyone she can and bombarding them with questions about the Festival and whether they'd been hurt in the fire—there, that's her!"

Viktor pointed suddenly at the small TV set perched at the other end of the kitchen counter. It had been turned on earlier and forgotten, with the sound set to mute. Now, everyone exclaimed as they saw a young woman on the screen, standing in front of a familiar Georgian manor house, holding a microphone and talking earnestly to the camera.

"That's Huntingdon Manor!" Lisa gasped. "Quick, turn the sound back on!"

Caitlyn hurried to comply, and they all watched, mesmerised, as the reporter's voice came out of the set, loud and clear:

*"...coming to you from Huntingdon Manor, which was the scene of chaos only a few hours ago, when a 'freak wildfire' at their Samhain Festival nearly resulted in mass panic and the loss of lives. According to eyewitnesses, the fire seemed to be caused by a malfunction with the pyrotechnics used in the live entertainment show accompanying the bonfires—"*

"What? 'Live entertainment'?" spluttered Tara. "That was magic, you stupid cow!"

"Shhh!" everyone shushed her.

"...luckily, the fire was contained by the quick action of some of the performers and no one was seriously hurt. A bull that was taking part in the festivities is believed to have gone on a stampede, although once again, fortunately, it appears that no one was injured. Here with me is one of the visitors at the festival..."

The camera cut to the reporter holding her microphone up to a plump woman who was saying:

"...oh no, it was fantastic! Most exciting event we've been to in ages. I mean, it's true, things got a mite hairy for a while, but I don't think we were in any real danger. They got the situation under control fairly quickly. And I must say, the show that was on before the fire started was fabulous. Really good acting and special effects; you'd almost think it was real magic—"

"What about the stampeding bull?" asked the reporter hopefully. "Did you see him try to gore anyone?"

"Don't be daft!" the woman laughed. "Ferdinand is the sweetest, gentlest creature you'd ever meet. Yes, he was a bit rattled by the fire—who wouldn't be?— but he didn't hurt a fly."

"Oh... right." The reporter looked almost comically disappointed at the lack of juicy drama. "So you *wouldn't be hesitant to attend such festivals in the future?"*

*"'Course not!" said the woman staunchly. "Can't wait to come back to Huntingdon Manor for next year's Samhain Festival." She gestured to her children, who were hovering in the background, pulling faces at the camera. "The kiddies are hoping that the Manor might put on something for Christmas, actually..."*

The camera cut to the reporter now holding her microphone up to a familiar grey-haired man in a sombre pinstriped suit.

*"...with me now is Inspector Walsh of the local CID. Am I right, Inspector, in saying that this fire is only the latest in a string of unfortunate events which have occurred here at Huntingdon Manor? There have been various deaths and mysteries connected to the Fitzroy estate and the accompanying village of Tillyhenge... Some are going so far as to suggest that this whole place is cursed by black magic!"*

*"Nonsense," said Inspector Walsh testily. "There is no such thing as magic. While what happened at the Festival today is regrettable, it is a completely different incident to the previous cases involving the Manor. Those were actual crimes, and I am pleased to say that my team have been successful in wrapping up all the murder investigations—"*

*"Not all," said the reporter quickly. "The case of the young man who was found dead in the Manor Library*

*only a few days ago is still unsolved. I heard that you
may have a suspect in custody for that? A Benedict
Danby?"*

*"Mr Danby is helping us with the investigation, yes,
but the death of Percy Wynn may not have been due
to foul play after all. It appears to have been a tragic
case of accidental overdose."*

*"Oh." The reporter looked crestfallen, then she
perked up again and said: "But the death of Daniel
Tremaine at the Mabon Ball last month still hasn't
been solved, has it? And I believe that is related to the
strange woman who mysteriously turned up at the
Cotswolds Infirmary this morning. Will you be
charging her for the murder?"*

*"Well, the investigation into that is ongoing—"*

Inspector Walsh broke off suddenly, seized by a
coughing fit. He took out a handkerchief and turned
away from the camera for a minute. Caitlyn glanced
across the room and was surprised to see Tara
looking intently at the screen, her lips silently
moving. *What is she doing? Is she casting a spell?*
Caitlyn turned back to look at the TV just in time to
see Inspector Walsh face the camera once more. He
cleared his throat and said:

*"As I said, the investigation on that case is
ongoing... However, it appears that we may have
been too hasty in our assumption of pre-meditated
murder. Daniel Tremaine was a serial womaniser who*

427

*was known for cruelty and violence, and it is very likely that the woman who is under suspicion for his murder was acting in self-defence."*

*"You mean... you won't be pressing charges against her?"*

*Inspector Walsh hesitated, then said: "Yes, that is correct. I am considering the case closed."*

As the news moved on to a rail strike in the north of England, Caitlyn switched the TV off, then turned back to look at Tara again. Her mother met her eyes with an innocent air, but not before Caitlyn saw the edges of her lips curl up in a self-satisfied smile. She felt a surge of reluctant admiration for her mother's chutzpah. *I don't believe it—she's just bewitched the police into dropping all charges against her!*

No one else in the room seemed to have noticed Tara's machinations. They were all busily talking about the reportage on the Samhain Festival. Lisa, in particular, was beaming with delight, unable to believe that the impending PR disaster had somehow turned into a publicity boost for the Manor.

Everyone moved to sit down at the table, the jolly mood boosted even more by the favourable news report and Lisa's relieved delight. The room hummed with conversation and laughter until the Widow Mags held up her hand, signalling for silence. One by one, the guests stopped talking and a hush descended over the table. Bertha began passing a bottle of elderberry wine, but Mosley whisked it out of her hand before she could protest and proceeded to walk around with great ceremony, pouring each glass with a flourish. When he had finished and returned to his seat, everyone raised their glasses in a silent toast.

Caitlyn closed her eyes as she sipped the wine. It was rich and fruity, with an earthy sweetness overlaid by the natural tartness of the elderberries and accompanied by the faint floral aroma of elderflower blooms. She opened her eyes again to see the Widow Mags about to set her own glass down— then the old witch paused, her gaze riveted on the open back door of the cottage. Caitlyn swivelled her head around, wondering what her grandmother was looking at.

She saw nothing but an empty doorway leading out into the night, with a glimpse of the herb garden behind the cottage and the moon in the night sky beyond. Puzzled, Caitlyn looked back at the Widow Mags and was even more bemused to see the old witch incline her head and smile slightly, her eyes still fixed on the doorway—as if welcoming someone in. And yet there was no one at the door.

Frowning, Caitlyn turned to see if anyone else at the table had noticed the odd interlude, but everyone was too busy helping themselves from the platters and savouring the food; no one was paying any attention. She turned once more to look at the doorway and then caught her breath as something shimmered into view.

A figure. Shadowy, spectral, as ephemeral as mist.

Between one blink and the next, she saw him: a handsome young man with dark hair and a sensitive mouth—and those hazel-green eyes which were so familiar. Hazel-green eyes exactly like hers. Caitlyn's heart began to hammer in her chest as she watched the young man walk down the length of the table and take his seat at the empty place. She glanced around the table, but no one else seemed to see him. Even the Widow Mags was now absorbed in eating a slice of venison pie and was paying no attention to the other end of the table.

Her heart beating unsteadily, Caitlyn gazed back at the "empty" seat, and this time, the young man looked up as well. Their eyes met. Slowly, he raised his glass to her and gave her a gentle, proud smile.

Caitlyn felt her heart turn over in her chest. It was as if she had known that smile her whole life. She smiled tremulously back, and when she blinked again, he was gone. But somehow, she knew that Noah was still there—she could feel his presence, even though he was no longer in sight.

It might have only been a year ago that Caitlyn had learned she was adopted and begun her search for her real family, but in a way, she felt like a part of her had always been searching... searching for something she couldn't name. Somewhere to belong. Someone to belong to.

Now, as she sat here at the table with her mother, grandmother, aunt, cousins... *and father,* Caitlyn felt a sense of peace settle over her, and she smiled: she was home.

***

The dumb supper went late into the night, the quiet hush over the table broken only by the soft clink of cutlery and occasional sighs of contentment. When everyone had eaten their fill, Bertha rose to serve the desserts (Mosley being expressly forbidden to rise from his seat again!). Caitlyn hurried to help and felt a rush of pride as she watched everyone enjoy the desserts, especially the Widow Mags's sumptuous chocolate cake.

Returning to the counter to fetch some extra napkins, Caitlyn happened to glance out the open back doorway—then paused as she caught sight of a movement in the trees at the edge of the woods. She frowned, and before she realised what she was doing, she had stepped out of the cottage, the extra napkins forgotten. Walking to the edge of the herb garden, she peered out into the woods beyond. *Was that something pale moving between the trees...?*

Caitlyn realised suddenly that she had stood here before, in this exact same spot, six months ago when she had first arrived in Tillyhenge. There had been a murder, a body found dead at the stone circle, and whispers of sightings of the White Stag—a mystical creature believed to appear to those about to set off on a journey of new beginnings. Then, too, she had stood like this, straining her eyes, trying to see into the darkness—and she had been rewarded by a glimpse of that magical, otherworldly creature. Now, Caitlyn looked eagerly again for the pale form that she was sure she had seen moving through the trees: a graceful body and majestic head crowned by a magnificent set of white antlers...

She took a step forwards, then another. And another. She was just about to step into the woods when a familiar deep voice sounded behind her:

"Caitlyn?"

She whirled to find James standing a few feet away, looking at her quizzically.

"What are you doing out here? Is everything all right?" he asked.

"Yes... I thought I saw..." She trailed off, throwing another glance over her shoulder. The woods stood dark and silent, no magical creature slipping between the trees. She sighed and walked back to rejoin James at the edge of the Widow Mags's herb garden. "Nothing... never mind."

James took both her hands in his. "Actually, I'm glad you slipped away. It gave me an excuse to come out here to look for you." He gave a rueful laugh. "It's a bit anti-social of me to say this, especially on a night that's supposed to be all about family and community, but it's nice to be alone together at last. I feel like we've barely seen each other in recent days! There's been no chance to talk properly, and there are so many things I want to tell you, things I've been thinking about."

"I know. It's all been a bit crazy." Caitlyn smiled shyly up at him. "But hopefully everything will settle down now and we'll have loads of time to catch-up... starting tomorrow! Shall we go for a picnic in the grounds of the estate—just the two of us—and you can tell me everything you've been thinking?"

"Well, actually..." James gave her a whimsical grin. "I was hoping to tell you one of the things I've been thinking about... right now."

Caitlyn looked up at him, slightly puzzled. "Now?"

James nodded, his grey eyes tender. "Yes, I've been thinking that there's a prophecy I have yet to fulfil."

"What do you mean?"

"Well, when I was a young boy, I was told that, one day, I would meet a beautiful witch and marry her..."

Caitlyn's breath caught in her throat.

"Do you... do you have a witch in mind?" she asked, her heart beating fast.

"Oh yes," said James, smiling into her eyes. "And I hope when the time comes, she might say yes?"

Caitlyn slid her arms around his neck and pressed her lips to his, whispering softly, "I think she will."

THE END

# *From the Author:*

*Thank you for being on this incredible journey with me, following Caitlyn's adventures in the magical world of "Bewitched by Chocolate". Your support and enthusiasm for the characters and stories have both warmed and inspired me these past 7 years.*

*I hope that you've found as much joy in exploring this world as I've had in creating it. From Caitlyn's first steps into the enchanted chocolate shop to her growth as a young witch embracing her heritage, I've had such fun writing about the mysteries she's solved, the family secrets she's uncovered, and the myths, legends and magical creatures she's encountered (not to mention the scrumptious chocolate treats she's made and eaten!).*

*Though it's bittersweet to say goodbye, I hope the magic in these stories will linger with you—perhaps the next time you taste a particularly delicious piece of chocolate or spot a fuzzy fruit bat online (or in real life!), you'll wonder if there's enchantment everywhere, just waiting for us to see it.* ☺

*Wishing you a sprinkling of magic, a dash of mystery, and plenty of chocolate in your days ahead!*

*Hsin-Yi*
*(H.Y. Hanna)*
*P.S. Don't forget to sign up to my newsletter so you don't miss any exciting new books from me!*

# ABOUT THE AUTHOR

USA Today bestselling author H.Y. Hanna is the author of over 30 mystery novels, many of which have been translated into several languages. Her stories are filled with suspense, humour, and unexpected twists, as well as quirky characters and animals with big personalities! She is known for bringing settings vividly to life, whether it's the historic city of Oxford, the beautiful English Cotswolds or other exciting places around the world.

After graduating from Oxford University, Hsin-Yi tried her hand at a variety of jobs, including advertising, modelling, teaching English and dog training... before returning to her first love: writing. She worked as a freelance writer for several years and has won awards for her poetry, short stories and journalism.

Hsin-Yi was born in Taiwan and has been a globe-trotter all her life, living in a variety of cultures from the UK to the Middle East, the USA to New Zealand... but is now happily settled in Perth, Western Australia, with her husband and a rescue kitty named Muesli. You can learn more about her and her books at: www.hyhanna.com

Join her Newsletter to get updates on new releases, exclusive giveaways and other book news!

**https://www.hyhanna.com/newsletter**